...la Jackson is a *New York Times* bestselling author
...re than one hundred romance titles. Brenda lives
...ksonville, Florida, and divides her time between
...y, writing and travelling. Email Brenda at
...rbrendajackson@gmail.com or visit her on her
...te at brendajackson.net

...1 Vivian Award finalist and DEIA activist in the
...e industry, **LaQuette** writes sexy, stylish and
...onal romance. She crafts dramatic, emotionally
...es that are deeply pigmented by reality's paintbrush.

...Brooklyn native writes unapologetically bold,
...er-driven stories. Her novels feature diverse
...ole casts who are confident in their right to appear
...page.

THE OUTLAW'S CLAIM

BRENDA JACKSON

CINDERELLA MASQUERADE

LaQUETTE

MILLS & BOON

Scripture taken from the Amplified Bible (AMPCE), Copyright © 1954, 1958, 1962, 1964, 1965, 1987 by The Lockman Foundation. Used by permission.

First Published in Great Britain 2022
by Mills & Boon, an imprint of HarperCollins*Publishers* Ltd
1 London Bridge Street, London, SE1 9GF

www.harpercollins.co.uk

HarperCollins*Publishers*
1st Floor, Watermarque Building,
Ringsend Road, Dublin 4, Ireland

The Outlaw's Claim © 2022 Brenda Streater Jackson
Cinderella Masquerade © 2022 Harlequin Enterprises ULC

Special thanks and acknowledgement are given to LaQuette for her contribution to the *Texas Cattleman's Club: Ranchers and Rivals* series.

ISBN: 978-0-263-30389-6

1022

MIX
Paper | Supporting
responsible forestry
FSC™ C007454

This book is produced from independently certified FSC™ paper to ensure responsible forest management.

For more information visit: www.harpercollins.co.uk/green

Printed and Bound in Spain using 100% Renewable electricity at CPI Black Print, Barcelona

THE OUTLAW'S CLAIM

BRENDA JACKSON

To the man who will always and forever
be the wind beneath my wings and the
love of my life—Gerald Jackson Sr.

In memory of my childhood friend and soror,
Lynda Ravnell. Losing you this year was hard,
and I will forever appreciate the memories.
Rest in peace.

One

"I now pronounce you husband and wife. You may kiss your bride."

Maverick Outlaw grinned broadly as he watched his brother Jess pull his new wife, the former Paige Novak, into his arms, as if determined to kiss the lips right off her face. None of the onlookers seemed surprised at such a strong display of passion. Not even their father, Bart.

It had shocked the hell out of some when Bartram Outlaw had shown up for the wedding. It really should not have, since it was one of Bart's sons getting married. However, the Outlaw brothers would be the first to admit that their father was ornery as hell and pigheaded to a fault. There were other words that could describe him, but since none of them were nice, Maverick decided not to think about them today.

Maverick was just glad their old man was here and

trying to be friendly and sociable. Maybe that was helped along by the beautiful woman at his side, Claudia Dermotte. She was as friendly, sociable and outgoing as they came.

A few hours later, after all the wedding photos had been taken and the wedding dinner had been served and eaten, Jess and Paige escaped to change into their traveling clothes. They would be leaving to begin their month-long honeymoon, beginning in Dubai.

Maverick swore he'd never seen Jess so happy. There was no doubt in Maverick's mind that although marriage seemed to agree with some people, he was not one of them. He liked his life just the way it was, and he enjoyed being a bachelor. His goal was to remain that way for quite a while. Maybe even forever, since he didn't have to worry about continuing the Outlaw line. His married brothers seemed to be doing a good job of it.

"I noticed you kept your eyes on the old man today like the rest of us."

Maverick glanced over at his brother Sloan and nodded. "I don't know why we even bothered when he's with Claudia. Dad never acts like an ass when he's with her."

"True. That goes to show he can be a decent human being when he wants."

Maverick nodded again, knowing that was true. He wished he could say their father's bark was worse than his bite, but *that* wasn't true. Bart Outlaw was known to take a huge chunk out of a person's ass whenever he was inclined to do so.

Maverick took a sip of his champagne and glanced over at their father. Claudia's hand was firmly in Bart's as she moved toward the newlyweds, who had just reappeared. When they reached Jess and Paige, of course, it was Claudia who made the first move and gave the couple goodbye hugs. Maverick then watched his father give Jess and Paige hugs as well. If he hadn't seen it with his own eyes, he would not have believed it. When did Bart ever hug anyone other than Claudia and their sister, Charm?

"I'd be damned," Sloan said, obviously seeing the exchange as well. "Although he looked stiff as hell doing it, I can't believe the old man actually hugged them."

"I honestly think that stunt he pulled with Cash and Brianna scared the shit out of him," Maverick said, remembering how their father had tried to break up the couple. "He finally realized how close he came to losing one of his sons when Cash was ready to disown the old man."

"I agree with you there," Sloan said. "Maybe that's why he didn't have anything to say when I announced I was marrying Leslie."

Maverick had four brothers, and all were here and accounted for. He also had one sister. He knew some people found it amazing that all six Outlaw siblings were as close as they were, considering each of them had a different mother. Bart had been married to five of the women, and when the divorces became final, his attorneys made sure he was given custody of his five sons. Maverick, at thirty-two, was the youngest son.

Garth, at forty, was the oldest, and he and his wife, Regan, were the proud parents of a seven-month-old son name Garrison. Regan's father had been the corporate pilot for his family's company for over forty years. When he retired, Regan had taken over. Just as Garth had taken over as CEO of their family's multimillion-dollar business, Outlaw Freight Lines, when Bart had retired. Or more specifically, when the company's board threatened to oust Bart if he didn't step down.

Jessup—or Jess, as he preferred to be called—was thirty-eight and became the politician in the family when he went to Washington four years ago as a senator from Alaska. Everyone was happy for him and Paige, who was an actress in Hollywood and sister to their cousin Dillon Westmoreland's wife. Paige had turned twenty-nine today and wanted to get married on her birthday.

Cashen, who preferred being called Cash, was Bart's third-oldest son and at thirty-six was married to Brianna. They were the proud parents of two-year-old twin boys. Cash and his family made their home in Wyoming on a ranch he'd inherited from his mother.

Sloan was brother number four and had gotten married five months ago. He and his wife, Leslie, maintained dual residences in Wasilla and Fairbanks, Alaska. Sloan had had no problem informing the family—the day of his wedding, mind you—that he intended to have his wife pregnant by Christmas. Since that was next month, Maverick could just imagine how the couple spent most of their free time.

Last, but not least, there was his sister, twenty-seven-year-old Charm. She was the youngest of Bart's children, and being the only girl, she was definitely the apple of their father's eye. To this day, Charm's mother, Claudia, was the only woman Bart had ever loved and the one he couldn't handle. And…she'd been the only mother of his children Bart hadn't married, but not for lack of trying.

Hell, their father was still trying. Maverick and his siblings always got a kick out of seeing Bart court Claudia. They figured the reason she hadn't married Bart after all this time was because she needed some sort of affirmation that he had changed his manipulative ways. If that was true, then there would never be a marriage because Maverick and his brothers couldn't see his father turning over a new leaf any time soon, or ever. Just like a leopard couldn't change his spots, they doubted their father could change the ingrained nature of his character.

Sloan walked off, and Maverick was alone again. At least for the time being. There was no way he could ever be totally alone among his Westmoreland cousins. There were too many of them. Besides that, the wedding and the reception had been held in a section of Denver the locals referred to as Westmoreland Country.

Dillon, the oldest of the Denver-based Westmorelands, had built this mega building and named it Westmoreland House. The building, which could hold over three hundred people easily, was meant to be used for special occasions, events and family get-togethers.

Hearing oohs and aahs, he glanced over to where several relatives were admiring his cousin Bane's three-month-old babies. It was the second set of triplets for Bane and his wife, Crystal, and all six kids were a perfect combination of the two of them, though they all had their father's hazel eyes.

Maverick's cell phone vibrated. He had turned off the ringer during the wedding ceremony and now wondered who would be calling him. Most of his female acquaintances only had the number to his burner phone. Anyone he considered important was here, attending his brother's wedding.

Except for Phire.

He felt a slow roll in his stomach after pulling out

his phone and seeing it was her, Sapphire Bordella, the woman who'd once been his friend with benefits.

He and Phire had met in Paris three years ago, when he'd been on a business trip. They had been attracted to each other immediately. He had quickly discovered she was someone he could talk to and enjoyed spending time with—both in and out of the bedroom. They were friends who understood each other, and at the time neither had been looking for anything permanent. One thing they had in common—they both had domineering fathers. Maverick knew how to handle his, but Phire had yet to learn how to handle hers. He was convinced the man was as much of a manipulator as Bart. Possibly even more so.

A year ago, Phire had decided it was time for her to pursue a serious romantic relationship. By mutual agreement they had ended their FWB relationship. However, they had maintained their close friendship and would often call each other to see how things were going. Lately, he'd noticed her calls had become infrequent. He had assumed she'd met someone and things had gotten serious, and he'd been delegated as a part of her past.

"Phire?"

"Yes, it's me."

Maverick heard the strain in her voice. "Is everything alright?"

"No."

That single word stoked his ire at whatever was bothering her. The one thing Phire would never admit to was not being okay. He walked to an area in Westmoreland House where he could hold a private conversation. When he entered an empty room, he realized it was the huge playroom Dillon had added to the design of the building so the youngsters in the family could have a place to enjoy themselves. This room looked like an indoor playground.

"What's wrong, Phire?" he asked, closing the door behind him.

There was hesitation before she said, "I know we're not together anymore, but I need to see you, Maverick."

He heard the urgency in her voice and glanced at his watch. "I'm at my brother's wedding in Denver, but I can be in Paris in—"

"I'm not in Paris—I'm in Texas."

"You're home?"

"I told you this ranch hasn't been my home in years, Maverick."

Yes, she had told him that a number of times. "Alright. I have my plane. Just give me time to refuel and I'm coming to Texas."

"I hate for you to leave the wedding."

"The reception is about to end, and Jess and Paige will be leaving for their honeymoon in a little bit, anyway."

"If you're sure it won't inconvenience you."

A part of him knew Phire could never inconvenience him. "It's no problem. I can fly into Austin's airport and—"

"No, I prefer meeting you someplace else."

"Where, then?"

"Dallas. I can leave here for Dallas in a few hours."

"And I'll meet you there. I'll make all the arrangements and text them to you."

"Okay, and thanks, Maverick."

"Don't mention it. I'll see you soon."

After he clicked off the phone, he checked his watch

as he left the room. He hoped to have all his questions answered as to what was bothering Phire in a few hours.

"And just where do you think you're going, young lady?"

Phire didn't bother to glance up from tossing items into her overnight bag. The last thing her father needed to know was that she had plans to meet Maverick. The best thing she'd done over the last three years was to keep Maverick's identity shielded from her father.

When he had ordered her home from Paris a couple of days ago, all he'd said was that she should come home immediately. Once she had arrived at the ranch, it didn't take long to find out why she'd been summoned. He had selected the man he wanted her to marry.

Phire's mother had passed away when she was twelve. Less than a year later, her father, Simon Bordella—an attorney turned rancher—sent her to live with his older sister in Paris. He hadn't even sent for her to come home during the holidays or summers. If it hadn't been for her aunt, Phire honestly don't know what she would have done. Lois Priestly had been a godsend for her.

As Phire got older, two things became crystal clear. Although her aunt Lois never had anything bad to say about Phire's father, she'd never said anything good about him, either. There had definitely been a disconnect in the brother-sister relationship. Granted, there was a fourteen-year difference in their ages, but Phire would have thought they'd have a closer sibling bond.

More than once she'd tried getting her aunt to talk about it, but she never would. The only thing Aunt Lois would say, was that whatever was done in the dark would eventually come to light. Phire often wondered what she meant. Another thing her aunt had warned her about was to never to cross him.

When Phire finished high school at seventeen, her father had finally sent for her, saying he wanted her to attend an American university. After college, Phire decided to make her home in Paris, and at the age of twenty-one, nothing her father did or said could make her change her mind. She reminded him that she was now an adult and old enough to make her own decisions. Besides, why would he want her around when he hadn't before?

After she'd been living back in Paris for a year, her aunt had a massive stroke, which left her without speech and paralyzed in the legs. That meant Aunt Lois was in need of constant attention in a long-term care facility. When the funds for Aunt Lois's care ran out, a frantic Phire had no other choice but to reach out to her father, convinced he would come to his sister's aid.

Simon Bordella had agreed to provide the funds for his sister's care, but not out of the goodness of his heart. He'd told Phire that he would only agree to help on one condition—Phire would agree to marry whatever man he chose for her without any questions asked.

At first, Phire thought he was joking. When she saw he was not, she was appalled. It was only when the doctors stressed what could happen to her aunt without proper long-term care that, out of desperation, Phire agreed to her father's terms.

"I asked, where do you think you're going, Sapphire?"

She turned around. "I need to think, and I can't do it here."

"What is there to think about? I kept my end of the

agreement and provided the best care possible for Lois. Now it's time you kept your end of the deal."

Phire narrowed her gaze at him. "I had hoped you wouldn't hold that agreement over my head. I'd begun thinking that you were providing the best of care to Aunt Lois because she is your sister."

"Well, you thought wrong. Lois and I never got along. The only reason I've been paying those exorbitant fees for three years is because of the deal you and I made."

"Why, Dad? Why is it important for you to select the man for me to marry?"

"The reason doesn't matter. All you need to know is that now that you're twenty-five, it's time for you to settle down and Jaxon Ravnell will make the perfect son-in-law."

Phire frowned as she thought of the man she'd been introduced to last night at dinner. "Why? Because he's wealthy and you think he can be easily manipulated?"

Her father smiled as if he found what she'd said amusing. "Jaxon does have more money than he knows what to do with, so what's wrong with me helping him decide the best way to use it?"

Phire didn't say anything. She would admit that thirty-two-year-old Jaxon was definitely a handsome man. He was the CEO of several technology firms in Virginia and was in Texas looking for land to expand. Her father had met him a few weeks ago at one of those Texas business meetings, where the red carpet had practically been rolled out for Jaxon.

Over dinner last night her father had tried his hardest to sell Jaxon on the idea that he needed to invest some of his millions by buying up a lot of the land in the area. Mainly land her father owned that was adjacent to the ranch.

She'd always been good at reading people, and it had been obvious to her—even if hadn't been to her father—that Jaxon *wasn't* a man who could be easily manipulated. For some reason, she had a feeling Jaxon was actually playing her father by pretending the opposite. That was something she found rather interesting.

What her father had said earlier was true. He had made sure her aunt had the best of care in one of the finest facilities in Paris. He had kept his end of their deal, and whether she wanted to or not, she would keep hers.

"I need you back here in two days, Sapphire. I could tell over dinner that Jaxon was taken with you. He said he'd be in the area for at least six months and you two should spend time together. I want a wedding to take place no later than the spring. Understood?"

When she didn't say anything, he continued, "Just in case you don't understand, maybe now is the time to tell you that I had Lois moved."

"You did what?" she asked furiously, crossing the room to her father.

"You heard me. Just in case you try to wiggle out of our agreement. Don't worry, my sister is still getting the best of care, just in a nondisclosed location. I won't tell you where until *after* you and Jaxon get married."

"You can't do that!"

"As her legal guardian, I can do whatever I want. Don't worry about your aunt. What you need to concern yourself with is getting Jaxon to make you his wife by spring. As far as I'm concerned, there's nothing you need to think about. However, if you feel the need to get away to accept your fate, then by all means, do so. But I expect you back in two days with a smile on your face, ready to convince Jaxon that you are the best thing that could ever happen to him."

When her father walked out the room, Phire sank down on the bed.

Maverick checked his watch as he paced the confines of the hotel room. He hadn't expected to arrive in Dallas before Phire and had texted her all the information she needed, including the fact that a hotel key in her name was at the check-in desk.

He knew everyone was wondering why he'd left Denver unexpectedly, when he and his brothers had planned to remain in Westmoreland Country for another two days. His brother Sloan had made a wisecrack that it must have something to do with a woman. His brother was right on that account. What Sloan was wrong about was in thinking this was a hookup.

Maverick considered Phire more than that.

From their first meeting it had been easy to see she was unlike any woman he'd ever known. In addition to her striking beauty, she had wit and a personality that drew him even when he hadn't wanted to be drawn. And the more he had gotten to know her, the more he'd appreciated their friendship. Entering into a FWB relationship had been the first of its kind for him. Before Phire, he would never have considered such a thing.

As he waited for her arrival, he couldn't help but recall when they'd first met. It had been his and Garth's second night in Paris, and Maverick had decided to check out the nightlife at a pub someone had recommended. Since the place was a few blocks away and it had been a beautiful night in April, he'd walked.

As Maverick gazed out the hotel window at downtown Dallas, he let himself remember when he'd met Sapphire Bordella. It was a night he would never forget…

Two

Paris, France
Three years ago

"Welcome to DuRands. What can I get you?" the bartender asked when Maverick slid onto the barstool.

"Brandy," he said easily.

"Bottle or glass?" the woman responded with a grin.

Maverick couldn't help but return her amusement. Nor could he help noticing how gorgeous she was as he studied her with deep male appreciation. He had an eye for beauty and on a scale of one to ten, he gave her a twenty plus. She was stunning, and that said a lot since he'd met a number of striking women in his lifetime.

She wore little makeup and her mass of dark brown curls cascaded around her face, complementing her mocha skin tone. He didn't have to see the lower part of her to figure the rest of her looked just as sexy. And damn, she smelled good, too. He might have been bored to tears while attending those business meetings earlier today, but his interest was now piqued at the highest level. He'd never hit on a bartender before but there was a first time for everything.

"Do I look stressed enough for a bottle?" he asked, grinning, and noticed there was no ring on her left hand. He didn't believe in encroaching on another man's territory. A boyfriend who wasn't smart enough to put a ring on her finger was of no significance.

The woman tilted her head to the left and then to the right as if closely scrutinizing him, then said, "Not stressed, but you look like you have plenty of time to kill."

"I do, but if I tackle a bottle you might have to carry me out of here."

"I don't have a problem carrying you anywhere, mister," she said, flashing a pair of the most beautiful dimples he'd ever seen.

A crackle of energy passed between them with her words. He'd had women flirt with him before. However, there was something about *this* woman that had everything within him standing at attention…which meant it was a good thing he was sitting down.

"I need to know the name of the person who might end up rescuing me from a drunken stupor," he said, liking how the opening of her shirt hinted at a pair of awesome breasts.

She smiled again and a burst of need hit his stomach. "I'm Sapphire Bordella. However, my friends call me Phire."

"Phire," he said, liking how easily her name rolled off his lips. It was pronounced the same, but spelled differently from one of the classical elements. The one he was feeling now, burning him.

"And what's yours?" she asked.

"Maverick Outlaw."

She nodded. "Maverick. I like that. And are you one or the other? A maverick or an outlaw?"

He chuckled. "My family claims I am both, and from my escapades that often get me into trouble, I have no reason not to believe them."

She grinned. "Then I definitely need to keep my eyes on you tonight, Maverick, the outlaw."

"What about you? Are you a precious gem or are you as hot as the name *Phire* implies?"

She gave him one of those smiles that made a jolt of sexual energy rock him to the core. And her skin… He was tempted to reach across the bar and touch it to see if it was as soft as it looked. "I'll claim both. With that said, I'll be back with your drink."

Maverick watched her walk off, thinking he would definitely keep his eyes on her as well. It didn't take her long to return with his glass of brandy and their hands touched. Another jolt of sexual energy hit him. It had been his intent to grab a table to enjoy the live band, but he'd rather stay sitting right here at the bar and get to know Phire better. All he had was her name, but he definitely wanted more.

His brother Sloan had once called Maverick a man-whore, which hadn't hurt his feelings any. He liked women. They liked him. He didn't believe in lingering in any woman's bed for more than a few nights. He detested a clingy woman or one who thought a romp between the sheets came with certain rights. He was quick to remind them that it did not.

"So, are you American or French?" he asked, since

he detected both accents in her words but couldn't tell which was more dominate.

She glanced up from wiping off the counter. "American. Born in the heart of Texas. I assume you're American, although you have an accent I can't place."

"I was born in Alaska and still live there. In fact, my first trip to the lower forty-eight wasn't until I graduated from high school. I got my own plane and flew there myself."

"You own a plane and can fly it?"

He heard the amazement in her voice. He often used that tidbit as a conversation starter with women. The interest drew them in every time. "Yes. Due to Alaska's limited road system, the most common way for us to get around is by personal aircraft."

She smiled. "That's interesting."

"How long have you been living in Paris?" he asked, taking a sip of his brandy.

"I moved here when I was twelve, not long after my mother died. I guess my father thought raising a daughter was more than he wanted to take on, so he sent me to his older sister. I lived with Aunt Lois until I graduated from high school at seventeen. Then Dad sent for me because he wanted me to attend college in Texas."

"Where?"

"University of Texas in Austin. The day after I graduated, I returned here."

Maverick took another sip, finding her story interesting. Her father had sent her away at twelve, but his own father had had a different mindset. Bart hadn't minded raising five sons alone. "Do you still live with your aunt?"

"Aunt Lois had a massive stroke earlier this year

that left her paralyzed. She's currently in a long-term-care facility."

"I'm sorry to hear that."

"Thanks. Excuse me, I've got another customer."

He nodded and watched her talk to the guy who'd just arrived. From her greeting, the man was someone she knew. Possibly a regular. She proved the assumption right when she didn't ask the man what he wanted to drink. She knew.

She remained at the other end of the bar, chatting with the guy, and a part of Maverick felt peeved. He frowned. Lack of attention from a woman had never annoyed him before, so why did it now? Maybe because she could ignore him, but he couldn't ignore her. There was something about that soft-looking skin, that curly hair and those gorgeous dark eyes, that had him mesmerized.

A half hour later, she came back down to his end of the bar to see if he wanted more brandy. He said he did and while she was pouring, he asked, "You don't look old enough to be a bartender. How long have you been one?"

She smiled up at him. "I'm twenty-two and actually I'm not a bartender. At least not usually. The couple who owns this club are the parents of a good friend of mine. Their regular bartender called in sick so they asked if I could help out."

"You're good at it."

"Thanks. During my summers while in college, I would return to Paris and work here as a waitress. On those slow days, I learned the art of being a bartender. The DuRands know they can call me if they ever need help."

"And what do you do when you're not helping out here?"

"I work at a clothing boutique."

"Do you find that interesting?"

She chuckled. "I find anything having to do with clothes interesting. One day I plan to open my own shop."

"And I'm sure you will." He glanced at his watch. "What time do you get off tonight, Phire?"

She lifted an eyebrow. "Why?"

"I'd like to get to know you better. Thought we could grab a table over there and listen to the band."

She nodded, which to him meant she didn't have a problem with his suggestion. "The club closes at midnight, but I'm only needed until ten." She studied his features for a minute and then said, "And I'd like to get to know you better, too, Maverick, the outlaw."

While pouring a drink for another customer, Phire couldn't help but glance over at the man she'd flirted with off and on for most of the night. There was no reason to pretend she didn't find him irresistible, because she did. And he was a great conversationalist. She didn't want to think about all the men she'd gone out with who had bored her to tears.

She glanced at the clock and saw that in ten minutes, her shift ended. A part of her couldn't wait. She had noticed Maverick Outlaw the minute he had walked into the club—he was any woman's fantasy man.

He had to be every bit of six foot two and was handsome as sin. She wasn't sure what attracted her more, the darkness of his eyes, the slash of his eyebrows, the smooth coppery brown of his skin, the shape of his lips or that panty-wetting cleft in his chin. Or it could be that sexy-looking beard on his jaw. Another thing she'd noticed was how observant his gaze was. It had been on her most of the night and she hoped he liked what he saw.

She would admit he was the first man to not only grab her attention, but also to hold it. After her high school sweetheart, Jacques Fontaine, had broken her heart, she'd sworn she wouldn't become seriously involved with a man again. For the last four years, she'd done just that.

When she'd left Paris for college, Jacques had promised to wait for her, that she was worth the long-distance romance they would endure. By the end of her freshman year, his calls became infrequent. Then she had gotten the dreaded letter. Unfortunately, the letter hadn't reached her until his wedding day.

The lessons she'd learned from that heartbreak were to never engage in a long-distance romance and to never give her heart to another man.

The moment Maverick told her he was from Alaska and in Paris on business, she had checked off one of her "never do" boxes. Otherwise, not falling for him would be a challenge. He was a man a woman could give her heart to without a second thought.

"I'm here, Phire."

She glanced up and smiled at Clancy DuRand, the guy who'd been her good friend since the first year she'd moved to Paris. "Good, because I have a date."

He chuckled. "You mean that guy at the bar who hasn't taken his eyes off you for the past couple of hours."

She grinned. "Were you watching me through that one-sided mirror your father installed?"

Clancy smiled. "Of course. I've always looked out for you and old habits are hard to break."

"Whatever. Just for spying on me, you can start a few minutes early while I go get ready for my date."

"Who's the guy?"

"No one you have to worry about. By the way, how's Dionne?" she asked, wondering about his wife.

"She looks like a woman who's about to have twins."

Phire laughed. "She is a woman who *will* be having twins, dude."

"Don't remind me."

"I didn't. You brought it up, and I don't know why you're so worried. You're going to make a great dad to daughters."

"I hope so."

"You will. You got plenty of practice trying to keep up with me in school. Now hold down the fort and don't you dare interrogate my date or I'll never speak to you again."

"So you say."

"So I mean, Clancy." With that said, she handed him the bar towel and walked toward the back. She didn't have to glance over her shoulder to know Clancy was already making his way over to where Maverick was sitting. To interrogate him.

The loft above DuRands was where Clancy had lived before marrying Dionne and it was still unoccupied. It didn't take Phire long to use the facilities there to shower and change into another outfit. Then she released her hair from the knot on her head and applied new lipstick. Satisfied with her appearance, she left to join Maverick. He had turned around on his stool to take in the band getting into their third number. She would know since they were regulars and rarely changed their routine.

Maverick couldn't have heard her approach over the sound of the loud music, but he turned his head to look at her. His gaze was so penetrating she almost missed a step, and she was not one to be clumsy.

Phire never had a man look at her with such intensity. Total awareness of him seeped into every pore. She was aroused just from seeing him sitting on that stool, from being aware of the full length of him, from the top of his head to the soles of those expensive-looking shoes. And when he stood, he was taller than she'd originally assumed.

"I'm here," she said, when she finally reached him. She had to tilt back her head to meet his gaze.

He did a thorough sweep of her outfit before meeting her eyes again. "You changed clothes."

"I usually keep a change of clothes here," she said.

"That's convenient."

"For me, it's a necessity. The shop where I work is in the next block. I live quite a way from here and on those days that I prefer hanging out with friends or going to check on my aunt, it's easier for me to shower and change here than go all the way home and then come back."

"That makes sense."

"How did you know I was approaching? You must have awfully good hearing."

He smiled. "No, I picked up your scent."

"Oh." No man had ever told her something like that before.

"You want to find a place to sit?" he asked.

"I'd rather not. You've heard three of the band's numbers already, and I've been here for five hours. I need a change of scenery."

He cocked his head and looked at her. "Then where would you prefer going?"

She could tell from the look in his eyes what he was thinking. Having Clancy as a good friend helped since he'd been quite the rascal before meeting Dionne. "I missed dinner and I'm starving. It just so happens that my favorite café is right across the street. While I eat, you can tell me about all those bad things you've done to earn you the last name of Outlaw."

It didn't take Maverick long to know that he liked Phire, and not just because he desperately wanted her in his bed. He was enjoying his time with her. Just watching her eat was a total turn-on. Nobody ate French onion soup quite the way she did. Each time she brought the spoon to her lips was sensuality in motion.

"So there you have it," he said, continuing their conversation. "I was the youngest of five brothers and I wanted attention any way I could get it."

"So you were a real rascal."

He chuckled. "Yes, I'll admit that I was." He took a sip of his wine, and then said, "Clancy is your protector, I gather."

She chuckled. "He's the brother I always wanted is more like it. On my first day in school here in Paris, I was twelve and scared to death. He assured me everything would be alright. I believed him since he was the only one in my class who spoke English."

Maverick couldn't help but chuckle again. He'd been doing that a lot tonight. Not only was Phire gorgeous, but she was also entertaining. He had eaten dinner earlier with Garth and Regan, who had flown them both here as the company pilot, so he'd only ordered a glass of wine when Phire had ordered her soup.

"I hope Clancy didn't drill you too much," Phire said, interrupting his thoughts.

"I didn't mind. I have a younger sister, too. Charm is twenty-five."

"And you and your brothers get all into her business, right?"

"There was a time when we did, but we soon discovered Charm could take care of herself."

That was an understatement. Bart hadn't known Claudia was pregnant when their affair had ended and she left for parts unknown. Fifteen years later, she'd reappeared with Charm in tow, telling Bart that she couldn't handle Charm's sassiness anymore. He could deal with it. Bart's way of dealing with it had been to spoil Charm even more. That's when the brothers had taken a firm hand to their newly discovered sister. In the end, Charm had settled down. Thanks to her five older brothers, she definitely knew how to handle herself without their interference.

"So tell me about your life in Texas, Phire."

She shrugged beautiful shoulders barely covered by the cute blouse she was wearing. The moment he'd picked up her scent and turned to look at her in the sexy outfit she'd changed into, his breath had caught on a surge of desire so strong he'd wondered if he'd be capable of breathing again.

"My father, Simon Bordella, used to be an attorney in my grandfather's law practice. After my grandfather died, Dad sold the practice, stopped practicing law and tried his hand at ranching. All this took place before I was born." She paused. "I would love Texas more if my father wasn't such a tyrant."

Maverick lifted an eyebrow. "His name isn't Bart, is it?"

She smiled. "No, his name is Simon and there's nothing simple about him, trust me." She took a sip of her wine then asked, "I take it that your father, Bart, is a tyrant as well."

"Worse. But my siblings and I have learned how to deal with him."

"By just letting him have his way?"

"Hell no. Just the opposite. That doesn't mean he doesn't try. He's one manipulating old cuss."

"You say that with fondness and not an ounce of bitterness."

"It won't do any good. We understand Bart, or we try to."

"What about your sister? Does he treat her worse?"

Maverick rolled his eyes. "Hardly. Charm's the apple of the old man's eye. Definitely a daddy's girl."

He'd told Phire more about himself and his family than he normally would tell a woman, especially on a first date. And he did consider this a date. However, whether it ended with him in her bed, or her in his, was yet to be seen.

"I'll never understand my father."

He came close to telling her that at some point she would need to let it go. She was a grown woman living in Paris, thousands of miles away from Texas, so why did it matter if she understood her old man or not? For years, Maverick hadn't understood his mother, Rosalind. She'd been Bart's wife, whom he'd caught in an affair. Lucky for Maverick, there hadn't been any question that he'd been Bart's kid since he favored the old man more than any of the others. Right down to the cleft in his chin.

He glanced at his watch and saw it was close to midnight. He had intended to be in some woman's bed tonight and had hoped it would be Phire's. "It's getting late," he finally said.

"I know." She smiled over at him after she pushed aside her empty bowl. "So tell me, Maverick, the outlaw. Are you going to see me home like a nice gentleman would?"

Three

The sound of a muffler backfiring brought Maverick's thoughts back to the present. He was still staring out the hotel window. Christmas decorations were everywhere, and he found it hard to believe that Thanksgiving was next week.

He couldn't help recalling how that night with Phire had ended. After leaving the café, they had walked back to his hotel. Then he'd gotten the rental car and driven her home. Her car, she'd told him, was in the shop and she would be picking it up tomorrow. She had planned to take a rideshare home.

Phire had been right when she'd said she lived outside the city limits. He thought the stucco home, nestled among smaller chateaus in the countryside, was a really nice place. He especially liked the garden courtyard that led to her front door.

She'd told him her aunt had lived in the house for

years and how lonely it was without her aunt's presence. He knew from all the things she'd said that her relationship with her aunt was a close one, and other than her father, her aunt was the only living relative she had.

He had walked Phire to the door, and she'd invited him inside. Not one to waste time on formalities, the moment the door closed behind them, he had drawn her into his arms. The moment their mouths had connected, he'd been a goner.

That night they'd made love after she'd told him she had never done anything so promiscuous before—inviting a man she barely knew home for the night. She'd even told him that she hadn't shared a bed with a man in over four years and why. He knew all about the heartbreak she'd endured upon receiving her boyfriend's letter on the day of his wedding to another woman.

Another thing Phire had done before sharing a bed with Maverick was set the ground rules, which was something he usually did with women. She'd made it clear that the night with him would be just a night. She didn't do long-distance, long-term or long-lasting. In other words, they would be one and done.

By the next morning, he was convinced Phire had gotten under his skin in a way no other woman had. That night had started their friendship with benefits, which had continued for two years. He would hook up with her whenever he came to Paris, and he'd made it his business to return often.

During his visits, he'd often accompanied her to movies, concerts and dinners. He'd even gone with her to visit her aunt Lois. He knew how much she cared about her aunt. The older woman was in a very nice facility and definitely well cared for.

Phire had told him that her father was footing the bill for all her aunt's expenses. Maverick thought that no matter how much of a tyrant the man was, at least he'd had the decency to take care of his sister.

He rubbed his hand down his face while thinking that the real kick in the gut had come last year, when Phire suggested they end their FWB relationship. She wanted to start dating seriously. He'd been surprised since she'd sworn she would never fall in love again. But he knew she had a right to change her mind. After all, his brothers, Garth and Cash, whom he'd thought would never marry, had done so.

Maverick knew that although he wasn't in love with Phire and she wasn't in love with him, there was a bond between them. That's why he was here in Dallas. It didn't matter that their FWB relationship had ended over a year ago, and he hadn't spoken with her but a few times since. The bottom line was that she'd called and said she needed to see him, and he was here.

He turned around when he heard the key in the door. His heart rate increased as he watched it open. And there she stood. The woman he had thought about over the last year more than he should have.

The look on her face had him quickly crossing the room to gather her into his arms.

Phire inhaled deeply when she was enveloped in Maverick's warm embrace. He was the man who'd turned her world inside out within months of meeting him. His familiar scent calmed her in ways he would never know. He was the last person she should have called, but she hadn't been able to *not* call him.

"What's wrong, Phire?"

At that moment, Phire couldn't speak. Nor did she

want to. The only thing she wanted was for Maverick to hold her while she buried her head on his chest and fought back her tears.

She had tried putting distance between them at the first sign she was developing feelings for him. That's when she'd come up with the big lie that she needed space to start dating others. Falling in love with him would have made things hard because of that agreement she'd made with her father.

Her future was not her own so there was no reason for her to have any fanciful hope of anything ever growing between her and Maverick. Besides, he didn't love her. The only thing they'd shared for those two years was a friendship with benefits. There was no doubt in her mind that they still would be FWB if she hadn't ended things.

The thought of how miserable she'd been over the last year without Maverick made tears well up in her eyes. Her aunt's condition wasn't improving, and the doctors had told her to stop holding on to hope that it would. However, it had been enough for her aunt to recognize her during her visits and give her a smile. Phire had looked forward to that smile. Now, thanks to her father, she had no idea where her aunt was. Did her aunt know why Phire no longer visited her? The thought made more tears come.

"What's wrong, Phire? Please tell me."

Until Maverick had spoken, she hadn't realized she'd been sobbing into his chest. But she hadn't been able to help it. For two years he had been her strength. He'd been what was right in her world when everything else seemed to be tumbling down all around her.

When she didn't say anything, she suddenly felt herself being swept off her feet into Maverick's strong arms and carried over to the sofa. Maverick had booked a suite, and she'd noticed how big it was the minute she'd opened the door.

Cradling her in his arms, he held her tight while gently stroking her back. "Talk to me, Phire. Did you and that guy break up or something?"

She lifted her head, swiped at her tears and asked, "What guy?"

"The one you ended our relationship to begin seeing."

"There was never a guy."

He looked at her strangely and said, "Oh."

Realizing what she'd just admitted, she quickly said, "I never got around to meeting anyone. I was too busy."

He nodded. "Then has something happened to your aunt? Is that the reason you're back in the States for a while?"

She saw the depth of concern in the darkness of his eyes. He didn't love her, but their friendship had always been solid. She knew he genuinely cared. Pulling herself up, she straightened in his lap and wiped the tears from her eyes. "I'm sorry. I should not have fallen apart like that."

"You don't have to apologize for letting go if you needed to. I'm Maverick, remember?"

There was no way she could forget. He was Maverick, her outlaw. But he was also more. He was the man who had become her world even when he hadn't known it. She had looked forward to his visits, no matter how infrequent they'd become. He was a treat worth waiting for.

She had given him a key to her place, and there was nothing like coming home from work to find him there. They would spend time together as friends and lovers.

Maverick had a way about him that had her laughing at his antics one minute and screaming out his name in an orgasm the next. Their relationship had been unique. It had been special. Even Clancy had said as much. He had accused her of falling in love with Maverick even before she'd realized she was doing so.

"Yes, it's about Aunt Lois."

He nodded as he gently stroked the side of her face. "And?"

She fought back more tears. "I don't know where she is."

He frowned and then tilted his head to look at her with a confused expression. "How can you not know where she is? Is she not in that facility in Paris?"

Phire shook her head "Dad moved her and won't tell me where she is."

"Why would he do that?"

"Because he needs to make sure I keep my end of the deal and marry the man he's picked up for me."

Holding her steadily in his arms, Maverick straightened up in his seat. "I think you need to start from the beginning, Phire."

Although Maverick was trying like hell to hold his anger in check, he was having a hard time doing so. First, he was furious at Phire's father for asking her to agree to something so outlandish. The other part of his anger was directed at her. Not for agreeing to the arrangement, because he figured she would do anything to give her aunt the best of care, but that she hadn't told him anything about it until now.

"Why am I just hearing about this crazy-ass deal you made with your father, Phire?" he asked, not caring if she heard the harshness in his tone. It couldn't be helped, since he was fuming.

"It happened before I met you. In fact, it was the month before. I didn't even mention it to Clancy. All I was concerned with was making sure Aunt Lois received the best care."

She twisted in his lap to face him fully. "I honestly was hoping Dad would see how ridiculous his ultimatum was. And that helping with his sister's health care was the decent thing to do. I was wrong. My dad doesn't have a decent bone in his body. He's been biding his time and waiting for the right prospect to come along."

"So you're going to marry the man he picked?" he asked incredulously.

"What choice do I have, Maverick? If I don't then I might never see Aunt Lois again. Not knowing where she is, it's tearing me up inside."

He pulled Phire into his arms and held her when the tears began to fall again. Simon Bordella was an ass, not deserving to have Phire for a daughter or her aunt Lois as a sister.

"I understand, Phire, but at some point you'll need to stand up to him. After living with Bart for thirty-two years, I've learned that the only way to deal with a wannabe dictator is to stand up to them once and for all."

"I want to but I can't, Maverick. There's too much at stake. There is no doubt in my mind that if I don't give Dad what he wants I won't see Aunt Lois again."

"How can you even deal with the thought of what he's demanding that you do?"

"By reminding myself that I did agree to the deal. As crazy as Dad's ultimatum sounds, and I'll forever think he did it for the wrong reasons, he kept his end of the agreement. You've even commented about how

nice a place it was where Aunt Lois was being kept."
She paused while swiping at her eyes. "Then there's
Jaxon Ravnell."

He lifted an eyebrow. "Who's Jaxon Ravnell?"

"The man Dad has chosen for me to marry. Dad
invited Jaxon to dinner the first day I arrived home,
and practically every single evening since. He honestly
seems like a nice guy, and I think he's fully aware Dad
is trying to throw us together. My orders are to convince Jaxon that I'm the best thing for him."

She paused again. "For some reason I think Jaxon is
pretending to be easily persuadable, but he has no intention of letting Dad railroad him. There's something
about Jaxon that makes me thinks he's playing Dad."

Maverick didn't say anything for a minute. If what
she believed was true, then her father deserved it. What
Phire didn't deserve was to be caught in the middle. "I
still think you should stand up to your father."

"As long as I don't know where Aunt Lois is, I can't
and he knows it." She added, "I'm hoping Jaxon found
me not to his liking, anyway."

As far as Maverick was concerned, unless this
Ravnell guy was blind, there was no way he hadn't
thought Phire was beautiful.

"I don't want to talk about Dad and Jaxon anymore,"
she said. "I've missed you, Maverick. We haven't talked
in almost a year. To be honest, I wasn't sure you would
even take my call."

He looked down at her. "Why?"

"Because we agreed to end our FWB relationship."

"Do I need to remind you it was your idea, Phire?"
He wouldn't tell her that they shared a bond he couldn't
explain and an intense attraction he couldn't deny.
Whenever he thought of her in the arms of another

guy, it was like a knife being driven in his heart. He kept telling himself there should be no reason for him to feel that way when he didn't love her, but the feeling persisted nonetheless. Over the last year, he had thrown himself into his work, trying to get over her. He'd finally taken off a couple of weeks in August, when he had gone to visit his cousins in Napa Valley.

Instead of responding to what he'd said, she cuddled in his arms, and he held her as neither said anything else. For a minute he thought she had dozed off with him holding her. Then she shifted in his lap to gaze up at him again. The moment their eyes connected, he felt it. That crackle of energy that would pass between them when desire simmered, making the air hot and raw with need.

Whenever that happened, he became aware of how she felt in his arms, the heat of her skin and her scent. Especially her scent. He heard it when her breath caught, almost at the same time as his. He felt a yearning so sexual that his entire body began to ache.

"Phire."

He whispered her name as she leaned up and offered him her lips for a taste of what he knew was the sweetest, most delicious flavor any mouth could possess. At that moment, he could no more not give her what they both wanted than he could stop breathing.

"I have to give Dad what he wants, Maverick, so tonight has to be goodbye," she whispered when he brought his lips closer to hers.

Like hell it would be. There was no way he would allow her father to force her into marrying anyone. When she stuck out her tongue to lick his lips, his guts twisted, and he captured her mouth in his. He heard the low moan from deep within her throat and it did something to him. He hadn't heard it in a long time and had missed the sound of it.

Their kiss intensified and he became aware of her in every pore of his body, in every single cell. Somehow, he managed to ease off the sofa with her still cradled in his arms and their lips remaining locked. He broke off the kiss, and whispered the words, "I want you, Phire."

"I want you, too," she responded.

Satisfied that their thoughts, wants and needs were in sync, Maverick headed toward the bedroom.

Phire had meant what she'd told Maverick. She wanted him. She'd also meant it when she said this would be goodbye. She couldn't fight her father, not if she wanted to find out the location of her aunt. What if Jaxon didn't want to marry her any more than she wanted to marry him?

But all other thoughts left her mind the moment Maverick placed her on the huge bed. And then he stepped back and stared at her. He would never know just how much she loved him. It didn't matter if she ended up marrying Jaxon or some other man. Maverick Outlaw would always have her heart.

"Earlier you said you missed me. Well, I've missed you, too, Phire. I missed talking to you on the phone, flying to Paris knowing when I got there that I would see you, spend time with you, make love to you. I missed the sound of you breathing, inhaling your scent. I missed everything about you."

Whether Maverick knew it or not, his words touched her deeply, although she knew they were based on lust and not love. It didn't matter. Just knowing he'd come when she'd called meant everything to her. This was the goodbye she needed.

"I'm here now, Maverick. Please don't keep me waiting."

There could never be an emotional aspect to their relationship, but they'd always had the physical. But then, at present, they weren't even *in* a relationship. They weren't even friends who shared benefits. They were friends who had to say goodbye. Unlike when they'd ended their FWB relationship, and they had kept in touch. At least for a while. Until it had become painful to hear his voice. That's when she'd decided to fade from his life and let him assume she'd met someone else.

This time when they parted it would be permanent. She wouldn't be able to call Maverick again just to see him, be held by him. By then she would be someone else's wife.

Phire watched as he moved toward the bed, then sat on it to remove his shoes and socks. Afterward, he removed her boots and socks, gently easing them off.

"You have beautiful feet," he said throatily.

"Thanks. You have beautiful feet, too."

Maverick did and she would often tell him that. He reached for her and she came willingly, knowing he enjoyed undressing her. And she always loved the way he did it, because as he removed each piece he let her know how much he liked every inch of her body. Tonight was no exception.

When she was completely naked, he stood and stared at her. She sat back on her haunches in the middle of the bed and smiled up at him. Maverick, her outlaw. "Now it's my turn."

"Okay."

She scooted across the bed to him and began unbuttoning his shirt, taking her time. Knowing this would be the last time she performed this ritual made her chest fill with anguish and she fought back a sob. She loved him and she had to give him up. The last time she'd done so, she'd known that although she was giving up the benefits, there would always be the friendship. That wouldn't be the case anymore.

When she had finished with the last button, she eased the shirt off a pair of massive shoulders. She then gazed at the naked chest she loved. "Now for your pants. As usual, I'm going to need your help." She always had a problem sliding his pants down his aroused body.

"No problem," he said in a voice that was huskier than usual. She eased off the bed and went to him. Together they tackled the removal of his pants and then he stood before her as naked as she was.

Maverick pulled her into his arms and together they tumbled back on the bed as he covered her mouth with his.

Four

With his kiss, Maverick wanted Phire to know just how much he had missed her.

He had assumed she would be out of sight and out of mind, but she hadn't been. And no other woman he'd been with since they'd been apart had eradicated her from beneath his skin. He'd missed her taste and the way heat ignited between them before they could draw in another breath. Passion had always been more than within their reach. It took control with an intensity that had them both moaning before things even got started.

Like now.

The mating of their mouths seemed endless, as if they were making up for lost time. Over a year's worth. He continued to kiss her, hungrily, greedily, needing this as much as he needed to take another breath.

When oxygen finally became a necessity, he broke off the kiss and rested his forehead against hers, breathing deeply. Mentally, he knew he needed to slow down, but physically, he wasn't sure he could. He gently stroked the bare skin of her neck, before leaning in to lick the area, loving how her skin tasted.

"Maverick…"

"Yes, baby?" he answered.

He had gotten aroused even more from hearing her say his name. He skimmed his fingers over her upper body, reacquainting himself with her breasts. He cupped them in his palms. Lowering his head, he swiped his tongue across her nipples several times before covering a breast with his mouth to suck hard on it. Her body shivered beneath his mouth and that only made his erection harder.

"Two can play your game, Maverick, the outlaw."

Before he realized her intent, she pushed him on his back, her warm hands claiming just what she wanted. "It's been a while, Notorious," she said, talking to his throbbing member and referring to it by the name she'd given it. "Before you show me how much you've missed me, let me show you how much I've missed, you, too."

With that said, she eased him into her mouth while her fingers stroked his sensitive flesh. The loud moan that escaped his lips couldn't be helped. Nor could he stop himself from groaning her name and clenching the bed coverings. And when she ardently worked her mouth on him, he felt as if he was being driven out of his mind.

Over and over again, she brought him to the verge of ecstasy, and when he felt ready to explode, she refused to let go. She deliberately clamped her mouth down on Notorious while her tongue got greedier.

"Phire!"

He let loose and she still refused to let go. When he

managed to regain the sanity he'd lost to her mouth, he flipped their bodies.

He was about to thrust into her when she said, "Wait. I'm no longer on the pill."

He went still and stared down at her. "Why not?"

"I began getting headaches, so the doctor took me off them for a while. I didn't have a problem with that since I was no longer sexually active."

He nodded, eased off the bed and picked up his pants off the floor. "No problem. I've got condoms."

"Good." The mass of brown hair that covered her head was in disarray around her shoulders and the eyes staring back at him were filled with as much desire as he was feeling.

He smiled as he went back to her. "Since you wanted to get a taste of me, now is my time to get one of you," he said, scooting back onto the bed. Before she could close her legs, his head was between them.

His greedy tongue took delight in giving absolute attention to her clit. He knew she was feeling good when she lifted her hips off the bed and held tight to his head to keep him there. It wasn't long before he had licked her right into an orgasm.

Then he moved on top of her, groaning in anticipation. He went deep, and deeper still. Her inner muscles held him tight, trying to take him hostage, but he pulled back and began thrusting hard. Over and over again, refusing to let up or slow down.

He kept going and going and when she screamed his name, he let go. Thrusting harder, he felt the moment his semen released inside her.

What the hell!

Although it had never happened to him before, he knew that it had this time. Damn! The condom had bro-

ken and Notorious was living up to his name. And Phire
felt like fire. She didn't know what had happened, and
he was about to tell her when he felt her inner muscles
tightening around Notorious even more, milking everything out of him. She was doing a damn good job.
Too good. He was about to pull out of her, but then his
treacherous body responded and bucked straight into
another orgasm. When she screamed out his name, he
knew she had reached another high as well.

It was only when they were sated that he eased off
her and pulled her into his arms. He glanced over at
her and saw that her eyes were closed and her lips were
spread into a satisfied smile.

"Phire?"

"Hmm…"

"Open your eyes, baby. There's something I need
to tell you."

She evidently heard something in his voice that
had her slowly opening her eyes and looking at him.
"What?"

"The condom broke."

Maverick held Phire while she slept. After the shock
had worn off from his words, she'd said it wasn't the
right time of the month for her to get pregnant. That
relieved his fears…somewhat.

Since she didn't seem bothered by the accident, he
tried not to be, either. He'd gone to the bathroom and
dispensed of the defective condom. Since all the ones
in his wallet had come from the same package, he had
left her sleeping while he'd put on his clothes and gone
downstairs to the hotel's gift shop to purchase a new
pack.

She'd told him she wanted to spend the next two days

with him, and he wanted to make sure he not only had enough condoms, but that they were also ones he could depend on. Like he'd told her, nothing like that had ever happened to him before.

He doubted she knew just how good it felt having her back in his arms. Since ending their FWB relationship, he'd tried returning to his routine of being a perpetual womanizer but had discovered he couldn't. At least not to the degree that he had been before Phire. He'd found other women lacking.

Now, he glanced down at Phire and smiled at how her lips tilted at a seductive angle as she slept. Sleeping or awake, the woman was totally alluring. He recalled what she'd said about not being involved with anyone during the year they'd parted. She would never know how many nights he'd lain awake thinking about her. Phire was everything any man would need. Not only was she gorgeous, but she was also intelligent, thoughtful, loving and kind, which was evidenced by how she looked out for her aunt. There was no doubt in his mind that some lucky guy would appreciate having her on his arm. *In his arms.*

He hated admitting it, but deep down, part of him was glad she hadn't found her Mr. Right. He didn't fully understand why he felt that way, but the thought of her with another man cut him to the core.

Maverick had convinced himself it wasn't jealousy that made him feel that way. It was merely the fact that she was his friend, and he didn't want any man to ever hurt her again like that prick Jacques Fontaine had done. *And that included her father.*

There had to be something he could do. Even if it meant contacting his cousins, Quade and Cole Westmoreland. The two owned a security firm with international connections. Maybe they could find out where Phire's father had moved her aunt. Hopefully, Quade and Cole could even give an update on the woman's condition. That information could definitely give Phire peace of mind.

He glanced over at the clock. It was close to midnight. After he had returned from the gift shop, Phire had awakened and they'd ordered room service. After eating they'd showered together and made love all over again before drifting off to sleep. Now he was awake and his mind couldn't help but think about the defective condom. What if she had gotten pregnant? For him that would be a game changer. Before they parted ways, he would make sure she knew that. There was no way he would allow her to marry another man if she was carrying his baby. He didn't give a royal damn about her father or whatever plans he had for her and that Ravnell guy.

The one thing Maverick had vowed years ago was that he would not be like Bart and take a child away from its mother. Co-parenting was something he didn't have a problem doing if it came to that. Of course, there was another option, one that left a bad taste in his mouth. Marriage. He could marry Phire for their child's sake. That way he could have his child with him all the time. He would have Phire with him, too. The thought made him feel something he didn't want to explore...

There had to be another option. He wasn't the marrying kind. He was certain he and Phire could work out something, and keep what would be best for their child at the forefront.

Their child...

He might be putting the cart in front of the horse.

But if she wasn't right about the timing, the one thing an Outlaw knew was to always be prepared.

Phire knew the moment Maverick entered the bedroom. Although he wasn't saying anything, she knew he was watching her pack. Their two days of idyllic bliss had come to an end. She refused to look in his direction, afraid he would see the deep love she had for him in her eyes.

So instead, she thought about how much she had enjoyed the time they'd spent together. These had been the best two days and three nights she'd had in a long time. After their first night, they had gotten out of the hotel around noon, enjoyed a delicious lunch in the hotel's restaurant and gone shopping. She'd needed an outfit since he'd told her he intended to take her to dinner and dancing later that day.

Both had been fantastic. They'd gone to one of the fanciest restaurants in Dallas, the French Room. Afterward, they'd danced the night away at the Singer Nightclub. It felt good being in his arms while they danced, and more than once, he'd whispered how much he'd missed her. That had been the last thing she needed to hear when she knew their two days together were all they had.

It was way after midnight when they returned to the hotel. As soon as he'd closed the door behind them, they had quickly undressed each other and made love all through the night and most of the next day. On their last evening together, he had taken her skating.

For a while she had forgotten her troubles. It had always been that way whenever she spent time with Maverick. He had a knack for knowing what she needed. And he knew her needs weren't always in the bedroom.

However, those times when they *were* in the bedroom, he could definitely deliver.

"We need to talk, Phire."

She heard the seriousness in his voice and stopped what she was doing to look at him. His tall, sexy frame leaned in the doorway. He was shirtless and his jeans were riding low on his hips. They had made love for the last time less than an hour ago and she was missing him already.

"What do we need to talk about, Maverick?"

"I know you said you doubt that you're pregnant, but if you're wrong—"

"I'm not," she interrupted.

"But if you are, that changes everything. I want you to promise me something."

She lifted an eyebrow. "What?"

"That you'll contact me and let me know."

She frowned. "You think I wouldn't, Maverick?"

"I don't want to think so, but you won't stand up to your father. The man who sounds as ruthless as they come. After being raised by such a man myself, I can see your father trying to force you into not telling me or convincing you not to have the baby."

Yes, unfortunately, she could see that, too. "If I am pregnant, Maverick, which again, chances are that I'm not, but if I am, I promise to contact you."

What Maverick had said was true. If she was pregnant, then it would change everything. He was not a man who would walk away from a child he'd conceived, regardless of whether that conception was planned or not. On the other hand, if she was pregnant and didn't follow her father's orders and marry Jaxon, that meant she might not ever see her aunt again. Knowing such a thing was possible sent a chill through her.

Maverick must have seen her tremble because he crossed the room and pulled her into his arms. "If you are pregnant with my child, Phire, everything is going to work out."

She pulled out of his arms. "How can you even think that it will? You don't know my father like I do. There are things about him that my aunt would never explain to me. The only things she would say was that whatever was done in the dark would one day come to the light. She also warned me never to cross him."

He lifted her chin so their gazes could meet. "Doesn't matter. If you are pregnant, I will claim my child and there won't be anything your father can do about it."

Maverick would claim his child…but not her? She pushed the pain of his words from her mind. Although she loved Maverick, she knew he didn't love her. She also knew he would never marry any woman. He'd told her that countless times. Phire knew about his mother and how she had betrayed his father. For that reason, he didn't see the institution of marriage as anything he wanted a part of—ever. Not even for the sake of his child. His child would have his love, his name and everything else that came with being an Outlaw. There was no doubt that he would respect her as his child's mother and they would remain friends, but that would be as far as things went between them.

"So we're in agreement, Phire. If you're pregnant you will let me know."

It was a statement and not a question, but she nodded, anyway. "Yes, Maverick, I will let you know."

Five

Maverick glanced at the calendar on his desk. It was mid-January. How long did it take a woman to find out if she was pregnant? He had come close to asking his sisters-in-law, but knew he couldn't without raising anyone's suspicions, and Google hadn't provided any answers that made sense in his situation, so he'd waited it out. He was still waiting it out.

Going through the holidays had been hard. More than once he had been tempted to call Phire or text her, but he knew he had to be patient. Since she hadn't called, did that mean she *wasn't* pregnant? What he should have done was make her promise to call him, regardless of the outcome.

He tossed several paper clips on his desk while remembering their time together in Dallas. He didn't want to think about how she might have spent the holidays or with whom. What if her father was still using manipulation to bend her to his will?

He looked up at the sound of a knock on his office door. "Come in."

Garth stuck his head in the door. "Will you be joining us for lunch? You never did say at the meeting."

Maverick quirked an eyebrow. "I don't recall anyone asking."

Garth came into the office. "I did, but you seemed preoccupied."

Maverick would admit that he had been. This was one of those rare times when all his siblings were in Alaska. Since yesterday had been Martin Luther King Jr. Day, Jess and Paige had flown home to Fairbanks on Saturday morning. Cash, Brianna and their family had done so as well. "Will my beautiful sisters-in-law be joining us?"

Garth chuckled. "No. They made plans to go shopping."

"With the kids?"

"No. Claudia volunteered to babysit, and my son's nanny will be there to assist."

"Christ, you guys trust your kids around Bart? I can see him instilling into their young minds the importance of inheriting Outlaw Freight Lines."

Garth shook his head, grinning. "I doubt Claudia will let that happen. By the way, I just got a call from Walker. He arrived in town this morning, so he's joining us as well."

Maverick nodded. Walker Rafferty had been Garth's best friend since childhood. He and his wife, Bailey—who was a Westmoreland cousin—had twins and lived on Kodiak Island.

"So are you joining us?"

"Yes. Just tell me where."

"Loretta's."

Loretta's used to be both Jess's and Cash's favorite eating place. "Fine. I'll meet you guys there at noon."

A short while later Maverick had finished working on a document. After tossing it aside, he stood to get his coat when his cell phone rang. He recognized the ringtone. It was Phire. He couldn't pull his phone out of his pocket fast enough.

"Phire?"

"Yes, it's me."

"You have something to tell me?" He was anxious to know what she had to say.

When she didn't answer, he drew in a deep breath and slid down into his chair. "Phire?"

"I'm pregnant, Maverick. I honestly didn't think I was, even when I was late. But I just left the doctor and he verified it."

He could hear the panic in her voice. "Everything is going to be alright, Phire."

"You keep telling me that, and I keep telling you that you don't know my dad. He's still being relentless about me marrying Jaxon. He's only happy when Jaxon and I go out on dates, so I've been doing that a lot to appease him."

Dates? Knowing she and that Ravnell guy were going out—and from the sound of it pretty damn frequently—didn't sit well with Maverick. "And your father still hasn't told you where he's moved your aunt?"

"No. I can't imagine what Aunt Lois thought when I didn't come see her. Especially during the holidays. It was hard for me to pretend everything was okay when it wasn't."

Maverick picked up an ink pen on his desk and tightened his fingers around it. A part of him wished it was Phire's father's neck. Maybe he should tell her that he'd asked his cousins to check into things. He decided not to say anything yet since Quade and Cole had to wrap up a couple of important cases before they could take on his.

"I meant what I said, Phire. Your pregnancy is a game changer. I'm coming to claim what's mine. I want you to pack and be at the Austin airport tomorrow around three."

"I can't leave, Maverick."

"Why can't you?"

"I just can't. Not until I know where Aunt Lois is. If I left, Dad might retaliate and withdraw all the care he's been paying for and—"

"If he does that then I'll take over your aunt's medical expenses, Phire."

"I can't ask you to do that."

"You're not asking me, I'm volunteering."

She was quiet for a minute and then said, "I can't just take off with you, Maverick."

He frowned. Why couldn't she? Had she started falling for this Ravnell guy? "Why not?"

"Where will you take me? What will I do?"

"I'll take you wherever you want to go. Even Paris. And you won't have to do anything. You're giving birth to an Outlaw, and from now on, I'll take care of you."

"I don't need you to take care of me, Maverick. Look, I need time to digest everything. Like I said, I just left the doctor's office and I'm sitting in my car in the parking lot. I wanted you to know because I promised I would tell you, but I won't let you run roughshod over me."

Run roughshod over her? "I'm not doing that."

"Yes, you are, and I'm tired of people telling me what to do and expecting me to obey."

"Phire…"

"I'll call you back in a few days, Maverick."

A few days? "Phire, listen. I need you to—"

Click.

He moved the phone from his ear and stared at it. Had she just hung up on him? What the hell! And what did she mean about him running roughshod over her? He was trying to remove her from that toxic environment with her father. Couldn't she see that?

Maverick placed the phone on his desk and rubbed his hand down his face when the full impact of what Phire had said hit him. They had made a baby together and he was going to be a father. *A father.* He would be the first to admit that fatherhood had never crossed his mind, but now that it was a reality, a part of him was glad about it.

He leaned back in his chair and recalled how on Christmas Day, Sloan and Leslie had announced they were expecting and how happy the two of them were about it. Sloan had done what he'd sworn to do— gotten his wife pregnant by Christmas. Neither Maverick nor Phire had been trying. In fact, everything was his fault because of that defective condom.

As soon as he'd realized what happened, he should have pulled out. Instead, his greedy ass had lost control and kept right on going, thrusting his way into another orgasm. If she hadn't gotten pregnant from the first release, then the second had probably done the trick.

His cell phone rang, and he recognized Garth's ringtone. He picked it up. "Yes, Garth?"

"We're all here at Loretta's. Have you left the office yet?"

"No, I got an important call, but I'm on my way."

"Alright."

He clicked off the phone and stood. He trusted the five men he was meeting for lunch, and more than anything he needed their advice.

Phire was fuming. Maverick had a lot of nerve. How was he going to claim the baby without claiming her, too? Filled with anger, she couldn't drive any farther, so she pulled into the parking lot of a shopping mall, parked and then turned off her car to calm down.

What had she expected when she'd called Maverick? Had she honestly assumed he would mention the word *marriage*? That he would indicate that he not only wanted their baby, but also wanted her?

Well, he hadn't. All he'd wanted was to come get her because she was carrying his baby. He hadn't even said what he intended to do with her when he got her. Would he end up being as controlling as both her father and his? He was claiming her baby without any regard for what she needed or wanted.

She didn't know how long she sat in her car before she finally pulled herself together. She placed her hand on her stomach and for the first time that day, she smiled. Just the thought that a life was growing inside of her was a bit overwhelming, but also wonderful.

Today she had even heard her baby's heartbeat. She hadn't known such a thing was possible, thinking it was too early for that. But since she'd known her conception date, the doctor had told her a heartbeat could be detected after twenty-two days. It was the most beautiful sound she'd ever heard. Maverick hadn't given her a chance to tell him about the experience before he began stating his claim. Although his attitude had infuriated her, she still felt overjoyed at the thought of the baby she and Maverick had created.

Phire wished she could be totally happy. She would be if it wasn't for her father being a ruthless and manipulating ass. Just that morning he reminded her that March was the beginning of spring, which meant she didn't have long before she and Jaxon should announce their engagement.

Their engagement!

Although her father had successfully thrown her and Jaxon together every chance he got, Jaxon still wasn't biting. And she was glad. They'd gone out together several times, and she had a feeling he was truly trying to get to know her. However, he didn't seem any more eager to get into a serious relationship with her than she was with him.

He was always a perfect gentleman. Even when he kissed her good-night it was always on the forehead. If she didn't know better, she'd think he had a girl back in Virginia. If that was true, then why was he going along with her father to court her?

She could see her and Jaxon being friends rather than lovers. Even with his good looks and charming personality, he was not anyone she could fall in love with. Her heart belonged to Maverick, even if she was annoyed with him at the moment.

She yawned, feeling sleepy. The doctor had warned her such a thing might happen. Pregnant women had a tendency to sleep a lot. He'd also given her a number of prenatal books to read. She would hide them somewhere in her room to make sure none of her father's loyal household staff saw them and reported back to him.

The only good news for her was that her father had announced at breakfast that he would be leaving to go on a business trip and would be gone for a week. Although he no longer practiced law, in order to maintain his license, there were continuing education requirements he had to fulfill. She was glad he would be leaving to take those classes in Houston. She definitely needed the break from him.

Phire started her car to head home. Chances were, Jaxon would be coming to dinner yet again tonight.

Maverick glanced around the table at the five men. They had all finished lunch and were drinking coffee and enjoying a slice of Loretta's mouthwatering peach cobbler when he decided to drop the bomb.

"I'm going to be a father."

In unison, all the forks went still, and five pairs of eyes stared at him. It was Walker who finally spoke. Maverick figured his brothers were too busy picking their jaws up off the floor. "Congratulations, Mav."

"Thank you."

"Wait a minute! How in the hell did you get a woman pregnant?" Sloan bellowed in a voice so loud Maverick was glad Loretta had given them a private room in the back. They'd been coming here since their teens and she knew whenever the Outlaw boys got together—and then add Walker to the mix—it meant loud and boisterous conversations.

Maverick had to fight back a smile, the first he'd felt like having since getting the news Phire was pregnant. "The same way you got Leslie pregnant, Sloan."

Cash raised an eyebrow. "You were trying to get a woman pregnant?"

"No. The condom was defective," Maverick said.

"Is that what she told you?" Jess asked.

"That's what I know." He then stared from one

brother to the other. "Let me set something straight. The baby's mine. There is no doubt in my mind that it is because I know the night that I got Phire pregnant."

"Phire?" Sloan asked, staring hard at Maverick. "Isn't that the name of the woman you were with when you stopped speaking to me? Because I left Paris earlier than planned and you had to leave with me?"

Maverick rolled his eyes. "I don't recall that scenario."

"I do," Cash said. "I was on my way to Black Crow, Wyoming to prepare for that weekend when I'd invited all of you there with our Westmoreland cousins. I clearly remember that you called me, Maverick, whining, and saying you weren't speaking to Sloan because he'd rushed back to Alaska from Paris, cutting your time short with some woman named Phire."

Maverick frowned. There were times he wished his brothers didn't remember every single thing that concerned him. "Whatever."

"That was a good three years ago, maybe a little longer. I've never known you to stay with a woman that long. Usually, one night, no longer than a weekend, is your limit."

Maverick shrugged. "Phire is different. Her real name is Sapphire Bordella, and she's my best friend."

"You got your best friend pregnant?" Jess asked incredulously.

Maverick rolled his eyes again. "We were involved in a FWB arrangement."

"A what?" Walker asked with a confused look on his face.

"Friends-with-benefits arrangement," Cash answered before Maverick could.

"And when did this conception happen?" Sloan said.

"I hope it was *after* I got Leslie pregnant because I still intend to have the first Outlaw girl in that generation."

Maverick shook his head. Sloan had let it be known, to anyone who would listen, that he wanted his first child to be a girl. "I saw Phire the weekend of Jess's wedding. That's when it happened."

"So that's why you rushed away from the wedding," Cash said, grinning. "You were hot in the crotch."

"I didn't rush from the wedding. In fact, I didn't leave until after Jess and Paige. Anyway, I got Phire pregnant that weekend. She called today. That's why I was late getting here."

"So your best friend is pregnant with your child. What are your plans, Maverick?" Garth hadn't said anything before now. Leave it to his oldest brother to get down to business by wanting to know details.

"I told her to start packing because I was coming to claim what's mine."

"You're flying to Paris to get her?"

"No, I'm flying to Austin. She was living in Paris temporarily. She's from Texas. Her family owns a ranch there."

"In Austin?" Sloan asked.

"No, it's a small town outside of Austin called Forbes. Austin is the closest airport."

"Forbes?" Garth asked, scrunching his brow. "I've heard of that town before for some reason."

"So you're flying to Texas to bring Phire to Alaska?" Walker asked.

"That was my plan but…"

Maverick paused, then Jess prompted, "But what?"

Before Maverick could answer, Garth said, "Let me guess. You never did ask what she wanted to do. You told her what you wanted her to do, mainly to start packing. And that pissed her off."

Maverick quirked an eyebrow. "Yes, I did tell her that I was coming to Texas and claim what's mine."

Four of the men—namely Garth, Cash, Sloan and Walker—shook their heads as they stared at him. "The one thing you're going to learn about pregnant women, is that you don't order them around. You have to treat them gently. More gently than normal."

"Why?" Maverick and Jess asked simultaneously.

"Because they get overly emotional. I'm finding that out for myself," Sloan answered. "It has to do with an increase of hormones or something. They cry for no reason at all. Get mad at you about any little thing, and they like eating weird stuff. Like mixing pickles with ice cream."

"And they sleep a lot," Walker added.

"And heaven forbid if they're carrying twins. When they go into labor, they'll scream at you like everything is your fault," Cash added.

When Maverick didn't say anything, Garth asked, "You told her that you were coming to Texas to claim what's yours. Exactly what is yours?"

Maverick rubbed his hand down his face. "I just told you guys. She's pregnant and the baby *is* mine."

"We get that, Maverick," Sloan said. "What Garth is trying to find out is if at any time you let this Phire woman know you also claim her, too."

"No. I figured I didn't have to tell her that. I can't claim the baby without claiming her. At least not until I figure out what else I need to do."

"Hell, I hope you're not planning to do what the old man did. Take her to court for custody of the baby after it's born," Cash said.

"I wouldn't do that."

"You sure?" Jess asked. "You look like the old man more than any of us. I hope that doesn't mean you'll eventually start acting like him, too."

"I won't, and like I said, I won't take my child away from Phire. They are a package deal."

"Does she know that?" Garth asked. "Sounds like you didn't do a lot of talking, just a whole lot of claiming. Did you ask how she was doing? Assure her that you'd never take your child from her, like your father did to his five wives? Did you even ask if she wants to be pregnant? She does have a choice you know."

It occurred to Maverick that he hadn't taken the time to ask Phire how she was doing or how she was dealing with her father. No, he'd gotten her upset, to the point that she'd hung up on him. It was the first time she'd ever done that, and he would admit that he'd deserved it. Garth was right. Whether she wanted to be pregnant or not was her choice. He'd been too busy telling her what to do instead of asking what she wanted. Now he'd made a serious mess of things.

"Why do you have to rush off to get her?" Walker asked when no one said anything.

Maverick glanced over at Walker. "Because her father is trying to marry her off to another man."

"What! How old is Phire?" Cash asked.

"Twenty-five."

"Then she's old enough to tell her father to go to hell with that kind of nonsense," Sloan said.

"She can't," Maverick said.

"Why not?" Jess asked.

"Because he practically kidnapped her elderly aunt, who had a stroke a few years ago. It's the aunt who raised her. Her father moved her aunt from one long-term-care facility to another one, and he won't tell Phire where until after she marries the man he has chosen for her."

For the second time that day forks went still as five pairs of eyes stared at him. Finally, Garth said, "I think you need to start from the beginning, Maverick."

Phire glanced across the dinner table at Jaxon. As usual, he seemed to be hanging on to her father's every word, which put a smile on Simon Bordella's face. It also gave him an incentive to keep talking. It was obvious her father was trying desperately to get Jaxon interested in the land surrounding their ranch. Land that, she'd been told, had been left to her grandfather, passed on to her mother and subsequently to her father.

She moved her gaze back to her plate. This wasn't the first time her father had tried talking Jaxon into buying the land. However, tonight was the first time Jaxon seemed interested in doing so. She wondered why.

"So what do you think, Sapphire?"

She glanced over at Jaxon. "About what?"

"My buying all that land adjacent to this ranch."

She shrugged. "The decision is yours."

Jaxon nodded. "Do you plan to return to Paris to live?"

Before she could answer, her father quickly spoke up. "My daughter is home for good, Jaxon. In fact, just the other day she mentioned she didn't intend to leave the ranch ever again. That let me know she would want to one day marry someone interested in settling in the area."

Jaxon smiled. "Hmm, that's good to know," he said, picking up his wineglass and staring at her over the rim of it. If she didn't know any better, she'd think he was analyzing her. This wasn't the first time she'd gotten that impression.

"I have a favor to ask you, Jaxon," Simon said.

Jaxon put down his wineglass and smiled over at Simon. "And what favor is that?"

"I'm leaving Monday for Houston to take some continuing education classes, to retain my law license."

"Do you plan to begin practicing law again?"

"Heck no, but it will come in handy if I need to represent myself."

"Oh, I see," Jaxon said, and Phire figured he really did. Her father was tight with his money.

"I'll be gone for a week and there's something I need you to do."

"And what is that?" Jaxon asked.

"I know you'll be busy with your own affairs during the day, but I'm hoping in the evenings you'll find time to check on things here."

Jaxon chuckled. "Not sure what help I'll be since I know very little about ranching."

Simon waved off his words. "I'm not talking about my ranch per se. I have a capable foreman for that."

"Then what exactly are you talking about?" Jaxon asked.

"Sapphire. She will be here all alone while I'm gone. My daughter is my most precious jewel, and I need to make sure she is taken care of. That way I won't have to worry. You could even use one of the guest rooms while I'm gone."

Phire almost choked on her bite of steak. Her father couldn't get any more accommodating than that. He was inviting Jaxon to move in here while he was gone? And that BS about her being his most precious jewel nearly made her gag.

"I appreciate the trust you've placed in me, Simon," Jaxon said, smiling.

Phire glanced at Jaxon and met his gaze. He then switched his gaze to her father, smiled and said, "Looking after Sapphire will be my pleasure."

Had she misjudged Jaxon Ravnell? Was he just as manipulative as her father? Even more cunning? Did she have a say in the matter? What if she didn't want him here?

Later that night, Phire got out of bed, unable to sleep. Crossing the room, she went to the window and looked out into the darkness. She couldn't believe the nerve of her father, inviting Jaxon to stay here while he was away. And then to outright lie to the man about her wanting to remain in the area to live. If given the chance, she would move back to Paris in a heartbeat.

Gently rubbing her stomach, Phire knew she would go back there and build a life for her and her baby. At that moment her child was the only good thing happening in her life, and she would cherish it because she and Maverick had made it together.

Maverick.

She was tempted to call him, but he might not accept her call after the way she had ended their conversation earlier that day. She had hung up on him, for Pete's sake. She'd never done anything like that to anyone in her life. Never had a reason to do so no matter how mad she'd been.

She checked her watch. There was a three-hour time difference between Texas and Alaska. By her calculations it would be around 7:00 p.m. their time. She would call him because she owed him an apology.

But before she could call, her phone rang. From the tone, she knew it was Clancy. She had asked him to snoop around to see if he could find out anything about what facility her aunt had been moved to.

"Hello, Clancy. It's four in the morning there. What are you doing up?"

"Just got back from taking the folks to the airport. They're taking a cruise out of Barcelona."

"Good for them."

"I think so, too."

"Have you turned up anything on my aunt?" she asked him.

"Not a thing. I even had Dionne asking questions, but it seems everyone who works at that long-term-care facility is keeping a tight lip. I'm sorry, Phire."

"Don't be. I appreciate you and Dionne trying to find out anything for me. How are the twins?"

"My girls are fine and growing every day. I decided they won't ever date. No guy will be good enough for them."

Phire smiled, wishing she could have had such an adoring father while growing up. "Well, give them and Dionne my love. And thanks again for trying."

"Wished we could have been more help. When are you coming home?"

She nibbled on her bottom lip. Clancy knew her father was using her aunt to force her into marrying someone. However, she hadn't told him that she was pregnant with Maverick's child. "I'm not sure yet."

"Well, I hope you won't let your father force you into marrying someone against your will, Phire. That's plain ludicrous."

Clancy let her know how his parents were doing before they finally ended the call. She barely had time to place her phone down when it rang again. She couldn't ignore the increase of her heart rate when she recognized Maverick's ringtone. Was he calling to make more demands? State more claims? She knew as her baby's father he had certain rights, but she couldn't help wondering if he would do her like his own father had done and take her child away from her.

"Hello?"

"Hello, Phire, it's me. How are you doing?"

He sounded calm and not anxious, like he had earlier. "I'm fine. In fact, I was about to call you. I should not have hung up on you earlier today. I apologize."

"I'm the one who should be apologizing. I didn't even take the time to ask how you were doing or what you wanted." He paused. "Do you want to be pregnant, Phire?"

His question made her automatically rub her stomach. "Doesn't matter now, does it?"

"But do you want to keep it?"

His question made her hand go still. Was he suggesting that she not have the baby? Had he changed his mind and now wanted to wipe his hands of the child they'd made together? "Why are you asking me that, Maverick? Do you not want me to keep it? Are you suggesting that I get—"

"No!" he said, before she could finish her question. "That's not what I'm suggesting, and it doesn't matter whether I want you to keep it. It's what you want to do."

"It's your baby, too, Maverick. Do you want it?"

"Yes, I want it."

She released a sigh of relief. "And I want it, too. I intend to be a good mother."

"There's no doubt in my mind that you will be. And I intend to be a good father. I don't intend to be anything like your father or mine."

"That's good to hear because Dad's on a roll. He

knows he has me just where he wants me as long as I have no idea where he's taken my aunt."

"Well, just so you know, I've hired my cousins' security firm to locate your aunt's whereabouts."

"You did?"

"Yes. I refuse to have your father hold something like that over your head. And I meant what I said, Phire. I have no problem taking over the cost of your aunt's expenses."

She fought back her tears. Maverick didn't love her, but he was doing whatever he could to lighten her load. She knew why he was doing it. She was having his baby and no matter what, it was all about claiming what was his. "Dad's going out of town next week to attend an attorney seminar in Houston and he had the nerve to invite Jaxon to stay here while he's gone."

"Good, let him stay there, but that doesn't mean you have to be there, does it?"

"No, but where will I go?"

"I'd love to see you. I'm coming to Austin and will be staying with my cousins, Clint and Alyssa Westmoreland. They have a spread, the Golden Glade Ranch, that's about seventy miles outside of Austin. I'll be staying in one of their guest cottages. I'd love for you to join me. We do need to talk, Phire."

She nibbled on her bottom lip as she thought about what he'd said. She knew he was right. They did need to talk.

"Will you have a problem with getting away?"

"No. I'll tell Dad that I changed my mind about staying here while he's gone and will be flying back to Paris to check on things there. He won't like it, but at this point, I don't care. I don't like the idea of him inviting Jaxon to stay here without asking how I felt about it first."

"I don't like it, either, and I have a plan to outsmart him."

That sounded pretty good to her. "Okay, Maverick, what's your plan?"

Six

"You think I don't know what you're doing?" Simon said, glaring at Phire across the breakfast table.

She looked up from her meal. "And just what am I doing? I'm merely going back home to check on things."

His glare deepened. "You're deliberately defying me, and it won't work, Sapphire. In the end I will get just what I want. Paris is no longer your home. This is. And there's nothing for you to check on there. If you think you can go snooping at that long-term-care facility for answers as to your aunt's whereabouts, don't waste your time. They have my orders not to tell you anything."

Phire had discovered that fact when she'd called the facility last month, hoping there was something they could tell her. Even the nurse who'd taken care of her aunt, whom she'd gotten to know, refused to talk to her.

"Look, Dad, you're not the only one who can spring

a surprise on someone. You had no business inviting Jaxon to stay here while you're gone."

"I don't see why not. He's going to be your husband eventually. It's obvious the man is quite smitten with you and if you were to add enough pressure, I'd have that spring wedding."

She glared over at her father. "I won't be rushed into anything."

"Well, remember what I said. I won't tell you the whereabouts of your aunt until *after* you're married," he said, standing. He angrily threw his napkin on the table before storming out of the room.

Phire continued eating, refusing to let him ruin her day. She glanced around and saw several of the house staff eyeing her suspiciously. She figured her father had told them to keep an eye on her and report everything she did back to him. She was grateful her pregnancy wasn't causing her to have morning sickness. If anything, she was eating more.

A short while later she was looking through her closet to pack. She and Maverick had decided that there was no need to wait until after her father left for Houston on Monday to put their plan into motion. In fact, Maverick thought it would be better to do it before he left since he'd probably have her watched.

The one thing she did constantly was make sure her phone was with her at all times. She wouldn't put it past her father to have a member of his household staff check for messages to pass on to him. The young woman who came in to straighten her room, Massie, was friendly enough, but Phire had a feeling she couldn't be trusted.

As she began choosing what outfits she would take with her, she felt happy at the thought that not only would she be seeing Maverick, but she would also be spending an entire week with him. He'd given her instructions about how they would pull things off and she was ready. Just in case her father decided to check, Maverick was purchasing a ticket to Paris in her name with a flight leaving Saturday morning. That was just part of the plan.

She turned at the knock at her door. "Come in."

It was Massie. "Mr. Bordella wanted to let you know that Mr. Ravnell will be joining the two of you for dinner. You should look extra nice tonight."

"Did he say why?"

"I believe Mr. Ravnell is bringing a business associate."

Whatever. "Thanks for the message, Massie."

Phire frowned when the woman closed the door. She couldn't wait to leave on Saturday.

"Thanks for letting me know, Clint. I'll see you back at the ranch."

Maverick clicked off the phone. He'd figured Phire's father would doubt that she was leaving for Paris. As a favor, his cousin Clint Westmoreland, a Texas Ranger turned rancher, had begun tailing Phire the moment she'd entered the terminal. He'd recognized her from a photo Maverick had shown him last night.

Clint's phone call to Maverick was to let him know that he'd picked up on two other tails as well. Did Simon Bordella figure it would take two men to follow his daughter? According to Clint, the two men had ended their tail once she'd gone through the TSA security gate for Paris.

Little did they know, the Outlaws had TSA connections, thanks to an old former-marine friend of Garth's, Ollie Linton, who'd recently been promoted to regional director of Transportation Security Administration in the southwest region of the country. Ollie was instrumental in making sure Maverick's plan worked on this end. Now it was time for Maverick to do his part.

He walked through the airport terminal, ignoring the interested looks of women he passed. The only woman he wanted to see was Phire. He glanced at his watch as he continued toward the area where she would be waiting for him.

Frissons of fire raced up his spine with every step he took. But then, it had always been that way. Especially those times when he took a trip to Paris. When the plane landed, just knowing they would soon be breathing the same air did something to him.

Maverick then recalled their time together in Dallas. Although he wanted to curse every time he thought of that defective condom, he'd finally accepted that what had happened was meant to be. He hadn't planned on being a father this soon, or ever, but now that he was one, he honestly didn't know of any other woman he would want to give birth to his child.

Phire had all the attributes he desired for his baby's mother. Now he intended to do whatever was necessary to keep her out of harm's way, even if it meant dealing with her father. And he honestly didn't know what that Jaxon Ravnell guy was all about, but it didn't matter. Simon Bordella might think the man was in the picture, but Maverick had news for him.

Hopefully, it wouldn't be long before Cole and Quade discovered where Phire's aunt was being kept, and once that information was determined, he and Phire would decide what to do next.

He slowed his pace when he rounded a corner and saw her. She hadn't seen him yet, so he had a chance to slow his steps and study her. She looked beautiful, as usual, dressed in a long flowing skirt with a plaid jacket and boots. Today she was wearing her hair just how he'd liked it, flowing loosely around her shoulders.

Not for the first time, he wondered how a woman who was his best friend could cause such an abundance of desire to invade his body, in every pore and nerve. Just the thought that his child was growing inside of her had his heart racing at the wonders of nature. He'd meant what he'd told her on the phone that night before their call had ended. They would work through this because they had a child to protect.

Maverick wasn't sure what gave him away, but suddenly she turned to look in his direction, and she saw him.

Phire's breath caught the moment she saw Maverick. She blinked at first, making sure it was him since he was dressed in a way she'd never seen him before. In Western attire. He even had a Stetson on. If she didn't know for a fact that he'd been born in Alaska, she would have sworn he was a Texan through and through, all the way down to his boots.

Her gaze drifted over him as he continued walking toward her. She liked the way he looked in his Western shirt and jeans with the shiny belt buckle around his slim waist. She felt the heightened beat of her heart the closer he got, and heat curled inside her.

When he came to a stop in front of her, she nearly melted when he flashed a smile from beneath his Stetson. "Hello, Phire."

It always did something to her whenever he said her name, but today it was doubly so. And it didn't help matters that his dark, mesmerizing eyes were drifting over her facial features like a visual caress.

"Maverick. It's good seeing you."

"Then show me how good it is, beautiful lady."

She smiled up at him. It wouldn't be the first time she and Maverick had openly displayed their affection, and she figured it wouldn't be the last. Besides, today called for it. They would be sharing more than a kiss. They would be sharing the knowledge that together they had made something special. A baby.

She moved closer and stood on tiptoe to wrap her arms around his neck. That's when he captured her lips, kissing her with all the passion she'd come to expect. Anyone seeing them would assume they were lovers who'd been separated for a long time, instead of the best friends that they were.

Phire needed this. To be held in Maverick's arms this way and kissed thoroughly by him. It had been nearly two months since she'd seen him.

When he finally released her mouth, he smiled down at her. "Ready to go?"

Unable to speak, she nodded.

He took her hand, and they began walking. She felt protected with him. Maverick, and only Maverick, could make her feel this way. "What about my luggage?"

"It's been loaded on my plane. I told you about that friend of Garth's who's over the TSA in this region?"

"Yes."

"Well, he handled everything."

They had taken flights together before. He'd surprised her with a trip from Paris to Rome for her twenty-third birthday. However, this would be the first flight where he would be at the controls.

He'd told her he would fly his personal plane to Texas

and land at his cousin Clint's airstrip. He had arrived yesterday and had called her last night to give her additional last-minute plans. She hadn't lied when she'd told her father she would he flying out of the Austin airport. But she had lied about her final destination.

When they stepped through an exit door that led to where private jets and smaller aircrafts were located, he said, "That's my plane over there. We've been cleared to fly."

She glanced over at the silver plane they were walking toward. He'd told her it was a Cessna. The name *Maverick* was written in bold black letters across the door. "It's beautiful, Maverick."

"Thanks."

Once they reached the plane, he opened the door for her, and she was impressed with how comfortable the seats in the cockpit looked. He helped her up and then walked around to get in. She watched him, still in awe at how good he looked. Just like a real cowboy.

When he got inside, he glanced over at her after she had snapped in her seat belt. "Why were you looking at me like that?"

So he had caught her staring. "I can't get over the transformation of how you look in Western attire."

He grinned. "This is usually how I dress whenever I visit my brother Cash on his ranch or my Westmoreland cousins in Denver, Montana or here. It took some getting used to, but I like the Western look."

"You should because you wear it well."

"Thanks, I'm taking that as a compliment." He leaned in and brushed a kiss across her lips.

She settled back in her seat as he began working the controls and talking to someone at the air-traffic-control tower.

"You look good and you smell good, too. How are you feeling?"

Phire smiled over at him. "Thanks, I'm feeling fine."

"No morning sickness still?"

"No morning sickness, and I'm glad. That would have been a dead giveaway to Dad that I was expecting."

Maverick nodded before turning his attention back to the controls. "Our destination is the Golden Glade Ranch. We should be there in about fifteen minutes. So get comfortable and enjoy the flight."

Maverick glanced over at Phire. She had fallen asleep the minute his plane leveled off in the sky. He then recalled what one of his brothers had told him about pregnant women napping a lot.

He'd meant what he told her about how good she looked and smelled. Even now her scent was getting to him. It always had and he figured that it always would.

She had never met anyone in his family, not even his brothers, and he looked forward to introducing her to Clint and Alyssa. He hadn't explained the full nature of their relationship to them, but they knew him well enough to know that inviting Phire to spend time with them was a good indication that she meant a lot to him. She did. Even before she'd become pregnant with his child she had meant a lot to him.

Deciding to spend time with Phire at the Golden Glade Ranch had been a good idea, and he appreciated Sloan covering for him at work. Even Cash had volunteered to take on some of his duties. Maverick might give his brothers hell most of the time, but when he needed them, they came through for him.

He knew they would be landing soon. He thought of

his cousins, the triplets, Clint, Cole and Casey. Casey, the youngest and a female, lived with her husband, McKinnon Quinn, in Montana where they ran a horse-training facility.

Cole also lived in Montana with his physician wife, Patrina. Both Clint and Cole had learned to fly planes while working as Texas Rangers, so Clint said a runway on the ranch made sense. In addition to the security company Cole owned with Quade, he was also CEO of a helicopter-service company that provided transportation to the people living on the various mountains in Bozeman, Montana. One of which included Clint, Cole and Casey's father, Corey Westmoreland.

It was hard to believe it had been less than ten years ago that the Outlaws had discovered their Westmoreland cousins. Anyone around them for any period of time would swear they'd known each other all their lives. The connection had been automatic and immediate. The only person who still had a problem with it was Bart. But then, Maverick knew his father had a problem with anything he couldn't control. Except for maybe Claudia, he thought, grinning.

Maverick glanced back over at Phire and thought of the next seven days. His gaze lowered to her stomach and shivers went through him at the thought that a child—his child—was growing there. As if she felt him staring at her, she slowly opened her eyes and their gazes locked. Immediately, he felt that crackle of energy. And then he saw the blush creep into her features. It made her even more beautiful.

She straightened up in her seat and asked, "What's wrong?"

"Nothing's wrong. What makes you think there is?"

"You were staring at me."

He smiled over at her. "You were staring at me earlier, so I figured it was my turn."

"You, Maverick, the outlaw, need to keep your eyes on where you're going."

He laughed at that. "As you can see, there's no one else around. It's like we have the skies to ourselves."

She looked around again and nodded. "Yes, it does look that way, doesn't it? It's beautiful up here. This is my first time flying in a plane this small."

"I'm glad your first experience was with me."

Phire glanced at him and nodded. "I am, too." She paused. "Your cousins do know that I'm coming, right?"

"Yes." There was no reason to tell her that Clint had watched her when she'd arrived at the airport and had reported two different men tailing her. He would share that when they knew more. He wanted her to relax while she was here and not worry about anything.

"And they don't have a problem with you having a guest in your cottage?"

"No, and we won't be using a cottage after all. My cousin Casey has a nice home not far from the ranch house. When she heard I was coming and had invited a special lady friend, she insisted I use her vacant place to make sure you were comfortable."

"That was kind of her," she said.

"Yes, it was, and I took her up on her offer."

"Where does she live?"

"She and her family live in Montana, but she grew up on the Golden Glade. Their uncle, Sid Roberts—"

"Sid Roberts? *The* Sid Roberts?"

Maverick grinned. "Yes. I heard he was a legend in these parts."

"He definitely was. First as a rodeo star and then as a renowned horse trainer."

"Well, he willed all his land to his nephews and niece—Clint, Cole and Casey. Since Casey and Cole live in Montana, they're satisfied with building homes on the property to use whenever they come to visit since all three siblings have growing families."

He paused and then added, "I didn't tell Clint and Alyssa about your condition. However, I did tell my brothers, so they are the only ones who know for now." He worked at the controls. "Clint and Alyssa are looking forward to meeting you since I've never invited a woman anywhere before, so they know you're special."

"Tell me about them," she said.

He smiled. "Clint and Alyssa used to be Texas Rangers. On one undercover assignment they had to pretend to be a couple and get married. The marriage was to have been annulled at the end of the assignment."

"It wasn't?"

"No. Someone let that bit of paperwork fall through the cracks. It was five years before they discovered they were still legally married. Unfortunately for them, a judge refused to give them a divorce until they lived together as man and wife for thirty days."

"They did?"

"Yes. Alyssa moved from Waco to spend a month with Clint on his ranch. By the time the thirty days were up, they had fallen in love and decided to make their marriage real."

"Oh, that's so romantic. Do they have any children?"

"Yes. Four. The oldest is Cain, and he's twelve. Carolyn, who was named after Clint's mother, is nine, and the twins, Collin and Colton, are seven."

She nodded. "Multiple births run in your family, don't they?"

He smiled over at her. "Yes, we have a lot of twins

and several triplets. Does the idea of multiple births make you nervous?"

"Yes," she said, laughing. "But if I'm having two babies or three, it doesn't matter. I want our baby or babies."

"So do I. Now hold on because we're coming in for the landing."

Seven

Phire liked Alyssa Westmoreland right away. Her warm and friendly smile put Phire at ease, and Clint was tall, dark and handsome. He favored Maverick a lot. When she'd said that, Alyssa had laughed and told her about those strong Westmoreland genes. She couldn't wait for Phire to see the other Westmorelands and Outlaws together. It surprised Phire that Alyssa assumed it was a foregone conclusion that she would one day meet Maverick's other family members.

She was introduced to Alyssa's elderly aunt, Claudine, who was married to Chester, the man who had been Clint's cook and housekeeper for years. Chester had been a widow when he'd been smitten with Claudine when she'd flown in for the renewing of Clint and Alyssa's wedding vows. It had taken six years for Chester to win her over, and for her to move from Waco to Austin.

The older couple had built a beautiful home on a piece of Golden Glade property that Clint and Alyssa had given them as a wedding gift. It was far enough from the ranch to give them privacy and close enough for them to visit as often as they liked.

"You're going to like Casey's home," Alyssa said.

"I'm sure I will, and I appreciate you letting me spend time here with your family."

"We're glad to have you."

Alyssa's words were still on Phire's mind when they left in Maverick's rental SUV. He told her Casey's home was a few miles from Clint's, and that a lot of land surrounding the Golden Glade was used as a reserve for wild horses.

It wasn't long before Maverick brought the vehicle to a stop in front of a beautiful two-story home with a wraparound porch. "The house is gorgeous."

"Yes, it is. The door is unlocked, so go right on in while I bring in your luggage," Maverick said, opening the car door for her.

"Okay." She smiled up at him. A man wearing a Stetson did something to her every time.

Placing her purse strap on one shoulder, she strolled up the walkway and went inside. The furnishings and decor had a sturdy Western flair, and everything looked like it belonged. A stunning staircase led to another floor and she figured that's where the bedrooms were located.

She crossed the room to the window and looked out at the huge lake. Across the way she could see the roofline of another house and figured it belonged to the other triplet sibling, Cole.

"Well, what do you think?"

She turned and met Maverick's gaze. "What I see is amazing and the view of the lake is so picturesque."

"Wait until you see the canyon. Now that's a magnificent sight," Maverick said, placing her luggage in the middle of the living room. "Come on and let me show you around."

He gave her a tour of the huge eat-in kitchen and dining room, the mudroom, the laundry room and the wine cellar. He told her about his cousin's vineyard in Napa Valley, and because of it, there was never a chance of any of his relatives running out of wine. Phire then followed him upstairs, where six bedrooms were located—five on one wing and a primary suite on the other that was huge, nearly the size of the other five rooms combined.

"That was kind of your cousin to let us stay here," she said as they headed back downstairs.

His smile widened. "I would be the first to say that all my cousins are kind. When we met them a few years ago, my siblings and I were amazed at just how kind and genuine they were. They treat us like we've always been a part of the Westmoreland family, and we can't help but feel good about that."

"And you should. Being born an only child, I always envied those with a large family. I always felt alone."

He pulled her closer to his side. "You won't ever have reason to feel alone again, Phire. I'm going to make sure of it."

Maverick then leaned down and kissed her.

This was the second kiss they'd shared today. Phire doubted it would be the last, and she was looking forward to more. Maverick had the ability to kiss the panties right off a girl, which was why she usually went without wearing any whenever he spent time at her place. He'd said he liked knowing she walked around her house with no undies.

When he deepened the kiss, her hands went to his broad shoulders, loving their firmness beneath her fingers. She wasn't surprised when she felt his palms on her backside, stroking her cheeks through the material of her skirt. Maverick had a way of turning a sizzle into a scorcher.

Phire knew she had to end things before Maverick had her spread out on that bed. Or she might be the one to spread him out. Neither option could take place until they talked. She broke off the kiss, but he still was nibbling her mouth. "Maverick?"

"Mmm?"

"We need to talk." Within seconds of saying those words, she was the one taking his mouth again, running her hands over his muscled body. His hands were on her backside again, and he eased up her skirt, little by little, while he deepened the kiss.

When he had hiked her skirt to the point where his fingers were now easing between her legs, she broke off the kiss again, trying to catch her breath. "We do need to talk, Maverick."

He pulled back to look at her and his smile was so sexy it almost made her melt to the floor. "Okay, we'll talk. But just for the record, it won't take a week for us to talk, Phire."

She tilted her head and looked at him. Was he letting her know that he had sexual plans for her this week? Whatever plans he had were dependent on how their talk went. They needed to concentrate on their child and not each other.

He eased her skirt back down, and then took her

hand to lead her over to the love seat. "Okay, let's talk," he said, sitting down and pulling her into his lap. She moved away to sit beside him. If they were going to do some serious talking then they needed distance.

"Tell me again how you've been feeling," he said, stroking the side of her face with his fingertips.

Trying to stay focused, she said, "Not counting sleepless nights, intense anger I feel for my dad whenever I see him and spouts of anxiety whenever I think of Aunt Lois, I'm doing fine."

Maverick frowned. "None of those things are good for you in your condition, Phire."

"That's not good for anyone in any condition, Maverick. But there's nothing I can do for now."

"Yes, there is."

"What?"

"You can marry me as soon as it can be arranged. Will you, Phire? Will you marry me?"

With those words, Maverick had just offered a commitment to a woman, a commitment he'd sworn he would never offer. But he knew this wasn't just any woman. This was Phire, his best friend. The woman who was full of sunshine and warmth on even the coldest of days. The one woman whose smile could brighten his entire world. But, more importantly, she was the woman who was pregnant with his child.

He would admit that first he'd thought claiming his child didn't mean getting full custody. Co-parenting would have suited him just fine. He was in a financial position to provide them with whatever they wanted or needed. It didn't matter to him if Phire lived in the States or in Paris, he would take care of them. And he would only be a flight away since he intended to be a part of his child's life. He trusted Phire enough to know she would never keep his child from him and he would have access to him or her whenever he wanted.

So when had thoughts about that sort of arrangement changed? When had he decided he preferred that they get married? Probably after he'd talked to her the night they'd made plans to spend this time together. The moment he had heard her voice he'd known he didn't want to live apart from her and his child. He wanted more. He wanted them to be a constant part of his life.

He studied her reaction to what he'd said. She'd stared at him without blinking. Now she was blinking a lot…as if she thought she must not have heard him correctly.

"I can't marry you, Maverick."

Her words crashed into his thoughts. They weren't what he'd wanted to hear. "And why can't you?"

She released a deep sigh. "Think about it, Maverick. We're best friends, not lovers."

He couldn't help but smile at the absurdity of that. "We're best friends who were lovers, which resulted in a pregnancy." As he said those words he couldn't forget how Jess had looked at him incredulously and asked, "You got your best friend pregnant?"

Yes, he definitely had. Now he'd just asked that same best friend to marry him. "Like I said, we're best friends, Phire. However, I will admit that thoughts of having you naked beneath me have crossed my mind more than a few times today."

She rolled her eyes. "We both enjoy sex. In fact, I want more of it now that I'm pregnant."

Maverick could tell by the look on her face that she hadn't meant to reveal that fact. Sloan had told him such a thing was possible during the early months of pregnancy. He wondered what she would do when he wasn't there. Would she turn to that Jaxon guy?

"You're not sleeping with anyone else, right?" he asked.

She frowned at him. "Anyone like who?"

"Anyone."

Her frown deepened. "I told you I haven't slept with anyone since we ended things, Maverick. I know I told you I hoped to meet someone and get serious, but I never did. And do you honestly think I would sleep with someone else knowing I was pregnant with your child? You should know me better than that, Maverick."

"I do, but I had a moment of panic when you mentioned your desire for sex had increased."

"It has, but that doesn't mean I want it from anyone else. Just you." She nibbled on her bottom lip. "So can we reinstate our FWB relationship this week?"

He stared at her. Did she honestly think after making a baby together and his proposal of marriage that they could ever go back to being friends with benefits? "I want more, Phire, and I still want you to tell me why we can't get married."

She didn't say anything. Instead, she looked out the window. When she glanced back at him, she said, "It would ruin our friendship, Maverick, and I don't ever want to lose you as my best friend."

The moment Maverick realized Phire was serious, he took her hands in his. When he felt them shaking, he pulled her into his arms, and when he heard a sniffle, he tightened his hold. "Don't ever think that will happen to us, Phire. We'll be best friends for life, regardless."

She drew away from him and swiped at her tears. "I'm sorry, Maverick. I've been crying a lot lately. All these extra pesky hormones."

He pulled her back into his arms. "What have you been crying a lot about? Has the thought of being pregnant made you sad?"

She pushed back to look up at him. "No. Although we didn't plan for this baby, it is the brightest part of my life. It's all the other stuff that often weighs me down. I try not to think about it, but can't help doing so."

"And it's all that other stuff I want to protect you from, Phire. You don't deserve the crap your father is putting you through. It's bad enough he won't tell you where your aunt is, but trying to force you into marriage is crossing the line. If you're going to marry anyone, it should be me."

"Yes, but…"

He raised an eyebrow. "But what, Phire?"

Phire looked away again, trying to regain her composure. How could she tell him that the real reason she couldn't marry him was because everything he wanted to do for her was because of the baby? He would offer her the moon so that their baby could be protected and cared for. But he didn't love *her*. It wasn't his fault that she loved him so much and it broke her heart that he couldn't love her back.

"Our baby would have parents who didn't love each other."

"But we do love each other, Phire. We just aren't *in love* with each other. You and my baby are the most important people to me right now."

"But why do we have to get married, Maverick? Shared custody would work for us."

Maverick didn't reply, but she could see his agitation. Why? Didn't he know she was trying to make things easy for him? Why should he give up his womanizing ways because she was pregnant with his child?

Instead of commenting on what she'd said, he glanced at his watch. "Let's go for a drive."

She lifted her brow. "A drive?"

"Yes, I want to show you around the Golden Glade."

Knowing Maverick like she did, she figured he was only dropping the subject for now. There was no doubt in her mind that he would pick it up later when he thought he would have the upper hand.

Standing, she said, "Okay, a drive sounds wonderful. But I need to use the bathroom first."

When she returned a short while later, Maverick was no longer standing by the love seat, but had moved over to the window. "I'm back."

He turned around and smiled at her. "So you are. And about our earlier conversation."

"Yes?"

"I don't want you to feel like I'm rushing you into anything, Phire. Just promise me you'll think about my marriage proposal."

She nodded. "Okay, I promise I will."

"And just so you know, I'm taking a month's leave from work."

"Why?"

"To hang around to be close to you in case you might need me for anything."

There he was, being thoughtful again. "Anything like what?"

"Anything. I don't like the thought of you not sleeping at night and feeling stressed."

"It can't be helped until I find out where Dad has taken Aunt Lois, Maverick."

"And what about Jaxon Ravnell?"

If she didn't know better, she would swear Maverick sounded jealous. But she did know better. "I'm still trying to figure him out. He seems to be a nice guy, but then a part of me feels he's up to something and could be just as manipulative as Dad."

"Don't think about any of that now. I want this week to be a relaxing and peaceful one for you." Taking her hand, he said, "Come on and let me show you around the ranch."

Eight

"I can't believe how beautiful the Golden Glade is," Phire said when they returned a few hours later. Surprising her with a packed lunch that Chester and Claudine had prepared, Maverick had chosen a spot near the south ridge for them to have a picnic. All around them had been the open range, fields and meadows, and he showed her the reserves where all the wild horses ran free.

"Whoever's idea it was to build those cute outhouses in several locations on the range must have understood the needs of a pregnant woman."

Maverick grinned as he took off his Stetson and placed it on the rack by the door. "I understand it was Alyssa's idea. She designed them and had them built specifically for the men and women who work on the ranch. A lot of them spend most of their days on the range, and she wanted to not only make things convenient for them, but also nice to look at."

"They are and that was really thoughtful of her. I like her."

"And she likes you," he said, heading for the kitchen. A cold beer sounded nice about now.

"How do you know?"

"She told me." He stopped walking, turned around in time to see the huge smile on Phire's face. And those dimples he loved. His eyebrows drew together. "Why are you smiling?"

She shrugged and shoved her hands into the pockets of her skirt. "Because I am."

He recalled her telling him that she'd never had any girlfriends while growing up in Texas. Her father didn't allow her to socialize with any of their neighbors. When she moved to Paris, most of the girls in her class didn't bother to befriend her because they didn't speak English. He figured that's why she appreciated Alyssa's friendship. He couldn't wait for her to meet Charm and the other women in the Westmoreland family. There was no doubt in his mind they would like her, too.

"I think I'll take a nap now. Which guest bedroom will we be using?" she asked.

Maverick hadn't wanted to assume they would be sharing a bed again until they had a more in-depth discussion about their baby business. Evidently, she felt they had said all that needed to be said for now.

"Whichever one you want to use." It honestly didn't matter which bedroom he slept in as long as she was in there with him.

"I like the bedroom with the window facing that huge lake," she said, walking over to the window and looking out. "That other house across the water belongs to Cole, right?"

"Yes, that's Cole's place," he said, coming to stand beside her. "He and his family come down often to visit, especially during the winter months, to escape the Montana cold. But they don't come as much as they used to since their kids are in school."

She looked up at him. "How many kids do they have?"

"Three, which includes a set of twins," he said, gently pulling her against his chest.

Her eyes widened. "More multiple births?"

He chuckled as he leaned in, still cradling her in his arms. After placing a kiss on her forehead, he said, "Yes, if only you knew how many others there are. Not sure if I mentioned that Cole's wife, Patrina, delivers babies."

Phire's eyebrows arched. "She's a midwife?"

He chuckled. "No. Patrina is an ob-gyn and has her own practice in Bozeman. You will get to meet her later this week."

"I will?"

"Yes. Clint mentioned that Cole and his family will be flying in on Saturday. He has his own plane as well. In addition to Westmoreland Security Firm, he also owns a helicopter service in Bozeman."

"He sounds like a busy man."

"That he is."

She wrapped her arms around his neck. "Thanks for lunch, Maverick. I'm one of the lucky pregnant ones— not only do I not have morning sickness, but so far there's nothing I eat that upsets my stomach. Those sandwiches were delicious."

"You'll have to tell Chester and Claudine that at dinner."

She smiled. "I will, and thanks for inviting me here. I needed to get away. Now maybe I'll sleep better at night."

He leaned in and brushed a kiss across her lips. "Hmm…don't be so sure of that."

"Why not?"

"Have you forgotten how much I enjoy middle-of-the-night sex?"

She chuckled. "No, in fact I'm counting on it. I told you about the increase in my sex drive."

"Yes, you did, and I intend to take care of that while you're here."

A smile played at her lips in a way that made him want to devour them.

"Then there's no doubt I will sleep better this week." Then after a breathy sigh, she asked, "So will you take a nap with me now?"

"Do you want me to?" he asked her.

"Yes."

Maverick swept her off her feet and into his arms, and decided he would have that beer later.

When Maverick placed Phire on the bed, she couldn't help smiling up at him. When her doctor first told her some women experienced an increase in their sex drive during the first and second trimesters of pregnancy, she'd brushed it off as one of those things that wouldn't happen to her. But it had. Erotic dreams of Maverick would wake her up at night, only because they were never fulfilled to the extent they would have been in reality.

"Are you going to take off your clothes or do you

want me to do it for you?" he asked in a voice so husky it sent vibrations shooting right to her core.

If he did it, Phire doubted she would last because he liked touching her all over after discarding her clothing. She honestly doubted she could handle that right now. He stood there with his arms folded across his chest in a stance that was so sexy, she had to clench her thighs together or come from the sight of him. His gaze fixed on her as if he wanted to eat her alive.

"I'll take off mine and you take off yours, and let's see who's the fastest," she said. They had played this game before, numerous times, and she'd always finished before him. A woman might take the longest to get dressed but it was a different story when it came to undressing. Besides, when she'd worked in that boutique in Paris, the owner used to host fashion shows and she was one of the models. The one thing a model knew was how to do a wardrobe change quickly.

"Baby, you're on."

She eased up on the bed and began removing her clothes. First her blouse and bra, and then her skirt and panties. Her boots would take the longest because of the zipper.

"I'm done, Phire."

She jerked up her head, and sure enough, he was totally naked. Her womb contracted with intense need just from the sight. "How did you finish before me?"

He chuckled as he moved toward the bed to help with her boots. "My secret."

She glanced over at his pile of clothes and when she didn't see his briefs, she turned back to him and cocked an eyebrow. "Have you gone commando on me, Maverick the outlaw?"

"You're asking too many questions, Sapphire."

"Whatever." He seldom called her *Sapphire*, but whenever he did, it sounded a lot nicer off his lips than her father's. Even the way Jaxon had said it hadn't done anything for her.

Maverick's hand began stroking her legs and she stopped thinking.

"I love your legs."

"I know." That was one of the things he always did—compliment her legs. Reaching up, she cupped his chin and gazed into his dark eyes. Her heart was racing, and she couldn't slow it down.

He eased them both back against the pillows. "I just want to hold you a minute and get to know my child, Phire."

His words touched her and when he began caressing her belly, she fell in love with him even more. Her pregnancy might not have been planned, but she so wanted this child because it was part of Maverick.

Adjusting their positions, he placed a kiss in the center of her stomach and whispered, "I am your daddy, little one, and I love you."

Phire couldn't stop the tears that sprang in her eyes. His words were so special because he was claiming their child, not out of possessiveness but out of love. And it was love she felt and she believed her child felt it, too.

After placing several more kisses on her stomach, he pulled her into his strong arms. And when his mouth came down on her, she was ready, parting her lips on a desirous sigh. His tongue took hold of hers, moved around her mouth, possessing and claiming.

It had been nearly two months since they'd shared a bed. Two lonely months for her but being here with him now was worth the agonizing wait. All her thoughts dissolved with every stroke of his tongue.

His hands had moved back to her stomach and were gently stroking her there again. He pulled his mouth away and looked down at her. "Making love to you… the way I usually do, won't hurt the baby, will it?"

Phire knew why he was asking. Not that he was ever rough, but when it came to making love, he was always thorough and intense. Just the way she liked it. His thrusts were always hard, reaching her to the hilt, and making every cell in her body yearn in primitive hunger. She loved the feel of the solid length of him going in and out in rapid succession.

"No, nothing you do to me will hurt the baby. It's all good." Just looking at his aroused body let her know he would be alright.

"You sure?"

"Yes, I'm positive. The doctor said that whatever I was doing before I could continue doing. I can even continue horseback riding as long as I don't get risky with it."

He gave her a look that meant he would have something to say about her riding a horse, so she decided to save that discussion for another time. Especially when her gaze lowered to his chest. Unable to help herself, she ran her fingers through the curly hair. She always loved how it felt, and for her it was such a turn-on. Like she really needed something else to get her aroused.

"Maverick," she whispered.

"Yes, baby?"

"Make love to me. I need you so much."

"And I need you, too, Phire," he said, nibbling at her throat before licking around her mouth.

She couldn't help but moan, parting her lips in an invitation he didn't need. He was well aware of what his tongue did to her. His hand moved upward to her breasts, which were sensitive since she'd become pregnant. Those same breasts that could trigger an orgasm the moment his mouth touched them.

To prove her right on that account, he sucked on a nipple and a multitude of sensations swept through her, sending her body into a mind-blowing explosion. She screamed his name when an orgasm slammed into her. Before she could recover, she met another head-on as he kissed her other breast.

By the time he'd moved into position over her, she'd gotten needier. Her clit throbbed mercilessly with wanting him. After he devoured her breasts, he shifted to bury his head between her legs. Maverick had introduced her to oral sex and her womanly core hadn't been the same since.

He looked down at her. "How am I doing so far?"

Did he really have to ask after three orgasms? "You've yet to break a previous record," she said, "but you're off to a good start."

"I haven't even started," he said, holding tight to her gaze as his body eased into hers.

She trembled from the intimate contact and was tempted to break eye contact with him, fearful he would read what was clearly there. She loved him.

After he reached the hilt, he paused and stared down at her. She stared back. The darkening of his eyes revealed the extent of his desire and the firm set of his jaw showed the degree of his control. She could feel every inch of him, throbbing and ready. So what was he waiting on? What was on his mind?

She was about to ask when he captured her lips in a kiss that was unparalleled to any before. It was full of something deep and substantive, but for the life of her, she couldn't define just what that was. All she could do was return it and enjoy the moment.

Then he began thrusting into her, a little too easy at first, but when she lifted her hips off the mattress as an indication she wanted him to go deeper, he finally obliged. "Maverick…"

They moved together in perfect harmony. They were spontaneous combustion that had been ignited and now they were all but ready to blow. Their bodies were ablaze with desires, with wants and needs. Suddenly, her entire body fragmented into a thousand pieces, each making her stomach curl.

There was an intensity in this lovemaking that had never been there before. This was unadulterated, unyielding, relentless passion.

She screamed out his name at the same time he threw back his head and hollered hers. Phire knew she couldn't fall more madly in love with someone she already loved, but if such a thing was possible, it had happened to her.

"Ah, baby, you just don't know what you do to me, Phire," Maverick whispered against the side of her neck after easing off and taking her into his arms.

"Probably the same thing you do to me." With Maverick, she knew how it felt to be all woman because he was all man. "You satisfied its mama, so our baby is smiling."

He touched her chin with his finger, and every nerve ending within her sizzled. It was as if she hadn't experienced four orgasms over the last hour. "That's good to know because its old man is smiling, too," he said, doing just that.

Neither of them said anything for a minute. Maverick just looked at her. She knew that hot look. It was the kind that drew her in and made her feel desired.

Warmth returned to the area between her legs, slowly seeping into her very core. He wanted her again and she wanted him again, too.

As if Maverick felt her heat, he leaned in and captured her mouth.

Nine

Phire glanced around the dinner table. Seeing the faces of Maverick, and Clint and Alyssa's family, was a lot more appealing than sitting across the dinner table from her father. Jaxon's company wasn't so bad, except those times her father all but threw her at the man.

"Phire, I understand your father has a ranch as well."

Alyssa's comment made Phire look across the table and smile. As she'd told Maverick, she really liked Alyssa. In addition to being friendly, Alyssa was kind. Phire thought she looked gorgeous no matter what time of day it was, and she certainly didn't look like she had given birth to four children. Four very active children. Another thing Phire noted was that Alyssa was very much loved by her husband. That was obvious by the way the couple interacted with each other.

Phire and Maverick had arrived for dinner early, and the moment Clint entered the house, after being out on the range most of the day, he'd gone straight to his wife and given her a huge kiss. Regardless of the fact they had an audience.

"Yes, it's on the east side of Austin, on the outskirts of Forbes."

"Has it been in your family long?" Clint asked her.

"I understand my maternal grandfather inherited the land from a client. The old man died without any family and willed it to my grandfather, who was his attorney at the time."

"That's sad that the man died without any family," Maverick said.

Phire realized this was the first time she'd ever shared that bit of information with him, mainly because she never liked talking about her home in Texas. The ranch had seemed less like her home the longer she'd lived in Paris.

"Yes, it was. But it stayed in our family. My father was a young attorney who worked for my grandfather. I'm told my mother had left home to attend an all-girls college in Atlanta. When she came home after graduating, she and my father met, fell in love, and the rest is history."

For the life of her it was hard to believe her father could fall in love with anyone but himself. Phire might have been young when her mother died, but she never remembered seeing her parents act as affectionately with each other as Clint and Alyssa did in front of their kids.

The conversation then shifted from her to Alyssa, who talked about her job as a freelance website designer. "I love what I do and have a nice clientele. I work around Clint's and the kids' school schedules."

Clint then explained how he'd ended his career as

a Texas Ranger to run the ranch full-time, and how he and his siblings started the Sid Roberts Foundation to save wild horses in memory of his uncle.

"Did your uncle have any children?" she asked him.

"I can answer that," Chester said.

"Only because Chester believed the woman's story," Clint added, shaking his head.

Phire was intrigued. "What story?"

Clint glanced over at Chester. "By all means share your theory with Phire, Chester."

"It's more than a theory, Clint. I totally believe Sid has a child out there. I'll never forget the day that letter came here to Sid. It was from a woman telling him that she'd given birth to his son. She stated she didn't want anything from him but felt that telling him was the right thing to do. She didn't provide a return address, so Sid had no way of finding her to corroborate her story. He did hire a private investigator, who couldn't find the woman."

Phire nodded. There had never been a question in her mind that she would tell Maverick she was pregnant. "Why are you so sure there was a child somewhere when the private investigator couldn't find anything?"

"Mainly because I never trusted the guy Sid hired as the PI."

Clint chuckled. "What Chester really means is he didn't like the guy."

"No, I never liked him. You and your siblings weren't even walking yet, and he was only coming around, every chance he got, because he was sweet on your mother. Although she never gave the man the time of day. Smart girl, that Carolyn."

Alyssa's aunt Claudine served the most delicious raisin-bread pudding that Phire had ever eaten, and it was served with the best coffee she'd ever had. More than once, her and Maverick's gazes met across the dinner table, and she would remember how their nap had turned into one bout of lovemaking after another.

After dinner Phire joined Clint and his family while the older kids told them how excited they were to see their Uncle Cole and his family who would be visiting in a week. Then Alyssa read the younger two a story. Listening to Alyssa brought back so many memories for Phire of her own mother reading stories.

"You okay, Phire?" Maverick asked her when they returned to the house later that night.

"Yes, why do you ask?"

"You didn't have a lot to say on the drive back here."

"I was just thinking about Alyssa's interaction with her children. It reminded me of my mother. I recalled her reading me bedtime stories. She was a good mother." She paused. "The best thing Dad did was to send me away to Aunt Lois after Mom died. My aunt took good care of me and all I want to do is take good care of her. But because of Dad's manipulations I feel so helpless in doing that, Maverick."

He pulled her into his arms. "I told you I hired my cousins to find your aunt. We will beat your dad at this game he's playing."

We... She hadn't wanted Maverick to take on her problems, but a part of her was glad he cared enough to do so. She knew his main concern was the baby. He didn't want her to get upset because of her condition. "And you honestly think they will be able to find her?"

"If anyone can, they will. They have a great team working for them."

His words gave her hope. "Thanks, Maverick." She

pushed back and looked up at him. "So what are our plans tomorrow? I hope it includes horseback riding."

She saw his concerned look. "Trust me, Maverick. I can ride a horse as long as I'm careful. That's one of the first things I asked the doctor. I knew Dad would become suspicious if I stopped riding Salem every morning."

"Salem?"

"The Arabian horse my mother gave me for my twelfth birthday. It was the last gift I got from her. He was just a foal then, and I ride him every day when I'm home. So will you take me riding tomorrow?"

"If you promise to be extra careful."

"I promise."

He smiled down at her. "Okay then, we'll go horseback riding."

"I'm ready."

Maverick turned around and his breath caught. Phire had stepped onto the porch looking like a bona fide cowgirl. Since she'd worked in a boutique while living in Paris, he'd seen her in a number of sexy outfits. He'd even seen her in jeans. However, this was the first time he'd seen her in total Western attire. In addition to the Western shirt and jeans, she was also wearing a denim jacket with fringes, cowboy boots and a cowgirl hat that sat prettily atop her head.

"Is anything wrong, Maverick?"

He blinked, realizing he'd been staring. "No, nothing's wrong. You look fantastic."

"Thanks. Whenever, I dress like this around Dad, he claims I don't look enough like a lady to suit him. He prefers seeing me in dresses."

To be honest, Maverick preferred seeing her in nothing at all. He was liable to get aroused all over again just from thinking about their lovemaking after they'd gone to bed last night. They hadn't been able to get enough of each other. "Well, I think you look gorgeous and sexy. Does it matter what your old man thinks?"

She shook her head. "Nope. Not this week, anyway."

Maverick knew that if he had his way, it would never matter. "Here are the horses. Clint brought them over earlier."

She came down off the porch. "They're beautiful," she said. "Which one will I be riding?"

He handed her the reins. "This one. Her name is Buttercup, and she's Alyssa's daughter's horse."

"She's a big horse for a nine-year-old-girl," Phire said, scratching the animal's head and then patting her coat. "And she's beautiful." She then gazed at the horse and said in a calm, low-pitched voice, "Hello, Buttercup. I promise to treat you well."

Phire seemed to have a way with horses, which meant she was used to them. Although he'd known how to ride, he'd never done as much of it until he'd become a partner in Cash's dude ranch.

"Ready?" he asked Phire.

"Yes, I'm ready."

He helped her up on her horse and then mounted his. "In addition to new territory, we'll cover some of the same areas we covered yesterday by SUV. However, today we get to go through trails and paths that a car can't take us."

They rode at a slow pace while he told her about his brother's dude ranch in Wyoming. He then told her more about his Westmoreland cousins and how his father still refused to accept them as family. After they'd ridden a while, he said, "Let's dismount over there. I want to show you something that I didn't yesterday."

"Okay."

They brought the horses to a stop near several trees. He got down first, and after making sure they had tied the reins of both horses to a tree, he assisted her. When their bodies touched it was as if they hadn't made love most of yesterday and last night. Intense fire ignited in his loins, rushing through every part of him. He looked at her mouth and wanted to taste her lips, right then and there, beneath the Texas sky. Phire was like an aphrodisiac. The more he got, the more he wanted.

He saw the way her lips trembled and knew she wanted this kiss as much as he did. He decided to put them both out of their misery. He leaned in and took her mouth with the greed of a man who was about to have his last kiss, or the first one after months of going without.

Either scenario painted a picture that could serve as the reason why his mouth was devouring hers. The sound of her moaning only kindled the flame as she hungrily kissed him back. Her tongue moved in sync with his, stroke for stroke.

He finally forced himself to end the kiss, otherwise he would have eased her down to the grassy ground and made love to her. That wasn't a good idea when Clint or his men could wander into this area anytime.

"Why did you stop?" she asked him in a pouty voice.

He released a deep breath and pressed his forehead to hers. "You, Sapphire Bordella, will be the death of me yet."

She leaned back and smiled up at him. "I hope not, because I need you around to help raise our child."

He didn't say anything. Was she hinting at the possibility that she would marry him, or did she have co-parenting on her mind? He tightened his lips, otherwise he would be tempted to ask her. He'd told her he would not rush her into making a decision and he wouldn't. Even if he was tempted like hell to do so, he would be patient.

"Come on and let me show you something that's pretty remarkable," he said, taking her hand and leading her toward an edge that looked down into a massive valley.

"Oh, my goodness," she said, and he could hear the amazement in her voice. "You're right, Maverick. That is pretty remarkable."

That's how he'd felt when he'd first seen it. Thousands and thousands of wild horses running free. While they watched the animals, he told her more about Clint's determination to save as many of them from being slaughtered as he possibly could.

"I'm glad he's doing so," she said, leaning her shoulder up against him.

He glanced down at her. "Tired?"

"No. I just like it whenever I can touch you."

Maverick smiled at that admission. "Baby, you can touch me anytime." He tightened his arm around her.

Yesterday, while making love to Phire, he had realized something. He had fallen in love with her. Maybe he'd always loved her and was just getting around to accepting it. Either way, just like with her pregnancy, the realization that he loved her was another game changer. He would use this week to convince her to marry him. He would indulge in something he'd never done with a woman. A courtship.

"Will you be taking another nap with me later today?" she asked, breaking into his thoughts.

He smiled down at her. "Do you want me to take a nap with you again today?"

"Um, that would be nice."

Maverick thought it would be nice as well.

Ten

Phire stepped onto the porch in the early morning sunlight to drink her glass of milk. Before her pregnancy, it would have been tea or coffee, but those days were over. At least for a while.

She smiled at the thought that Maverick hadn't gotten up yet because she had worn him out. When he'd awakened her before sunrise thinking he would get a good ride off her, she had flipped him on his back and gotten a good ride off him instead.

It was hard to believe she only had two more full days to spend here with him. She definitely didn't look forward to returning to her father's ranch. But at least she would have good memories of the time spent here not just with Maverick, but with Clint, Alyssa and their family, too.

Maverick had planned something for them to do every day. There had been picnics, horseback rides and cooking lessons. She couldn't help but smile at the latter. Alyssa's Aunt Claudine had offered to teach Phire how to make several dishes that she had fallen in love with, and to her surprise, Maverick had asked to be included.

Then there were those days they just relaxed and watched television, or went swimming and hiking. He'd made sure everything was done in moderation so as not to tire her out. However, her favorite activity was nap time because they always did more than take a nap. And, of course, she enjoyed bedtime when they would make love to the point of exhaustion, and then she would sleep through the night like a baby. And he would wake her up during the predawn hours for more sexual delight.

Tonight they would accompany Clint and Alyssa to a barn dance at one of their neighbor's ranches. She was looking forward to going, even if there would probably be more square dancing than line dancing. While in Paris, she and Maverick went dancing often, and people complimented them on how well they danced together.

"So this is where you ran off to."

Phire turned at the sound of Maverick's deep voice. Her gaze immediately latched on to his bare chest and the jeans riding low on his hips before moving back to his handsome face. She was convinced that nothing looked sexier than Maverick Outlaw in the morning. But then he looked pretty darn nice at night as well.

"I didn't run off," she said, smiling. "You'd gone back to sleep and your baby needed some food."

He grinned as he walked over, placed a kiss on her lips and gently rubbed her stomach. "And what did you feed it?"

"Eggs, bacon, pancakes and milk," she said, holding

up her now empty glass. "I cooked enough to share and kept them warming in the oven."

"Thanks." He glanced down at her stomach while still caressing it. "You don't look pregnant."

She laughed. "Well, for your information, I can't snap my jeans anymore, so I've gained weight."

He grinned. "Are you sure it's all baby and not those dinners we've been enjoying?"

Phire laughed. "I have been eating a lot since coming here," she said. "Chester and Claudine's meals are so delicious." And she truly meant that.

"How often will you be going in for checkups?" he asked, still gently stroking her stomach.

"Every four weeks for now."

"When is your next appointment?"

"In a couple of weeks. Why?" she asked, tilting her head to look up at him.

He met her gaze. "I'd like to go with you. Hell, I'd like to go with you to every appointment."

She patted his cheek. "That's kind of you."

"Hey," he said, grinning broadly. "I have a vested interest in our baby."

She tried not to let his words dampen her spirits. He had a vested interest in the baby, but not in the baby's mother. Although he had asked her to marry him, she knew that was for the baby's sake. She was Maverick's best friend and knew more than anyone of his plans never to fall in love and get married. That would not change just because she was pregnant with his child, and if she married him, he would eventually come to resent her for it.

"What are your plans for today?" Maverick asked, taking her away from her thoughts.

"I overheard Clint invite you to watch him break in one of his stallions today so I'll give you a break."

"You don't have to do that since I'd rather spend the day with you."

And she'd rather spend the day with him, too, but the last thing she wanted to do was get used to Maverick's presence. Next week she would be alone again to deal with her father. "Thanks, but Alyssa and I are going shopping in Austin since I didn't pack anything fancy enough to wear to the dance tonight."

"I see."

Was she mistaken or did he sound disappointed? She figured she must be mistaken.

"I'm glad that's over," Maverick said, pulling off his Stetson and wiping his forehead with the back of his hand. He was convinced he'd aged a good ten years. He and a number of Clint's ranch hands had gathered around the corral to watch Clint break in one of the meanest horses Maverick had ever seen.

Clint had told him the horse, Vicious Cycle, was an offspring of Vicious Glance, who'd been one of the most mean-spirited horses his father, Corey Westmoreland, ever owned. At least the horse had been until Clint's sister, Casey, had broken him in. Several of Clint's men had gotten hurt trying to break in Vicious Cycle, so Clint decided it was his time to try.

Maverick would admit he'd been nervous as hell when he'd seen the horse, but it had taken a skilled horseman like Clint to show the animal who was master. "Hell, man, you had me scared. I thought I would have to tell Alyssa that you had broken every bone in your body trying to tame that beast."

Clint threw back his head and laughed. "You have so little faith in your cousin's abilities?"

Maverick grinned. "Let's just say that horse looked ready to eat any man alive who tried taming him."

Clint chuckled. "I was trained by the best."

"And now you're training your sons."

"And daughter. Like Casey, my little Carolyn is determined to learn anything her brothers do." Clint leaned against the post and eyed Maverick speculatively, then asked, "What about you? What future plans do you have for your child?"

Maverick returned the Stetson to his head and didn't say anything. He knew none of his brothers had mentioned Phire's pregnancy to anyone and he hadn't, either, so he wondered how Clint knew.

Before he could ask, Clint said, "My wife has been pregnant three times and I know the signs, Maverick. Phire might not be experiencing morning sickness but needing a nap every day and frequent bathroom breaks are sure signs as well." He chuckled. "But to be totally honest, I overheard her tell Alyssa about her condition the other night."

Maverick raised an eyebrow in surprise. Phire hadn't mentioned that she had shared their news, but he was glad she did. "My future plans for my child are to make sure it gets everything it needs and wants," he said, tilting back his hat from his forehead and looking over at Clint.

"What about your child's mother?"

He shoved his hands into the pockets of his jeans and released a ragged breath. "Same thing. I want to make sure Phire gets everything she needs and wants. I love her, Clint, and have asked her to marry me. However, she hasn't given me an answer yet."

Clint nodded. "She does know you want to marry her because you love her and not because of the baby, right?"

Maverick then rubbed his hand across his face. "I haven't told her I love her, if that's what you're asking. Phire doesn't love me and things between us are rather complicated at the moment. That's why, other than my brothers and Walker, I haven't told anyone about her condition. It has to do with her father."

Clint frowned. "What about her father?"

"He's trying to force her to marry someone else. A wealthy man he thinks he can control. That's the reason I had you watch to see if she was being tailed at the airport. And you saw that she was."

Clint's frown deepened. "Phire is allowing her father to manipulate her that way?"

Maverick released a disgusted sigh. "Not by choice." When Clint gave him a strange look, and knowing he hadn't told his cousin everything about Phire's father, he said, "I think I'd better start from the beginning."

Phire glanced at herself in the full-length mirror. She loved the purple dress she'd bought while out shopping with Alyssa. It wasn't too fancy, and it had a definite Western flair, especially with her cowhide boots. It was short with an inch of lacy hem. When worn with the matching lace jacket, the entire ensemble had a layered look.

She liked how it fit loosely at the waist because, regardless of whether Maverick could tell or not, her stomach was a little pudgy. Pretty soon she would be showing and even if her father didn't notice, his loyal staff would. She had to tell him and deal with what she knew would come.

"You're wearing my favorite color and you look absolutely gorgeous."

She turned from the mirror and smiled when Maverick entered the bedroom. He had finished getting dressed before her and looked handsome in his jeans, white Western shirt and black cowhide blazer. "You look pretty dapper yourself, Maverick, the outlaw."

He threw back his head and laughed. "Thanks. I missed spending time with you today."

His words made her feel good because she'd missed spending time with him as well. But then, to let him know she understood what he really meant, she said, "The baby missed spending time with you, too."

"And my baby's mother didn't?"

She chuckled. "Of course, I did, but I know you really like hanging around me because of the baby."

He frowned. "I don't know how you could think that when I hung around you for two years when there wasn't a baby."

Yes, he had. But there hadn't been any pushback on his part when she had suggested they end things. To change the subject, she said, "How long do you think the dance will last?"

"Not sure. Just in case you want to leave early, we're taking our wheels."

"You know the way?"

"Yes. This won't be the first barn dance that Tyler and Emma Baker have given that I've attended. They give one every year. They're a nice couple and you'll enjoy yourself."

Phire nodded. Alyssa had said the Bakers were childhood friends of Clint and his siblings. "I'm looking forward to meeting them."

Less than an hour later, Phire discovered Maverick

had been right. She liked Tyler and Emma immediately. They had a huge ranch and were the closest neighbors to Clint and Alyssa. The couple had a lot of stories to share about growing up with the Westmoreland triplets. Phire found each one amusing, especially when Tyler told them how Clint and Cole tried keeping the guys away from Casey.

There was a lot of food and Phire was convinced the barbecue spareribs, cooked on an open pit, were the best she'd ever eaten. To her surprise, the dancing wasn't what she'd thought. There had been no square dancing, but line dancing and regular dancing. Tyler and Emma said they might be ranchers, but both had left home to attend college at a university in New York. They admitted the four years away from Texas had been fun as well as a culture shock. Although they'd enjoyed it, ranching had been their blood, and they'd returned home after college ready to get married and take over Tyler's parents' cattle ranch when the older couple retired to Florida.

Phire enjoyed dancing with Maverick. Although he was tall and muscular, he had smooth moves. The moment they'd entered the party, all the feminine attention was drawn to him. Obviously, he knew some of the women since they called him by name. But then, she couldn't blame them for thinking he was eye candy personified. Hadn't she been mesmerized by him the moment he'd walked into DuRands that night in Paris?

Tonight, dressed in Western attire, he looked like a dangerous and sexy outlaw. She could imagine him living back in the 1800s, a card shark and woman-getter. They would gravitate to him in droves, and he would have his pick. Even tonight he could have done that very thing.

Those women bold enough to approach him, as if she was not standing by his side, were introduced to her by Maverick. He called her his best friend. A number of them gave her a side-glance, as if they didn't believe it. Then there were those who had assumed that meant they could flirt shamelessly with him right in front of her. One such woman, Kim, had been so sickening that Phire excused herself to grab a cup of punch and left Maverick to the woman, since it was apparent Kim intended to keep his attention any way she could.

"You okay?" Alyssa came to stand beside her.

Forcing a smile, Phire said, "Yes, I'm fine. The party is fun, and I enjoyed dancing."

"And you do it very well. You and Maverick look good together."

"Thanks." Phire glanced over at Maverick, who was still engaged in conversation with Kim. "And now he and Kim look good together."

Alyssa rolled her eyes. "Don't worry about Kim. Maverick is a smarter man than that. Kim has a reputation around these parts."

Phire figured that might be true, but Kim was definitely working hard for his total attention. The only good thing was that she wasn't getting it. Maverick would stare over at Phire every so often as if to make sure he still had her within his radar. Why? Wasn't Kim enough? But then, deep down she knew why. She had something he wanted. His baby.

That was why he had suggested they spend time together while he was visiting his relatives on the Golden Glade. If she hadn't called and told him she was pregnant, he would have had no reason for wanting to see her. Things would be just like they'd been for the last year, when they hadn't had any contact with each other.

Okay, she would admit he'd reached out to her a number of times, but she hadn't returned his calls. He hadn't known the reason she hadn't done so was because she'd been trying to protect her heart.

At that moment the band struck up a slow number and Clint, who'd been across the room talking with a group of men, made his way to Alyssa and pulled her toward the dance floor. Phire didn't want to see Maverick doing likewise with Kim.

"Dance with me." It was Maverick's husky voice, close to her ear, and she felt his masculine arm around her waist.

She was about to tell him that she didn't want to dance with him, but the last thing she wanted was for him to know how jealous she'd been of Kim.

"Sure."

He led her to the dance floor and something came over her. A bond between them that Kim couldn't take away. This was the first slow song tonight and she was the one he was dancing with. Not Kim or any of the others, but her.

Knowing that calmed her somewhat. But still, she asked, "Where's Kim? For a minute I thought she was going to dominate your time all night."

"Well, you thought wrong. I'd tolerated her for as long as I could."

"Yeah, you really looked like you were in pain," she said smartly, and then wished she hadn't when he slowed his steps and looked down at her.

"You were the one who left me with her, Phire. Why did you do that?"

"I figured you might want to spend some time alone with her."

He snorted and drew her tighter into his arms. "That's bullshit and you know it."

Maybe she did, Phire thought. But she felt jealous, anyway. Kim was pretty and could stay looking pretty nine months from now. Phire, on the other hand, would began to resemble a whale.

When the dance ended and another slow song followed, she and Maverick remained on the dance floor. Since he didn't seem to care what message that was sending out to anyone watching them—namely Kim and those other women—she decided not to care, either.

She loved him so much, and at this moment she wanted to tune out everything and just concentrate on this—being held by him and knowing from the feel of his aroused body that she was the woman he wanted.

For now.

Would that ever be enough for her? The desire and not the love? Even if she would be the mother of his child?

"Are you ready to leave, Phire?"

She raised her head off his chest and looked up into dark, aroused eyes. The music had stopped, and people were returning to the dance floor for a line dance. She nodded.

He walked her to the car and opened the door. He then leaned in and fastened her seat belt. "Thanks, Maverick."

"For you, anytime." He brushed a kiss across her lips. Straightening, he closed the door and she watched him walk around to get into the driver's side.

Phire tried to push to the back of her mind that she wanted things from life that Maverick didn't want. Just because she was having his baby wouldn't make him want those things any more than he had before. But he did want their baby. The thought that she was the woman who would be having his child should have given her comfort. But more than anything, she also wished she was the woman who had his heart.

He had asked her to marry him, but she knew she couldn't. It wouldn't be long before he discovered what she knew. The baby was not enough to hold a marriage together.

She deserved more and so did he.

*ne and knew Eve. Today, it hurt to have her leave, to know
that she'd be returning to the Double D ranch. But it would be a
day or more before the real plans got under way, and when she
had it wholly inside of her head, he told himself, he'd...*

*She had asked him to carry him over the threshold, to
pretend. But this was just some game and he just wished
it... Why? Everybody told her that at. Don't ruin it, he
wanted...*

"So," he claimed, "am I going to tell you?"

Eleven

"Are you okay, Phire?" Maverick asked, glancing over at her when they pulled into the yard and brought the SUV to a stop.

She turned toward him. "Yes, why do you ask?"

"You haven't said anything since we left the Bakers' ranch."

She shrugged and looked away, out of the vehicle's window. "I guess you'll be glad to see me leave so you can hook up with Kim."

Maverick frowned, wondering what Phire was talking about. "Why are we even discussing her, Phire?"

"Because she wants you and I could tell she intends to have you."

"And you believe that's what will happen?"

"Why not? I don't have any dibs on you."

He wondered if Phire realized she sounded jealous. That was surprising to him since she wasn't the type.

Besides, she had no reason to be jealous of another woman when he loved her but she didn't love him.

"Did you want to sleep with her tonight, Maverick?"

What the hell! "What kind of question is that for you to ask me, Phire?"

She turned to glare back at him. "A logical one. Earlier this week you asked me to marry you for the baby's sake. Did you not?"

He frowned. He didn't recall his marriage proposal mentioning anything about the baby. "I asked you to marry me, yes."

"Well, after tonight there's no way that I can."

Maverick shook his head, thinking he'd clearly missed something here. "And just what happened tonight to make you reach that conclusion?"

"I'm your best friend, Maverick. I, of all people, know how much you like women. We ended things almost a year ago and I'm sure you went back to your old womanizing ways. It won't be fair for you to give that up just because I'm pregnant and you think marrying me is the right thing to do."

His frown deepened. What made her assume she knew what he thought? Well, it was time he told her what he *really* thought. "I'm beginning to suspect the only reason you don't want to marry me is because of that Ravnell guy."

"What about Jaxon?"

"Maybe he's holding more of your interest that you're letting on."

She released a disgusted sigh. "How can you even think such a thing?"

"I can think it because you're trying to come up with some BS as to why we shouldn't get married," he said, trying to keep the anger from his voice.

"BS? The reason I gave you should be sufficient."

"Well, it's not."

"Then, that's your problem and not mine." She flung open the vehicle door and got out. He stared out the car window and watched as she walked to the house. He wondered if she realized he had the key, and she wouldn't be able to get inside without him.

He knew the exact moment she realized it, when she stopped in front of the door, looked over her shoulder and glared at him. "Well, are you coming?"

He had a good mind to say he wasn't coming, that he was going back to the party to spend time with Kim. For her to even think such a thing must mean she was having one of those pregnancy-related, emotional moments that Sloan had warned him about.

Deciding not to piss her off any more than he already had, he kept quiet as he got out of the vehicle and walked up the steps. She moved out of his way when he reached the door, and the moment he opened it, she entered and headed straight up the stairs for the bedroom.

"I think we need to talk, Phire."

"I don't want to talk to you, Maverick," she said over her shoulder as she continued up the stairs. Moments later, he heard the bedroom door slamming shut.

Maverick rubbed a hand down his face, feeling frustration seep into his every pore. After grabbing a beer out of the refrigerator, he sat on the back porch. Gazing out at the lake, he wondered how a night that had started out so promising could end up going all wrong.

After his talk with Clint earlier that day, he had felt better about the situation with Phire and had even considered telling her how he felt about her. But tonight, she'd pretty much made it clear that they shouldn't get married because there was nothing between them other than the baby.

Hell, she could speak for herself because there was love on his end, even if there wasn't on hers. Maybe he could deal with a partly loveless marriage because he had enough love for the both of them.

"Maverick?"

He turned when he heard the sound of Phire's voice. He'd been so absorbed in his thoughts that he hadn't heard her open the back door. But there she was, and the moonlight highlighted her beauty. "Yes?"

"I only have one more full day here, and I don't want to spend it with us mad at each other."

He heard the break in her voice and knew he didn't want that, either. "Neither do I." He placed his beer bottle on the porch's banister, then opened his arms and she quickly came to him. She held him as tight as he held her. It was as if neither of them wanted to let go.

"Make love to me, Maverick."

He preferred that they talk, but he heard the gentle plea in her voice. If making love would calm whatever storm was raging within her, then he would give her anything and everything she wanted.

Sweeping her off her feet and into his arms, he carried her back into the house.

After making love, Maverick held Phire tenderly in his arms while she slept. Their lovemaking had been so explosive, he was still feeling aftershocks. Although it had been physical, for him it had been emotional, too, because a new element had been thrown into the mix. Love.

He closed his eyes when he remembered placing her on the bed and how quickly they'd gotten out of their clothes. Afterward, she had clung to him as if he was her lifeline. It was then that he'd decided no matter what, he *would* be her lifeline. He'd never let a controlling, calculating, scheming father get in the way of anything they wanted. That's the way he'd handled Bart and he had no problem doing likewise with Simon Bordella.

The one thing her father probably wouldn't be counting on was the likes of an Outlaw standing up to him. For the sake of the woman he loved and their child she carried, he had no problem doing so. It was time to confront the BS, and he would.

"Maverick…"

He glanced down at her when she whispered his name in her sleep, smiling at the realization that, even when her mind should be at rest, it was on him. It was the same with him. He had her on his mind and dreamed about her all the time. He couldn't see that changing. Ever.

"Maverick?"

He glanced down at her and saw she was awake. "Yes, sweetheart?"

"I hate to be a bother, but these hormones are at it again. Please make love to me once more."

He stroked her cheek. "You would never be a bother, Phire. Making love to you at any time is my pleasure and I will always try to make it yours."

On Sunday, Phire couldn't believe her week with Maverick had come to an end and she was now packing to return home. It had been fun, just what she needed. Yesterday, Clint's brother Cole had arrived with his family. Just like Phire had taken to Alyssa immediately, it had been the same way with Dr. Patrina Westmoreland. The kids had been glad to see each other and had taken off to do fun activities. Cole, Clint and Maverick left to go riding on the range and that gave the three women time to spend together.

Patrina had known Phire was pregnant without her saying a word about her condition. She'd been happy to ask Patrina a number of questions and appreciated the woman's willingness to provide answers. Patrina shared that her mother, grandmother and great-grandmother had been midwives, and that although she'd been trained to follow in their footsteps, she'd decided to go to medical school to offer her patients the best of both worlds. It had been lovely to get to know both women better.

"Expect me at your father's ranch in a week, Phire."

Her head jerked up from packing to see Maverick leaning in the doorway. She was surprised by what he'd said. "What do you mean?"

"I'm coming to claim what's mine."

She rolled her eyes. "Please don't tell me we're back to that again."

Especially not after a night like Friday and a day like yesterday, she thought. After making love numerous times Friday night after the barn dance, they had slept late yesterday before getting up, showering together and preparing lunch, since it had been too late for breakfast. That's when they had joined Clint and Alyssa at the main house, where she'd met Cole and Patrina.

Knowing she would be leaving today, last night's lovemaking had practically been an all-nighter. Whatever she'd needed, Maverick had delivered.

"We never left the issue. You were mistaken about my claim only being about the baby, Phire. I'm claiming you, too."

She glared at him. "I am not an object to be claimed, Maverick. Now you're really acting like an outlaw."

Why did a smile suddenly appear on his lips? What part of what she'd said had he found amusing? She slowly drew in a deep breath when he eased away from the doorjamb and stalked toward her. She couldn't stop her gaze from traveling all over him. He didn't look at all like an Alaskan. Dressed in his Western wear, all the way down to his boots, he looked totally Texan. This wasn't the first time she'd wondered if he had Texas blood running through his veins.

He came to a stop in front of her. "I hope I'm acting like a man who cares very much for the woman who is having his baby. A woman who means a lot to me."

A woman you don't love.

She knew the best way to handle Maverick was not to be argumentative, since he was in one of his possessive moments. But still, the last thing she needed was for him to confront her father about anything, especially now.

She leaned against the bedpost. He was so sexy, just looking at him made her weak in the knees. "Maverick, promise me you won't do that."

He crossed his hands over his chest. "Only if you promise me that you won't let your father talk you into marrying someone else."

"I won't do that. I'm merely trying to play along with Dad for now." She saw some of the tension leave his features.

Maverick stroked her cheek. "I'm not trying to be difficult, Phire."

She loved the feel of his hand on her face, spreading heat all through her. "Aren't you?"

"No. I worry about you and refuse to let anything happen to you."

She nodded. "I promise to take care of myself for the baby's sake."

"Why do you center everything around the baby?"

She wondered how he could ask her that when everything *was* about the baby. "No reason."

He nodded. "Are you ready to join everyone for lunch before we leave?" he asked.

"Yes."

Maverick would be flying her back to Austin in his plane. Her father had texted her that he had returned to the ranch yesterday and that he would be the one picking her up from the airport. She wondered why. Even when she'd returned to the States from Paris, he had never bothered picking her up. She would like to think he was softening, but she knew that probably wasn't the case. However, it did make her curious.

"Phire?"

She glanced over at Maverick. "Yes?"

"You're okay?"

She drew in a deep breath, smiled and nodded. "Yes, Maverick. I'm okay."

It was much too soon, to Maverick's way of thinking, when he landed his Cessna at the Austin airport. His week with Phire was over and he wasn't ready to let her go. Especially when he knew the chaos she would be enduring. More than once during the flight he'd been tempted to fly them straight to Alaska, but there was no way to do so without her consent and she wouldn't be giving it. More than anything, he hoped his cousins' security firm could locate her aunt, and soon. Phire's happiness and peace of mind meant everything to him.

"Thanks for inviting me to the Golden Glade, Maverick, I had a great time. The Westmorelands are awesome. I enjoyed their company."

He tilted back his Stetson and gazed over at her. He was in no hurry for them to get out of the plane. "What about me? Didn't you enjoy my company as well?"

She gave him a cheeky grin, the kind he always adored. "I always do. You, Maverick, the outlaw, are something else." She leaned in and whispered, "You weren't even bothered with the increase in my sex drive."

He couldn't help but chuckle. "Whatever you want, I will deliver. Always have and I always will. And while your mouth is so close to mine, at least I can claim this for now."

"Yes," she said, inching her lips even closer. "I have no problem with the outlaw's claim there."

"Good." Maverick captured her lips with his. At that moment, he needed all of her, the full Phire effect—his baby growing in her womb wasn't enough. He wanted her to feel the love even if he knew she wasn't ready to hear it.

He finally broke off the kiss and rested his forehead against hers. "I'm going to miss kissing you anytime I want. Those seven days have spoiled me."

"They have spoiled me as well, but I definitely won't complain." She rubbed her stomach and added, "Your baby enjoyed spending time with its daddy, too."

Maverick couldn't help his huge smile. That always happened whenever she spoke of their baby being his. Now if he could get his baby's mother to think of herself as being his, that would make his life complete.

"I think if we don't deplane, the airport police will wonder things about us," she said, breaking into his thoughts.

"Let them." He looked around and then frowned. "But I'm curious as to why that guy who just got out of that private plane keeps staring over here at us."

When she sucked in her breath sharply, Maverick asked, "What is it?"

Her face looked troubled. "That guy…"

"What of him?" Maverick asked, watching the man walk into the terminal and get lost among a ton of others.

"That was Jaxon. I forgot he has a private plane. He must have taken a trip when he saw I didn't intend to stay at the ranch while he was there. Do you think he saw us kissing?"

"I'm pretty sure he did," Maverick said, not really caring.

"I need to explain things to him."

Maverick frowned. "Why?"

"Because I can just imagine what he thinks. He was at dinner that night I announced to Dad I'd be flying to Paris. Now he knows I lied about that and that I'm allowing Dad to manipulate a relationship between us even though I'm kissing another man. I honestly don't know his angle in all this, but deep down I think Jaxon is nice guy."

"Since you think he's a nice guy, will you come totally clean and tell him that you're pregnant with my child? Will you tell him about what your father is doing, forcing you into a relationship with him?"

When she didn't say anything, he frowned. "That's what I thought," he said, trying to hold back both his disappointment and anger.

He then got out of the plane to walk to the other side to help her out.

Twelve

"Hello, Sapphire. How was your trip to Paris?"

Phire stopped walking and turned to the man who'd appeared by her side. In a way, she wasn't surprised, and figured he'd been waiting to intercept her right before she exited the airport.

"Jaxon," she said, pushing back windblown hair from her face. "I'm sure you know I didn't go to Paris."

"Why did you feel the need to lie? I'm sure you're well aware that your father is trying his hardest to get something going between us."

She had news for him. Her father intended to get them married. "Yes, I know that."

"Then why are you letting him when you're involved with someone else, Sapphire? I'm not the type of man to encroach on another man's territory."

"I couldn't tell you the truth and Dad doesn't even know about him."

"Why? You're too old to be sneaking around, don't you think?"

"Yes, but there's a lot about the situation you don't know, Jaxon."

"Then tell me. I think I have a right to know since your father is all but trying to dump you into my lap every chance he gets."

Phire was about to say she wasn't ready to tell him anything when a voice from behind them caught her off guard. "Well, it's good seeing the two of you together."

She watched as her father approached. She looked away as the two men shook hands. Her father didn't bother giving her a hug since he'd never done so before. "Hello, Dad."

"Sapphire."

Was she mistaken, or was that anger in his eyes behind the huge smile plastered on his face? "When did the two of you meet up?" her father asked.

"Just now," Jaxon said. "I had to take an unexpected trip home and ran in to her outside of baggage claim. I was just trying to talk her into having dinner with me tonight."

Her father beamed. "Dinner? I think that's a swell idea."

"I'm tired from my flight," she quickly said. She was in no mood to have dinner with Jaxon. He had questions, and she wasn't ready to provide any answers.

"Nonsense. You've always had a bundle of energy, Sapphire. I think the two of you should go out."

"Like I said, Dad. I'm tired," she answered more firmly.

Before her father could say anything else, Jaxon intervened. "You have my number, Sapphire. If you feel better later and change your mind about dinner, please call me." He then turned to her father. "I'll see you around, Simon." He then walked off.

She was about to ask her father where he was parked, but the anger she'd seen in his eyes earlier now covered his entire face. "This way, Sapphire," he snapped.

He was silent until he'd placed her luggage in the trunk and they were inside the car. That's when he turned to her and said, "It's obvious Jaxon is taken with you. I don't know what kind of game you're playing, but it better end here and now, Sapphire."

She lifted her chin. "I have no idea what you're talking about."

"Then let me tell you. I know for a fact that you didn't go to Paris, but hung around town because you were seen on Friday by one of my household staff out shopping in Austin with some woman. I can only figure that you refused to stay at the ranch while I was gone, knowing I had invited Jaxon. I can't believe you could be so foolish. That would have been the perfect time to seduce him."

"Seduce him? Why would I want to do that, and what father would suggest such a thing to his daughter?"

Instead of answering her, he said, "You're running out of time, Sapphire. I told you I wanted you married to Jaxon before spring. Since you're being difficult, you leave me no other choice."

Phire felt a dip in her stomach. She recognized that manipulative look in his eyes. "What do you mean?" she asked. Her throat suddenly felt so thick she could barely swallow.

"It means unless your engagement to Jaxon is announced in thirty days or less, I'll make sure you never see your aunt again. In other words, I'll make sure you never know where she is. So I suggest you call Jaxon and let him know you're feeling fine and would love to join him for dinner."

* * *

Maverick tossed his empty beer bottle into the recycling can. Leaving the kitchen, he went into the living room. Everywhere he went had Phire's scent. He missed her already, but then that's how it had always been whenever he'd left Paris to return to the Alaska. He would fondly refer to them as Phire-withdrawals. Sharing a bed with her had always been vigorous, energetic and dynamic. And now, with her increased sexual drive, those times were even more robust.

And unforgettable.

He liked being the man she wanted to take care of her needs, and he had told her that if she needed him again, he was a phone call away. As far as he was concerned, he'd always had an increased sex drive when it came to her. He recalled the many times he would intentionally rearrange his work schedule just to fly to Paris even when his family hadn't known his reasons.

Although he'd pretended otherwise, he'd known the exact situation Sloan and Cash had been referring to when they'd reminded him of getting mad at Sloan for cutting their business trip short. Maverick now figured he'd loved Phire then but hadn't known it.

Alyssa had called earlier, inviting him to dinner, but he'd turned down the invitation. The last thing he wanted tonight was company because he wasn't in the mood. He recognized the caller when his phone rang. It was Garth. He pulled his phone out of his jeans pocket. "Yes, Garth?"

"I'm calling to see how you're doing and how things are going with you and Phire Bordella."

Maverick rubbed a hand down his face. "Phire was here with me on the Golden Glade for a week, and I flew her back home today. She still hasn't told her father about us or the baby. She's afraid he'll make it impossible to visit her aunt. She still has no idea what facility he had her transferred to."

"Has Quade or Cole found out the whereabouts of her aunt yet?"

"No. Cole and his family arrived at the Golden Glade yesterday, but he can work from anywhere since they've got men out in the field. I'm hoping they find out something soon."

"Sounds like Phire's under a lot of pressure, Maverick, and that's not good in her condition. I hope you're not adding to it."

He hoped not, either. "I'm trying to be patient, Garth, but there's a side of me that wants to show up at her father's ranch and claim what's mine. Both Phire and my baby."

"Have you asked Phire to marry you yet?"

"Yes."

"And she has agreed?" Garth asked.

"No. She thinks I only want to marry her for the baby."

"And you don't?"

"No. I love her, Garth." There, he'd said it. The only other person he'd admitted that to was Clint.

"Glad you've finally accepted your feelings for her. I could tell."

Maverick lifted an eyebrow. "How?"

"By your possessiveness." Garth chuckled and then added, "I've never known you to claim anything or anyone. That's a first for you."

He would agree. It was a first.

Phire looked across the table at Jaxon. She had called him just as her father had ordered and told him she wasn't as tired as she'd thought and would go to dinner with him. He had picked her up and taken her to one of the upscale restaurants in downtown Austin.

They had finished their meal and had just ordered dessert. He'd had wine and she'd ordered tea, something Patrina had assured her was okay to drink while pregnant.

"Are you ready to tell me what's going on with you, Sapphire?"

She'd known he would get around to asking questions sooner or later, and to be quite honest, she still wasn't ready to tell him anything. But she should and she would. She couldn't pretend any longer. Besides, it wouldn't be long before her pregnancy began showing.

"What exactly do you want to know, Jaxon?"

He leaned back in his chair. "Are you seriously involved with someone else?"

Now that was a good question. She honestly didn't know how serious her involvement with Maverick was, so she would answer as best she could. "If you're asking to determine if I'm available for marriage, then the answer is no. I can't marry you or anyone."

"Is there a reason why?"

"Yes. I refuse to marry someone I don't love or who doesn't love me."

He nodded. "Fair enough, since that's my position as well. However, your father believes two people can marry without love."

"Yes, I know that's what he thinks."

Jaxon took a sip of his wine and then asked, "What about that guy I saw with you earlier today?"

"We're only friends."

"Oh, I see."

Phire could just imagine what he was thinking.

Friends didn't kiss the way she and Maverick had kissed. She put down her teacup and said, "He's a friend that I've fallen in love with. He only wants friendship. I knew that and fell in love with him, anyway."

"Does he know you want more?"

"No. I knew from the beginning how he felt about serious relationships. My heart should have taken heed, but it didn't." She paused. "There's something else you should know."

"What?"

"I'm pregnant with his child."

Phire was taken back by the coldness that suddenly appeared in Jaxon's eyes. "Was it you and your father's plan to pass the child off as mine?"

"No," she said quickly. "I would never do anything like that. Dad doesn't even know that I'm pregnant."

Jaxon didn't say anything for a long moment as he studied the contents of his wineglass. He finally asked, "Does the father of your baby know?"

"Yes."

"And?"

She wondered what business it was of Jaxon's. And why she felt the need to tell him? "And he asked me to marry him."

"So you're getting married."

He'd said it as a statement and not a question. "No. I told you earlier I can't marry a man who doesn't love me. I love him, but he doesn't love me."

"And you're sure of that?"

"Yes."

He was silent for a while, then said, "Earlier today, at the airport, you said something about there being a lot about the situation involving your father that I don't know. I'd like to know what that is so I can deal with it and him. Especially since there won't be the wedding between us that he's counting on happening."

Phire decided it was time she completely leveled with Jaxon. They wouldn't be getting married so she had nothing to lose. "If I don't convince you to marry me, I might never see my elderly aunt again. Dad has threatened to keep her away from me."

Jaxon frowned. "Both you and your aunt are adults, so how can he keep the two of you apart?"

Phire released a deep breath. "My aunt, who is my father's older sister, raised me after my mother died."

"In Paris?"

"Yes. She had a severe stroke three years ago and has needed long-term health care. Dad agreed to foot all of her expenses on the condition that when he was ready to find me a husband that I would let him."

"And he's ready to marry you off now? Is that it?"

"Yes, and to make sure I do what he wants, he had my aunt moved to another facility in Paris and refuses to tell me where."

Jaxon frowned. "Are you serious?"

"Yes. So now you know why Dad wants me to marry you, and you also know why I can't do it."

Thirteen

"How about a game of poker?"

Maverick glanced over at his cousin Zane Westmoreland, who had arrived from Denver to pick up one of the stud stallions from Clint's herd. Whenever the Westmorelands got together, someone always brought out a stack of cards.

They had enjoyed a delicious dinner that Claudine and Chester had prepared, and afterward, the male cousins had gathered in Clint's office to enjoy a drink. They'd listened while Zane brought them up-to-date on how everyone was doing in Westmoreland Country. Then Cole had shared the same news with Zane that he'd shared with Clint and Maverick: McKinnon and Casey were having twin boys.

Everyone was elated when, due to groundbreaking research, a special medical procedure made it possible for McKinnon to be cured of a rare blood disease he'd inherited from his biological father. After three years of testing to make absolutely sure he couldn't pass on anything to a biological child, he'd had a reversal of his vasectomy. Within months, Casey had gotten pregnant. They had a son that they'd previously adopted, and everyone was happy for their family to expand.

There was a knock on the door, and when Clint called out for the person to enter, Alyssa stuck her head in, smiled at Maverick and said, "There's a man here to see you."

Maverick frowned. Other than his brothers and other Westmoreland cousins, no one else knew he was here. But Phire knew. Had something happened and she'd sent someone for him? Was it of such a serious nature that she hadn't been able to call?

In a somewhat nervous voice, he asked, "Did he say who he was?"

Alyssa nodded. "Yes. Jaxon Ravnell, and he's waiting in the foyer." She then closed the door.

The fear inside Maverick turned to anger. "What the hell. Why is Jaxon Ravnell here and wanting to see me?"

Hearing the anger in his voice, Cole asked, "Who's Jaxon Ravnell?"

"The man Phire's father has been trying to shove down her throat."

"Who's Phire?" Zane asked, curiously.

Maverick placed his glass of brandy on Clint's desk as he headed for the door. "Fill him in, will you, Clint? I need to go see what Ravnell wants."

"And I think I'll go with you," Cole said, following Maverick out of the office.

Clint and Alyssa's ranch house was huge and consisted of four spacious wings that jutted off from the living room. It seemed to take forever to reach the foyer, where Alyssa said the man was waiting. The walk had given Maverick time to wonder if perhaps something *had* happened to Phire. How else would the man know where Maverick was and why he was here? The thought made Maverick increase his pace. Cole, who was just as tall as Maverick, was right beside him, keeping up with his long strides.

When Maverick reached the area where the man was standing, he asked, "Is Phire okay?"

Obviously hearing the urgency in his voice, the man quickly replied. "Yes, Sapphire is fine."

Maverick let out a relieved breath. "Then why do you want to see me?"

The man, who Maverick noticed was just as tall as him and Cole, said, "Before I explain why I'm here, I think that first I need to introduce myself." The man then extended his hand.

Maverick thought about not taking it, but then did. "I already know who you are. You're the man Simon Bordella wants Phire to marry." Maverick turned to Cole. "This is my cousin, Cole Westmoreland." The two men shook hands and Maverick could tell Cole was sizing up Ravnell as much as he was.

"Yes, I'm the man Simon wants Sapphire to marry. However, I'm sure if you've spoken to Phire recently then you know that won't be happening. Not that there was ever a chance of it happening, anyway. Unbeknownst to Bordella, there's a reason I came to Texas and sought him out, and it has to do with you, Maverick Outlaw."

Maverick frowned. "Me?"

"Yes, you and the other Outlaws. Namely, your brothers, sister, and your father."

Maverick's frown deepened. "What the hell are you talking about? What does Phire's father have to do with the Outlaws?"

The sound of footsteps behind Maverick alerted him that Clint and Zane were now in the foyer as well.

"I'll be glad to explain things to everyone," Jaxon said, acknowledging the other two men and shaking hands with them. "However, I think it's time to tell you who I really am."

Maverick lifted an eyebrow. "Okay then, who are you?" Cole, Clint and Zane had come to stand by his side.

The man didn't seem bothered facing off with four men who matched him in height and build. "Like I said earlier, I am Jaxon Ravnell. But what I didn't say was that I am your cousin."

"Cousin?" four male voices asked simultaneously.

Jaxon Ravnell nodded. "Yes, cousin."

Clint then said, "I think we need to continue this conversation in my office."

"Are you claiming to be a Westmoreland?" Zane asked after everyone had settled in chairs around Clint's desk. An assortment of whiskeys were in decanters, and everyone was invited to help themselves.

"No, I'm not related to the Westmorelands," Jaxon replied.

"Then how are you my cousin?" Maverick asked.

"You're connected to the Westmorelands through Raphel Westmoreland. You and I are related through Clarice Riggins, the woman who gave birth to Raphel's child and later died in a train wreck."

Although Maverick hadn't read the private investigator's full report, he recalled bits and pieces of it.

"And how are you related to Clarice Riggins?" he asked Jaxon.

"My great-grandmother, Lorraine Parkinson, was her aunt. If you recall, the reason Clarice was on that train was because she was returning to Virginia. Her parents didn't accept her baby out of wedlock like she'd thought they would. She went back to be near her aunt Lorraine and try to make a life for herself and her baby in Virginia."

"I recall that Lorraine Parkinson was Clarice's mother's younger sister," Zane said. He was more familiar with the story than most since it had been his sister, Megan, who'd hired a private investigator, her now-husband, Rico Claiborne, to determine the details of what had happened to Clarice. He glanced over at Jaxon. "That means, your grandfather's biological mother was the woman who'd been Clarice's best friend at the time, Fanny Banks. He was the baby adopted by Clarice's aunt Lorraine."

"Yes that's right. His name was Elliott Parkinson. My mother was his only child, and she married my father, Arnett Ravnell. I am their only child."

Jaxon paused, then said, "What you might not know is that Clarice's father, Tillman Riggins, regretted not accepting his only daughter and her illegitimate baby. He caught the next train out of Forbes to go after her, to bring her and the baby back home. Unfortunately, Clarice's train derailed, and he didn't make it to the hospital until after she'd died."

"And that was after she'd given her child away to the woman on the train," Cole said. "A woman by the name of Jeanette Outlaw." He had read Rico's report as well.

"Yes, but Tillman Riggins never gave up looking for the child. He hired several private investigators, but once Jeanette Outlaw discovered someone was looking for the baby, she was on the run, fearful the child would be taken away from her."

"I can see her having that emotional frame of mind," Zane added, after taking a sip of whiskey. "According to the report, the woman had lost her own baby a year before that train accident and was probably still grieving from that. Then her husband lost his life during the train derailment. She probably considered the baby Clarice had given her as a blessing and refused to give it back. Not even to its biological grandparents."

"Yes, well, Tillman never gave up," Jaxon said. "Right before my grandfather died last year, he gave me a trunk full of legal documents that Tillman wanted him to have. One such document indicated Tillman had allotted a huge sum of money in his will to continue searching for the child he claimed was his heir."

"Okay, so Clarice Riggins's father looked for her baby and never found him," Maverick said, putting down his glass to lean toward Jaxon. "What does any of that have to do with Simon Bordella?"

"According to the legal documents left with my grandfather, Tillman's trusted attorney, Wylan Nader, was given instructions to continue looking for the child even after Tillman died. Like I said, such directives were placed in the will and funds set aside to do so. And from what I can see, Wylan Nader did as Tillman requested," Jaxon said.

Jaxon took another sip of his drink before continuing. "Ten years after Tillman's death, Wylan came down with cancer. That's when he instructed a young attorney who worked in his office to continue carrying out Tillman's wishes if anything was to happen to him. I have legal documents signed by that young attorney agreeing that he would continue the search, as well as make sure the ranch was kept in good shape until the Riggins heir was found."

Maverick sat up straight and looked at Clint. Immediately, he knew they were both remembering what Phire had told them at dinner that first day she'd spent on the Golden Glade. "Simon Bordella was that young attorney. Wasn't he?" he asked.

Jaxon nodded. "Yes. Bordella was that young attorney. As soon as Wylan Nader died, Bordella ended the private investigators' search and claimed all of the Riggins wealth as his own. That included the ranch and all the land surrounding it."

"And how was he able to get away with doing that?" Zane asked.

"First, he forged a document claiming Riggins gave Nader rights to do as he saw fit with the land if his heir was never found. When Nader died, Bordella stated the land belonged to Nader's daughter. Then to make sure no one questioned what he did, he married her."

"Phire's mom?" Maverick asked.

"Yes," Jaxon said. "Tillman Riggins's trusted attorney was Phire's grandfather. And there is something else I think you need to know."

"What?" Maverick asked.

"Bordella is not Sapphire's biological father."

Maverick blinked. "And you know this how?"

"From letters that Wylan Nader wrote my grandfather. Over the years the two established a rather close friendship through frequent correspondence. Tillman was adamant about my grandfather keeping a copy of every legal document. Obviously, Wylan Nader didn't apprise Bordella that he was doing so."

Jaxon adjusted his long legs in front of him. "In one

letter I read, Nader told my grandfather about his cancer and that he was prepared to die, but was concerned for his daughter. She had gotten pregnant while away at an all-girls school and he didn't intend to make the same mistake in the treatment of his daughter that Tillman had made with his. He said a young attorney in his office had agreed to marry her and be a good father to her child if Nader signed the law practice over to him when he died, free and clear."

"Good father, my ass," Maverick said through clenched teeth. "He's nothing but controlling. I would hate to think how he treated his wife."

"Phire has never said?" Clint asked Maverick.

"No. All she said was that she didn't think they were in love." Maverick studied Jaxon. "Why didn't you level with Phire and tell her what you told me?"

"Because when I arrived in town and saw how Bordella was trying to push a marriage between me and his daughter, and then after meeting her and seeing she wasn't giving him any pushback, I assumed that maybe she was in on his scheme," Jaxon said. "I decided to keep my eyes on the both of them."

He then added, "I had her followed her first week back home from Paris. Imagine my shock when the guy following her reported to me that she left and hooked up with you, Maverick, in Dallas. I couldn't understand how she could seem agreeable to something developing between us when she was having an affair with you. I immediately suspected that Bordella had found out you were a descendant of the Riggins heir and that with her help, he was covering all bases."

"When did you discover differently?" Zane asked.

"It soon became obvious that although her father was trying to push something between us, Sapphire wasn't having it. I can tell when a woman isn't interested in a man and it became quite clear to me, even if it wasn't to her father, that she wasn't interested."

He then added, "I knew for certain when Bordella made plans to go out of town and he invited me to stay at the ranch with Sapphire unchaperoned. If she had been in on her father's plan, she would have used that week to try to seduce me. Instead, she announced that she intended to go to Paris that same week. That ruined Bordella's plans for a seduction and I could tell he wasn't happy about it. I later discovered that instead of flying off to Paris, she was spending a week here with you."

When Maverick lifted his brow, Jaxon smiled. "Like I said, I was having her followed."

"I noticed," Clint said. "Maverick suspected her father would have someone following her, so as a favor to him, I was stationed outside the airport when she arrived. I saw two men tailing her instead of one."

Jaxon nodded. "One was my man Lockley, who handles all my investigations and security. The other was a ranch hand Bordella assigned to tail her when he didn't believe her story about going to Paris."

"So now you know the truth, that Phire is an innocent victim in all of this," Maverick said.

"Yes. She told me last night that her father is using her sick aunt to make her do everything he wants her to do."

"Do you know why Bordella is desperate to marry her off to some wealthy guy?" Cole asked.

"Yes," Jaxon said, after taking a sip of whiskey. "He's strapped for money due to a bad investment. To get out of debt he wants to sell the ranch and all the land surrounding it."

"A ranch and land that doesn't even belong to him," Maverick muttered.

"Right. He has until June to pay off his debt. Maybe he's fearful if he sells it, someone will discover that he got the ranch and land illegally. I guess he assumes if I become his son-in-law that I won't ask questions if he sold the land to me."

Maverick nodded. "Do you think he's a threat to Phire?"

"I won't say he's a threat, but I can see him getting pretty pissed off if a wedding between us doesn't take place in the time frame that he needs it to. Therefore, I would advise you to keep a check on her."

"I do that, anyway," Maverick said.

When the room got quiet, Zane spoke up. "So it sounds like this Bordella is claiming land and a ranch that rightly belongs to the Riggins heir, who was your grandfather, Maverick."

Maverick nodded again. "And with my grandfather's death that makes Bart the legitimate heir."

Cole snorted. "Good luck on that one. Your father refuses to claim any connection to Raphel Westmoreland, which means he won't claim a connection to Clarice Riggins, either."

Maverick took a sip of his drink. "You're probably right, but I think it's time my brothers and I confront Dad about his refusal to acknowledge his past. Once I tell them everything, my brothers will agree with me." He glanced over at Jaxon. "I'd like you to come to Alaska to meet my brothers and tell them what you've told us."

"That's no problem," Jaxon said. "I'll have my attorneys provide copies of all the legal documents and letters." He paused. "There is something else you need to know."

"What?"

"To weed out imposters who might have pretended to be the Riggins heir, Tillman had the necessary lab work done on Clarice's body, so that if the child was ever found they could do a blood test. Now, with DNA testing, it would be easy to determine if your father is the legitimate son of the Riggins heir."

"Yes, but the key is getting my father to agree to such a test," Maverick said, frowning. "Knowing Bartram Outlaw like I do, regardless of whether or not the test will prove things, he will refuse to do it. He's just that pigheaded."

The room got silent and then Jaxon turned to Maverick. "There is another matter I need to talk to you about and it's rather private."

Maverick was about to say that anything Jaxon had to discuss with him could be said in front of his cousins, but changed his mind. Standing, he said, "I was about to leave for where I'm staying while I'm here. We can go and talk there."

Fourteen

"Massie said you wanted to see me, Dad," Phire said, entering her father's office. She had been running water for her bath when Massie had knocked on her bedroom door and said he'd wanted to see her.

He had barely exchanged a word with her during dinner after inquiring about her date with Jaxon the night before. He was anxious to see if wedding plans had been made. Obviously, he didn't think a courtship or an engagement needed to take place before a wedding.

There was no doubt in her mind that Jaxon would not set foot on her father's ranch again now that he knew the truth. So where did that leave her with getting any information on her aunt? She had spoken to Maverick last night and he'd again given her hope that his cousins could find her aunt.

Her father finally looked up from the papers on his desk and stared at her. There was an angry expression on his features, but then that wasn't uncommon. The only time he wasn't angry was in Jaxon's presence, when he pretended the two of them had a great father-daughter relationship.

"Are you pregnant, Sapphire?"

She wondered how he knew. She didn't want to believe Jaxon had told him, but if not Jaxon, then who? "Why would you ask me something like that?"

"Because of these," he said, pulling her prenatal books out of a side drawer and tossing them on the floor in front of her. "Massie found them in your room."

Her anger flared. "She had no right to go through my things."

"Just answer the damn question," he snapped.

"I'm not answering anything."

"You will tell me what I want to know," he said, hitting his desk with his fist so hard it made Phire jump.

She saw anger in his face like she'd never seen before. "And what if I am?"

"Then for your sake, it better be Jaxon Ravnell's baby."

"It's not," she said, knowing she was affirming her pregnancy.

"Well, I don't care whose it is. You either make Jaxon believe the baby is his or get rid of it."

"What! I will do neither of those things."

"You will do what I say, Sapphire."

"No, I will not. Not even your threats about keeping me from Aunt Lois will make me," she said, her voice just as loud as his. "I refuse to let you manipulate me any further."

He came from around the desk to stand in front of her. "Who's the baby's father?" he asked. When she didn't answer, he all but screamed, "Tell me who he is."

She would not tell him anything about Maverick, but she did say something that was the truth. "A guy I met in Paris."

He stared at her for a long moment. "You're no better than your mother."

"What are you talking about?"

Instead of answering her, he went back around his desk. "I will give you time to think about which of those two choices you're going to make, Sapphire. Until you do, I forbid you to leave the ranch or have contact with anyone."

She moved to stand in front of his desk and placed her hands on her hips. "I'm twenty-five and not a child. You can't forbid me to do anything."

"You think not? Then think again. And to make sure you don't try reaching out to that girlfriend you went shopping with last week when I thought you were in Paris, I've asked Massie to confiscate your phone and—"

"You did what!" Not waiting for his answer, she rushed from the office to her bedroom to find the contents of her purse had been dumped on her bed. She heard Massie moving around in the bathroom. Phire then remembered she had placed her phone on the bathroom vanity while running her bathwater. She walked in just as Massie was picking up her phone.

"Give me my phone," she demanded.

The woman was startled by the sound of her voice, and when she threw up her hand the phone went flying across the bathroom and landed in the tub of water. Phire quickly moved to retrieve it while Massie rushed from the room. Phire grabbed a towel, hoping the water hadn't damaged it, even though it wasn't the newest model or waterproof. When she tried using it, she saw it wouldn't work. Frustrated, she walked out of the bath-room, intending to confront her father again, when she heard the sound of her bedroom door being locked. When had an outside lock been installed on her door?

Phire quickly walked over to her bedroom window. One of the ranch hands was stationed there. She couldn't believe it. Her father was holding her hostage, just like he had threatened to do. And she couldn't call for help.

"What do you have to talk to me privately about, Jaxon?" Maverick asked as he stared at the man sitting across from him at the kitchen table.

He'd suggested they ride in the same vehicle over to where he was staying. That way he could get to know the man better. It was obvious Jaxon was doing well for himself. Maverick would even admit to checking him out on the internet when Phire had first mentioned him. However, at no time had he thought he and the man were related.

Maverick knew that Jaxon's paternal grandfather, Jasper Ravnell, had started the Ravnell Institute of Technology over sixty years ago to work on techno-logical advances in higher learning. He'd read there was a waiting list to get a masters degree in technol-ogy management from the institute. Once in hand, most graduates were offered a six-figure job.

Jaxon's father spearheaded the business side, with Ravnell Technology, Inc., and to make sure they were getting the best of the best, over sixty percent of their employees were graduates of their institute. Both the institute and firm were located in Dumfries, Virginia. Considering the man's portfolio, no wonder Bordella wanted him for a son-in-law.

"It's about Sapphire."

Maverick frowned. "What about Phire?"

"She told me the two of you are good friends, so I thought I'd bring something to your attention."

As far as Maverick was concerned, he and Phire were more than *good friends*. "What do you need to bring to my attention?"

"Bordella found out that Phire didn't go to Paris like she claimed. She was seen in town shopping by one of his household staff, who reported it to him. The reason I know this is because, unknown to Bordella, my security firm got one of their men hired on as a ranch hand and he overheard the servants talking about it."

Maverick recalled the day Phire left the Golden Glade to go shopping with Alyssa. "When I talked to Phire last night, she said her father knew she hadn't gone to Paris but he thinks she was spending time with a girlfriend since she wasn't seen with a man." Maverick paused. "She also mentioned that she'd told you about the baby."

"Yes, she told me," Jaxon said.

"And something you said earlier isn't completely correct. Phire and I are more than friends—I want to marry her."

Jaxon took a sip of his coffee. "Yes, she told me you asked her to marry you. However, she also told me she doesn't plan to marry anyone who doesn't love her."

Maverick nodded. "I am in love with her," he said, seeing no reason not to admit it. Especially when he wanted Jaxon to know where he stood with Phire.

Jaxon put down his coffee cup. "I doubt she knows how you feel, Maverick."

Phire paced the confines of her bedroom, not believing that her father was keeping her here against her will. What in the world had come over him? Did he honestly think she would do anything he wanted after this? Not even her aunt would want her to allow him to treat her this way. That only made her wonder why he was so hell-bent on marrying her off to Jaxon. Granted, he liked manipulating people, but she had a feeling it was more than that.

She had planned to sneak into her father's office and go through his papers tonight to see if she could find anything that would tell her where her aunt was being kept. Now she could kiss that plan goodbye. Not only did he have some ranch hand stationed outside her window, but she also knew Massie was keeping the door locked.

She glanced at the clock on her nightstand. This was usually the time when she would be expecting a call from Maverick. He'd said he would call her tonight. Had he tried? Would he suspect anything when he didn't reach her? And just how long did her father intend to keep her here? She'd told Jaxon the truth, so chances were he wouldn't be coming back, and as far as her ending her pregnancy, that wouldn't be happening.

In the past, Maverick's possessiveness had teed her off. But now she would give anything for him to find a way to come claim her and his baby.

Why wasn't Phire answering her phone?

Maverick tried calling her for the third time that night. And she'd told him she kept her phone with her at all times.

He began pacing his bedroom. Okay, so Bordella wasn't Phire's biological father, but he had raised her, so Maverick wanted to believe that no matter how manipulative the man was, he wouldn't harm a hair on Phire's head.

Maverick drew in a deep breath and tried calling her again. Instead of ringing, it again went straight to voice mail. "Baby, call me and let me know you're okay."

He left the bedroom to pace the living room for a while. He jumped at the sound of his phone ringing and knew it wasn't Phire since she had a special ringtone. He quickly pulled out his phone and saw it was Jaxon. He wondered what he wanted when Jaxon had left here just a couple of hours ago.

"Yes, Jaxon?" he asked.

"I just got a call from the guy posing as a ranch hand on the Bordella ranch."

The hairs on the back of Maverick's neck stood up. He had a feeling he wasn't going to like whatever Jaxon had to tell him. "And?"

"Bordella is holding Sapphire hostage."

Maverick blinked. "What do you mean he's holding her hostage?"

"My guy didn't have all the details, but Phire has been locked in her bedroom and a guard is stationed outside her door and outside her bedroom window."

"What the hell! I'm leaving to go there right now and—"

"No, Maverick. I believe she'll be okay for tonight. I think we should come up with a plan. You might want to include your cousins on this. Start the coffee. I'm on my way."

Fifteen

The next morning Simon heard the knock on his office door and glanced up. "Come in." When he saw it was Massie, he asked, "What do you want?"

"Mr. Ravnell is here to see Miss Sapphire and he has a gentleman with him."

Simon immediately stood. He had hoped Jaxon wouldn't come around until he had talked some sense into Sapphire by showing her that he meant business. "Where are they?"

"I've seated them in the parlor."

"Good. I'll join them there in a minute. In the meantime, see to their comfort."

"Yes, sir."

It didn't take long before Simon walked into the room where the men were seated. They stood when he entered. "Jaxon," he greeted heartily with a huge smile on his face. "This is a surprise. I called you twice yesterday and when I didn't hear from you, I thought perhaps you were out of town."

"No, I was in meetings most of the day with representatives from my firm in Virginia. I'd like you to meet my cousin, who just arrived in town to visit me, Maverick Outlaw. Maverick, this is Sapphire's father, Simon Bordella." The two men shook hands.

"I want to introduce Maverick to Sapphire. Then he will understand why I am so taken with her. Is she available?"

Maverick had been observing Bordella's features and saw no sign that he'd recognized the Outlaw name. That meant the man had ended the search for the Riggins' heir without reading any of the private investigators' reports.

Another thing Maverick had noticed was just how pleased Bordella had been with Jaxon's admission of being taken with Phire. However, when Jaxon requested to see her, Maverick picked up Bordella's tension and figured Jaxon had as well.

"Ah, Sapphire isn't up yet."

Jaxon glanced at his watch. "It's almost noon. Is she ill?"

"No," Bordella said quickly. "She was up late reading, and I guess she decided to sleep in."

"Be careful of women who stay in bed late in the mornings, cuz," Maverick said, grinning over at Jaxon. "They tend to be lazy, no matter how beautiful they are."

Maverick could tell Bordella didn't like his comment because it put Phire's suitability for Jaxon into question. "My daughter is anything but lazy," the man said defensively.

"Never mind, Maverick," Jaxon said, grinning. "He has a warped sense of humor. We will visit with Sapphire another time."

"Or maybe not," Maverick said. "I need to introduce you to that woman I met on the plane. Now she was really classy—"

"I'm sure when I let Sapphire know you're here she will want to see you," Bordella interrupted. It was obvious he hadn't liked Maverick's suggestion of Jaxon meeting another woman.

Bordella gave Maverick an annoyed look, but Maverick didn't give a damn. He wasn't leaving here until he saw Phire, even if he had to tear this house apart to find her. He was still trying to control the anger he'd felt after receiving the call from his cousin Quade that morning. His men had found the whereabouts of Phire's aunt.

"Are you sure she will see us? I'd hate to inconvenience her," Jaxon said.

"No inconvenience. Just have a seat and I'll go get her." Bordella then walked off.

"I still say you need to marry a woman with more spunk," Maverick said to Jaxon, deliberately loud enough to reach Bordella's ears.

Phire glanced at her bedroom door when she heard it being unlocked. When it opened, her father was standing there wearing an anxious look. "Good. You're up and dressed already."

"What's good about it when I'm being kept here against my will?" she snapped.

Ignoring what she'd said, he closed the door and walked over to her. "Jaxon is here to see you with some relative of his. I want you to go out there and impress them both."

He'd gone off the deep end if he thought she would do any such thing. "I will not!"

"Yes, you will! I've instructed that facility where your aunt is being kept to discontinue her care when they get a call from me. You do know what that means if that happens, right?"

Yes, Phire knew, but then she remembered what Maverick had said about helping with her aunt's care. "Fine, just tell me where she is and I will begin taking care of her myself."

"Not only will I not tell you where she is, I'll remove her from Paris and you'll never find her. Maybe to some homeless shelter for ill people like her."

A pain settled around Phire's heart. "She's your sister. How can you be so cruel?"

Her father began laughing so loudly Phire thought he had lost his mind. "My sister? That's where you're wrong. Lois isn't my sister. She's my mother."

Phire's hand flew to her throat in shock. "Your mother?"

"Yes, my mother. She was raped at fourteen and gave me up for adoption. It was only after I became an attorney that I tracked her down living a good life in Paris. If she only knew the life I lived as a child in foster care... So don't you dare tell me how I should take care of her. She means nothing to me. The only reason I took care of her health needs was to use you to my advantage when the time came."

"Use me to your advantage?"

"Yes. Like I told you, Jaxon is loaded and I want him as a son-in-law. A marriage will take place between the two of you, whether you want it to or not."

"You're a ruthless man."

"I couldn't care less what you think of me. Just consider Lois and what will happen to her if you don't give me what I want. Now go out there so he can introduce you to his cousin. I have a feeling he places stock on what that jackass thinks, so you better impress the man."

"How can I pretend everything is okay and impress anyone?"

"That's for you to figure out. Just remember what's at stake. And if you give Jaxon reason to think anything is wrong, I will make that call and you won't be able to save Lois."

He looked at his watch. "I'll give you ten minutes and then I expect you to meet us in the parlor with a huge smile on your face." He glanced at her outfit, a pair of jeans and a top. "Change into a dress. One that makes you look feminine. I want him to see what a beautiful daughter I have."

Phire watched as her father walked out the door. She dropped down on the bed, thinking about what he'd said. Was he actually Aunt Lois's son? Her aunt had been raped at fourteen and had given up the child for adoption? It was obvious he held that choice against her aunt. But what would a fourteen-year-old have done with a baby?

Phire wanted to believe her father's words were lies, but she had a feeling he'd spoken the truth. Was that why her aunt had never spoken ill of her father? If what her father said was true, then her aunt was her grandmother.

Phire rubbed her forehead when she felt a headache coming on. Her father didn't know that Jaxon knew the truth. Phire was surprised he was here. And he had brought a cousin for her to meet? That didn't make sense. She was determined to give him some kind of sign that she needed his help.

Following her father's orders, she put on a dress. She combed out her hair and tried making herself look as pretty as possible. In less than the ten minutes he'd allotted, she walked out of her bedroom and headed for the parlor. The moment she entered, she came up short. Standing beside Jaxon, talking with her father, was Maverick.

What was Maverick up to? Was Jaxon in on it? How? Why? The three men turned, and she knew Maverick saw all the questions in her eyes. And she could clearly see the message in his.

I have come to claim what's mine.

It was as if he'd spoken aloud yet he hadn't moved his lips.

She moved toward Maverick and extended her hand, forcing a smile. "Hello. I'm Sapphire Bordella."

"And I'm Maverick Outlaw." He paused for a quick second. "You're right, Jaxon. She's beautiful." Maverick didn't want to let go of Phire's hand. It felt warm in his…and it was trembling. He studied her eyes and knew no matter what, he wouldn't leave here without her.

"You better watch your cousin, Jaxon, or he'll take your girl."

Maverick released Phire's hand after her father's statement. Although the older man had spoken in jest, he didn't know the half of it. Phire was already Maverick's.

Phire turned her attention away from him and gave

Jaxon a smile. "Hello, Jaxon, it's good seeing you again."

"Hello, Sapphire. Your father said you slept late this morning. Are you okay?"

Her smile widened. "Yes, I'm fine. Thanks for asking."

"Then how about lunch?" Maverick suggested. "I'd like to get to know you better, Sapphire. Jaxon has told me a lot about you."

"Lunch sounds great," her father said quickly. "I can have my cook prepare something here for everyone."

"No," Jaxon said. "There's a restaurant in town where I'd like to take Sapphire. Then afterward, she and I can show Maverick around. I want him to see where I plan to construct the Ravnell Building."

"Wonderful! I'd love to see it myself," Bordella said.

Maverick tightened his lips, about to tell the man that no one had invited him. He kept from grinning when Jaxon said, "Maybe another time, Simon. My cousin and I want Sapphire to ourselves. He is determined to get to know her before I make any decisions about our relationship."

Maverick could see the wheels turning in Bordella's head, trying to come up with a reason for Phire not to leave with them.

"I'll grab my purse," Phire said, and quickly left the room.

When Bordella moved to follow her, Jaxon reached out and touched his hand. "Are you okay, Simon? You seem agitated."

"No, no, I'm fine. I just need to remind Sapphire about something."

Maverick could just imagine what he needed to remind Sapphire about. "I'd rather we talk, Mr. Bordella."

"About what?" he asked, looking at Maverick.

"Jaxon said something about this lucrative investment deal you told him about. I've got a few millions to spare."

As he figured it would, Maverick's statement caused a gleam to appear in the man's eyes. "That's wonderful. I have some free time now and could join you for lunch."

Jaxon laughed. "Another time. Maverick intends to be around for a few days, and I can certainly bring him back for dinner."

"What about this evening?" Bordella said excitedly.

"That sounds good," Maverick said, knowing he had no intention of coming back for dinner.

"I'm ready," Phire said, returning.

"Remember our earlier discussion, Sapphire," Bordella said as Jaxon led her from the parlor.

She slowed, gave her father a faint smile and said, "Trust me, Dad. There's no way I can forget it."

As soon as the car pulled away from the ranch house, Phire released a deep breath and then turned in her seat to glance at Maverick, who was sitting in the back. "How did you know I needed you to come for me? And how do the two of you know each other?"

"It's a long story, and we'll tell you everything once I get you as far away from here as I can," Maverick said.

"Thank you," she said, first to Maverick and then to Jaxon. Her mind was still whirling with questions. When they were on the main road that bordered her father's property, she saw four other vehicles parked there. When Jaxon pulled the car to the shoulder of the road, several men got out of the other cars.

"Who are they?" she asked Maverick, as he was getting out, too.

"Friends of Cole and Clint. All Texas Rangers. They were here in case we had trouble getting you out of there. And the other guy, the one who is taller than me and wearing a brown Stetson, is my cousin Zane Westmoreland from Denver. He came to town to pick up a horse from Clint."

"Oh," she said, studying the man he'd referred to. There was a strong resemblance between him, Clint, Cole and Maverick.

When Maverick opened the door for her, Jaxon got out and said, "I'll go let the guys know how things went back there." He then walked to where Clint and Cole were standing while talking to the group.

When Jaxon left, Phire turned to Maverick. He pulled her into his arms and captured her mouth with his. She felt desire in every stroke of his tongue and returned the kiss with just as much greed as he put into it. She honestly hadn't known he would come, but he had. Although her mind was filled with a million questions, she was satisfied with this. Being thoroughly kissed by him.

When he released her mouth, he said, "I've been worried sick since not being able to reach you last night, Phire."

"My father's housekeeper took my phone and when I tried to stop her, it landed in a bathtub filled with water." She swiped at her tears and added, "I was hoping you knew that I needed you. This was one time when I wanted you to show up and claim me and your baby. How did you know Dad was keeping me against my will?"

"Jaxon called me."

How did Jaxon know? "But how did the two of you meet?" she asked him.

"We met when Jaxon came out to Clint's ranch to see me."

"But why? How?" she asked, not understanding.

"To inform me that he's my cousin."

"Your cousin? He's a Westmoreland?"

Maverick smiled. "No, and I'll explain everything as soon as I get you settled." He brushed back a strand of hair from her face and the tears from her eyes. "My top priority is getting you as far away from here as I can."

"Where are we going?" she asked, truly not caring as long as she was with him.

"I'm flying you home."

She lifted an eyebrow. "To Paris?"

He shook his head. "No. I'm taking you to my home in Alaska."

Sixteen

As the Outlaw Freight Lines company jet cleared the Austin runway and tilted its wings toward Alaska, Maverick glanced down at the woman who slept in his arms. He was certain he'd aged ten years last night after getting that call from Jaxon letting him know Phire was being held by her father against her will. He'd almost become the outlaw Phire often teased him about being. It had taken his cousins' calm demeanor, which included Jaxon's, to keep him from storming Bordella's ranch last night.

He had called Garth, who had contacted his brothers and the other Westmorelands, and let them know what was going on. They'd sent word that they were poised and ready for action if needed. He'd even gotten a call early this morning from his Navy SEAL cousin, Bane, stating he and his team members and friends, who were home awaiting their next mission, had no problem flying to Austin to rescue Phire. They could get her out without anyone on Bordella's ranch even knowing they'd been invaded.

Maverick had appreciated everyone's support and offers of assistance, but had told them to hold tight. He figured that he, Cole, Clint, Zane and Jaxon could handle things for now. Of course, that meant explaining to everyone who Jaxon was. His brothers and the Westmorelands were looking forward to meeting him.

Although Maverick had also told Garth to hang tight, he hadn't been surprised when his oldest brother had called first thing this morning to let him know that he and his pilot wife, Regan, were on their way to get him and Phire in the company jet.

Maverick and Jaxon figured once Phire didn't return to the Bordella ranch within a reasonable time, her father would suspect something was not on the up-and-up. For that reason, Jaxon had called Bordella before takeoff and told him that his cousin Maverick had been so taken with Phire that Jaxon had impulsively asked Phire to fly to his home in Virginia to meet his other relatives. She had agreed and they were on their way now in his company's jet.

Jaxon mentioned he would take her shopping when they got to Virginia and not to expect them back for a few days. Bordella was smart enough not to push back on Jaxon's impulsive actions and risk his ire. When Bordella asked to speak to Phire, probably to remind her again of his threats, Jaxon said he would have her call him back later.

Maverick cuddled Phire in his arms. She had dozed off the moment they'd boarded, and he figured she hadn't gotten much sleep last night. When they had arrived at the airport, he had introduced Phire to Garth and Regan, and told Jaxon he would see him in a few hours. Jaxon would be trailing behind them in his own private jet to Alaska.

Maverick drew in a deep breath as he gently caressed the side of Phire's face, intending never to let her out of his sight again. He wanted her to sleep for as long as she could because he was not in any hurry to tell her the rest of what he knew, especially about her aunt.

However, the first thing he wanted to do was make sure she knew how he felt about her. They had some serious talking to do. Knowing they had several hours of flight time ahead of them, he leaned back against the seat, stretched out his legs and closed his eyes as well.

In her sleep, Phire thought she heard Maverick's husky voice repeating her name while showering kisses along her cheeks and upper lip. She didn't want to open her eyes, fearful that when she did, her dream would end. So instead, she cuddled deeper into his arms to enjoy what he was doing. And when she began getting aroused, she moaned out his name.

"Wake up, baby, the plane has landed."

His words had her opening her eyes to stare into his dark ones. "Maverick?"

"Yes?"

She reached up to touch his bearded chin. "You're really here."

"Yes, I'm really here."

She glanced around and saw they were on a plane and then she remembered and jerked up in his lap.

"Easy, or you're going to fall out of my lap."

She looked up at him. "You held me the entire trip?"

"Yes. I needed to hold you."

Leaning up, she glanced out the window. "I'm really in Alaska?"

He chuckled. "Yes, you're really in Alaska."

She looked toward the cockpit. "Where's your brother and his wife?"

"They've deplaned already and are checking in with the tower. We will see them tomorrow."

"We will?"

"Yes. My siblings and I will hold our own meeting at my place before we meet with our dad. I want you there with me so I can introduce you to him."

"Attend a meeting with your dad? But I have nothing to wear. This is all I have. I didn't pack anything, remember?"

"Yes, I remember. It's been taken care of."

Phire lifted an eyebrow. "It has?"

"Yes."

Lifting her off her lap, he said, "My brother Sloan is bringing the car to the plane since you don't have a coat. For now, here's my jacket," he said, pulling off his blazer and placing it around her shoulders.

"What about you?"

He chuckled. "I'm an Alaskan and used to the cold."

When they stepped off the jet, a sleek car pulled up and a guy who resembled Maverick was driving. She blinked, thinking he favored Clint, Cole and that other Westmoreland guy she'd been introduced to. The one named Zane. They were all extremely handsome men. "Strong Outlaw genes," she said.

"No, strong Westmoreland genes."

He introduced her to his brother Sloan, who told her that his wife, Leslie, was looking forward to meeting her. It didn't take them long to get to Maverick's home, which was located less than fifteen miles from the airport. Sloan kept things lively during the drive, telling Phire that he and his wife were expecting their first baby in June and the doctor had confirmed they were having a girl. They were ecstatic about it.

Phire was impressed with Maverick's house the minute the car pulled into the driveway of a huge modern-style split level. The yard was completely covered with snow. She'd never seen this much snow ever. "Your house is beautiful, Maverick."

"Thanks. I bought it last year. Before then, I lived in a condo in town."

Since neither of them had luggage, Maverick swept her into his arms after they'd thanked and said goodbye to Sloan, saying the ice on his walkway was slippery and he didn't want her to fall. The moment he opened the door to his home, she was in awe. It was beautiful and the decor looked amazing.

"I have my cousin Gemma to thank for this. She lives in Australia with her husband, Callum. She did the decorating for me."

"She did an awesome job."

"I think so, too," he said, placing her on her feet. She saw the numerous shopping bags on his sofa and said, "Those are yours. I called my sister Charm, and she was more than happy to go shopping for you. I told her your size."

She glanced over at him. "And you know my size?"

He pulled her into his arms. "I believe I do."

He probably did, she thought, but she wondered if he'd taken into consideration that certain parts of her were beginning to expand. "I want to see what's all in those bags."

"Later," he said. "We need to talk."

She nodded. However, there was something she

needed from him first. The moment she'd entered the parlor at her father's home and had seen him, those overactive hormones had pushed her desire buttons. She wasn't sure how long they would stay here before she returned to Paris, but it didn't matter. She intended to get in all the lovemaking she could.

"I really want to do something else first, Maverick," she said, wrapping her arms around his neck.

"And just what is it you want to do, Phire?"

"Make love with you."

His smile widened as he swept her off her feet and into his strong arms. In no time he'd made it up the stairs and placed her on the bed. Glancing around, she saw just how spacious his bedroom was and his furniture looked big and sturdy.

She was about to ask him about the various framed artworks on the wall when he began undressing her. The moment he removed her dress and touched her breasts, any further questions evaporated from her mind. All she could concentrate on was what he was doing and how he was doing it.

"They look bigger."

She chuckled. "They are bigger."

"Will you be breastfeeding our baby?"

"Yes, I plan on it."

"Good. I'm sure, like its father, he or she will enjoy your nipples."

When he reached out and placed a hand on her stomach, the warmth of it against her skin made her moan. "If you do that in a few weeks, you'll get more than you bargained for."

He looked up at her. "What will I get?"

"Probably a kick. Our baby will start moving soon."

"I can't wait."

She rolled her eyes. "Only because you're not the one who will constantly be feeling those kicks."

"I could be feeling them if a certain part of me stayed inside of you the majority of the time."

Her pulse leaped as his words stirred a sensuous visual image in her mind. She tilted back her head to look at him. "Um…as nice as that sounds, I don't think it's possible. But for now, it is. The part about you being inside of me."

He eased away to remove his clothes and when he returned, he caressed her all over as if needing to verify the fact that she was there with him. The way he stroked her skin sent sharp sensations all through her.

"Maverick…"

"I'm here, baby, and I will always be here."

And then he straddled her and clutched her hips with his strong hands, while widening her legs with his knees. When he eased inside of her, filling her in a way that only he could, her body quivered in anticipation. When he began moving, going deep and then withdrawing in long, sinuous strokes, she couldn't stop the moans flowing from her lips or the way her nails dug deep into his shoulders. And she certainly couldn't bring an end to the way her inner muscles clenched him, increasing the pace of his thrusts.

"Phire!"

"Maverick!"

Together they were swept away in a high tide of turbulent waves. She screamed his name again when she felt his body fill hers with another hot release as they both came a second time. If she hadn't been pregnant before, she would definitely have gotten pregnant now. Their lovemaking had been so compelling, so needed and so draining.

As she closed her eyes, something he said earlier coaxed her into sweet oblivion. *I'm here, baby, and I will always be here.*

Seventeen

An hour or so later, Maverick watched as Phire came awake in his arms. She gazed at him before glancing around as if to remind herself where she was.

"Thanks, Maverick."

He knew what she was thanking him for. He leaned in and kissed her lips. "Never thank me for making love to you, Phire. The pleasure was all mine." Then with seriousness, he said, "It's time for us to talk now."

She nodded and pulled herself up in bed beside him. "Alright."

"First there's something you obviously don't know and maybe I should have told you long before now."

She pushed a lock of hair back from her face. "And what's that?"

"That I love you."

She nodded. "I know you love me, Maverick. I wouldn't be your best friend if you didn't."

He took her hand in his and met her gaze. "That's where you are wrong, Phire. I love you more than just as a friend."

She blinked. Then she blinked again, and asked, "What did you say?"

He had no problem repeating himself. "I said that I love you more than just as a friend. I love you as a man would love a woman he wanted, needed and desired. A woman he wants more than anything to spend the rest of his life with."

"Because of the baby?" she asked in a soft voice.

"No. I believe I fell in love with you a long time ago. I just wouldn't admit it to myself. Now I understand why I felt so hurt when you ended our FWB relationship."

"You felt hurt?" she asked, looking deep into his eyes, as if she couldn't believe what he'd said.

"Yes. We were doing good, enjoying a fantastic relationship, and then one day I arrived in Paris, and you announced you wanted to end things."

She nodded. "There was a reason I felt I had to do that, Maverick."

"I know. You were ready to seek a serious relationship with some other guy."

"That's the reason I told you, but it wasn't the truth."

He drew his eyebrows together. "Then why did you end things with us?"

"Because I had fallen in love with you even though I knew what we'd agreed to be from the beginning—just friends. I decided to end things to keep my heart from getting broken."

His hold on her hands tightened, as if he thought he had to keep her captured with them. "Are you saying you love me?"

"Yes. I've always loved you, Maverick. I think I fell

in love with you that night you walked into DuRands, although I'd convinced myself I would never love another man after what Jacques did to me. But I fell in love with you, anyway."

Maverick leaned down and brushed a kiss across her lips. "Well, I fought the idea of falling in love with you for as long as I could, but that week you spent with me at the Golden Glade made me realize what my feelings were for you. That's why I asked you to marry me. I want both you and my baby, Phire."

"I didn't know."

"Now, you do," he said, leaning toward her to capture her mouth with his. Their tongues dueled and mated, and desire stirred his insides in a way it had never done before. He always enjoyed kissing her, and realizing she loved him as much as he loved her affected him. And knowing his child grew inside of her was like the icing on the cake. But he knew there was something else she needed to know, and he needed to be the one to tell her.

He pulled back his mouth and met her gaze. "There's something else I need to tell you, Phire."

She nodded. "About how you and Jaxon are related?"

"That, too, but this is news about your aunt."

"My aunt?" she asked excitedly. "Did your cousins' security firm find her?"

"Yes."

A huge smile covered her face. "That's great! Where is she? I want to go to her, Maverick. I haven't seen her in months, and I need to see for myself that she's okay and—"

"Phire."

Evidently there was something in his tone that made her search his gaze intently. "What is it, Maverick? What's wrong?"

He tightened his hold on her hand and said, "Your aunt passed away, Phire. She died in her sleep in November."

"In November?"

"Yes. Your father ordered the facility not to inform you of your aunt's death. Instead, he called for you to come home immediately. Under the pretense that she was still alive, he hoped you'd do what he wanted you to do."

"Aunt Lois is gone?" Phire said in a soft voice as tears sprang into her eyes. "All this time Dad knew she was gone. How could he be so cruel?"

Instead of answering her, Maverick pulled her into his arms while she cried and inwardly cursed Bordella for what he'd done.

"Here, baby, drink this."

Phire took the glass of apple juice Maverick offered her. "Thanks." She didn't know how long she'd cried, but it had been until she hadn't had any tears left. And Maverick held her in his arms the entire time. He'd finally taken her out of the bedroom and brought her into the living room.

Maverick, her outlaw. The man she loved and who'd told her just an hour ago that he loved her. The news he had delivered about her aunt had been such a shock. "How could my father have lied to me about something like that?" That was the part she just couldn't get beyond.

Maverick eased down on the sofa beside her and pulled her into his arms. "I don't know, Phire. I can't imagine him lying to you that way and actually using his sister to bring you to heel."

She took a sip of her juice, then looked at him and said, "Aunt Lois wasn't his sister."

He quirked an eyebrow. "She wasn't?"

"No, she was his mother." When he eased her into his lap, she then told him what her father had shared. "She was only fourteen and he blamed her for giving him away. She was just a child, one who'd gotten raped."

"What made your father decide to hold you hostage?" Maverick asked her, gently stroking her stomach.

She frowned. "Massie found my prenatal books and told my father she suspected I was pregnant. He questioned me and I admitted I was. He said I was to seduce Jaxon into thinking he was the father or get rid of my baby. I refused to do either. That's when he had me locked in my room. What kind of father is he?"

"For one thing, he's not yours."

"What do you mean?"

While Maverick held her, he told her what Jaxon had told them about the letter her grandfather had written to his. "Now what Dad said last night makes sense," she said softly.

"What did he say?"

"He said that I was no better than my mother." She paused. "I'm glad he's not my biological father. Now I don't have to worry about our baby one day growing up and being anything like him."

"Me, too," Maverick said, grinning. "It would have been bad enough with Bart's blood running through his veins."

She leaned up. "Now will you tell me how Jaxon knows so much and how the two of you are related?"

For the next half hour, he held her while telling her everything, including why her father was desperate for her to marry Jaxon.

"Wow, that's a lot to take in," she said, appreciating him holding her the entire time. "Just think what would have happened if Jaxon's grandfather hadn't shared all those documents with him and he hadn't had a mind to set a wrong right."

"Yes, and I can't wait for my brothers and sister to meet him. You said in the beginning that there was something about Jaxon that made you think he was playing your Dad. Now we know that was the truth." Maverick eased her from his lap and stood. "There is something else that needs to be done to make this day complete."

She looked up at him. "What?"

"This." He then eased down on bended knees before her and took her hand in his. "I asked you before and you thought it was for the wrong reason. Now I'm asking you again, and I hope you know it's for the right reason. I love you, Phire. Will you marry me?"

Tears sprang into her eyes. "Yes! I will marry you."

He slid a ring on her finger, and the huge diamond nearly blinded her. "Wow! It's beautiful, Maverick. I love it!"

"I'm glad, sweetheart. The day after you left the Golden Glade, I took Alyssa and Patrina shopping to help me pick it out. I had every intention of asking you to marry me a second time and making sure you knew how I felt about you. I love you."

"And I love you."

"Time to celebrate the Maverick Outlaw way." Standing, he swooped her off the sofa into his arms and headed for the bedroom.

The next day, Maverick and Phire got visitors—all his brothers and their wives. She also got to meet his sister Charm and thank her for shopping for her. She liked Charm immediately, as well as Maverick's four sisters-in-law.

Everyone congratulated them on their engagement and the women told Phire how much they loved her engagement ring. It was decided that she and Maverick would get married before returning to Texas and have a reception a few weeks later.

She was surprised when Jaxon arrived. Maverick said the brothers had wanted to get to know him and hear everything he had to say. Most of which she knew Maverick had heard, but he listened again along with everyone else. Garth asked a lot of questions and Jaxon had copies of all the documents that were needed. At one point they'd placed a phone call to a man named Rico Claiborne, who was married to Zane's sister, Megan. Mr. Claiborne had been the private investigator hired by the Westmorelands to find more family members connected by way of Raphel Westmoreland.

After being placed on speakerphone, Rico told them how the trail went cold after he'd traced Jeannette Outlaw to Detroit. He'd discovered she had named the child Levy, after her deceased husband.

The mother and son remained in Detroit until Levy turned twenty-one and married. He and his wife had a son they named Javier—that was who they believed Bart to be. Their grandfather Levy had changed all their first names and fled to Alaska after discovering someone was looking for him.

It amazed Phire how well the brothers and their wives got along and how easily Jaxon was included as a family member. But then, she had to admit, they were very kind to her as well and everyone had easily accepted her as the woman Maverick loved and planned to marry. Everyone knew about her pregnancy and said they were happy for them.

"I hope you understand why I couldn't tell you anything about my purpose in Texas, Phire," Jaxon said after the meeting was over. She had prepared a number of French pastries that everyone enjoyed.

She smiled up at him. "I understand, especially when you thought I was a willing accomplice in my father's scheme. And just to think, you and the Outlaws are cousins. With all the information both you and Rico provided tonight, I wonder what happens next."

"Only the Outlaws can answer that. They're calling a meeting with their father tomorrow and asked me to attend."

Phire nodded. Maverick wanted her at the meeting, too. "Tomorrow's meeting should be interesting."

Eighteen

Bart entered the conference room and glanced around, seeing his sons, his daughter and his married sons' wives. Maverick observed that his father then saw two people he didn't know. Namely, Phire and Jaxon. "What's this meeting about and who the hell are those two?" he asked gruffly.

"Let's just take a seat, Bart. I'm sure you'll meet them soon enough," Claudia said in a soothing voice, as she entered the room with him. She sat down and he sat in the chair beside her.

Maverick glanced over at his brothers. They hadn't known if Bart would invite Claudia to the meeting, but he was glad that she was here. Claudia knew just how to handle Bartram Outlaw when he got too overbearing.

"Now that you're here, Dad, we'll get started," Garth said. "And to answer your earlier question, introductions are in order, and I'll let Maverick do the honors."

Everyone's attention shifted to Maverick. Before standing, he smiled at Phire, who was seated beside him. "Dad and Claudia, I'd like you to meet Sapphire Bordella, better known as Phire. She is the woman I love and plan to marry as soon as it can be arranged."

"Marry!" Bart exclaimed, his stare moving from Maverick to Phire.

"Yes, marry," Maverick said, glaring at his father. "Do you have a problem with it, Dad?" Everyone knew that of all Bart's sons, Maverick might be the most fun-loving, but he would be the one least tolerant of Bart's interference in his life.

Bart and Maverick's eyes held and then Bart said, "No, I don't have a problem with it. In fact, I want to congratulate the two of you."

Maverick fought back a smile and figured Claudia had given their father a hard kick under the table. "Thanks, Dad." It didn't surprise Maverick when Claudia got up from the table and came around to give Phire a huge hug.

When Claudia settled back in her seat, Maverick then introduced Jaxon, saying only that he was a family friend.

"Now, I turn the meeting back over to Garth," Maverick said, sitting back down, and then brushing a kiss across Phire's lips.

Garth stood. "The reason for today's meeting, Dad, is that we think the time has come for you to face some real important facts."

Bart frowned at his oldest son. "What facts are you talking about?"

"That we have Westmoreland blood running through our veins."

The room got quiet and when Bart didn't stand to

make a scene or storm out of the room, Garth continued. "Now more than any other time we need to know the truth, whatever it is, and accept it."

"Why?" Bart snapped.

"Because millions could be at stake," Garth said. The Outlaw brothers knew the mention of money would interest Bart.

"How so?" Bart asked.

"This is where we will let Jaxon explain," Garth said, then took his seat.

Jaxon stood. "Mr. Outlaw, I have reason to believe you're the Riggins heir."

Bart rolled his eyes. "First Westmorelands, and now someone by the name of Riggins wants to claim the Outlaws?" he said in a snort.

A smile touched Jaxon's lips. "I guess you can say that since your father was conceived by Raphel Westmoreland and Clarice Riggins."

When Bart opened his mouth to deny such a thing, Jaxon held up a hand to stop him. "Please let me present my proof before you state your denials, Mr. Outlaw."

Maverick and his brothers had fully expected their father to tell Jaxon just what he could do with his proof. When Bart glanced over at Claudia, Maverick wasn't sure just what unspoken communication passed between the two. But maybe it had been a warning from Claudia. All they knew was that after breaking eye contact with Claudia, Bart glanced back at Jaxon, nodded and then said in a brusque tone, "Okay, state your case."

Like an attorney in a courtroom representing Raphel and Clarice in a child-custody suit, Jaxon presented his case. Although nobody said a word, all eyes were on

Bart. Their father wore his poker face, which meant none of them had a clue what he was thinking.

Jaxon was good and there was no doubt in Maverick's mind the man had a law degree. The legal documents he had presented could not be denied. He effectively explained why Levy, his wife and their child fled from Detroit and changed their first names. Levy became Noah, his wife Elouise became Abigail and their son's name—Javier—was changed to Bartram. Upon arriving on Kodiak Island, Alaska, with little money, they were befriended by Walker and Lora Rafferty—Garth's best friend's grandparents. They had given them a place to stay and food to eat. In fact, it was the elder Raffertys who'd sold Bart's parents land to build their first home. The cabin on Kodiak Island that the Outlaws still owned.

A half hour later, Jaxon was still presenting documentation to substantiate everything he was saying. There was no doubt in anyone's mind that he was presenting a compelling case.

"I've heard enough!" Bart suddenly said, slamming his fist on the table. He stood and left the room.

Claudia stood, looked around at everyone and smiled. "I suggest we take a fifteen-minute break. I'll make sure Bart comes back."

True to her word, fifteen minutes later Bart and Claudia entered the room. After closing the door behind them, Claudia said, "Before you continue, Jaxon, Bart has something he needs to say."

Claudia sat down and the room was quiet, waiting for Bart to speak. For once he was not wearing a poker face. Anguish was etched in his eyes and his sons and daughter saw it.

Shoving his hands into his pockets, he looked at Jaxon. "I need to speak with my sons and my daughter privately."

Jaxon nodded and moved toward the door. When Phire, Regan and the other wives stood to leave, Garth said in a firm voice, "Our wives and fiancée stay. They are part of this family."

Bart opened his mouth to say something, then as if he thought better of doing so, he nodded "Yes, of course." He hesitated and then said, "For the past two months I've been seeing a therapist in New York."

Maverick was certain that although no one made a sound, just like him, his brothers were picking their jaws up off the floor.

"Something I saw at your wedding, Jess, left me totally shaken," Bart added.

"And what did you see, Dad?" Jess asked.

"It was a framed portrait inside that building where your reception was held. I had Claudia ask someone about it and they told her it was a picture of Stern Westmoreland, Raphel Westmoreland's son."

"What about the portrait?" Cash asked.

Bart didn't say anything for a long moment. "It was just like seeing my daddy. They were almost identical, right down to the mole above the lip. I couldn't believe it."

He paused again. "I'm not obtuse. I've seen the similarities between my sons and those Westmorelands, but I still refused to consider it could be true until I saw that portrait."

"Why did you get this sudden epiphany when you saw that picture, Dad?" Maverick asked. He wondered how his father would handle it when it was disclosed that Stern Westmoreland was Bart's father's half brother since they'd shared the same father, Raphel Westmoreland. That was the reason the two men looked so much alike. Those strong Westmoreland genes.

"Not only were his features almost identical to those of my father, but his eyes—it was like staring at my Dad. Like I said, seeing it shook me up real bad."

Everyone got quiet and then Sloan asked, "Dad, do you recall ever being called *Javier*?"

"No. And I've never known my father to be called *Levy*, either. He was Noah. And my birth certificate says I was born here, in Alaska, to Noah and Abigail Outlaw. But the one thing I do recall as a child is Dad buying that land from Walker's grandfather and the two of them building that cabin."

"Do you know why there's an underground tunnel and why Granddad had all those guns?" Maverick asked his father.

"Yes," Bart said. "He told me there were people who were part of some group, sort of like a cult, that wanted to change our identity and that if they ever showed up in Alaska looking for us that he would be ready."

Bart paused and then added, "While growing up, both my father and mother would tell me to protect the Outlaw name because we were Outlaws, and not to believe it if someone ever tried to tell me differently. Dad stressed the same thing to me on his deathbed and made me promise I would protect the Outlaw name."

The room got quiet again. Now Maverick understood and knew his siblings did as well. Jeannette Outlaw had pretty much brainwashed her son, Levy, into believing he was the biological son of her deceased husband, Levy Outlaw, Sr., for fear he would be taken away from her. It sounded like she concocted this big lie about a cult. No wonder the man had fled from the lower forty-eight to Alaska, believing he was protecting his family.

"After listening to Jaxon, you do see there's a possibility what he's saying is true, Dad, right?" Charm asked. "He has the documentation to prove it."

Bart glanced over at his only daughter and his face softened. "I don't want to see it because that would mean my father lied to me, Charm, and my father would never have lied to me."

"He probably told you what he believed was the truth," Maverick said. "His adoptive mother felt she had reason to keep him away from the biological grandfather looking for him, the man who wanted to take him away from her. That's why she lied. Her son was all she had."

Maverick wondered if his father recalled that he'd acted that same way when the Westmorelands first reached out to them. They'd been grown men, yet Bart had acted as if they were children and had forbidden them to have a relationship with the Westmorelands. And he'd honestly expected his directive to be followed.

"I promised Dad on his deathbed that I would uphold the Outlaw name and its legacy," Bart said. Everyone could hear the pain in his voice.

"Just because we have Westmoreland and Riggins blood running through our veins doesn't mean we aren't Outlaws, Dad," Garth said. "We *are* Outlaws. Nothing will ever change that."

"Garth is right, Dad," Jess said. "We are Outlaws and there's nothing wrong in discovering we're related to others. After meeting Jaxon, we're claiming him as kin the same way we do the Westmorelands."

The room got quiet and then Maverick said, "We would like you to hear the rest of what Jaxon has to say.

Tillman Riggins never gave up looking for your father. He even put a clause in his will for the search to continue after his death. He left money for that to happen. Money that Phire's father has misused over the years."

Bart raised an eyebrow as he glanced across the table at Phire. "Your father?"

"My stepfather," she corrected.

"In order for you to stop Simon Bordella and claim what was rightfully Granddad's, and now yours," Sloan said, "you have to admit you are the Riggins heir."

"Well, what do you think your father will do?" Phire asked Maverick when they returned to his house later that day. Jaxon had returned to the meeting and Bart had listened to what he had to say without interrupting.

"Jaxon certainly did a great job explaining everything and he had all the legal documents to prove it," Maverick said, closing the door behind them. "I talked to my siblings after the meeting. We knew there was a reason Dad refused to accept the Westmorelands. Now we see it was more than him being ornery and pigheaded."

"Well, I think it's admirable that he decided to seek help with a therapist."

"Don't get it twisted, Phire. I'll bet a million dollars seeing a therapist wasn't Dad's idea, but Claudia's."

Phire dropped down on the sofa to remove her boots. "Is there really a cabin with an escape tunnel and an arsenal of weapons?"

Maverick came to sit down beside her, reached over and placed her legs in his lap to remove her boots for her. "Yes. My siblings and I never knew the reason for the secret passageway or why an arsenal of guns was kept there. Now the mystery has been solved."

Maverick dropped her boots to the floor. "Are you ready to marry an outlaw?"

Phire couldn't help the smile that spread across her face. "Yes. When?"

He smiled. "Is tomorrow soon enough? Since there's a three-day wait in Alaska, let's fly to Canada tomorrow to get married."

"That sounds good to me," Phire said, wrapping her arms around his neck. "Jaxon said Dad keeps calling, wanting to talk to me. That's what he gets for trying to take my phone. Since it's damaged, he can't reach me."

"Jaxon did mention your father keeps calling him. He told Bordella that you're extending your stay until this weekend. That will give us time to get married and wait for Bart to decide what he will do."

"I guess Dad's hoping I'll use that time to seduce Jaxon so he'll think my baby is his." Phire didn't say anything for a long moment. "What happens if your father doesn't admit to being the Riggins heir? Will Dad get to keep the ranch and land?"

"Not if me and my siblings can help it. It would be less messy and an easier process in court if Bart cooperated. However, if he doesn't, my siblings and I can certainly prove we're descendants of Levy Outlaw. We've decided that with or without Bart, we're going to handle your father. There's no way I'm going to let him get away with what he did, especially to you."

"I now pronounce you husband and wife. Maverick Outlaw, you may kiss your bride."

Maverick pulled Phire into his arms and captured her lips. He'd figured it would be just the two of them with Garth and Regan as witnesses. But when they'd landed in Vancouver, the rest of the Outlaw brothers and their wives, along with Charm and Jaxon, were waiting on them.

When he released Phire's mouth, he whispered, "I love you, Mrs. Outlaw."

She smiled up at him. "And I love you, Maverick, my outlaw."

After the ceremony, everyone joined them for dinner at a restaurant not far from the chapel where they'd gotten married. The food was great, and Maverick wanted to pinch himself knowing he had married his best friend and they were having a baby.

Garth excused himself from the table when his cell phone rang. Maverick figured it was some kind of business call. When Garth returned moments later, he said, "Well, I'll be damned." Everyone looked over at Garth when he sat back down at the table with his phone still in his hand.

"What?" Maverick asked.

"That was Bart, and he intends to go to Texas to claim what's his."

Nineteen

Simon glanced up when there was a knock on his office door. "What is it?"

Massie opened the door and stepped inside. "Your daughter has returned."

"About time," he said, standing. "Is Jaxon with her?"

"Yes, along with several others, including that man who came with him the last time."

Simon nodded. "Where are they?"

"I've seated everyone in the parlor. There's something else you should know."

"What?"

"Your daughter is wearing a wedding ring. A very expensive-looking one."

A huge smile touched Simon's face. He'd known when Jaxon had whisked Sapphire off to Virginia that there had to have been a plan behind it. For a while, he'd been worried that Sapphire wouldn't do as she was told, but things had worked out just the way he'd wanted. "Those other people with Jaxon are probably other family members. Tell Cal to bring out the best wine and whiskey. This calls for a celebration."

When Massie closed the door, Simon came from around his desk and leaned against it. With Sapphire married it should be easy enough to persuade Jaxon to buy all that land. Like he'd told his servant, today was one to celebrate.

Drawing in a deep, satisfied breath, he left his office and headed toward the parlor.

"Remember, Dad, let Jaxon do the talking," Maverick told Bart, who merely grunted a response.

All Maverick's brothers were there. Also present were Clint, Cole and Zane. Zane was supposed to have left to return home days ago, but said there was no way he would return to Denver with all the action about to go down.

Also present was Jaxon's attorney, along with the Outlaws' attorney. Based on the proof Jaxon had in his possession, both attorneys had worked together for the last two days to obtain proper documentation certifying Bart as the rightful descendant of the Riggins heir.

For once, Bart hadn't questioned the Westmorelands' presence. Maverick and his brothers figured it was because of the test results that had come back yesterday that showed Bart's DNA was a match for both Raphel and Clarice. They were able to get Raphel's DNA verification by way of the Zane Wesmoreland. He'd been more than happy to assist.

Such a revelation had to have had a jarring effect on Bart. They were glad Claudia was there to give him whatever support he needed. Hopefully, those therapy sessions would help him come to terms with his true family history.

"Jaxon and Sapphire, you have returned."

Everyone's attention was drawn to the man who'd entered the parlor. Simon smiled at everyone, and then his gaze went back to Jaxon. "I assume these people are your family."

"Yes, they are," Jaxon said, smiling, and then he began making introductions.

"I understand you and Sapphire have news for me," Simon said. It hadn't gone unnoticed by everyone that other than acknowledging Phire when he'd entered the room, he hadn't approached her with a hug.

"And what kind of news do you think we have for you, Dad?" Phire asked, smiling. Maverick wondered if her father found it odd that she was standing beside him and not Jaxon.

"I'd think that wedding ring on your finger says it all, Sapphire."

"Not quite, Simon," Jaxon said with a smile that didn't quite reach his eyes. "What I didn't mention during the introductions was that Mr. Barnett is my attorney and Mr. Coker is the Outlaws'."

Simon's eyebrows drew together. "Attorneys? Surely you're not going to tell me any nonsense about a prenuptial agreement."

Jaxon chuckled. "Of course, I wouldn't tell you any such nonsense. However, I am telling you that you have twenty-four hours to vacate these premises, leaving everything as it is and making sure you take all your servants with you."

A deep frown settled on Simon's face. "What the hell are you talking about?"

"Just what I said. We have proof that for the past twenty-five years you have been living on property that doesn't belong to you," Jaxon stated.

"That's a lie. If this ranch doesn't belong to me then who in the hell does it belong to?"

Before Jaxon could answer, Bart came forward and

in Bart Outlaw fashion got in Simon's face. "It belongs to me, so get your thieving ass off my land."

Simon stared at Bart. "And who the hell are you supposed to be?"

"Bart Outlaw." He hesitated for just a second, then added, "My father was the Riggins heir. Anything that was to have gone to him, I'm here to claim today."

And while her father was too shocked to speak, Phire said, "I know about Aunt Lois. You had me thinking she was still alive to try and get me to do whatever you wanted. And just so you know, I didn't marry Jaxon. I married Maverick Outlaw, the father of my baby."

"And you're sure you're okay, baby?" Maverick asked Phire, slowly breaking off their kiss. They had checked into a hotel in downtown Austin, while other members of the family joined Clint at the Golden Glade. Bart and Claudia had left to return to Alaska and the attorneys remained behind to file more paperwork with the courts.

"I'm fine. Sorry if I shocked your dad when I announced my pregnancy."

"Don't worry about Bart. He loves seeing the Outlaw family increasing."

"That's good to hear, and I tried to warn you that Dad wouldn't leave willingly."

Yes, she had, and he was glad Clint had the Texas Rangers on stand-by to escort Simon off the premises. They would join the family at Clint's ranch tomorrow for lunch. Then his brothers and their wives, along with Jaxon and Charm, would fly with them to Paris. Everyone understood Phire's need to give her aunt a proper memorial service.

Regardless of whether the woman had been her aunt or her grandmother, Phire loved her and appreciated her giving her the love she had needed after losing her mother.

"Well, Simon Bordella's insolence got him arrested," Maverick said, pulling her into his arms and smoothing his hand down her back, then lower to her backside. When he shifted his stance, he knew she felt the hardness of his erection poking into her middle. "And Bart doesn't intend to let him get away with anything. He'll have to make restitution for any funds he used illegally."

"Serves him right. While listening to Jaxon state all my stepfather had done, it made me glad he wasn't my biological father. It also made me appreciate my grandfather for being Tillman Riggins's trusted attorney and for him having the hindsight to send all those documents to Jaxon's grandfather."

"Me, too. Without Jaxon's intervention, and letting the Outlaws know what was going on, your father would have gotten away with it," Maverick said, sweeping Phire off her feet.

He was glad his father had had the decency to thank Jaxon, and it had made his brothers feel good when he had welcomed the man to the family. They'd warned Jaxon not to get too giddy about it, since it might end up being a curse more than a blessing. You never knew with Bart.

He placed Phire on the bed. "You think my son or daughter is ready for another visit from their old man?" he said, unbuttoning his shirt.

"They would welcome your visit at any time. It was kind of the Outlaw ladies to help me plan our wedding reception. They know we can't put it off too much longer if I want to fit into a nice gown."

The reception would be held on Cash's ranch in Wyoming since February wasn't the best time for anyone to travel to Alaska. After he completely undressed himself, he then reached out for his wife. She had been this Outlaw's claim, and he would never regret making it.

Epilogue

Phire glanced up at the man who was holding her in his arms while they shared a dance. He was not only her best friend and husband, but he was also her everything. "Thanks for making arrangements to have Clancy and his family and the DuRands fly here. That meant a lot to me."

Maverick smiled down at her. "I figured it would. I told him of my plans when we flew to Paris for your aunt's memorial service. I also told him not to tell you because it was a secret."

"And it was a wonderful one."

"And you're okay with us living in Alaska and not Paris?" he asked, holding her close.

"Yes, but then there's no other place I'd rather be than where you are. Sloan's wife, Leslie, has given me the name of her doctor and I plan to call him when we get back from our honeymoon." Before leaving Texas, Phire had kept the appointment with her doctor. The look on Maverick's face when he'd heard their child's heartbeat had been priceless.

She paused and then said, "It was kind of your father to give us the ranch and the land it sits on as a wedding gift."

Maverik nodded. "Yes, it was, but then look at how much land he kept. Over two thousand acres. I have a feeling he'll be giving each of my other brothers and Charm acres of their own as well. Even after that, Dad will still have plenty land left for himself."

Phire glanced across the room to where Bart and Claudia were talking to Dillon and his wife, Pam. At least Claudia was doing the talking—Bart was just listening. Maverick had said his father wasn't all that sociable and finding out about his family history hadn't changed that about him. "Do you think your father and Claudia will eventually get married?"

Maverick followed her gaze. "Yes, one day. There's no way Dad will let her get away a second time. Enough about everyone else—let's talk about us. Are you ready for our honeymoon?"

They would be flying out tomorrow for Jamaica. He said he wanted to take her someplace where there was a lot of sunlight since when they returned to Alaska, the days would be short and cold. "Yes, I'm definitely ready. I even got a bathing suit. I figured I better wear it now while I can still look sexy."

When the music came to an end, he pulled her closer. "Baby, you'll look sexy even if it's the day before you deliver our baby." He then lowered his head to hers for a kiss.

Jaxon took a sip of his champagne while watching the woman across the room talking with Zane. He had met most of the members of the Westmoreland family and wondered who she was. He thought she was beautiful, or *striking* was a more appropriate word.

"You're enjoying yourself, Jaxon?"

He nodded to Jess. "I'm fine. There are a lot of Westmorelands."

Jess chuckled. "Yes, there are. Now you can imagine how my brothers and I felt meeting them for the first time. They are a right friendly group who are big on family. I understand Dillon welcomed you to the Westmoreland family and introduced you to the Atlanta and Montana Westmorelands."

"He did, but he really didn't have to do that since I'm not related to them," Jaxon said, taking another sip of his champagne.

"You're related to us, which makes you related to them. That's the Westmoreland way."

"And what about that woman standing over there talking to Zane? Is she a member of the family?"

Jess followed his gaze. "That's Nadia Novak and, yes, we consider her a member of the family." He then studied Jaxon and said, "But not to the point where you can't approach her if you're interested."

Jaxon switched his gaze from Nadia back to Jess. "You sure? You did say she was considered part of the Westmoreland family."

"Yes, I'm sure. I can say that with certainty since my wife, Paige, is Nadia's sister. And so is Aidan's wife, Jillian, and Dillon's wife, Pam. Three out of four sisters married Westmoreland men."

A smile spread across Jaxon's face. "You don't say?"

"I do say. However, I'll give you fair warning— Nadia is as feisty as they come."

Jaxon chuckled. "I love feistiness in a woman."

Jess threw back his head and laughed. "Then you'll

definitely love Nadia. Come on and let me introduce the two of you."

Jaxon followed Jess across the room. He had a feeling that after meeting Nadia Novak, his life would never be the same again.

"All your sons are now married, Bart, to strong women. You have to feel good about that."

He looked over at Claudia. "I am. They are married and producing more Outlaws."

"Now all that's left is Charm to marry."

Bart snorted. "I'm not ready for that."

"Well, you need to get ready. She'll be thirty in a couple of years."

Bart frowned. "And?"

"And I think it's time you tell her what you did all those years ago. It's best she hears it from you and not find out on her own."

"I did the right thing, Claudia. She was too young to think herself in love. It was utter teenage nonsense."

"She might not agree with you about that, especially when she discovers what you did to break up her and Dylan Emanuel."

Bart didn't say anything for a moment. "I might lose her if I told her."

"And you might lose her if you don't tell her."

Bart glanced across the room, to where Charm was talking to Cash and his wife Brianna. Charm was his pride and joy and the thought of losing his only daughter was a pain he couldn't endure.

He'd done what he thought was best, and he'd leave it at that.

* * * * *

CINDERELLA MASQUERADE

LaQUETTE

To my only princess, Mackenzie.
You're the jewel of your auntie's eye.

One

"Absolutely not!" Zanai James shook her head and crossed her arms as she stared down her best friend in the whole world, Morgan Grandin. Considering the smile spreading on her friend's lips, Zanai was doubtful Morgan was taking her objection seriously. She never did.

"Come on, Zanai," Morgan fake whined as she stepped from behind the counter of her boutique, The Rancher's Daughter, and stepped in front of Zanai. "This is the party of the year. Anyone who is anyone attends. People start ordering their costumes nearly a year in advance to make sure they're prepared for the masquerade ball. You've spent years dodging this event, it's time for you to stop hiding."

Self-conscious about the truth her friend was hurling at her, Zanai looked down at the top of her very sensible Mary Jane–styled shoes.

"Morgan, I appreciate what you're trying to do. But it won't work. I don't fit in to spaces like these. Books, science, research, those things all make sense to me. Small talk and flirting are foreign concepts. Hell, I can't even bat my eyelashes properly. I look like I'm having some sort of seizure when I do."

"Zanai," Morgan huffed as she placed her hands on Zanai's shoulders. "You're beautiful and smart. People will love you if you just give them the chance to."

Zanai shook her head. "People find me awkward and boring."

"Hey, don't talk about my best friend like that. You're neither."

Zanai smiled at Morgan, loving how protective she was. "I didn't say I *was* awkward and boring. I said people *find me* to be so."

When Morgan's lifted eyebrow revealed she didn't get the distinction, Zanai continued. "Morgan, that wasn't a self-deprecating comment. I like the fact that I'm a nerd. I wear that badge proudly. It's just I'm smart enough to know other people don't appreciate that quality in me. So I stay away from them and live my best STEM life."

Morgan gave her a sad smile. Zanai knew her friend didn't pity her. Morgan just didn't think it was healthy for anyone to spend so much time alone.

"Zanai, you promised your aunt you wouldn't let your light be snuffed out by work and that pack of wolves masquerading as your family."

Guilt and grief tugged at the edges of Zanai's heart at the mention of the only loving influence she'd had in her life since her mother died when she was a child. Her mother's sister Déjà was everything bright and beautiful in Zanai's bleak little life. Losing her earlier in the year still weighed so heavily on her that she wondered if she'd ever truly recover from the loss.

"That's a low blow, using my dead aunt to manipulate me. I see now why you and Ryan fight so much. You don't let anything go."

"Encourage, not manipulate," Morgan corrected. "And Ryan is hardly a paragon of virtue. He's a thick-headed neanderthal that I'd sooner…"

Zanai couldn't hide the devilish grin blooming on her face. Morgan wasn't the only one in the room who knew how to get a reaction out of her best friend.

Morgan was usually sunshine and rainbows hopped up on sugar on most days. However, the mere mention of Ryan Carter's name and Morgan lost all her chill. Though her friend would never admit it, Zanai suspected Morgan's dislike of the man had more to do with mutual attraction than anything else.

"We are not talking about Ryan or how infuriating he is. We're talking about how wonderful you are and how you need to live a little."

"I know." She huffed and walked over to a nearby settee in the fitting area. "I just don't know how to be at these things. I don't fit in. While other girls were figuring out how to be sociable proper ladies, my nose was stuck in a book. I don't know how to act or dress for these kinds of events. I'd be so out of place."

Morgan sat down next to her, wrapping a protective, comforting arm around her shoulders. "Your nose being stuck in a book helped you become a stellar developmental psychologist for neurodivergent kids. The good news is you're rich enough that you can pay for someone to do your hair and makeup. Also, your best friend in the whole world owns a boutique shop and has connections in the rag industry that also includes clothing fit for a queen. So, if you promise to let me have my wicked way with you, I'll make sure you're the prettiest girl at the ball."

Zanai looked at her friend with a skeptical glare. Morgan had that same determined look in her eye that always seemed to be there when she was about to do something that would probably land Zanai in the middle of something she'd more than likely want to shake Morgan for later.

Zanai closed her eyes and gathered just enough strength to tell her friend no when her gaze landed on Morgan's face practically glowing with excitement. Like always, she could never deny Morgan anything when it made her eyes light up like the star on a Christmas tree.

"Fine, Morgan. Do your worst."

Three days later, Zanai stood in front of a mirror in Morgan's closed shop in absolute awe of her reflection.

"Morgan, how on earth did you pull this off in only a few days?"

The satisfied gleam in Morgan's eyes revealed the obvious pride she had in her creation.

"I told you I'd make you the prettiest girl at the ball."

Zanai stared at herself in front of the mirrored wall, barely recognizing the reflection shining back at her.

Her dress was a strapless ball gown with a scoop neckline bodice that accented her shapely torso and cinched her waist. The floor-length skirt was made of layers of chiffon falling into perfect folds. The dress was gorgeous, but the bright red color is what took Zanai's breath away.

"Morgan, I don't recognize myself."

Her friend clapped beside her as she let out an excited squeal.

"It's a masquerade ball, silly. You're not supposed to recognize yourself. Let me get your accessories and we'll be ready to leave."

Morgan handed her a small silver clutch then draped the matching cape over Zanai's shoulders. Although the cape was made of a single layer of sheer chiffon, it made Zanai feel less exposed. Once again, her friend knew just what she needed.

Morgan swept Zanai's long dark curls over one shoulder before securing a sparkling crown on her head then sliding a red masquerade mask onto her face.

Zanai had to admit, she was stunning. She definitely looked like she belonged at the ball. Now, all she had to do was keep her mouth shut, and maybe folks at the Texas Cattleman's Club wouldn't recognize what an outsider she truly was.

Jayden Lattimore sipped his glass of champagne as he leaned on the bar looking out at the sea of people in the large ballroom. As always, it looked as if most of the elite in Royal had shown up for this annual ball.

Even with some portions of their faces being covered with a mask, Jayden could make out almost everyone milling around the room. With boredom clawing at him, he looked around to see if there was anything for him to get into before he made his exit.

Coming from one of the wealthiest families in Royal, he'd fulfilled his duty by showing up. But he wasn't about to spend his entire night bored to death at this excuse for grown rich folks to play dress up.

He was about to take another sip from his glass when a vision filled his gaze. A queen dripping in red stood at the entryway. He couldn't tell if she was purposely pausing for dramatic effect, or if she was just getting her bearings as she entered the room. Either way, more than a few heads turned to take in the elegant, yet sexy monarch gracing the rest of them with her presence.

Jayden was about to make his way over to where she stood when she stepped inside of the room and headed in his direction.

That suited him just fine. Usually, he was too easygoing to chase a woman. The truth was, coming from old money while standing at more than six feet with good looks meant he didn't have to chase anyone. Women came to him, not the other way around.

But even though she was literally approaching him, there was something about her air of mystery that intrigued Jayden enough that his interest in talking to her went beyond the usual cursory notice he had in the women he encountered.

"At the risk of sounding cliché, may I get you a drink?"

The masked queen glanced up at him with sultry deep brown eyes, and something akin to a sledgehammer slapped him in the center of his chest, forcing him to fight against the urge to take in a gasping breath.

"No, thank you." She answered quickly as she leaned into the bar and looked around the room. "I'm waiting for someone."

Disappointment flooded him. It would figure this alluring creature was attached.

"My friend needed to speak to someone out in the hall. She's going to meet me here shortly."

Jayden could feel a smile burgeoning on his face. She was here with her friend. Well, that changed everything, didn't it?

"Seems your friend's delay is my good fortune.

Spending a few moments in the presence of the loveliest woman at the ball is no hardship at all."

He waited for the practiced dip in her head, the expected response ingrained in most of the women from the upper class of Royal. Feigned humility was something that was taught from the cradle. But not this woman. She stared at him openly as if she were trying to figure out what was going on in his head.

"Thank you for the compliment. But half my face is covered in a mask, how on earth can you tell if I'm beautiful or not?"

Her question was so blunt it amused him. She was definitely not using the normal script for an encounter like this.

"Wow," he laughed before taking a sip from his glass. "You don't hold back, do you?"

She blinked, then tucked an errant strand of hair behind an ear, making the ruby and diamond earrings dangling from her ears sway back and forth. When she tipped her head to the side and looked up at him, her eyes softened to a warm brown. "I'm sorry. I didn't mean to offend you. Small talk just isn't my strong suit."

He waved a dismissive hand. "No apologies necessary. It's actually quite refreshing to have a woman speak her mind to me. It levels the playing field if I know what she's thinking." He extended his hand, hoping against hope she would accept it. When she did, a spark of something unrecognizable but potent burned through his palm spreading like wildfire through his system.

"I'm Jayden Lattimore." He pointed a finger from the hand still holding his glass. "Otherwise known as the Phantom."

"I kind of figured that from the white mask that covers half your face."

He shrugged. "Well, when you've been to enough of these, you eventually run out of interesting costumes. A classic is easy to put together yet acceptable in these rarefied circles."

He didn't let go of her hand and he wasn't ignorant to the fact that she hadn't taken hers away.

"And you are?"

She formed her lips into the perfect O that made him contemplate how much he'd love to see her sultry mouth take that shape under an entirely different set of circumstances.

"It's a masquerade party, the point is to conceal one's identity."

Jayden couldn't help the smile tugging at the corners of his mouth. Whoever she was underneath that mask, she had a quick mind and a sharp tongue. Two characteristics he suddenly decided were his absolute favorite in a woman.

"Don't be that way, darlin'. How are we ever going to get to know each other if you don't tell me who you are? I'm at this party every year and I can tell you I've never seen you here or at the Texas Cattleman's Club, period. So, forgive me for being so taken by your breathtaking beauty that I'm clamoring to know your name."

She looked away briefly before bringing her gaze back to his. When she did, there was a twinkle of something mischievous in it that made his heart race and his blood run hot.

"But if I told you, I'd miss out on the fun of watching you try to figure out who I am. I'm not sure I can willingly give that up just to satisfy your curiosity."

"Trust me, my queen. My curiosity isn't what I want satisfied."

He waited a beat to see if his words offended her. He wasn't trying to be a smart-ass. Well, okay, he was definitely trying to be a smart-ass, but he wasn't attempting to offend her. Any worry he had about disrespecting her slipped away when her smile broadened.

"Seriously," he continued. "I'd love to find out who that lovely mask is concealing."

"Why?"

He narrowed his gaze as he contemplated his answer to her question. She was gorgeous in all that red. The way the fitted bodice clung to and lifted her small breasts definitely played a role in him wanting to know her better. But it was more than that. The way she looked at him, he could tell she wasn't the average socialite that attended these sorts of parties. There was something deeper and brighter shining through that drew him in.

"I want to know who you are because I want to know what to call you when we leave here and spend a little time together."

"Presumptuous, aren't you?"

He shrugged. "Confident. You've been here for a few minutes and you haven't attempted to get away from me yet. If I was getting on your nerves, something tells me you'd have found a way to shut me down by now. Besides that, I don't chase women. If a woman tells me she's not interested, I move on to the next. If you're not interested, all you have to do is say so."

There, he'd thrown down the gauntlet, placing the ball firmly in her court. Whatever happened next would be her decision, and more than anything he hoped her desires were aligned with his.

"There you are." Jayden's attention was pulled away by the intrusion. He felt the red queen's hand slip from his, leaving him with a strange sense of loss he couldn't understand.

He shook his head before looking at the woman interrupting them. Even with her face covered by a lace half mask and her red hair covered by a white-blond wig, he could recognize Morgan Grandin no matter her disguise. She was his best friend's sister and they'd spent enough time together as kids that he could pick her out of a crowd anywhere.

He glanced over Morgan's shoulder and saw Vic following closely behind.

"Two of the Grandin siblings, as always, your timing is perfect." Jayden hoped his words sounded as sarcastic as he'd meant them to.

"Jayden, can I speak to you for a minute?"

Apparently, Vic hadn't picked up on the bite he'd intended his greeting to have.

"I'm kind of in the middle of something, Vic. We can meet up later."

His friend placed a hand on his shoulder, pulling his attention from his red queen in front of him.

"This is important, Jay. It'll only take a few minutes."

Jayden cut sharp eyes at Vic before returning his gaze in the red queen's direction. Unfortunately, by the time he did, his mystery woman was quickly walking away with Morgan.

"Thanks for the cockblock, my friend."

"In that outfit, you'll easily locate her once I'm done talking." When Jayden groaned, Victor held up a hand to quiet him. "Just hear me out so you can get back to your mystery lady and I can get back to Aubrey."

At the mention of Vic's fiancée's name, Jayden could

see the bright spark of joy flooding the man's gaze. Who could be mad at him when he looked that damn happy?

"Speak your piece so I can get back to what I was doing before you so rudely interrupted me."

"Someone's in a pissy mood." Vic raised a brow as he watched Jayden carefully.

A strip of red caught his eye and he quickly turned to see if it was the intriguing woman who'd held his attention, who was still holding his attention even now.

It wasn't her, and that realization brought him more disappointment than it should have. Considering they hadn't spent more than five minutes in each other's presence, he truly shouldn't care. Apparently his brain hadn't gotten the memo, though, because here he was trying to look around Vic to see if he could get her in his sights.

"I can see your focus is elsewhere." When Jayden didn't answer, Vic smiled because he'd known Jayden so long, he didn't need a verbal response to know what was going on in Jayden's head.

"I can see why you're so taken, but I really need you to bring it in. I need your help."

"With what?"

"I think I've figured out a way to get Ryan and Morgan together."

"Ryan and Morgan? Really?"

Ryan was a good friend of Jayden's. Although he knew Ryan was a decent man, he had really strong opinions and an authoritarian personality. Jayden wasn't completely convinced pairing him with Morgan, a woman who walked her own path despite what anyone else thought, was the best idea Victor had ever come up with.

"Come on, Jayden, it's obvious the two of them are

seriously into each other. And if my sister is going to be with anyone, I'd rather it be a man I know actually cares about her."

Jayden agreed. He loved Morgan like a sister and Ryan was his friend. And although Jayden knew Vic wanted what was best for his sister, he had his suspicions about his motives.

"He does care about her, but I feel like your motivation is also grounded in the fact that you're so deliriously happy with Aubrey you're trying to match up everyone around you."

Vic didn't outright deny Jayden's claim, he just continued on as if Jayden hadn't said anything.

"They fight like alley cats." Vic's observation was an accurate one. Morgan and Ryan couldn't be in each other's presence more than two seconds before they started arguing about something. It was oddly entertaining, yet somewhat exhausting, to watch. "I'm just tired of their bickering. Besides, what's wrong with wanting the people around me to be as happy as I am?"

"Nothing," Jayden replied. "Just keep your busybody matchmaking focused on your sister and leave my love life alone. I have no intention of being the next one on your list."

Having laid down the law, Jayden huffed loudly hoping to move this conversation along so he could find his red queen.

"What do you want to do, Vic?"

"I'm gonna send Morgan a message she'll assume was meant for Ryan. When she texts back, I'll tell her to disregard the message, it wasn't meant for her. She'll never be able to resist coming back over to try to force an explanation out of me. She'll no doubt come back over here to make me clarify my meaning. When she's within earshot, we let her overhear us talking about how much Ryan is into her."

Jayden tapped his finger against his champagne glass before speaking. "You really think that'll work?"

"It will work." Vic didn't give Jayden a chance to respond before he was pulling his phone from his pocket and tapping out a quick text.

Jayden glanced over Vic's shoulder, watching Morgan make her way back to the bar sans the red queen. He noted his disappointment at the stranger's absence and sighed.

He could pretend it was just his curiosity that allowed him to care this much about the mystery woman's absence, but he knew it wasn't. There was something in the depths of her dark eyes that had taken hold of Jayden. And he knew he wouldn't be satisfied until he was able to explore it.

"All right, man. She's almost in position," Jayden noted quickly. "Let's get this done so I can get on with my evening."

"And back to that exquisite woman in red?"

His friend's penchant for being a pain in the ass was beginning to grate on Jayden's nerves.

"Do you want my help or not?"

Vic threw up his hands in surrender. Satisfied the subject had been dropped, Jayden swallowed the last of his champagne in one gulp.

"Good. Let's get this over with before Aubrey comes looking for you."

Vic waited until Morgan was safely within earshot before he began.

"It's such a shame that Ryan would never admit his true feelings to Morgan. It's obvious he's into her, and if she was actually paying attention, she would realize it too."

"Attraction that powerful can be hard to admit." Jayden saw Morgan stop from the corner of his eye. His words had definitely caught her attention. "Especially if you're afraid the other person will reject you."

Vic gave Jayden a knowing nod before continuing. "You're right. But they're both going to end up miserable for no reason at all. It's such a waste."

"You can't force people to do what's in their own best interest, Vic. Ryan and Morgan will either figure this out, or they won't. There's nothing you or anyone else can do about it."

Morgan stopped before turning on her heel and heading back in the direction she'd come. When she was far enough away, Vic smiled, happy his plan appeared to be working.

"I'm glad you're pleased. Now get out of my way so I can get back to what I was doing before you rudely interrupted me."

Jayden's body was thrumming with the anticipation of finding his mystery woman in red.

"Don't worry, friend. We're almost there. We just gotta do one more thing to get this plan underway."

Jayden sat his empty glass on the bar top then narrowed his gaze at his friend.

"What more do you want from me?"

"We gotta go find Ryan and tell him the same thing."

"I feel like we're back in elementary school passing notes between these two in class. All that's missing is the 'check yes if you like Ryan' box."

"Don't be so cynical, Jayden. Love is in the air. We're just helping it along."

Two

"And you're sure about this?"

Jayden kept his mouth shut, leaving opportunity for Vic to answer Ryan. This was his plan after all. Jayden saw no reason his friend shouldn't do the heavy lifting in this little scheme.

"Ryan," Vic continued, "no one knows my sister like me. All that annoyance is just frustration. She's really into you. She just doesn't think the feeling is mutual, so she lashes out."

From the corner of his eye, Jayden saw a flash of bright red. He turned to see his red beauty walking in the opposite direction.

"Hey, y'all. Excuse me for a moment. I've got something to take care of."

He didn't know whether his friends had agreed or not. Almost as soon as he'd spoken, his long legs were carrying him in the red queen's direction, eating up the distance between them.

"There you are. I finally found you." His words made her stop, pausing briefly before she turned around to face him.

"Found me? I wasn't aware I was lost."

"You were to me." That comment bought him a sincere smile that warmed him from the inside out, compelling him to step closer into her personal space.

"Dance with me, darlin'."

She watched for a moment, her silence stretching out so long he worried that she might actually deny his request. But at the last possible moment, she extended her hand to him and he clasped it in a gentle but firm grasp before pulling her into his embrace.

The music was slow as they swayed back and forth pressed so tightly together there was no clear line where she ended and he began.

"You still haven't told me your name. Who are you under that mask, my dear queen?"

"A little intrigue is good for the soul."

He chuckled at her response. "I'm almost certain that's not how that saying actually goes."

Her nonchalant shrug kept their banter going. "That doesn't mean it's not true. The beauty of this night is we can be anything we want to be. So, it doesn't matter who I really am. It only matters who I want to be in this moment."

He looked down into her gaze, feeling a little buzzed. He hadn't consumed nearly enough alcohol to feel any of its effects. The only thing he could attribute it to was the alluring woman in his arms.

"And who do you want to be in this moment, m'lady?"

She smiled again, drawing him closer into her web. He could feel her luring him in, but could do nothing to stop it. The truth was, he didn't want to.

"The woman dancing with you."

He was careful as he tightened the circle of his arms, like he was touching something breakable. It wasn't that he thought her too delicate for his touch. The gleam of need and burning desire flashing in her eyes revealed everything he needed to know about how much she could handle.

No, this wasn't about her being too fragile. It was about fear. His fear to be precise. He was afraid that if he was too abrupt, it would shatter the moment, the cocoon they'd made for themselves in the middle of the dance floor. They were surrounded by other bodies, but somehow, it was just the two of them swaying back and forth.

He looked down at her, moving a hand slowly from the dip of her back, up past her shoulder until his fingers found their way into the soft strands of her hair.

She purred for him the moment his fingertips grazed her scalp and the sound of her pleasure was so tempting, so damn powerful, it nearly overtook his senses.

His thumb grazed across one of her dangling ruby and diamond earrings he'd glimpsed when they'd met at the bar. They were a flash of fire and ice tied together in an intricate design where neither could be extricated from the other.

His body stiffened at the thought of their limbs being tangled together in a similar fashion. He internally chastised himself. He'd just met this woman. His needy response to her presence was a bit much, especially for a laid-back person like him who always went with the flow.

"You are the most exquisite being in this room to-night."

She smiled up at him, putting those sultry matte lips of hers on full display, making him fight their pull.

"I'm already dancing with you. You don't need to butter me up at this point."

He splayed his hand against the small curve in her back, looking down at her with all the intensity he could muster.

"I'm not trying to schmooze you."

"Then what are you trying to do, Mr. Phantom?"

"This."

It was the only warning he gave her as he leaned down, pressing his lips to hers. Although, it was some-what of a chaste kiss—they were standing in the middle of the Texas Cattleman's Club after all, and he didn't need the busybodies of Royal reporting back to his mama about her youngest son pushing the boundaries of public appropriateness yet again. Even though it was just a peck, his flesh burned with need the moment his lips touched hers.

He wanted more, and with the way she moaned so beautifully, full of a powerful want that mirrored his own, he aimed to get as much of her as he could.

He was about to deepen the kiss when the music stopped and the lights came up just a bit. As lights brightened outside his closed lids, he could feel her pulling away from him. Not just to politely end their connection, but to free herself of his embrace.

"I'm sorry. I shouldn't have done that."

He could feel his brow pulling into a sharp V. "What, kiss me back? Trust me, darlin', I have no regrets about it. In fact, I was hoping we could do it again."

She stepped back, bringing a respectable amount of

distance between them. There was something akin to panic in her eyes that set him on edge.

"I'm sorry. I have to go."

"Wait, did I do something wrong? Did I overstep?"

She shook her head, granting him a shaky smile. "You did absolutely nothing wrong. It's just time for me to go."

As he attempted to step forward, he felt a hand grip his shoulder from behind, drawing his attention away. When he saw it was Vic interrupting, he turned away from his friend, but by then it was too late. His mystery lady was gone.

Jayden dropped his head, pinching the bridge of his nose as he tried to quell the annoyance at Vic growing in his belly.

"You have the worst damn timing, Vic."

When Jayden opened his eyes, the light glinted off of something sparkling on the floor. Bending down and scooping it up quickly with adept fingers, he recognized it instantly. Not only had his real-life Cinderella absconded from his embrace and his view, just like in the fairy tale, she'd left something behind.

"What's that?" Vic's fiancée Aubrey questioned, making Jayden aware of her presence for the first time.

"The only clue I have to figure out who the lady in red is behind her mask."

Vic gave him a remorseful look. "I'm sorry, man, I didn't mean to interrupt. I just wanted to show you how well our plan is working."

"Our plan?" Jayden folded his arms and tilted his head. "Don't blame this on me. This was all you, Vic. I just went along for the ride."

His friend shrugged, apparently too satisfied with himself to notice Jayden wasn't exactly in the best of moods. Vic pointed to a far corner in the room where Ryan and Morgan seemed to be getting along quite nicely.

"That was almost too easy." Vic's gloating was beginning to get on Jayden's nerves. Not because he didn't want to see Morgan and Ryan happy together. If for no other reason than stopping their incessant bickering, Jayden would be thrilled if those two actually found their way to each other.

But in watching the two of them whispering closely together, Jayden could see all the possibilities of what could be, and it made something inside him ache with the need to explore his own possibilities with the stranger in red too.

"I hope it works out the way you want, Vic. But you're gonna have to deal with the rest of this on your own."

"What's going on, Jayden?"

Jayden rubbed his thumb across the large ruby at the bottom of the elongated earring as if it was a divining rod that could lead him to the one he wanted to be with.

"I have a Cinderella to find."

Three

"So, are you gonna drink that coffee or just stare at it? If it's the latter, let me just take it off your hands."

Jayden broke free of his daydream just in time to see his older brother, Jonathan, reaching for Jayden's coffee cup.

"Fratricide is a real thing. Don't make me have to show you."

Jonathan snatched his hand away from Jayden's cup with a snarky grin plastered on his face.

"You still 'round here moping because of your mystery lady? You sure she was even real? Maybe you had one too many cocktails at the club and you just imagined her."

"Did Vic and Morgan imagine her too? Because they saw her as well."

Jonathan's smile spread wider as his shoulders began to shake with laughter.

"What?" Jayden didn't bother trying to keep the annoyance out of his voice. Although it was usually the younger brother's prerogative to annoy his older sibling, right now, those roles were definitely reversed and Jayden didn't like it one bit.

"It's just, I've never actually seen you care this much about anything. You're always so laid-back and easygoing, without a care in the world. It's been three days since that masquerade ball and you can't stop obsessing over the 'red queen,' as you call her."

Jayden couldn't deny his brother's observation. There wasn't much that could get under his skin. He just wasn't built that way. But he couldn't deny the truth in Jonathan's statement. He was obsessing.

"I can't find anyone who knows who she is." He shoved his hand in the back pocket of his jeans, pulling the ruby and diamond earring free. "No one recognized her earring either. It's like she's disappeared."

Frustration coiled around his spine, making him sit straight on the breakfast bar stool.

"In a small town like Royal, where everybody knows everybody else's business, finding this woman shouldn't be this hard."

"Maybe she doesn't want to be found." His brother's observation was logical, but methodical thinking wasn't what Jayden was going for right now.

"Then let her tell me that to my face. Until then, I'm gonna see if I can track Morgan down and get her to tell me anything. The red queen mentioned they were friends. I figure Morgan should know something. She wasn't around when I went by the Grandin ranch and she hasn't been answering her phone at the boutique. With as busy as she seems to be, I figure a surprise visit is the best way to catch up with her."

"Catch up with or interrogate her?"

Goodness his older brother was annoying.

"Probably a little of both." Jayden's honest answer made Jonathan shake his head with pity.

"I hope this woman turns out to be worth all this effort you're putting in. Because as tied up in knots as you seem to be over her, and as useless as you've been at doing ranch work since you met her, I'm afraid it will break you if you find a pumpkin instead of a queen."

"You and me both, Jonathan."

"Please stop pretending that bowl of chicken salad is so interesting you can't pay attention to me."

Zanai looked up from the colorful and leafy display of vegetables and protein at Morgan's interruption. She found her friend staring at her from across the table with a cat-who-ate-the-canary grin slapped on her pretty mouth.

"I haven't the slightest idea what you're talking about. You invited me out to lunch, I presumed I was supposed to eat."

"Lunch, my great-aunt Tilly," Morgan groused. "I'm sitting here trying to tell my best friend about my drunken escapades with Ryan, and your head is miles away."

Damn, Zanai certainly hadn't been listening if she'd missed that.

"You slept with Ryan?"

Ryan and Morgan fought like predators in the wild kingdom, each trying to assert their dominance as ruler of the land. The fact that Zanai hadn't soaked up every juicy detail meant her mind had to be on something else, or someone else, as it were in this case.

"Maybe I did. Maybe I didn't. You should've been listening."

Zanai bowed her head in deference to Morgan. "I'm so sorry, Morgan. I can't seem to keep my head on straight today. Please tell me this story again because I need to know how you and your mortal enemy ended up in bed...together...with neither of you killing the other."

Morgan's face beamed with mischief, which ratcheted up Zanai's need for the details.

"I never said we slept together. I said we had escapades. Most of which were fueled by alcohol," Morgan replied. "Lots of alcohol. But I'm not repeating that story again until you give me the details on what or who has you so distracted."

Zanai opened her mouth to deny the accusation in Morgan's pointed gaze, but before she could come up with anything to say, Morgan raised her manicured finger to interrupt her.

"Three days, Zanai. It's been three days since the masquerade ball here at the club. It's been three whole days since I watched Jayden Lattimore kiss you in the middle of the dance floor. I'm your best friend. If anyone is supposed to get the scuttlebutt about this, it's me. You can hold out on everyone else, but not me."

Zanai closed her eyes briefly, shaking her head at her friend's antics. "Careful, Morgan, you're sounding like one of the old gossips in this town."

"Since I have a vested interest in your well-being, it's not gossip. It's concern for my oldest friend."

Zanai laughed at that. "I'm not your oldest friend. My father didn't pack up my life in Brooklyn and drop me off in this one-pony town until seventh grade."

Morgan threw up her hands in mock frustration. "Fine." She audibly exhaled for emphasis. "You're not my oldest friend, just my dearest. And as such, you owe me this. What happened? One minute one of the richest and most eligible bachelors in Royal was kissing you and the next you were running out of the TCC so fast, you lost your very expensive ruby and diamond earring. Spill it."

Zanai dropped the fork in her hand and shifted in her seat. She'd tried hard to forget everything about her time at the ball, everything that reminded her of how awkward and out of place she really was.

"It was…" Zanai thought back to the handful of moments she'd spent with Jayden and sighed. "Magical."

Morgan gave a delighted squeal that had several people looking in their direction.

"Tell me everything," Morgan commanded.

"Jayden was funny and sweet, and so handsome, I could hardly notice anyone else in the room."

"I'm not surprised. Even when we were kids, he's always been a charmer."

Zanai wouldn't argue Morgan's point because as smooth as that man was, his talents for making a woman feel as if she were the only person in the room had to be cultivated from birth.

"Being in front of a man like that has always—"

"A man like what?" She let Morgan's question hang in the air unanswered. A mistake on her part. It only gave her friend fuel to keep going.

"Zanai, please tell me how Jayden is different from any other man in Royal?"

"He's wealthy, he's handsome, he has status in the town."

"Zanai, you do realize your father is one of the richest men in town?"

She leaned back in her chair, part of her resolve bleeding away at the mention of her father.

"Yes, Morgan. My father is very rich. But Jayden's family has old money wealth. We're two different classes of people in the eyes of most folk in this town. My father couldn't buy the prestige and respect the Lattimores have, and trust me, he's tried."

"You really have to get over this nonsense, Zanai. You've been in Royal for fifteen years now. You belong here. Stop letting the snobs in this town tell you otherwise."

That was much easier said than done. Zanai had been reminded from the moment she stepped foot in Royal that she didn't belong. Between the people in town treating her like an afterthought and her father and stepmother constantly reminding her of why she didn't measure up to everyone else, being a resident of Royal hadn't been easy for Zanai at all.

"I know you can't see it, Morgan. Your beauty, your old money and, to some degree, your race give you status in this town. To your circle, it doesn't matter how much money my father makes. I'm still the Black girl from Brooklyn invading their social club. I'll never measure up."

Morgan flipped a long tendril of red hair over her shoulder. It was a clear sign she was gearing up for a fight. Well, that and the angry blush she could see creeping up Morgan's neck to her face.

"I don't give a damn what anyone says or thinks. You're the best thing that's ever happened to this town. You belong here. And as progressive as Royal is, I know this is still Texas, so I'm not blind to how unpleasantly narrow-minded some of our residents are."

Morgan's eyes locked on hers with flecks of fire dancing in them. This was her protective mode. Morgan was a fighter, and she always fought for those she cared most about.

"Being so closely tied to the Lattimores over the years, it's almost impossible to not see how race plays a role in status in this town. I've had a front row seat to some of the downright horrible things people say and do. But those people don't matter. You do. And the way Jayden kept his eyes on you all night, I'd say you matter very much to him too. So stop with this 'I don't belong' nonsense. It seemed like you were into whatever was happening between you and Jayden. What happened to change your mind?"

Obviously, they weren't going to get past this because Morgan wasn't going to drop it. Deep down, Zanai couldn't be upset. She'd kissed one of the princes of Royal at the ball. It was probably the closest thing to a fairy tale she'd ever experience. Of course she wanted to share the magic of that moment with her best friend.

"You're right. Jayden is a charmer. But more than that. There's this quiet intensity about him that's so noticeable. He doesn't seem to care about what the rest of the world is thinking, and in our circles, that's so refreshing. To be the focus of that intensity, it was…intoxicating."

"Then why run away?"

"Jayden didn't recognize me at the ball. And even if he did, he only knows me peripherally through you. We've never actually had a conversation. No matter how much money my father has, I'll never be a socialite. All I care about are the kids from work. My idea of a fun night is starting a new book. I'd bore Jayden to death. So, when he kissed me, I decided to end it there so our stark differences couldn't ruin it later. Most people in this town think I'm a shy weirdo. After that kiss, I just couldn't bear the thought of Jayden thinking that too."

Morgan slid her hand across the table to clasp Zanai's, lending her comfort and strength the way she always did.

"We both know there's nothing shy about you. You're reserved because some really nasty people have shown you how little appreciation they have for your interests and talents. That's not your fault. It's theirs."

She squeezed Zanai's hand and offered her a concerned smile.

"You've protected yourself and there's nothing wrong with that. I just worry that in your quest to keep the asshats away, you're going to miss out on knowing a really great person like Jayden, and more importantly, you'll rob him of the opportunity of getting to know someone as wonderful as you."

Morgan's warmth cloaked Zanai like a familiar, fuzzy blanket. The chill of her fears dissipating underneath its comfort made her count her blessings for Morgan Grandin's presence in her life.

Zanai was about to say as much when she glanced up and saw the subject of their discussion entering the club.

"Oh, my goodness, Morgan. Did you set this up?"

"Set what up?"

Morgan turned her head to see what Zanai was referring to. Zanai could tell the exact moment her friend zeroed in on the intended target because when Morgan brought her attention back to Zanai, that wicked grin of hers was back with a vengeance.

"Morgan, did you tell Jayden to meet us here?"

The woman shook her head. "No, I didn't. But I certainly wish I had the forethought to do so. This is about to get interesting."

"No, it's not." Zanai spoke through clenched teeth, trying hard to keep her voice from rising above a whisper.

Morgan was about to say something else, but by the time she was able to speak another word, Jayden was standing at their table smiling down at them with the same wicked grin he'd worn for most of their interaction at the ball. Only this time, half his face wasn't covered with a mask and she bore its mesmerizing full strength.

"Afternoon, ladies. I'm sorry to interrupt your meal, but if I may, I need Morgan's help with something."

The tension in Zanai's body relaxed just a bit. He wasn't here for her. That should be a relief, and to some degree it was. But more than anything, disappointment began to set in and she realized a big part of her wanted him to be looking for her.

Jayden shoved his hand in his pocket, and then opened a flat palm in front of Morgan. "Would you happen to know who owns this?"

Jayden glanced at Morgan as he waited for her answer. There was a flash of recognition and mischief in her eyes that made him hopeful he was closer to finding his Cinderella.

"Yes, I know exactly who you mean."

Zanai was sipping from a large glass of water and quickly began coughing.

"You okay, Zanai?"

He intended the question as a cursory politeness, something you do automatically when you see someone having a bit of difficulty. But then she watched him for a long pause before answering. "I'm fine. Water just went down the wrong way."

He stared intently at Zanai, which was something altogether different. With her long and wavy dark hair and deep brown complexion with reddish undertones, it was difficult not to recognize her beauty. A beauty that seemed to call to him, transfix him to the point that he felt ensnared, trapped in its presence and unable to do anything but let his sight linger upon her.

She dropped her gaze to the offending glass of water sitting in front of her and it was the only reason her hold over him loosened.

Jayden shook his head, trying to get his bearings. He'd known or rather known of this woman for fifteen years. Never had he felt so drawn to her. Never had he noticed just how captivating the depth of her dark brown eyes were or how tempting the graceful line of her neck was.

Zanai had always been a bit standoffish for his taste. Almost every time he'd encountered her, she'd had her nose in a book as if she couldn't be bothered to interact with the people around her. Her tendency to be so serious always left him cold, so he'd never taken the opportunity to say more than *hi* and *bye* when in her presence.

Today was different, however. There was something different about the way she looked at him. It was as if she were finally seeing him and allowing him to see her.

"Jayden, you were asking about who that earring belongs to?"

Morgan's voice barely registered as he stared into Zanai's deep brown eyes. There was a familiarity there that went beyond the very casual acquaintance they'd shared over the years. It was strong, tethering him to her, nearly blocking his senses from detecting all other stimuli.

"Ah, yeah," he answered as he closed his eyes attempting to mentally set himself free from Zanai's hold. "While we were dancing, she—"

He intended to glance down at the earring in his hand when he saw the light breaking through the wall of nearby windows glint off of Zanai's wrist.

There, accentuating her delicate wrist was a ruby and

diamond bracelet that looked eerily similar to the lost earring he had in his hand. He was no jeweler, but the cut, color and setting of the stones, the platinum metal, the resemblance was too great to ignore.

"It was you."

Zanai looked up at him with a mix of fear and disbelief in her eyes.

"What was me?"

"Zanai, you're the red queen."

She sat there with her eyes wide and her mouth open, and Jayden knew instantly that he wasn't wrong. He'd known that from the moment he spotted her bracelet, but her expression of shocked disbelief gave it all away.

She tried to recover, shaking her head and looking as if she were about to mount a defense for his accusation. But when he held the matching earring next to the bracelet on her wrist, they both knew her charade was over.

"Why'd you run out like that?"

He tilted his head in expectation of an answer. However, Zanai couldn't seem to find her words if her hanging jaw was any indication.

"I wasn't feeling well and Zanai was kind enough to take me home." Morgan's excuse wasn't enough to pull his attention away from Zanai. Even though he was about to reply to Morgan, he kept his gaze firmly locked onto Zanai's bewildered face.

"Didn't I see you with Ryan later that evening?" He reached for his phone, pulling it out and making a display of looking through his contacts. "I could always call Ryan and see if I'm mistaken or not."

Morgan gave him the same nervous smile she did when they were kids and he'd caught her playing with his video games without permission. She was busted and she knew it.

"Well," Morgan's voice cut through their fixed gazes. "It seems like you two have a lot to talk about. I'm just gonna slip out and leave the two of you alone."

When neither of them said anything, Morgan stood, smiling as she looked back and forth between him and Zanai. "I'll call later tonight, Zanai."

When she was standing beside Jayden, she playfully swatted him on the arm. "You'd better behave."

Without taking his eyes off Zanai, he nodded. After the way she'd run off at the ball, he couldn't afford to let her out of his sight for fear she'd run again. Although he knew that wasn't the only reason he couldn't take his eyes off of her.

There was something drawing him to her. Something primal, pulling at his insides, making him hyperaware of everything from the tempting way her long lashes fluttered against the smooth brown skin of her cheeks, to the short, quiet breaths she took as she stared back at him.

He let a few long seconds pass after Morgan's departure before he sat in the seat across from Zanai.

"Ja-Jayden," she stammered. "There's been some mistake."

He held up a hand to stop whatever it was she thought she was doing with what appeared to be a half-assed explanation in the works.

"The only mistake was letting you get away from me. I just need to know one thing, Zanai."

She swallowed, her eyes still wide with the surprise of discovery.

"What's that?"

"Why you left?" He watched her in silence before speaking again. "I need to know why you ran away from me at the ball."

Four

"Mr. Lattimore, if you'll be joining Dr. James, would you like me to bring you a menu?"

Jayden briefly tore his eyes from Zanai's face to be polite and answer the server standing at their table.

"No, thank you," he replied. "I won't be staying long."

When they were alone again, he tapped his fingers on the table waiting for Zanai to fill the empty silence spreading between them.

"As I said, I don't plan on being here long, but that doesn't mean I'm leaving without an answer. What happened three days ago, Zanai? You spent the night flirting with me, and then after I kissed you, you ran off. What kind of game were you playing?"

She was barefaced except for soft pink lip gloss that reminded him of how kissable her lips were. Simple elegance was how he'd describe her. So beautiful without any enhancements that she was absolutely stunning when she wore makeup and adorned herself in finery.

How he hadn't noticed how striking she was before this moment was beyond him. Perhaps it was because his ego had taken a hit when she'd run off at the ball. Or maybe his sisterly view of Morgan had blinded him to how attractive he found her. Whatever it was, he was mentally kicking himself for not noticing how lovely she was.

"I wasn't playing a game."

He lifted his brow, calling her on her lie without saying a word.

"Okay, fine," she capitulated, throwing up her hands before placing them quietly against the table. "I was playing a game and I'm sorry it was at your expense. I just got caught up."

He leaned in. "In what, exactly?"

Her gaze drifted from his and she focused on a single spot on the table instead. "In the feeling of having someone desire me, be so interested in me he'd seek me out in a crowded room and try to monopolize my time."

She shrugged, lifting her eyes and face to him so he could see a slightly embarrassed blush coloring her cheeks.

"Men like you don't look at women like me that way. Being treated like that was intoxicating."

He shook his head. Something in her tone rubbed him the wrong way and it annoyed him that he couldn't quite pinpoint what it was.

"Men like me, women like you, what the hell are you talking about, Zanai? We've known each other for years."

"Yeah," she replied. "But in all the time we've known each other, we've never spoken more than a handful of words at a time. We're best friends with siblings, but we hardly know each other at all. Up until I put on some makeup, a mask and a red dress, you hardly knew I existed. Hell, as close as we were on that dance floor, you didn't even recognize me. That's how invisible I've been to you all these years."

He sat straighter in his chair carefully processing what she was saying. "You can't call me shallow for not recognizing you in one breath and put yourself down in the next. What the hell, Zanai?"

She tucked her bottom lip between her teeth and every muscle in his body clenched with need as she swiped the pink tip of her tongue across it, seemingly soothing where her teeth had gently scraped across her skin.

What he wouldn't give to press his lips to hers again.

"I'm not trying to insult you and I'm not putting myself down. It's just a fact. I'm not your type. I'm not most people's type. I get that. It was just nice to see how the other half lives for once. I'm sorry if I got a little carried away by letting you kiss me."

She wasn't wrong about not being his type. She was intellectual, an academic. She did important work. That wasn't to say he wasn't attracted to smart, professional women. He certainly was. But Zanai always seemed as if she wasn't concerned with dating and social activities.

He'd thought it was because she was shy. But after spending time with her at the ball, he wasn't so sure that was the case. It dawned on him that maybe she was so distant because she didn't think anyone wanted to be close to her.

"I'll accept your apology if you accept mine."

Her brow furrowed as she let her curious gaze slide down his face.

"What on earth do you have to apologize for?"

"For not recognizing how absolutely alluring you are until three days ago."

Her eyes went wide, blinking repeatedly as she appeared to digest what he was saying. He had to admit, since Zanai was always in control, always so focused, it was empowering to know he could knock her off her game like this. He liked it so much, he figured he should keep the game going as long as he could.

"Let me rectify my mistake. Have dinner with me, Zanai."

She opened her mouth to speak. It took a few tries, but she finally figured out how to push air through her vocal cords and produce sound.

"Are you asking me out on a date?"

"Indeed, I am."

"When?"

He leaned in, brandishing the lopsided grin his granny called sweeter than sugar. "The sooner the better. Tonight."

He was about to stand up when she reached across the table to grip his arm. He wore a long-sleeved button-down shirt, but even through the material, he could feel the heat of her touch burning through to his skin.

"Jayden, you can't just ask me out to dinner. I mean, we've known each other for fifteen years and have never shown any interest in each other. This doesn't make any sense."

This was a sight to behold. The cool Dr. Zanai James flustered and out of her element. He could definitely get used to this.

"Zanai, I didn't appreciate brussels sprouts when I was sixteen either. That doesn't mean my tastes haven't matured as a thirty-one-year-old man. You're a gorgeous, accomplished woman. Why wouldn't I or any man be interested in you?"

She shook her head as dismay threaded her brows.

"You were attracted to a costume, Jayden. Not the woman in it. That wasn't the real me."

"I don't believe that."

She stared at him open-mouthed with her tongue stuck to the roof of her mouth.

"Sure, the costume is what caught my attention. I don't think I've ever seen a more beautiful vision than you in that red dress. But it was the conversation and the banter that made me want to know the woman in the dress more."

He reached across the table, placing a gentle hand over hers before lightly squeezing it in his palm. The feel of her, even in this very unsexy way, stoked his desire like gasoline poured onto a wildfire.

"I think, maybe for the first time, you were being more you than you've ever been. That costume gave you the freedom to let the real Zanai come out to play. And quite frankly, I want to spend more time getting to know that woman.

"Meet me at Sheen tonight for dinner. My friend Charlotte is the chef there. I'm sure she can get us a table even on such short notice."

With a quick widening of her eyes, she scanned him as if she was trying to figure out how to fit the pieces of his puzzle together.

"You're serious about this? You want to go on an actual date with me?"

"Darlin', there are only a few things in life I'm serious about. My family, my friends and my food are of the greatest importance to me. If I'm inviting you to share in either, it's a pretty big deal. What do you say?"

She gave him one more assessing look before one corner of her sexy mouth curved into a half smile.

"I say yes."

"Why on earth did I let you talk me into this?"

Zanai could hear Morgan's amused giggle coming through her AirPods as she smoothed nervous hands down the front of her dress.

"I wasn't even in the room when you accepted Jayden's invitation. How is this my fault?"

"If you hadn't pushed me to attend that stupid ball, we never would've run into each other in the first place."

"Not true," Morgan countered with her blunt, matter-of-fact tone. "You're at my house and around my family all the time. You would've run into Jayden casually like you have any other time. Only this time, you couldn't hide away in my room like you usually do."

"I have no idea what you're talking about. I don't hide from Jayden. We've barely spoken to each other over the fifteen years I've been in Royal."

Yes, they both had a connection to the Grandin family, but that didn't make the two of them friends. They were friends of friends, who nodded hello whenever they crossed paths.

"Jayden has barely noticed me in all this time. He's never paid me much mind. The only reason he's interested now is you put me in a dress that made my cleavage look awesome."

Morgan's loud sigh, a sign that Zanai was testing her patience, seeped through the phone. "News flash, you have great cleavage. You couldn't hide it even if you were wearing a turtleneck. Accept it, the only thing that put you on Jayden's radar was the fact that you looked him in the eye and said more than your compulsory

'Hello, Jayden' when you saw him. You let him see what I've always known, you're pretty great. So, stop being nervous and go out there and have a good time. You can do this. But more importantly, you want to do this."

Zanai inhaled slowly through her nose then exhaled through pursed lips, trying to calm herself down. Morgan was right, she did want to do this.

She took another look at herself in the mirror. Fashion had never been her forte. She didn't know what was in season or on trend. But the simple fitted LBD with the square neckline and spaghetti straps accented her modest curves.

"Just be yourself, Zanai."

If she were going to be herself, something was missing from this outfit. She walked over to the corner where her cardigans hung and pulled a red one off the rack. When she glanced at her reflection in the mirror, she felt a sense of calm wash over her. She looked fashionable, like she was comfortable in her own skin.

If this evening had a prayer of being moderately successful, she needed to be herself. Well, the parts of her that weren't awkward and standoffish. She wasn't ashamed of those parts of her personality. Unfortunately, those traits kept people away, and as she stood there smiling at herself in the mirror, she realized she didn't want to push Jayden away.

Besides, the few moments she'd spent pretending to be the belle of the ball were exhausting. There was no way she could keep that up for an extended period of time. Tonight, for better or worse, Jayden Lattimore would get to meet the real Zanai James, whoever that was.

"Morgan?"

"Yes."

"Thank you for always pushing me to exist in the world we live in. I know I don't make it easy, but I appreciate it. No matter how tonight turns out, I don't regret going to that ball. I got to be Cinderella for a night. Who could be mad at that?"

"Well, well, well." Jonathan nearly sang the words coming out of his mouth. "Look at the number two son."

Jayden walked into the kitchen looking for his older brother. He found Jonathan standing in the center of the room leaning against the large granite counter with Alexa and Caitlyn flanking him on each side.

"Wow." Alexa walked over to Jayden, walking around him in a circle as she assessed him. "You're actually wearing something other than jeans and cowboy boots?" She waved her hand up and down, noting the button-down shirt, blazer, slacks and dress shoes he wore. "Where exactly are you going?"

Jayden was about to say something smart to his younger sister, but the lawyer in her would have an even better comeback so he didn't bother. He realized she wasn't exactly wrong in her observation. Jayden reserved dress clothes for weddings, funerals and events held at the Texas Cattleman's Club.

His family's business was the land they lived on, making his office attire of a T-shirt or a plaid shirt, jeans and broken-in cowboy boots his go-to. But the usual wouldn't do for tonight.

"Who you getting cute for?" Caitlyn stepped over to where Jayden and Alexa stood.

"Are you here again? Don't you have your own place? A whole man to get back to? Where's Dev anyway?" Jayden asked.

"He'll be here in a few minutes." Her reply was quick

and served with a wide grin. "Now back to you. What's with the outfit?"

Jonathan responded, "He's got a date with Zanai James."

"Zanai?" Alexa echoed, tilting her head to the side as she looked up at Jayden. "Morgan's friend? You're actually going out with her tonight?"

Jayden stepped around his sisters, heading for the center of the room where his brother stood. "What's that supposed to mean, Alexa?"

She shrugged, sharing a knowing glance with their sister before turning her dark brown eyes back to him.

"She's not exactly your type, Jayden?"

"What exactly are you trying to say about Zanai?" Alexa was bold. She didn't ever mince words, so he was certain she wouldn't hold back on an explanation. But as he waited for her to speak, he could feel the slight twinge of something dark growing inside him, daring his sister to say anything bad about Zanai.

"She's quiet and rarely does anything to draw any attention to herself. She's a lovely woman, no doubt. But kind of reserved for your tastes, don't you think?"

He could feel his body tensing, gearing up for an argument he didn't want to have. Usually, he'd just ignore Alexa. But tonight, her observations annoyed the hell out of him.

"Watch your mouth, Alexa."

His sister raised up her hands in surrender and softened her voice as she walked over to where he was standing.

"Hey, that's not a slight against Zanai. It's more of an observation of your dating practices. You don't go for the quiet girls. You like 'em loud, brash and ready to have fun at the drop of a hat. As little as I know about her, that for certain isn't Zanai."

Jayden nodded as the anger bled out of him. "You're right, she's usually quiet. But I got a glimpse of the fun person she's been hiding all these years. I think deep down, that's the real Zanai."

"So, what, you plan to dig deep until you get to the real her?" Caitlyn's question drew his gaze to hers across the room.

"Yeah," he confirmed. "I think all she needs is someone to give her a little encouragement and show her how to have fun."

His brother chuckled and his sisters groaned in unison.

"And let me guess—" Alexa stepped closer "—you're that someone? You're the man that's going to teach her how to be one of the cool kids in Royal?"

He nodded. That was exactly his plan.

"What is this?" Alexa continued with a tinge of heat in her voice. "The Royal edition of *She's All That*, but with Black people?" She huffed, walking away from him as she shook her head. "You can't change who a person is with a makeover, Jayden. And I worry if Zanai would want to date a man who wanted to change her into something he thought was more suitable."

He could see Alexa's point, but somehow his plan hadn't sounded as superficial in his head.

"Don't act like women don't do the same thing. How many times have I heard you and Caitlyn talk about a woman upgrading a man? How is this any different?"

His sister narrowed her gaze and pointed it at him like a sharp dagger. If he were a smart man, which he obviously wasn't for even attempting to have this conversation with both his sisters in the room, he would've kept his mouth shut, gotten the keys to his brother's car like he'd intended and headed out to meet Zanai. But today he chose stupidity, so here they were.

"Let me tell you something, big brother." He inwardly cringed. Any time Alexa began a sentence with that phrase, it meant she was about slay you with her sharp tongue. "When a woman upgrades a man, he consciously changes because he wants to be worthy of her, and the enhancements are usually something external like his wardrobe or his status. You're talking about fundamentally changing someone's personality so she can be worthy of you and meet your superficial standards for your arm candy. That's not the same thing."

Caitlyn nodded, walking closer to their sister, standing in solidarity. "Alexa is right, Jay. Zanai isn't a piece of clay for you to mold. She's a real person. If you're not into her as she is, you might want to leave her alone. No one likes to feel unworthy."

There was something about the way Caitlyn spoke that made Jayden wonder if she had any personal experience with the topic at hand. The thought that someone had made his baby sister feel unworthy raked against something in him. Luckily Caitlyn now had Dev who treated her like a queen.

Did he see the hypocrisy in his reaction? Absolutely. But that was his right as a big brother to be protective of his younger sisters no matter the circumstances.

"Thank you for the lecture, ladies. However, all I came in here for were the keys to Jonathan's Bentley. If I stay here any longer, I'll be late."

His brother dangled the keys in the air and Jayden grabbed them as he made a hasty exit. Just as he was about to step out of the kitchen, he heard Alexa's voice filling the air.

"Zanai is a person, Jayden, not a pet project. Remember that when you're trying to make her more suitable for you to date."

He pretended not to hear her as he continued his trek out of the kitchen and down the hall, which eventually opened into the foyer. As he stepped through the door, for a split second, he wondered if he shouldn't call the whole thing off. At that moment, his phone vibrated in his pocket notifying him of a text from Zanai.

Leaving now. Can't wait to see you there.

His stomach sank. His sisters were right. This woman was too innocent for the likes of him. But the idea of her waiting with anticipation for him stroked his ego in a way he couldn't ignore. He was a bastard. That was for certain. But he would be the lucky bastard spending time with one Zanai James, and he wouldn't turn that down for all the guilt in the world.

He tapped out a quick message before heading for his brother's car in the circular driveway.

OMW. Looking forward to seeing you too.

Five

Zanai sat quietly in the waiting area of the restaurant. She was a tad early and their table wasn't ready yet.

Overeager much, Zanai?

Was she already coming off as desperate? Their date hadn't even started yet and she was already being weird.

This was a mistake. She stood up, intending to march right out of the restaurant, get her keys from the valet and run away before Jayden could get there. But as she turned toward the door, she saw Jayden's solid body fill the entrance and somehow her feet wouldn't obey the signals from her brain screaming for her to run.

"Zanai." His voice was deep and smooth like a fine scotch poured over ice. He took in the sight of her. She could feel his tantalizing gaze sliding down every inch of her body. "You look…amazing."

His last word hung in the air as he continued his appraisal, swiping his tongue against his bottom lip as if he'd found a mouthwatering treat.

"Th-thank you." She cleared her throat, hoping that her stammer appeared more like the result of a pending cough rather than the bellyful of nerves currently dancing in her abdomen.

"Have you been waiting long?"

She shook her head. "Only about five minutes. I'm obsessive about punctuality, so don't worry."

He didn't respond, not verbally anyway. Instead, he let his gaze openly pass over her again. He looked hungry. And if she wasn't imagining things, he was hungry for her.

Zanai hadn't had a stable of men in her life. She'd dated a few, but nothing serious ever came of their brief associations. Before now, she'd never witnessed a man look at her with so much desire that she could almost feel his heated stare licking at her skin.

"Mr. Lattimore, welcome back to Sheen." A young man dressed in a high-end suit stood next to them, breaking the spell Jayden was weaving around her. "Your table is ready, sir. Would you and the lady mind following me?"

Jayden simply nodded, putting his hand at the small of her back. It was a simple gesture, one he'd probably made thousands of times with the women he knew. But it nearly short-circuited her brain, leaving her unable to do more than fall in step beside him.

The host sat them in a corner booth which, coupled with the dim lighting of the room, gave them privacy. She was grateful. The last thing she needed was the vicious Royal rumor mill getting wind of whatever this was happening between them.

She gently chewed on the inside of her cheek trying

to squash that idea as soon as it tried to form. There was nothing happening between them. Jayden was fascinated with a dress, makeup and a fancy hairdo. Free of those things, he'd quickly get bored with her like everyone else did.

"Everything okay?" His voice reached her first, followed by the warm sensation of his large palm surrounding her hand. The satisfying heat traveled through her skin, infusing her blood, and spread throughout her body like hot tea on a blistering cold day in Europe or the Northeast.

"Yes." She managed to shake herself free of the daze his touch invoked. "Why do you ask?"

He let his gaze slide down her face as if he were trying to assess more than her words. "You're just different than you were at the ball."

The red flags her fear had tried so hard to warn her about were snapping hard in the metaphorical wind. She'd been waiting for this. It was the obvious result for anyone who'd been paying attention.

"The ball was make-believe. I played dress-up and danced with the most eligible prince in Royal. But at the stroke of midnight, my fairy godmother's magic wore off and I turned back into a pumpkin. That's usually what happens in fairy tales. Why are you so surprised?"

She waited for the awkward discomfort that usually followed when people realized she didn't possess the ability to engage in polite small talk. But to her surprise, Jayden didn't shrink back. Instead, he simply nodded.

At first, she thought he was agreeing with her and a little bit of sadness slightly quelled the happy buzz she'd had all day. But as a spark of mischief filled his dark eyes and his lips bent into a cocky grin, she realized he wasn't agreeing with her at all.

"I call bullshit."

Her eyes widened. Not at his use of profanity, but that he didn't seem to be distancing himself as expected. Instead, he leaned in, locking his amused stare with hers before sliding his thumb over the back of her hand.

"On what exactly?"

"I don't think any of that nonsense about you turning into a pumpkin is true. What I saw in you the night of the ball can't be faked. I think that was the real Zanai James finally escaping from the aloof, distant prison you keep her locked in."

She'd spent years learning how to keep her face expressionless when she heard things that shocked her. But sitting here in front of Jayden's penetrative gaze, she was finding it hard to keep her features schooled into a neutral palette that gave nothing away.

"You know, if I didn't know any better, I'd think you'd earned a PsyD right along with me. That was some first-class psychobabble right there."

"You would know, Dr. James, wouldn't you? That deflection tactic was top-grade. It's obvious I'm dealing with a pro."

"My professional abilities aside, it still doesn't make anything you're saying about me true. I'm not the woman you spent a few moments with at the masquerade ball. She doesn't exist."

He leaned back in his chair, still smoothing his thumb gently along the back of her hand. The motion was rhythmic and soothing, distracting her from the nerves she knew she should have in a situation like this.

"Oh, I beg to differ." His smile brightened and she found herself responding in kind, like her face muscles were somehow in sync with his, obeying his commands instead of hers.

"Do you, now?"

"I do. In fact, I think she does exist. I think she's the real you. This watered-down facsimile of you is who you pretend to be, although I'm not sure why."

Her free hand cut through the air in a dismissive wave. "Seems you've got me all figured out then. What will we do with the rest of our evening if you've discovered all my hidden quirks in the first ten minutes of our night?"

He leaned in, his smile relaying something powerful with just a tinge of naughtiness. He lifted her hand to his mouth and graced her knuckles with a delicate kiss.

"Don't worry." His eyes burned with restrained passion and she had to remind herself they were in a public place. The intensity of his gaze was like a match to kindling, searing her entire body with the blaze of one look. "I'm sure I can come up with something."

She swallowed trying to push the difficult knot sitting at the back of her throat down so she could manage to speak.

"Your theory that I have some inner princess trapped within is unfounded. I don't mean to let you down, but I'm a boring plain Jane. From my ponytail to my barely there pink lip gloss, I'm as predictable as they come."

"But what if you're wrong?" His query was like a sledgehammer to her midsection, making her instinctually want to fold her frame in half. "And for the record, I don't think you have an inner princess. I think you're a full-blown monarch in your own right."

If nothing else, this man was good at telling a woman what she wanted to hear. Because even she couldn't deny how much she wanted his words to be true.

"What if you do have a queen inside that just hasn't been convinced to come out to play yet?"

She nodded, not because she agreed with him. The most interesting thing about Zanai was her name, and she wasn't responsible for that. If her late mother had known how bookish and uninterested in society her only daughter would be, she was sure *Zanai* wouldn't have been the moniker the new mother had chosen.

"Hear me out before you completely dismiss my theory. I think the reason your queen was on full display that night was because your majestic side was given a chance to be free. Once she was free, everyone around you, most of all me, had no choice but to be awestruck."

She had to admit, she liked his theory a lot better than her own. But there was no way she could buy into it. She knew herself too well to believe that kind of magic existed in her.

"So, because I dressed like a queen and felt like a queen, people treated me as if I was a queen? It sounds good, but I don't buy it. It's too preposterous to be true."

"It is true. And if you give me the chance to remind you of what it was like to be that queen, remind you of who you really are, I have no doubt her majesty will appear again."

She shook her head. What he was saying made absolutely no sense. But even still, his words had sparked something bright and impossible to ignore inside. There, where there was once quiet reserve, now burned a new, fiery hope. A hope she wasn't entirely certain she could ignore anymore, especially not when he was looking at her with his perfect, sexy smile and smoldering eyes.

She cleared her throat. "I'm afraid you're going to walk away from our time together disappointed."

"Doubtful," he countered. His shoulders were stiff with conviction and his smile beamed with confidence. He believed every word he was saying. This wasn't an act. "And after we finish our meal, I plan to convince you to follow me home so I can prove it."

She stared openly at him. Not because she was offended, quite the opposite. She was completely taken in by the possibility of what he was proposing and hoping in the end he was right.

"This is a beautiful view. So many stars tonight." Jayden leaned against the railing of his condo's balcony in the city proper as he watched Zanai take in the evening sky.

"I love ranch life. The open space, the working with your hands, the backbreaking labor, all of it gets my blood running. But the twinkle of a night sky in the city is somehow soothing to me."

The corners of her mouth tugged until a full-blown smile spread across her lips. "The quiet at night was the hardest thing for me to adjust to when I moved here from Brooklyn. Listening to all the crickets chirping so loudly kept me up all night."

She kept her gaze focused on the night sky, but he could see her smile dimming slightly even from her profile.

"We moved here very soon after my mother died. I'm sure my insomnia had more to do with that than the crickets, but still. Those little buggers wouldn't let me get any sleep. It's why I used to beg my father to take me with him whenever he had to travel for business. That noise, no matter if we were in Tokyo, Paris or London, there was always this buzz that soothed me."

"I didn't know you traveled so much."

"Yeah, it was one of the reasons I never really bonded with any other kids here besides Morgan. I was never really around. I just wanted to be with my dad. He hadn't remarried at the time, so he took me with him."

"What about school?"

"His business was on the rise by then. He wasn't as wealthy as he is now, but he could afford private tutors. They made sure I kept up with my work when I was away from school."

She looked up at him, a somber cloud draped over her face even when she attempted to share a forced smile with him.

"It wasn't all bad, if that's what you're thinking. I'd traveled most of the world by the time I was eighteen and I learned to speak several languages by immersing myself in other cultures versus reading a textbook. To tell you the truth, the only thing I missed about this town was Morgan."

Standing there in the moonlight, her beauty was breathtaking. But the stoic grace she used to hide her pain drew him to her, made him want to bring her joy to shove away the clouds that hung over her.

He lifted a finger to a loose tendril of hair blowing in the warm, gentle breeze of the night. "Hopefully, I can make you see there's more to miss about this town than Morgan."

She turned to him then, her gaze penetrating through his defenses and finding its way to the buried parts of him he'd never let a woman see. His association with women was about fun. Never anything of substance, never real. But the way her gaze burrowed through him until it hit something solid and consequential had him questioning his own good sense.

"Oh, yeah? What else is there besides Morgan?"

"Not *what*," he answered, "but *who*. Morgan's your

friend. Hopefully there's some space in your life for a new friend like me."

A light bubble of laughter escaped her lips, bringing a softness to her features he hadn't been able to detect in the restaurant.

"We've known each other for fifteen years. I think that disqualifies you as *new*."

"We've spent a handful of moments together through mutual acquaintances, Zanai. That hardly counts as friendship. Admit it, we've never taken the time to really get to know each other. I think it might be fun to give it a try now."

She turned to the Royal skyline again, taking a break from whatever this game was the two of them were playing. He understood her need to distance herself. If she were feeling any of the desire and pull that he was, taking a moment to attempt to break the spell was the prudent thing to do.

"Fun seems to be important to you. You've got a reputation for being a 'good time' guy in Royal."

She turned around, staring directly at him at first before allowing her gaze to dip slightly. That wasn't a slip—everything he knew about Zanai spoke to her being very intentional. The words she spoke were careful and precise. Even when she was behind a mask, her words were almost as exact as a surgeon's scalpel. So that slip of her gaze wasn't anything to ignore. Brief though it was, he'd bet everything he owned that the good, sensible Dr. James was checking him out.

"Darlin' I'm not *a* 'good time' guy. I'm *the* 'good time' guy. No one in this town can show you a better time than me."

"So, you're not proposing anything serious? Just fun, right?"

He stepped closer to her, seeing some unrecognizable thing in her eyes that made him want to be nearer. He lifted his hand, cupping her cheek, and softly stroked the skin beneath his thumb. It was something he'd done to women a million times before. But when she closed her eyes and leaned into his touch, everything about this moment felt new to him.

He'd known going into this Zanai wouldn't be like his other conquests. Their mutual connections to the Grandins meant he had to tread carefully to some degree. The last thing he needed was Morgan pissed at him for breaking her best friend's heart.

"Zanai, I'm not a playboy. I don't seek to collect women and I don't treat them poorly. My grandmother, mom and sisters would have my hide if I did, and trust me, I don't need that kind of stress in my life. But when I find a woman I like, and if she's willing to have a little fun, I'm all for showing her the best time I can."

The playful smile on her face eased the tension the turn of the conversation had brought. Something he was certainly relieved about.

"Are you close to the women in your family? The few interactions I've had with the Lattimores, it always seemed like you were a close bunch."

"We're all pretty tight. My dad and brother too. Even my grandfather, although he sometimes forgets." For the Lattimores, it was them against the world. Not that they didn't form cherished relationships outside of their kinship—the Grandins were proof of that. But the Lattimores always supported each other, no matter what.

"Even though my siblings can be a pain and always give me crap, I couldn't imagine my life without the three of them. But you've got sisters, so I'm sure you get what I'm talking about."

"I wouldn't exactly say that."

There was a cautious but distant look in her eye that immediately drew his concern.

"I'm fifteen years older than my half sisters"

"Half sisters? People still make those kinds of distinctions about family?"

It was only after the thought leapt out of his mouth that he realized his words might come off as insensitive. But the slight pallor of sadness that briefly cloaked the brightness in her deep brown eyes wouldn't let him deviate from the conversation.

"My stepmother does." Her response was spoken in a matter-of-fact manner. But again, the distant look on her face made him think this was much more important than she was relaying.

"There's friction between you and your stepmother?"

She looked back over the skyline, seemingly needing to break away from his prying gaze. "Not like you think. We're not mortal enemies or anything like that. I've just never been her priority. I'm a reminder that she isn't the first Mrs. James and she doesn't like playing second fiddle to anyone. She and Sanford really focus on the family they've created together. I've never really fit into that dynamic so well."

Again, her delivery was very benign, as if she were ordering a ham sandwich instead of talking about the dysfunctional aspects of her family.

"You speak like that dynamic is somehow your fault. I remember Morgan saying you lost your mother at twelve and within a year someone else was taking her place in your family. The adults around you should've seen how difficult that was for you."

She shifted her weight from one foot to the other, leaning her forearms on the railing and clasping her hands together in what seemed like an effort to contain any emotions that might arise.

This definitely wasn't first-date conversation material. He was prying. He knew that. But his need to know her, all about her, made him keep pushing for more.

"I don't think it was at all intentional. I'm an odd duck that my stepmother couldn't really understand. I was withdrawn and had little interest in all the supposedly quintessential girl things Estelle believed a proper little girl should like. It was just easier to leave me and my books be and mold her daughters into perfect socialites from birth."

"You must have been very lonely."

He turned around. With his back facing the open land, he planted his elbows on the balcony railing as he looked down at her. There was still this impassive look he couldn't make heads or tails of.

"I was. But it was a great lesson on how to exist when you're invisible to the rest of the world. Morgan is the only person that's ever seen me and appreciated me for who I am. I shudder to think who I would've become if she hadn't been part of my life to remind me it was okay to like books instead of social climbing as a pastime."

"What does Sanford have to say about all of this?"

Her father was a corporate raider who'd amassed as much money as some of the old money families in Royal.

"Not much," she replied. "It would make Sanford's life much easier if I was the little socialite my little sisters are being raised as. He didn't have all that much tolerance for a sensitive, quiet girl who just wanted to be left alone with her books. Nothing about me makes sense to him. Not my interests, not my career—"

"Wait," Jayden interrupted, facing her again. "You're

a doctor. How could he possibly have a problem with that? Sanford seems like a man who likes bragging rights. I can only imagine that having a kid who's a doctor gives him ample things to brag about."

"If I were the right kind of doctor, I imagine he would."

"Right kind?"

She huffed, bringing her eyes to his, accompanied with a weary smile.

"I'm a PsyD, not an MD. So to him, I'm not a real doctor. Even as a psychologist, he probably would've had more respect for me if I'd gotten the almighty PhD. He thinks me getting a PsyD, because my intent was to be a therapist instead of a researcher, is some sort of intellectual failing."

Jayden found himself unconsciously tightening his fists into tight balls. The idea of anyone treating Zanai like that rubbed him raw on the inside. All it took was talking to the woman for five minutes to see how intelligent she was. Her own father calling her otherwise didn't sit right with him.

It didn't seem right, but it wasn't exactly a surprise either. Sanford was big and larger than life. A man who didn't think twice about saying exactly what was on his mind with little care for the people around him. He reminded Jayden of a Black Asa Buchanan, a character on the *One Life to Live* soap opera his grandmother used to watch when Jayden was a kid.

There was also an air about him that made it easy to believe he wasn't above doing questionable things to get the results he wanted in business and in life.

Jayden's few interactions with the older man had left him cold. The thought of him being that harsh and abrasive with Zanai surprisingly set him on edge.

"You are a brilliant doctor and your father should be proud of your accomplishments. The work you do at the clinic, providing therapy for special-needs kids, that's important, Zanai. Don't ever let anyone tell you different."

She shrugged, waving a dismissive hand in the air before speaking. "It all happened a long time ago and I don't think there's any real way to fix it now. I'm used to it. I don't let it get to me. But never mind all that."

Her smile brightened and the way it lit up her face put him at ease.

"You were saying something about a good time before we got started on all this."

He mirrored her smile, finding it was difficult to stand in her presence and not want to smile and celebrate the light coming from her.

"Not-so-subtle topic change." He wagged a finger at her. "That's okay, I can take a hint. I didn't mean to bring down the mood."

"Don't sweat it. I'm glad I got the chance to talk to you about it. I don't often get that chance to confide such things to anyone else except Morgan. But I'd be lying if I said I didn't want to know more about this good time you mentioned previously."

Recognizing her topic change as a need to cover the exposed parts of her, he willingly switched gears, bringing fun Jayden back to the forefront.

"I will always show you a good time. But I need to make sure we're on the same page here."

"Let me guess." She opened her eyes, staring so intently at him, he could feel her gaze burn through him. "This is only about fun and you don't want any strings?"

That should've been what he was going to say. It had been every other time he'd found himself in this situation with a woman. But somehow, the words coming out of Zanai's mouth didn't sound right to him.

"Don't worry. I'm a big girl. I'm not expecting anything more than fun."

Her delivery wasn't cold. In fact, the warmth of her gaze and the wide smile she was wearing made his blood simmer. But something inside him wished he were the kind of man who would prove Zanai wrong. Because even he could realize that there was something so inviting about this woman that any man would be fortunate to possess.

He was about to say just that when he was reminded that this was his best friend's kid sister's best friend. Things could get messy really quickly if he weren't careful.

He met her gaze, determined to be present in the moment, and decided on a course of action. Better to be careful and let her assume there were no expectations than give her hope for something he wouldn't deliver on. But as he leaned in, pressing his lips to hers, he knew this wouldn't be as simple as *a good time*.

She was hesitant at first. Some men might have interpreted that as inexperience. Perhaps it was. He couldn't recall her being attached to anyone in town. But it didn't read as naïveté, it was more like caution. Like she needed to keep things reserved for some reason unknown to him.

That just wouldn't do. Not since he knew what her skin felt like pressed against his. He needed more, and he would have it.

He wrapped an arm around her waist, pulling her flush against him, before slipping his hand from her face to the base of her neck. He waited a beat for her to get used to him, and when she didn't show signs of discomfort, he tightened his hold and deepened the kiss.

He was perfectly in control until she snaked her arms

around his neck, pulling him closer so that there wasn't an inch between them. And when she moaned, like the taste of him against her tongue was the most decadent experience of her life, everything in him wanted to press for more, feel more, taste more of the exquisite creature in his arms.

He pulled away, his rib cage expanding to satiate the air-hunger his lungs were experiencing.

"Exactly how much fun are you willing to have tonight, Zanai?"

There was a flash of something hot and defiant in her eyes that sparked flames in the already hot Texas air. He couldn't help the wicked grin tilting his lips when he recognized it. That thing he'd seen in her gaze at the masquerade ball, the thing that had drawn him to her even when he didn't know her identity.

"As much fun as you're willing to give me."

Hot damn! The woman she kept hidden from the rest of the world just showed up with a hunger in her eyes that rivaled his. This was who he wanted to get to know.

That need to know her had his body hardening in his slacks. Good manners be damned, he didn't care that his arousal was obvious. As far as he was concerned, he wanted her to be fully aware of what she was doing to him.

He slid his hands to her hips, applying just enough pressure to let her know he didn't want her to move, to give her time to get used to the idea of what he hoped they both had in mind.

When she pressed her hips into his, grinding her mound against his cock, he lifted a brow as he looked down into her playful gaze.

"If fun is what the lady wants, that's exactly what she'll get."

Six

Zanai, how the hell did you get here, girl?

If she had the answer to that question there'd be no need for her to keep repeating it over and over in her head.

Her night had started off with a lovely dinner at one of the most popular new restaurants in town, and somehow, she'd gone from a casual dinner and drinks to straddling Jayden Lattimore on his living room couch, topless, with his face currently buried in her cleavage.

As far as nights go, this wasn't a bad thing. But she certainly hadn't expected this. Speaking of the devil with his face in her cleavage, Jayden must have noticed her mind was drifting, because he chose that moment to place a trail of searing kisses against her skin until his plush lips pressed against the curve of her neck. He nipped at the flesh there, applying just the right amount of pressure that her sex clenched and her hips snapped forward searching for the friction she so desperately needed.

"Someone's eager."

Eager didn't quite describe what she was. She wasn't even undressed—not completely anyway—and her body was on fire. She was downright desperate to put out the flames. The only problem was Jayden seemed determined to draw out her desperation as if it turned him on to see her so undone.

If she were more sophisticated, more adept at situations like this, maybe she'd know the right way to tell him to stop teasing her and move this show along. Unfortunately, she wasn't that experienced when it came to matters of seduction. She'd had sex, but this wasn't just about the physical act. This was something altogether different and there was no way she couldn't recognize that.

Subsequently, there was also the added problem that the way Jayden teased and played with her body was so delicious, she didn't want to rush through that either.

His hands pushed her dress up over her hips, exposing heated flesh to the air, making her shiver in delight and anticipation. That anticipation stoked her desire, and by the time he'd slipped gentle fingers beneath her silk panties, she was halfway to climax.

A desperate mewl escaped her lips and she could feel his satisfied smile spreading against her neck. He was enjoying her destruction. Zanai was a proud woman, she almost always avoided situations that made her look like a fool. But as his digits slipped between her slick folds and the pads of his fingers found her clitoris, her pride went running out of the room and all she cared about was the next shock of pleasure that would rip through her.

He didn't disappoint. His fingers played her like an expert musician, coaxing her to the edge of satisfaction but denying her completion, keeping the movement of his composition on tempo until she'd reached the final bars, and her climax peaked with a sharp crescendo that had her calling his name. Caught up in the euphoric harmony he'd written across her flesh, she rode the wave of pleasure until the very last note had come to a strong end.

As she came back to herself, thoughts of how desperate and needy she must look began to creep into her mind. She closed her eyes, trying to shrink back and find some way out of this awkward predicament she'd found herself in.

"No, don't do that."

His words pulled her gaze to his. She didn't have the chance to speak, not that she could if she wanted to. She was completely mesmerized by the heated spark in his eyes.

"You have nothing to be ashamed of. Everything about this moment is beautiful, including the way you just lost yourself in my arms."

Zanai fought the audible sigh she could feel gathering in her chest. Could this man be any more sexy? If there was a way he could be, she was certain Jayden Lattimore would find it. As if the soothing way he'd coaxed her through her orgasm wasn't enough to spark her arousal all over again, his reassuring words made sizzling heat burn through the layers of her skin.

Without thought, she pressed her lips to his as she slid her hands down his chest until her fingers reached the belt buckle at his waist. She was about to pull it free of its clasp when his hands stilled hers.

"Don't you want me to—"

"I most certainly do." His breathing was labored, as if the very act of speaking hurt. "But not tonight. I meant what I said about coaxing your inner queen out into the open. I'm going to treat you like a queen until you finally accept that's who and what you are."

She'd heard and understood every word he'd spoken, and somehow, she still couldn't believe his intention. Outside of Morgan, none of the elite of Royal had paid her this much attention before, least of all her own family.

"Why is this so important to you, Jayden? What do you get out of me embracing my 'inner queen,' as you call her?"

He snaked his hand around the base of her neck and pulled her forward, slamming his mouth against hers and drinking from her very essence.

"Oh, the answer is so very easy, Doctor. This is a selfish ploy. For my own self-interest, I want you to be everything you felt free enough to be at that masquerade ball for one simple reason. The fierce creature I danced with is the sexiest woman I've ever seen, and I want her back so I can do all the wicked things to her that my lecherous mind thought up while we were on that dance floor."

Her pulse raced as fire spread throughout her body. She was being utterly undone by this man's words, and she didn't care one bit. The warning bells were clanging in her head that letting Jayden in was dangerous. She'd carefully orchestrated everything in her life to have the things she wanted most: complete her undergrad and graduate work, pass her state licensure exams, build a mental health clinic for those that didn't traditionally have access. That's it and that's all.

There was only one problem now—Jayden was included in that very specific list of things she had to do. And more than anything, she knew that fiery desire he seemed to stoke in her meant at some point, all of this would fall apart.

Seven

Zanai tensed as she heard her father's and stepmother's voices float into the hallway. She was usually gone by this hour of the day, but a late night with one Jayden Lattimore last night and she'd snoozed her alarm one too many times.

As a twenty-eight-year-old professional, there was no reason she should have to skulk out of her house to avoid her disapproving parents. But when your father was Sanford James and he seemed to disapprove of everything about you, it was much easier just to leave before he awoke.

Recognizing she couldn't stand in the middle of the hallway all day, she smoothed one hand down the front of her button-down shirt as the other tightened around her tote bag. With her shoulders pulled back, she continued her journey down the hall to her intended target of the front door.

She'd made it one step beyond the dining room's entryway when she heard her father belt out her name.

Zanai paused midstep, part of her determined to pretend she hadn't heard Sanford.

"I know you heard me, gal."

And he knew she hated to be called that too. Sanford was born and bred in Brooklyn, just like Zanai. His use of the word *gal* when directed at her annoyed the hell out of her because it was always meant to diminish her, to put her in her place. She knew it and so did her father.

She turned on her heel, walking through the dining room entryway to find Sanford and his wife, Estelle, seated at the grand table at the center of the room.

"Father, Estelle, good morning."

Neither of them looked up from their plates nor immediately spoke. And like always, the silence made her want to shift from one foot to the other in discomfort.

"You got in rather late last night," her father commented as he used his utensils to cut through the food on his plate.

Sanford James didn't ask questions. He made statements in a way that compelled the people around him to offer up explanations. This time was no different.

"I was working." She kept her voice neutral, hoping her father wouldn't pick up the scent of blood in the water. "The clinic is in need of funding, so I had to schmooze a potential benefactor last night."

Sanford slowly raised his eyes to hers, his cold, hard glare piercing through her like a dagger.

"You and that damn clinic. You are Sanford James's daughter. You asking for handouts from these old money snobs in Royal makes me look bad, Zanai."

She shook her head as frustration bubbled up inside of her.

"Father, we've been over this. Me being a therapist at the clinic doesn't have any bearing on you or your business."

"That's where you're wrong," Estelle interjected. "It's a clinic for the indigent. For a man of your father's status, what does it say if his daughter is dealing with the dregs of society every day?"

Zanai's sharp gaze slammed into Estelle's. Usually, she did her best to stay out of the woman's way. Incurring her stepmother's wrath always meant triggering her father's as well. This morning, however, she couldn't seem to get a proper hold on her anger as it twisted inside her.

"Being poor isn't a crime, Estelle. I work with innocent kids who are neurodivergent, not criminals. They shouldn't be punished simply because they weren't born into privilege or didn't marry into it."

Estelle blinked at her, the shock on her face clear and unmistakable. Zanai was filled with a brief swell of pride before she realized what she'd done.

"Don't talk to your mother like that, Zanai."

"She's not my mother. She's your wife." The words slipped out before she could stop it and she had to wonder what the hell was going on with her today.

A few hours in Jayden's presence was already screwing with her head and causing her to put herself on her father's radar, which was never a good thing.

"Don't speak about Estelle that way. She's sacrificed too much to take care of you."

That wasn't exactly how Zanai remembered it. The only time Estelle paid attention to Zanai was while she was trying to become Mrs. Sanford James. The moment the deal was sealed, she ignored Zanai like a forgotten toy shoved in a basement storage room.

"Father, I don't wish to fight with either of you. All I ask is that you respect my choice to work at the clinic. It's where I'm most needed."

"Where you're most needed is where I say you're needed." Sanford's voice filled the large room, nearly making everything from the chandelier crystals to the silverware shake. "You need to be using any talent you have to help me get into the good graces of these big-wigs around here. If you're not doing that, you're a waste."

She'd heard these words before too many times to be shocked by the amount of cruelty they were dipped in. But even though she expected them, it didn't stop them from hurting her either.

She swallowed, any fight she had in her disappearing into the ether. She simply nodded her head and said, "Yes, father," in a quiet voice before turning toward the door and slithering out of the house in shame.

She sat in her car, wishing beyond reason that she possessed the qualities Jayden had insisted she had. If there were ever a time for her inner queen to show up, it was now. But sadly, her absence made Zanai fear what she'd always suspected—that queen was a figment of Jayden's imagination and hers.

"Hey, you. How's your day going?"

Zanai smiled as Jayden's easy baritone drifted through her phone. "It was a little rocky this morning, but it's getting exponentially better at the moment."

"I'm glad to hear that. I'm going to choose to believe I'm solely responsible for making it better."

He didn't have to try to take credit for it. He was the reason, plain and simple. After her exchange with her father and Estelle that morning, her focus was off and she couldn't seem to get half of what she needed to done. But just hearing his voice pushed back the dark clouds lingering over her all day.

"You are so full of confidence, aren't you?"

"Of course I am," he quipped. "I'm Ben and Barbara Lattimore's baby boy. That's all the reason I need to be confident."

"You're a mess," she playfully mocked him. "You know that, right?"

His amusement filled the line, washing over her like a warm blanket that kept out the cold. "I've been called worse."

She was sure he had. But by his easygoing demeanor, she couldn't imagine it had ever bothered him.

"What can I do for you, Mr. Lattimore?"

"Direct and straight to the point, good Doctor. I like that."

She liked being able to be this way with him. But she wouldn't admit it. Not because she didn't want him to know she enjoyed the effect he had on her, that wasn't it. She didn't want him to know just how pitiful she was when it came to being direct with someone like her father.

"If you're getting off work at a reasonable time today, how would you feel about having dinner with me at the ranch?"

"You mean, with your family?"

She could feel a slight flash of panic rising in her. From everything she'd ever known about the Lattimores, they were a lovely group of people. But after dealing with her own family this morning, having to take on someone else's, no matter how nice they were, wasn't on her agenda.

"Don't sound so nervous. It's not that kind of dinner. If you wanna eat with the Lattimore clan, I can arrange that. But I was thinking something more private. If you can get here in the next hour, we'll have enough daylight left to eat outside."

She could feel the nervous tension slipping away as he described his plans. Oh, there was still tension, but a different kind that began to grow at the thought of spending alone time in a quiet place with one Jayden Lattimore.

"I just saw my last patient. Let me go home to shower and change and I can meet you in an hour."

He moaned softly through the line and she couldn't help but giggle like a schoolgirl. "I promise you won't regret it."

His reassurance wasn't necessary. She knew beyond a shadow of a doubt that she would enjoy every minute of her time spent with him.

Eight

The Lattimore ranch was a huge display of sprawling greenery for as far as the eye could see. She drove slowly up the path taking in the colorful garden and landscaping design. It was lush and lavish, not unlike the property she lived on. But where Sanford and Estelle's design style was ostentatious and cold like a museum, the Lattimores' home, even from the outside, looked welcoming and lived-in, like they actually took time to enjoy their wealth.

She pulled up slowly to the front of the house, cutting the engine and praying that whatever Jayden had in mind tonight, she wouldn't goof it up by being her usual awkward self.

She was still reeling from their time together in his apartment. Everything in her had wanted to continue. Why wouldn't she? She'd never felt so desired in all her life.

Zanai's sex life, for lack of a better word, sucked. She'd dated a couple of men throughout college and graduate school, but her time with them hadn't felt anything like the heated touches she'd shared with Jayden.

Everything about him, from the way his dark brown eyes made her feel seen in places she hadn't realized she possessed, to the way she burned when his skin met hers, was electric and addictive.

A few moments in his arms and she couldn't stop herself from thinking about him. And that was a problem. If his touch was this powerful and they hadn't actually had sex yet, how far gone would she be when she actually knew what having his body joined with hers felt like?

The certainty in that thought didn't slip her notice. She wholeheartedly intended that they would cross that threshold of intimacy. However, wanting it this badly worried her. If she was this needy already, how much more control would she lose when Jayden finally gave her what she wanted?

He's not the "forever" kind of guy, Zanai. This is just fun to him. You'd do well to remember that before you get your heart broken.

As if on cue, the object of her musings stepped through the grand doors, making his way out onto the circular driveway and walking over to the driver's side of her car.

"Hey, beautiful." His face was all aglow with easy charm, lulling her into what felt like a powerful trance.

How many women had he given that lazy smile to? How many more would know that simple pleasure after her?

Unwilling to entertain the idea for fear of ruining their time together, she focused instead on him, turning her face to the side and giving him a wide grin.

"I bet you say that to all the girls you invite here."

He leaned down into her window, giving her a quick peck on the lips. "That would be a bet you'd lose. I've never brought anyone to the main house."

While she sat stunned, trying to figure out if he was just feeding her a line or telling the truth, he squeezed her hand, giving her that roguish grin again that seemed to warm all the cold, dark places inside her.

He has to practice that. There's no way his smile became that devastating without years and years of practice.

"The main house is currently filled with my siblings, who will take any chance they have to make me look bad in front of company. So we're gonna have to eat out on the deck of my cottage. Follow me." She watched him get in his pickup truck, and she pulled out behind him on the gravel road leading away from the main house.

After a short drive, they arrived at their destination. This time she took in more details. The cottage was a mix of modern and rugged. Wooded cabin-like walls, a mounted flat-screen television, a large sectional in the middle of the room and decorative artwork throughout. The open floor plan was inviting and stylish.

"The main house appears huge on the outside. Aren't there enough rooms for all of you to remain in the house?"

With their hands entwined, he ran his thumb over her skin, making it hard for her to focus on anything but the places where their flesh touched.

"We do each have rooms in the house. But having my cottage means I get to be selfish and not share you with anyone else. Come on, I haven't shown you my favorite part yet: the back deck."

She followed his lead to a large square-shaped deck. The wood was painted a reddish brown with plush lounge sofas in three of its four corners filled with pillows in various shades of brown. The last corner housed a large grill that looked as if it belonged in a restaurant rather than someone's backyard.

"I take it someone enjoys their barbecue?"

Pride beamed on his face. Even in the dimly lit backyard, she could still see excitement glowing in his eyes.

"I'm a Texan, darlin'. Grilled meat over an open flame is kinda what we do."

She nodded, pointing in the direction of the grill. "You any good with that thing? Or is it just for decoration?"

His jaw dropped and he placed a hand over his heart. "You wound me with your words, woman. I come from a long line of pit masters. I might be useless in a kitchen, but I'm a king on a grill."

"You got proof or should I just accept your word for it?"

"See, those sound like fighting words to me. She's already heated. You go take a seat and I'll grab everything I need from inside."

Amusement flowed through her as she appreciated this playful side of him. "Someone's confident in his skills."

He shrugged. "Because I'm amazing at everything I do." He stole a quick kiss and disappeared back into the house, leaving her grinning wide despite her earlier reminder to play it cool. Jayden was a player, admittedly so. But that didn't mean she had to let herself get played. *Keep it light and fun, Zanai. That's the only way you walk out of here unscathed.*

"On everything I love, that was the best barbecue I've ever had."

"I told you my skills were unmatched."

He watched her lean back in her seat with her hand on her stomach. "I can't remember the last time I've been this full. You truly are skilled, Jayden."

"I know."

Her shoulders shook with laughter and it warmed him that she could tell he was joking. Sometimes his confident, yet easygoing manner came off as arrogance. But the way amusement beamed in her eyes, he could tell she understood this was just him being him.

"I don't think I can move. I'm stuffed."

"Good, that means I've done my job as grill master tonight. Rest up a few minutes while I clear the table."

She attempted to stand, presumably to help him with their used dishes.

"Nope," he admonished. "You're a guest, and it would be bad manners for you to lift a finger. I live to serve you, my queen."

He worked as quickly as possible to clear the table, rinse the dishes and get the dishwasher situated. He didn't want to spend one moment longer than necessary away from Zanai, but dried barbecue sauce on flatware was not fun and Josie, the family housekeeper, would have his head if she found a speck of dried food on those dishes.

When the machine was humming, he grabbed two longnecks from the fridge and headed back to the deck, to Zanai.

He couldn't remember exactly when spending even a few moments away from her became such a hardship. Thinking back, he couldn't pinpoint a specific moment, he only knew that when he was away from her for any amount of time, he felt antsy, unsettled.

The idea of being this attached to any woman didn't sit well with him, not usually anyway. But Zanai James had somehow changed things for him. He wasn't ready to admit this was anything more than fun. Yet, he wasn't foolish enough to ignore how tightly wound around her finger he was becoming either.

He found her standing, looking beyond the deck at his gazebo, which had a firepit in the center of it.

"It's cool enough to sit by the fire tonight if you'd like."

At the sound of his voice, she drew her gaze back to his.

"I don't want you to go through all that trouble if you hadn't already planned to do so."

"I told you, I live to serve you. It's really no trouble at all."

He took her hand, helping her down the few steps from the deck before leading her to the gazebo.

He handed her the beers in his hand and set about starting the fire in front of them. In short order, the small flames began to warm the cool night air and he took his seat next to her, grabbing the beer she offered to him as he relaxed into the cushions.

"So, how was work today?"

Incongruence weighed heavily on her delicate features and he wondered if he'd touched a sore spot by bringing up her work.

"You don't have to do that."

"Do what?"

"Ask about my work like it's interesting."

"I'm confused," he replied. "Why wouldn't I find what you do interesting? You've practically built that clinic from the ground up and given kids who need good mental health care a means to have it even if their families can't afford it."

She took a long sip of her beer and he surmised it had more to do with avoidance than thirst.

"I do. But most people aren't interested in talking

about the mental health profession as light, after-dinner conversation."

He threaded his fingers through hers, resting their entwined hands on his thigh.

"Zanai, you could've chosen to treat rich socialites who treat therapy like a fashion accessory. Instead, you treat a very specific population that's often overlooked. No to mention, for all the wealth in Royal, there are still parts that struggle with poverty. Don't think I haven't noticed that you started your clinic in an area that's 90 percent Black and Brown people, where poverty hits hardest in these parts."

He wasn't exaggerating. The clinic was on the edge of town, physically removed from the pretty parts of Royal that thrived at the town's center. Setting up shop there had to have been an intentional choice.

"It's not just that," he continued. "You know the stigma in Black communities when it comes to mental health care. So many of us suffer undiagnosed and untreated mental health conditions and we never seek help because we falsely believe therapy isn't for Black folks."

The widening of her eyes told him he'd hit the nail on the head again.

"That was the very reason I'd gone into the mental health profession. I'd seen the effects firsthand of the disproportionate amount of care in our communities.

"Some of it is because of lack of access. But there is a large portion who, even though access isn't an issue, they won't seek help for fear of the stigma in the community."

He leaned down, pressing his lips to hers, feeling the warm buzz of his beer being chased with the intoxicating taste of her. He gentled the kiss, pulling away from her before giving her still-entangled hand a squeeze.

"You are obviously dedicated to your work and to

this issue. How could I not be interested in hearing about the work you do when it's so important, and obviously so important to you?"

There was something distant in her eyes, a fog covering up the bright light he'd witnessed all night.

She shifted in her seat, pulling her hand out of his and picking away at the label on the beer bottle.

"It's important to me because of all the reasons you listed. But it's also important to me because my mother died of an undiagnosed mental health condition."

Her voice, the statement, it was all detached, as if this was strictly a clinical matter that wasn't personally linked to her. She could've been talking about any of her patients from the cool tone of her voice.

It didn't matter to him how distant she sounded. Wherever she was taking this conversation, everything in him screamed at him to give her support.

So he did.

He leaned over, wrapping his arm around her shoulders and tugging her into his side.

"My mother was so beautiful, giving and kind. She truly loved life. But being in an unhealthy relationship with my father eventually took its toll on her.

"She loved me, and was the best mother to me. But looking back on it with a clinical eye, I can pinpoint the many depressive episodes she had. My aunt begged her to get help and when she wouldn't, she begged my father to get her help. Unfortunately, he was too busy trying to build his empire. He thought having a wife in treatment would embarrass him and negatively impact his business."

Tiny tremors began to course through him and he couldn't tell if the vibrations were coming from him or Zanai. Either way, he tightened his hold on her, trying his best to let her know he was there for her.

"When I was eleven, she was in a car accident where she sustained back injuries. The injuries weren't severe enough to be debilitating, but her doctors gave her pain pills to ease her discomfort."

She shifted again, somehow burrowing herself deeper into his side. He rubbed his hand up and down her arm, trying to soothe her.

"She became addicted to those pills. And because they were prescribed, they didn't have the negative association illicit drugs have, so no one recognized there was a problem. Yeah, she said she was using them for her back pain. But looking back I can see she was just self-medicating to get through her depressive episodes.

"A year later, she died of what was documented as an accidental overdose of prescribed medication. But the days leading up to her death make part of me feel that maybe it wasn't so accidental after all. Not the way she kept reminding me that no matter what, she loved me. That her choices were her own flaws and not mine."

"You think she committed suicide?"

"The truth?" she huffed, as if finally unburdened by a heavy weight. "I don't know. I'll never know. Because her death was filed as accidental, her insurance company paid out three million dollars. Two-thirds of it went to me in a trust that paid for my education and helped me start the clinic, leaving the remaining million to Sanford. He used that money to start his business. He built his empire on the death of his wife."

Jayden's interactions with Sanford James were very limited. Sanford was a corporate raider. Thankfully that meant there wasn't much crossover between their respective areas of business. However, what little he did know of the man, Jayden had never liked.

After listening to Zanai, it was hard to find any re-deeming qualities about him.

"Losing my mom the way I did left me with so many unanswered questions about my own mental health. So when girls my age were learning to be social butter-flies, I was reading everything I could on depression and other mental health conditions."

"Because you wanted to make sure you weren't suf-fering the same symptoms yourself."

Silence hung between them. It wasn't awkward where either of them felt they had to fill the space. Instead, it was full of understanding, of compassion, of need.

As his arm tightened around her shoulders, pulling her into his frame, she wrapped her arms around his waist as if he were an anchor. And as much as part of him screamed at the intimacy of it all, he was glad she somehow instinctively knew she could lean on him.

"I'm sorry." She whispered those words while her face was pressed against his chest, and although quietly spoken, they seeped through his chest wall and some-how managed to wrap themselves around his heart.

"What on earth are you apologizing for?"

"Ruining the evening. You asked me how was work, and I go on and on about my dysfunctional family. I guess you can see now why this dating thing doesn't really work for me. I don't know how to do any of this."

"Zanai, look at me."

She complied, sitting up, bringing her soulful gaze to his. There was pain there. It wasn't fresh as if it was an open wound, but chronic, like she'd been carrying it for so long and now she was weary.

"Don't ever apologize for who you are. There's noth-ing wrong with you, then or now. Socialites are overrated. And if I cared about being with one, I certainly wouldn't be here with you. It's you I want, and nothing you can tell me about your past is going to change that fact."

She watched him, seemingly scanning every inch of his face. She was obviously trying to make sense of him, attempting to figure out why he wanted to be there so desperately. He could see her questions filling her dark brown eyes and it angered part of him that people had treated her so poorly, her baseline expectation was that no one wanted to be around her.

"You have to say that. Otherwise, your little social experiment won't work."

Something hot and angry sliced through him, causing him to pull out of her embrace. He could see by her pinched brow that he'd caught of her off guard. He didn't care.

"Zanai, if this were a social experiment, I'd be trying to make you into something you're not."

She shrugged as uncertainty danced in her eyes. "Isn't that what you're trying to do?"

He shook his head. He'd meant it when he'd told his sister he wasn't trying to change Zanai. But apparently, he needed to explain himself more if both women, women that he respected, seemed to think so.

"I'm not trying to make you into something you're not, Zanai. I'm trying to bring out what I already see there. The strength, the regal beauty, the fortitude to be an agent of change and provide help and a voice to the voiceless. That's who I see you as, Zanai. The only thing that's different about me is that I want to honor and celebrate who you are. I want to bask in your light. So please, stop comparing me to all the foolish people that have worked so hard to dim it."

Her expression was unreadable, and he worried that if he let her wallow in her thoughts, she'd withdraw from him again.

A kiss was the only answer. If she wouldn't listen to his words, then maybe he could convey his feelings through touch.

He'd intended the kiss to be patient and reassuring. It didn't quite work out that way, however. As soon as his lips pressed against the soft cushion of her mouth, gentle went out of the window and need moved right in, putting its feet up and getting comfortable.

The taste of her, like the barbecue they'd eaten, was sweet and tangy, with just the right hint of spice that slowly burned through his system catching him unaware before exploding into flames.

He tore his mouth away from hers in an effort to regain his composure. He was on fire and if he didn't get control of this situation, he'd strip her right here and have her in the gazebo. But he wanted more for her, more from her too.

Her brown skin was gleaming with a reddish glow as she attempted to catch her breath and his ego did a little happy dance because she was just as undone as he was.

"You are really something, Mr. Lattimore."

"I am," he replied. "Now, if I could only get my siblings to acknowledge that, all would be right in my world."

A conspiratorial grin spread on her face as she leaned into him. "Well, they won't hear that from me. I think if too many people acknowledge that, your ego might not be able to fit comfortably in another room."

He couldn't argue with her. Not with the way her smile delighted him and her touch made him burn. Everything about Zanai James did it for him, and he knew part of that was knowing that he absolutely did it for her as well.

Nine

"Okay, spill it. I need all the details."

Zanai looked up from the fashion magazine she'd plucked from a nearby table, squinting as she tried to figure out the meaning behind her best friend's outburst.

"I'm not sure I know what you mean."

"You've been out with Jayden Lattimore almost every night this week and you haven't called me once to tell me how it's going."

Understanding dawned, causing Zanai to nod in acknowledgement of her friend's claims.

"It's been great."

Morgan walked from behind the counter and flipped the sign on the door to the "Closed" position before she came to sit down next to Zanai in the empty store.

"That's it? You're dating the most eligible bachelor in Royal and all you have to say is 'It's been great'?"

"It *has* been great." Zanai shrugged. "Jayden is the perfect gentleman, a perfect Prince Charming."

"And that's why you're being all nonchalant about this? You don't believe he's real, do you?"

Zanai sighed loudly as she closed the magazine in her hands and tossed it back on the nearby table.

"He's a charmer. He knows how to make people feel good around him, especially women. None of this is real."

Her mind drifted back to the evening she'd had dinner at his cottage a few nights ago. That night had certainly felt real. From the good food and conversation, to the profound way he'd supported her while she revealed the circumstances of her mother's death, every second of it had felt real and tangible. And it was terrifying her.

Morgan simply shook her head and threw up her hands in frustration. "You can't be serious. I know Jayden, he does not do repeats. He certainly doesn't bring women to the Lattimore ranch. Yet, he's done both those things for you. Why can't you believe this is real?"

Because if it's real, then it can go away, then it can hurt me.

She already knew what it was like to lose someone special in her life. She didn't want to add Jayden to the mix. So if she planned to protect herself, and she did, she couldn't take any of Jayden's advances seriously.

"I wouldn't categorize Jayden as a player. But he's not looking for anything serious. He's been very clear about that. We're just enjoying each other's company for the time being. There's no need to complicate this more by trying to figure out if the man is sincere in his pursuit of me."

Morgan sat there with her mouth open and eyes wide. Her disbelief was evident and warranted. But Zanai could never let her know that, not when it meant Zanai would inevitably cry all over Morgan's shoulders when Jayden finally was through playing with his new toy.

"You're unbelievable. Only you could get the man every other single woman in this town is clamoring for, and you're acting like he's a cheap wine cooler when he's really a fifty-year-old perfectly aged scotch. How can you be so detached?"

"I'm simply not letting my emotions get the better of me. That's not the same thing as being detached, Morgan."

A flash of light illuminated Morgan's eyes. "So you do have feelings for him?"

Of course she did. Especially after that night in his gazebo.

It had felt so wonderful to, even for a moment, lay her burdens in his arms. However, when she'd gone home alone that night, she'd ached for him so terribly, she'd hardly slept.

That need for him, the strong, addictive thing that was growing in her belly, demanding she satisfy this hunger, that was the thing she had to fight against. Because becoming dependent on a man who could never love her like she needed to be was a fool's game. She'd watched it destroy her mother, and she vowed it would never be her.

Not now, not ever.

Jayden walked into the Royal Diner aching for a burger and fries. Yes, he could've made that at home, or asked the family chef to make it for him up at the big house. But he'd needed to get out of his house and talk to someone about everything that was happening with Zanai.

He scanned the restaurant, relaxing his shoulders as a sense of relief descended upon him once he glimpsed his friend Ryan at a booth in the back of the eatery.

In a few strides, he was sitting down next to a man he'd known for a lot of years. Ryan's blond hair and blue eyes belied the grumpy bastard that he truly was. Right now, though, it was that blunt, unaffected persona that Jayden needed the most.

"Hey, man, thanks for meeting me." Jayden's words were met with a grunt and a nod. More amused than offended, Jayden smirked at his friend's response.

Their server came and placed fresh cups of coffee in front of them and quickly took their orders. Once alone, though, Ryan glanced up at Jayden with just enough impatience or intolerance, at this point he really couldn't tell which, swimming in his gaze.

"You wanna get to the point why I'm out here in downtown Royal instead being back on my ranch?"

"Same old Ryan," Jayden muttered to himself. "I needed some advice."

"And you're coming to me?" Ryan's query made Jayden snicker. "You must be desperate. What about Vic?"

Jayden shook his head at the mention of his best friend's name.

"Not for this. Not yet anyway. Vic and Morgan are thick as thieves, and if I tell Vic what's going on, I have no doubt it will spread like wildfires on dry land."

Ryan sat up then, realizing how serious this situation must be.

"I've been hanging out with Zanai James for the last bit."

"Is hanging out a euphemism for dating or sex? I need the clarification."

Jayden's wry laugh didn't put Ryan off. The man still stared at him waiting for an answer.

"Dating," Jayden replied, "and some serious petting. We haven't gotten to the sex part yet, although I presume that's coming soon."

Ryan waved his hand in a "hurry up and spill it already" fashion to get Jayden to get on with the full story.

"Things are getting a bit hot and heavy, and I wanted to talk about the pros and cons of that. You think you can spare a moment for me?"

Something softened in Ryan's face, as if he was somehow less annoyed with Jayden's need to talk. He sighed deeply and sat back in his chair.

"What's going on, man?"

"I… This woman."

"If you're dating her, I assume that's a good thing, right?"

Jayden wasn't so sure about that. He didn't do serious relationships, ever.

"It feels good."

Ryan looked at him, nodding as if he was processing some sort of calculation in his head.

"And that's the problem, right? It feels good and you don't know what to do with that."

"Well…yeah," he hedged. Briefly taken aback by Ryan's uncharacteristic display of emotional awareness, Jayden reached for the cup of coffee their server had poured before she took their orders to the kitchen. "That's oddly perceptive of you."

"Choosing not to deal with people's nonsense is not the same thing as being unaware, Jay."

Jayden leaned back in his chair, his jaw dropping open ever so slightly with disbelief mixed with a bit of suspicion.

"Fine." Ryan threw up his hands before letting them lightly hit the table in front of them. "We both know I'm not that enlightened. Let's just say, I did something really stupid lately that's got me thinking about things I wouldn't normally waste a thought on."

Jayden couldn't disguise his amusement at his friend's response. This sounded more like the Ryan he knew, so stuck on doing things his way he rarely recognized anything or anyone around him.

"Care to elaborate?"

Ryan shot him a sharp glance that Jayden found more comical than he should have. It possibly made him a bad friend, but it made him feel better that he wasn't the only person walking around rethinking everything he thought he knew about himself.

"No, I don't." Ryan crossed his arms, an attempt to conceal how affected he was by whatever was going on with him. "Truth is, I couldn't if I wanted to. I'm out of my depth here, so I can't possibly give you any advice on how to handle your own situation."

Ryan's response hung in the air while their server returned with their food. Once they were alone again, Jayden looked up at his friend with a bit of commiseration in his chest.

"I don't know exactly what's going on, but if you need to talk about it, you know I'm here, right?"

Ryan shrugged a dismissive shoulder, but Jayden could see the appreciation swimming in his eyes.

"Thanks, man," he grumbled around a forkful of food as if he didn't really want Jayden to hear him. "'Preciate it. Just wish I could be some help to you."

So did Jayden, but it seemed he was going to have to figure this one out on his own. Unfortunately, he had the feeling that he'd better come up with a plan soon enough. He'd started out this thing hoping to have an impact on Zanai. But he'd never accounted for the fact that just being in her presence could somehow alter who he was too.

Out of any useful ideas, he picked up his fork and tucked into his food. No sense in dwelling on something when he hadn't a clue what he was dealing with in the first place.

Sure, Jayden. Ignore it, pretend that there's no problem at all. That always works, right?

"Lunch has arrived, m'lady."

She looked up from the bag of takeout Jayden had placed in her hand and smiled. Her day had started with a mountain of work and very little time to do much more than jump from one patient's session to the next. Days like this meant she'd have to cancel the prior lunch plans she'd made with Jayden.

Refusing to let her cancel, he'd shown up to the clinic with takeout from the diner in hand. He'd given her the food, kissed her on her cheek and said for her to call him if she got a moment later.

So overwhelmed by his kindness, she'd barely recognized his intention was to leave.

"You're not going to eat with me?"

"You're busy, and I'm not here to be a distraction. I just wanted to make sure you had enough fuel to keep doing what you do."

She fought to keep her jaw from dropping. A grown, self-possessed man who didn't need to be the center of a woman's world. Was she dreaming?

He'd just turned toward the door to leave when he looked back, tossing a wink over his shoulder and disarming her even more than his impromptu lunch delivery.

"By the way, are you free this weekend?"

"Yeah. You wanna do something?"

"Possibly. I'll give you the details when we talk on your way home."

Exciting anticipation whirled in her belly. So much so, she wasn't even going to allow her head to tell her she shouldn't be excited by such small things. All this man had done was bring her takeout and promise to talk to her on her ride home. But the more time she spent with Jayden, the more she realized it was the small things that she liked so much about him.

"You up for a trip tomorrow?"

If she weren't driving, she would've glanced down at her phone to make sure she'd heard him correctly.

"A trip where?"

Since they'd started whatever this was they were doing, Jayden always called her so he could keep her company on her trips home.

The clinic was only about thirty minutes from her house, hardly enough time to feel lonely on the road or get into any real danger. But she was still grateful to hear his voice nonetheless.

"To New York. We could catch a play, see the sights and then have a nice dinner."

Her brows knit together before a cautious smile spread across her lips. "Jayden Lattimore, is this your attempt to wine and dine me?"

"It most certainly is. After a day like today, you deserve it. The question is, are you going to let me?"

Her smiled widened. "Most definitely."

"Great." The excited lilt in his voice made warmth

spread through her. Why did such simple things endear this man to her more and more?

"Meet me at my house first thing in the morning and we'll head out."

"Will do." She nodded and smiled to herself with the hope of something decadent dancing in her head. Her expectations were high, just as he'd intended if she were gauging his voice correctly. The fun part was going to be spending an entire day watching him deliver on everything his words promised.

The truth was, he already had surpassed her expectations with the simple gesture of bringing her lunch when she was too busy to get it herself earlier today. This was just dessert on top of an already decadent meal.

As they continued their call, finalizing their plans, she wondered how on earth she'd ever managed to live without such treatment all her life.

Ten

"You're from New York, I can't believe you're so unfamiliar with your surroundings."

Zanai laughed as they milled through the throng of people in Times Square, heading back to their nearby hotel.

"I'm from Brooklyn. Totally different place from what you call New York."

"What I call New York? I'm not sure what you mean by that."

She slid her hand down from his forearm until her fingers were intertwining with his. "Tourists call this 'New York' or 'New York City.' Those of us who were born and raised here call it 'Manhattan.' And when you're from Brooklyn, for the most part, you only go into Manhattan when you have to. There are just too many folks out here, most of them tourists like you."

With their fingers interlaced, he squeezed her digits lightly, before offering her a smile. "So Brooklyn is like the Wild West of New York."

She shook her head. "No, it's actually to the east of Manhattan." Her matter-of-fact tone had the desired effect, tugging a generous grin onto Jayden's face. "Manhattan is beautiful, but it can be so noisy and chaotic, dealing with that on a daily basis can be a little tiresome. Sometimes you just want a much more relaxed vibe."

He nodded, stepping aside so she could walk through the revolving doors first.

He waited until they'd made their way on the elevator and then stepped off at their designated floor before continuing the conversation.

"I can see how the city could be a bit much on a consistent basis. Sometimes you just need to relax and breathe."

He pulled out his keycard, tapping it against the lock and waiting for the requisite light to flash green before he turned the knob and held the door open for her.

Forever the gentleman, he stepped aside and let her walk in first.

Almost immediately, she noticed something was off. The lights were dimmed with an artificial candlelit glow covering the entire sitting area.

In the center of the room was a small square table draped in a velvet cloth, adorned with a chrome champagne bucket and elegant crystal drinkware.

"What have you done, Jayden?"

When she turned around, he was standing there in a relaxed stance, his feet spread wide with his hands shoved in the pockets of his trousers, looking as smooth and unaffected as he could be.

"You work hard, and from what I can tell, you hardly

take any time to indulge yourself. I just wanted to make sure you took a few moments to do so while we were here. Not to mention, after spending most of my time with cows and horses and their respective aromas, it's nice for me to enjoy fancy digs too."

There was something about the way he said the world indulge that made her shiver with expectation. It wasn't overtly sexual in nature, but there were some heated undertones there that alluded to the potential this night could hold.

She looked into his eyes, his gaze so powerful, she could feel herself falling endlessly the more she stared at him.

She tore her eyes away from his to give herself a brief reprieve, and that's when she saw them. Rose petals scattered across the floor leading from the table to his room in their suite.

"You really went all out, huh?"

He stepped closer. "I told you, a queen deserves the very best. Let's eat, and then we can see how the rest of the night unfolds."

The weight of his focused gaze on her was too much to bear. It wasn't just on her, but somehow burrowing through her, seeing the absolute truth of who she was: a scared and lonely woman who'd built walls around herself to keep the world out.

"So, what are we celebrating?" She walked over to the table, picking up the glasses and nodding toward the chilling bottle in the bucket. He continued to watch her for a moment before he stepped forward and made quick work of popping the cork.

He dropped his gaze for the few seconds it took him to fill their glasses, and once the bottle was settled back in its icy nest, he was right back to watching her.

"As always, we're celebrating you." He gently touched his glass to hers before taking a measured sip of the bubbly liquid and setting his glass down on the table.

"Zanai, you don't have to be nervous. I set all of this up because I thought you'd like it. But nothing I've done means I expect you to sleep with me. Whether we spend the night eating snacks and watching TV or pleasuring each other until we're both too tired to move, it's your choice."

He tilted his head as if he were calculating something. Whatever conclusion he'd come to, his expression softened a bit. The need that seemed to be running just beneath the surface of his skin was still there, providing his dark complexion with a reddish tint that made her have to fight to keep her hands to herself.

He extended his hand until his palm was caressing her cheek, resulting in a decadent sigh that spilled from her lips involuntarily.

"What's going on in that beautiful mind of yours?"

She pressed her face into the warmth of his hand, his touch instantly soothing the nerves in her belly. If she could just stay like this and not think this to death, she'd probably have the best time of her life.

"I've enjoyed our time together. And by the way I so easily go up in flames every time you touch me, I hope you know, wanting this is not the problem."

"Then what is? Because I definitely see hesitation in your eyes. As much as I want you, I won't take what isn't freely given. There's no joy in that for me. So what's holding you back?"

She swallowed, closing her eyes briefly to gather her strength before locking her gaze with his.

"This is going to sound so immature and unsophisticated, but I'm just afraid this will change things between us."

She could see his brow pulling into a tight V as he continued to search her face for answers, silently prodding her to continue.

"You call me a queen, Jayden." She took a sip of her champagne, hoping it would provide her with just a touch of some of that liquid courage she'd heard so much about. "But the truth is, the time we've spent together has been the only instance in my life where I've felt like one."

"And you think once I get what I want, all that goes away?"

Said out loud, his assumption sounded ridiculous, but that didn't make it any less true.

"I don't think that's your intention." Even though she whispered those words, they bounced off the wall like percussion sticks clanging against a cymbal. "But I would be lying if I said I wasn't afraid of that outcome."

She expected to see his face contort into anger at the thought of not getting what he obviously wanted, what she wanted too.

Instead of anger, however, the fire in his eyes softened to a warm glow that seemed to permeate through her skin, soothing the fear that tried to take root inside her.

"Zanai, I want you. I've made no secret of that. But I'm not treating you this way just to get you into bed. I genuinely enjoy spending time in your presence."

Removing his hand from her cheek, he stepped closer, plucking the champagne glass from her fingers and settling it next to his on the table.

"I won't lie to you and say I'm looking for forever. But whatever this is, one night certainly won't be enough. And even though I'm certain I would enjoy every second of getting to explore your body, it would not define our relationship or convince me to treat you as anything less than the queen I believe you are."

His voice was so husky, his lower register settling over her like a comfy weighted blanket, making her feel safe.

He pulled her to him then, pressing his lips gently against hers as if he were trying to avoid spooking her into retreating. But the way the simple peck made molten fire slide through her veins, singeing every cell in her body, there wasn't a chance in hell she was going to walk away from this.

As if to prove the point to herself, she slid her hands up the front of his chest, loving the way the soft fabric of his Henley clung to his lean but muscular frame, but hating that it kept her from all that glorious flesh beneath it.

Her hands continued their journey until her arms were wrapping around his neck and she was closing any space that dared to stand between them.

He welcomed her into his embrace, sliding his hands from her shoulders down to her waist, pulling her against him in that wonderful way she'd become accustomed to.

She deepened the kiss, needing so desperately to taste him, all of him if he'd let her. The fear of reprisal that seemed to be her constant companion throughout her life seemed to disappear. All that remained was instinct and need, and she surrendered any will she had to deny that fact.

Her tongue licked inside his mouth and he moaned so deep she could feel the rumble of his voice against her chest.

She pulled away slightly, finally breaking the kiss, and lifted her eyes up to him. Her usual need to keep herself hidden was gone. She wanted Jayden to see her. Not just her flesh, but into her heart where hidden emotions she dared not speak, not yet anyway, rested deep in the caverns of her soul.

Panting as she tried to draw life-giving air into her burning lungs, she spoke in a ragged voice. "We're wearing…too many clothes."

He didn't patronize her by asking her if she was sure. The way she was holding onto him for dear life had to convey her desire. But if that didn't, she'd gladly start the process of stripping him where he stood so there was no doubt she wanted him naked and available to her.

"Darlin', that's a problem that's easily fixed." That flirty "devil may care" crooked smile of his was there and any concerns about this being awkward slipped away.

He pushed her hands down until they were at the bottom of his shirt and she took it from there. She made quick work of pulling it off, and stepped out of her dress even faster.

She was standing there in her lace bra and panties, exposed and nearly naked, but instead of feeling vulnerable, she felt empowered.

His eyes were transfixed, seemingly committing every detail of her form to his memory.

"If you're just going to stare at me all night, this is going to end up being pretty unsatisfying for the both of us."

"See—" he held out a hand to her, pulling her into his strong arms "—that's where you're wrong. I plan to enjoy every damn second of this."

She shivered. That wasn't just a statement, bravado

to make himself sound tough and masculine. It was a promise, a vow that they'd both receive unspeakable pleasure from the time they would spend in each other's arms.

As she looked up at him, all she could do was smile. Because for the first time in her life, she was ready to indulge in all the feel-good she could find in his arms.

Jayden struggled to keep his desire in check. They'd made it from the sitting area in their suite to the large king-size bed in his room faster than he could say his name.

Their hands and limbs were everywhere, stripping their remaining clothing. From the first moment he'd laid eyes on her, even behind a mask and a costume, he'd known she'd make him burn for her.

He pulled away from her, needing to slow things down. He'd spent so much time dreaming about this, fantasizing about what it would feel like to finally have her naked under him.

He'd had just a taste of her passion when he'd brought her to climax with his fingers at his condo. But like the old saying went, a taste will only make you mad. Except the madness he'd fought with every fiber of his being had nothing to do with anger, and everything to do with the need he felt all the way down to his cellular level.

He gentled their frenzied kissing, sipping slowly from her lips like he would a fine wine. When she mewled for more, he pulled back, loving the small moan of desperation that crossed her lips.

He kissed the shell of her ear, moving down to the silky skin of her exposed neck that called to him. He grazed it with his teeth, loving the needy shiver that vibrated through her body.

He smoothed eager hands up her sides and around to her slender back, making quick work of the clasp of her bra. When he looked down to find her full flesh practically begging for his attention, his plan to keep things slow so he could savor every inch of her went out the window.

He grasped the back of her thighs, lifting her until her legs were wrapped around his waist as he walked them over to his bed. As soon as she was positioned on the soft bedding, he kissed his way from her full lips charting a path that led down her collarbone, through the valley between her breasts. He was tempted to continue straight down to his prize, but a glimpse of one pert peak drew his attention, detouring his journey.

One flick of his tongue and Zanai arched up seeking more contact. If she wanted more, he would give her more and then some. He alternated between licking, sucking and molding his hands to the shape of her breasts. With the decadent sounds of her pleasure heightening his own, he quickly made his way down her torso, past the natural dip in her waist, until his lips reached her sex.

One gentle pass of his tongue over her clit yielded him a full-body shudder that stoked his own need. Never had a partner's reactions in bed turned him on so much. He didn't dare think about the implications of why that could be so. If he did, he might be tempted to put enough distance between them so he could gain control of himself again, and leaving the cradle of her tempting body wasn't something he could willingly do.

She was so soft, so hot, responsive, her reactions to his touch were just as heady as the feel of her flesh against his, fueling his need to continue.

He drew slow circles at her entrance with deft fingers as he increased the pressure of his tongue against her clit, slipping one finger in and moaning at the scalding heat that greeted him. His eager cock twitched at the thought of what all that delicious warmth would feel like wrapped around him.

Eager to find out, he added another finger, stroking and scissoring inside her. The sweet sounds of her pleasure filling the room, he focused his efforts, determined she would climax at least once before he satisfied his need to be inside her.

Certain he wouldn't have to wait too long given how her hips were swiveling, matching the rhythm he set with his fingers and his tongue, he added a third finger, stretching her, reveling at the way she possessively wove her digits through his hair, tugging him closer to her. And when her body seized and her ragged voice pierced the silent room, satisfaction spread through him as she broke apart beneath his touch.

He wasted no time pulling away from her. Normally he'd indulge in a moment of just holding her as he watched her come down from her peak. But tonight, he made quick work of finding the condoms he'd packed in anticipation of this moment.

Sheathed, he climbed back onto the bed, taking her mouth in his as he positioned himself at her entrance. It was the only reprieve he could offer considering how her body called to him.

He pushed forward, parting her folds as her heat slowly surrounded him.

"Damn, baby."

The sheer bliss of this moment had him questioning his ability to resist her this long. He'd believed it would be good between them. How could he not when the very sight of her grabbed at something unrecognizable in him?

He tried to sit, be still for a moment, savor the experience of their joining. But she chose that moment to squeeze him, demanding he move and there was no way he could resist.

The next stroke better than the last, he surrendered to their mutual need, driving inside of her until he was buried so deep, he could hardly tell where she began and he ended.

Every stroke, every desperate touch, every tortured sound had Jayden on edge, fighting back a climax that was closing in on him all too soon.

He glanced down at her, finding something akin to mischief flickering in her eyes, and that's when he saw it, the spark of his red queen that he'd met at the masquerade ball.

She wrapped her arms around his neck, pulling him closer to her, locking her legs around his hips, and used his body weight to pivot, switching their positions.

He had been quite all right with being the one in control. He'd assumed it was what Zanai wanted. That apparently was his mistake because the long sigh that escaped her lips as she slid down his length was nearly his undoing.

"Take what you want."

"I plan to."

He couldn't help the smile her declaration garnered.

As she began to move in earnest, driving him closer and closer to the brink, he lost himself in the decadent swivel of her hips and the searing heat of her body encasing his. When his eyes connected with hers, he realized this moment was so much more than just physical pleasure.

There was something that simply delighted his soul to see the indulgent, cocky grin plastered across her face. And when she gazed down at him, giving him a sly wink just before she tightened around him, he was lost. Her release driving him to his own, he raised his hips to meet hers.

Needing more, more contact, more pleasure, more everything, he dreaded the climax closing in on him just as much as he relished it. Too lost to the elusive sensation, he quickly pulled her beneath him. His fierce pace elicited sensual cries so wanton it was like she was somehow reaching inside of him, rearranging everything he knew to be true about himself and making him into a new creation all her own.

And no matter how scary that thought was, he couldn't help but hold on to it as she called his name. The sultry sound pushed him over the edge into bliss and he crumbled into a million pieces. He wasn't sure if he could ever be put back together again.

As his body struggled to find its way back to normalcy and the warmth of satisfaction spread through him, he realized he couldn't care less if the scattered pieces of his soul couldn't be reassembled. To be broken by this woman's pleasure was so satisfying, he'd willingly let her violently grind him into dust if it meant he could feel this way again.

He dropped to the bed, pulling her into his side and loving the sense of completion that flooded him as she wrapped herself around him and sighed.

Yeah, he was gone. A fact that should've terrified him. But instead of fear, the only thing he experienced was bone-deep satisfaction.

"When we get back tomorrow, will you be in a rush to get home or can you spare a bit of time?"

She pondered the question from the comfort of the plush bed as he stood at the foot with nothing but a phone in his hand and a towel hanging low around his waist.

"I'm sorry, what did you say? I was a bit distracted by you in a towel."

The naughty gleam in his eye cranked up his sexy factor even more than his exposed carved abs.

"That's good to know that my body distracts you. I'll have to use that to my advantage sometime soon. But seriously, do you need to rush back home on Sunday when we get back?"

She shook her head. "I'll probably just go over a few case files if nothing else comes up. Why?"

He didn't speak right away, which she could admit, made her slightly concerned so she prodded him again. "Why do you ask?"

He lifted his phone. "My brother just texted me. My parents are having an impromptu cookout and since you'll be there already to pick up your car, you may as well get a plate too."

Whatever she was expecting him to say, it certainly wasn't that.

"Wow, Jayden. You know when Black folks invite you to the cookout, that means you've been accepted into the fold. You sure you want to expose your family to an odd duck like me?"

Her voice had a nervous lilt to it she hoped he'd attribute to her inept attempt at a joke.

"Zanai." The weight of his voice filled the room, pressing hard against her chest, making it increasingly difficult to breathe. "There's nothing odd about you, and I really wish you'd stop saying that. If you hadn't noticed, I'm kind of fond of you, and your self-deprecation aggravates me because I know none of it is true."

"Jayden, I was just joking."

No, she wasn't.

"No, you weren't." She watched him take in a long breath before he spoke again. "I don't know if this is just nerves on your part or Sanford actively working to make you believe that every wealthy person in Royal is a blue-blooded snob who will turn up their nose at you. Either way, it's bullshit and I need you to stop."

His voice was edged with something rough and demanding that should have annoyed her. Instead, it made her feel warm and welcomed.

"There's nothing wrong with you. And there's certainly nothing wrong with you that would give me pause for bringing you around my family. My family is far from perfect. Yet despite our net worth, we've managed to remain a down-home group of folks whose only concern with breeding is for the damn horses on our land. You suggesting otherwise is an insult to them and me."

He closed his eyes for a moment, taking in a slow breath to rein himself in before he continued. "Zanai, you're beautiful, kind, strong and determined. And those are the reasons you can come to the cookout."

By the time she processed what he was saying, she slowly pulled herself up onto her elbows before positioning herself against the pillows adorning the bed. She bore an uncontrollably wide grin on her face that had nothing to do with her excitement over the invitation and everything to do with the man she was talking to.

"Thank you, Jayden." She tried to keep her voice steady so she didn't sound like the grinning idiot her aching face muscles told her that she was. "I'd like very much to come to the cookout."

"Good, we're due to land around noon. That means the ribs should be done and the beer should be cold by the time we get back to the ranch. It's an all-day affair, so if you have anything to wear to work on Monday morning in your bag, you should probably stay at the cottage with me."

"Jayden, it doesn't matter how late it finishes. I can drive myself home. There's no sense in me putting you out."

There was a sinister quality to the wry laugh that billowed from his chest and throat. "I'll have to share you for a good portion of the day with my family. You spending the night means I get to do two of my favorite things: eat my mama's cooking and spend a night pleasing you."

She was about to comment on how sweet and unsettling it was for him to mention sex with her and his mother's cooking in the same breath, but as he placed his phone on the foot bench and crawled up the mattress until he was holding himself above her, the ability to make coherent sentences almost slipped away until her next thought plowed through her lust-dazed brain.

"Are you sure I should stay? I don't need your mother thinking I'm some trollop trying to corrupt her baby boy."

"Corrupt, huh?"

Goodness, that mischievous grin lifting the edges of his full mouth was like a drug, taking her mind, and hopefully her body, on a trip. "I kinda like the sound of that."

"I just bet you do. But despite your apparent penchant for debauchery, I plan to make a good impression on your family."

"If you insist." They both laughed. At that point she realized it was getting easier and easier to let her guard down around him. She had to admit, it felt good. But

part of her wondered just how long she could expect
this good thing to last.

He lowered himself on top of her body and she rev-
eled in the heated press of his skin against hers.

She wanted to attribute the strange feeling that
seemed to start in the middle of her chest, spreading
through her whole system, to the comfort of his weight
above her. But deep down, she knew that wasn't it.

Too afraid to name it, she simply delighted in the satisfied sigh that slipped past her lips as his mouth and
tongue found the curve of her neck.

"You really are something else, Jayden Lattimore."

He beamed as his hand slid up her thigh, his fingers
tightening their grip on the flesh there.

"And don't you forget it."

Eleven

"You're sure your family's okay with you bringing a guest they don't know?"

"Zanai, you're an extra mouth for my mama to feed. She'll never be mad at that. That woman gets joy outta feeding folks I will never understand."

"That's not an answer, Jayden."

He snickered as he pulled up through the opened gates of the Lattimore ranch.

"If you knew my mother, you'd know it really is an answer. My family knows you're coming, Zanai. I've had to threaten each of them to be on their best behavior or suffer my wrath."

She tried to keep a straight face but inside of two seconds of his declaration, she fell into a bout of laughter. Jayden was the most carefree person she knew. She didn't believe he had the capacity for that kind of anger, to be honest.

"Stop worrying. Everything will be fine. And at some point today, I'm sure someone from the Grandin ranch will probably pop by. We're always infiltrating each other's lands when there's a grill firing up."

That did make her feel better. Although Morgan hadn't mentioned any plans to drop by, Zanai wouldn't be upset if her friend surprised her, providing Zanai with an impromptu wingman to help her ease her way through this gathering.

"You ready?"

She nodded, and put her hand on the door handle, quickly garnering a scowl from him as she did.

"You will not make me look bad in front of my mama by opening your own car door. She taught me better than that."

She tried hard to press her lips into a flat line, but the good mood between them had the corners of her mouth curling despite her efforts to prevent it. "So, you're only being chivalrous because your mother can see?"

He leaned over, stealing a brief kiss before gifting her with a bright smile. "Of course not. I'm way too selfish for that. I'm doing it because it's an excuse to hold your hand when I help you out of the car."

She could feel her amusement tickling the muscles in her face, demanding she smile even when she was trying to maintain a modicum of seriousness.

"You are too slick for your own good."

He stole another kiss. "No such thing." He winked at her, making her heart beat a little faster. He quickly made his way out of the car and to her side, offering her an eager hand to help her out of the vehicle.

He was right, the electric current that zapped through her when his hand connected with hers was more than worth the brief moment she had to wait for him to walk around and open her door.

When she was standing, he took her hand and placed it on his forearm before gifting her with a devilish grin.

"Let's do this."

She nodded, surprised that the unease she usually experienced whenever she was walking into unfamiliar social situations hadn't yet appeared. She could only guess that her mind was so preoccupied with how good it felt to have her hand pressed against him that it didn't have time to freak out about mingling with perfect strangers.

She knew who the Lattimores were, of course. Although there was a lot of wealth in Royal, Texas, there weren't many Black families with the kind of money and prestige the Lattimores possessed.

It would've been impossible not to recognize them. But even though her own father was a wealthy Black man in this town, there'd been few opportunities for her to mingle with the great Lattimore clan until now.

They walked up the steps and into the large house. The first thing she noticed when she was inside was the warmth that welcomed you once you stepped across the threshold.

From the first time she'd seen the outside of the house when Jayden had invited her over for dinner, she could tell this was a home. There were no marble columns greeting her. Instead, there was a long and wide porch with a swing attached at each end, inviting you to sit down and rest awhile.

She'd known then this was a place where a loving family resided. Walking inside, seeing all the rich burgundy and brown colors, shades that were both bold and soothing, she understood this was a place of comfort and not just a display of how large their bank account was.

They made their way quickly through the large, bright kitchen with its endless counter space stacked with covered aluminum chaffing pans. She couldn't help but be amused at the sight of them. These weren't the expensive kind you saw at the catered events of rich people who wanted to "rough it" by eating outside on the deck or poolside. These were the kind her aunt Déjà up in Brooklyn would get from the local dollar store. She always said the food seemed to cook the best in those pans.

While she was still musing about the novelty of rich folks using cheap pans, they stepped through a slide door that led to an impressive brick-and-stone patio.

It was simple, yet elegant, as was the furniture positioned sparsely throughout the space.

Jayden walked them over to the farthest corner of the patio where his parents were standing. She'd never met Ben and Barbara Lattimore nor any of their remaining three children face-to-face. They were the Lattimores, so of course she knew who each of them was, but this was the first time she'd actually have a proper introduction.

As they approached the grill, Barbara, a sixty-something-year-old woman with a thick and curvy build and dazzling gray hair peppered with a few remaining dark strands, smiled heartily. Even from this considerable distance, Zanai could see the gleam of the woman's bright white teeth.

The simple action put Zanai at ease, stopping the growing ball of nerves that was throbbing in her chest.

Meeting the rich and notable could be tricky in these parts. For various reasons, many didn't particularly welcome outsiders. But the exuberance in this woman's eyes made Zanai feel at home before they'd spoken their first words to each other.

Barbara tapped her husband, Ben, on the arm to get his attention. He was a solidly built man, tall, with low-cropped salt-and-pepper hair. She could definitely see how he could be an imposing force if he wanted to be. But when he turned around to see who his wife was pointing to, his dark brown clean-shaven face slipped into the same easy smile his wife wore.

"Mama, Daddy, I'd like you to meet a good friend of mine. This is Dr. Zanai James. Zanai, my parents, Ben and Barbara Lattimore."

Zanai went to extend her hand when Barbara gave it a dismissive shove before opening her arms and tugging Zanai into a warm hug.

When Barbara let her go, Ben wrapped an arm around Zanai's shoulder, tugging her in for a quick side-hug.

"Hello, Mr. and Mrs. Lattimore. Thank you for welcoming me into your lovely home."

"Look here, young lady." Ben's terse tone was belied by the broad grin on his face. "We don't stand on ceremony 'round here. I'm Ben and this is Barbara."

"He's right," Barbara continued. "You're among friends. So go grab you a plate and pile up on some of that food over there on the table. As soon as we're done with these ribs, we'll come join you."

Zanai reciprocated their friendly smiles. "Thank you. I look forward to it."

"Are Grandma and Grandpa around? I want to introduce them."

His father shook his head and a flash of sadness sparked in his eyes. "Your grandpa was a bit flustered, so Grandma took him upstairs for a nap. If he's feeling better, I'm sure they'll be down later."

Jayden nodded, then walked her over to the long, rectangular table where more covered aluminum pans rested.

They made quick work of filling their plates, giving her only a short moment to glance up and see the calm happiness that seemed to settle over Jayden.

Even from his profile she could see he was more relaxed. He was a laid-back person by nature, but here, he seemed even more comfortable if that were possible. With heavy plates and bottles of water in hand, they turned toward a long picnic bench in the middle of the deck where Jayden's older brother, younger sisters and three people she knew were his siblings' love interests from her conversations with Morgan sat watching them walk over.

"Zanai, this is my brother, Jonathan, and his better half, Natalie. This is my sister Alexa and her shadow, Jackson, and this is Caitlyn and her beau, Dev. Y'all, this is Dr. Zanai James."

"Doctor, huh?" That came from Alexa, a slender brown-skinned beauty with a long mane of jet-black curls. If it wasn't for the teasing gleam in her eye, her question might've put Zanai on edge. "That means you're smart, right?" Not waiting for Zanai to answer she continued, "So please explain what the hell you're doing with this guy."

Zanai couldn't help the honest snicker that bubbled up her throat and leapt out of her mouth. "Well, he makes me laugh. That in and of itself is a priceless skill."

Jonathan's eyes widened as he extended his hand to Zanai. "You hear that, Jay? She actually thinks you're worth something. That's a first."

He playfully winked at Zanai before shaking her hand. "I'm his older, much more handsome brother, Jonathan. It's very nice to finally meet you up close and personal."

"Ditto what he said," Alexa interjected. "We've seen you around town with Morgan, but I don't think any of us have ever had the chance to actually interact with you."

Royal was a small town, even Zanai couldn't manage to go completely unnoticed in it. "I'm a bit of a homebody. Being out and about in Royal can be a bit much for me."

"I can certainly understand that." Caitlyn gave her a delicate hand to shake. "Being around people takes up a lot of energy I don't always have."

Caitlyn patted an empty spot on the bench next to her. Getting the feeling Zanai had just stumbled on to a kindred spirit, she accepted the invitation and sat down next to Caitlyn while Jayden sat on the opposite side of the table where Alexa and Jonathan sat.

"Don't you pity me now that you see what I have to contend with when I'm around these folks?"

Pity him? No, pity wasn't what she'd call this feeling at all. Even as she smiled and enjoyed the good-natured ribbing that only became more robust once his parents joined the table, Zanai didn't pity Jayden. She envied him.

As his family made jokes at his expense, there was this unmistakable thread of love that connected them all.

Zanai had never been part of something like that, not even when her mother was alive. Witnessing the simple way a family interacted when they loved each other scratched at the secret longing she'd carried for years. But even as she ached for this kind of affection in her own family, watching it play out so easily amongst the Lattimores made warmth radiate throughout her body.

I could get used to this.

The thought was like pouring ice-cold water down her spine. No matter how nice this was, she couldn't allow herself to get accustomed to it. Jayden was here for the fun and nothing more. To forget that would be the worst mistake she could make.

As if he could sense there was an unspoken shift in her, he tossed a slightly concerned look across the table, silently asking if she were all right.

She wasn't. Not when everything she'd ever dreamed of having was sitting right here at this table. Life had already taught her this sort of happiness wasn't for her. But the draw of Jayden's smile and the shared laughter of his family dragged her back into this pool of good feelings and comfort. It was so powerful, her brain kept screaming at her to get out while she still had the chance, while she still could protect herself.

She took a deep breath, putting on her best smile and nodding, hoping he couldn't detect her reservation any longer. No matter how dangerous this was, she couldn't pretend she wasn't enjoying every second of it.

So, as warning bells in her head went off, she willfully ignored them, grabbing her fork and tucking into the potato salad on her plate—which she was certain was the best she'd ever tasted. She'd pay for that act later, of that, she was sure. But for right now, consequences be damned, she allowed this close-knit family to submerge her in their sincerity.

* * *

The sky was turning dusk. Usually, he loved a good sunset as much as the next person who treasured the wide-open spaces in Royal. But tonight, each inch the sun dropped below the horizon meant he was closer to tomorrow arriving and Zanai leaving for work. He just didn't want that.

"What's on your mind, little brother?" Jonathan's voice intruded on his thoughts, making him pull his attention away from Zanai as she sat with his sisters talking.

"Nothing."

"You may have that pretty therapist smitten, but not me. What are you really thinking?"

As much shit as Jonathan gave him, he was a great big brother to Jayden. He'd always been there, always had his back. If there were anyone in this world who he could share his thoughts with, it was him. Not to mention, Jonathan's ability to find something good with Natalie after going through hell during his marriage to his ex also made him the ideal person to have this conversation with.

"Honestly, I don't know."

"This woman has you that twisted up, huh?"

"We're really just having fun, Jonathan. But I'd be lying if I said I wanted it to end anytime soon. There's just something about her that makes me want to keep her close."

His brother hung a playful arm around Jayden's neck and pulled him into a half hug, half headlock. "Then go with it. Do like you usually do and enjoy it. Don't overthink it."

His brother was right. Jayden was king of letting things unfold as they naturally would. But in this case, for some reason his head hadn't clued in yet. The idea of not doing something to ensure this feeling lasted didn't sit right with him.

He was so uncomfortable with the idea, he was itchy and tight in his own skin thinking about it. Deep down he knew that just letting things happen as they were supposed to could mean this good thing he was enjoying more than he should would eventually disappear from his life.

He leaned into his brother's hug, turning and pulling Jonathan into his embrace. "Thanks, man."

"Anytime."

He disengaged from his brother's arms and walked over to Zanai. He tilted his head toward the other end of the patio, and she quickly followed his lead, excusing herself from his sisters.

"You ready to go?"

She gave him a weary smile. "No, actually. I'm having a great time. But it is getting late, and I should probably get some rest before I turn into a pumpkin."

"I'm sure you'd make the prettiest pumpkin in all of Royal."

"You're either drunk or on your way to a sugar coma after all that sweet potato pie you were putting away."

"Nope, we've been here for about four hours and I've only had two beers and I've eaten more than a football team, so I'm completely sober."

He slid his hand down her arm until he was linking his fingers with hers. They remained that way as they said their goodbyes and made their way to the front of the house where his car was parked.

"Did you really enjoy yourself?"

There was a tenderness that settled over her face as the apples of her cheeks rose with her smile.

"I did. Your family is amazing, by the way. Thank you for inviting me. I didn't realize how much I needed a day like this."

"You're busy helping people who need it. You deserve a day of fun and food."

They finally reached his car, but instead of reaching for the door so she could pull her overnight bag from the back seat, she brought her soft brown gaze up to his. Even in the dim lights that illuminated the driveway during the night, he could see something burning in her eyes that made his skin tingle and his cock twitch.

"You really need to stop looking at me like that."

"Like what?"

He couldn't tell if the innocent expression on her face was real or a ruse. Either way, it made desire lick at his insides, making him desperate to touch her no matter if they had privacy or not.

"Like you want something I desperately want to give you."

Initially, he thought his response must have shocked her. That was the only way he could make sense of the slight drop in her jaw resulting in her mouth opening just the smallest bit. But then his eyes traveled down the length of her face to her graceful neck and he saw her pulse jumping just beneath her skin.

Zanai was a slim woman, but even with her build, if her pulse was visible, her heart had to be drumming along at a fierce rhythm.

Drawn to it, he lifted his hand, allowing his thumb to caress the area. No, he wasn't touching her in a clinical manner like a medical professional would. He was gently dragging his thumb back and forth across the spot, searching for much more than signs of life, but signs of the same need burning through his own cells.

Without thinking, he snaked his fingers around the back of her neck, pulling her to him as he pressed his lips to hers. They were outside, in the view of any of his family who might've chosen that moment to walk by. But the fire growing inside him once his flesh met hers was too great to be concerned with things like getting caught by nosy onlookers.

That was especially true once she inched her fingers up the sizzling skin of his arms, her palms lying flat against his shoulders before snaking around his neck, keeping him pressed against her.

It was a bold move for someone as reserved as Zanai and the thought that she was so turned on she'd forget herself in an open space did unspeakable things to him. It made his already-scorching blood boil, the resulting pressure racing through his body looking for an outlet, finding none save for his cock, making it twitch with more than simple interest, but need.

The sparks they ignited turned into a burning flame. If he had common sense, he'd retreat to safety, putting as much distance between him and her as possible. However, his brain was too filled with the haze of lust to allow for any pragmatism. Instead, he gripped her hips, loving the natural curves that seemed to fit perfectly in his hands, tugging her to him so she could feel exactly what she was doing to him.

A long moan trickled across her lips and into the night air, charging it with need. He kissed her harder, walking her backward until she was against his car. He pulled his lips from hers, placing a path of kisses from her chin to the shell of her ear.

"You have no idea how much I want you."

His voice was raspy, as if he'd been drinking or yelling for so long that the delicate flesh of his throat was rubbed raw from overuse.

"Actually, I'm pretty sure I do." She flexed her hips, pressing against his stiffening cock. Surprised by her forwardness, he worried if this was too much for her and he should pull away. But then she slipped one hand around the base of his neck while placing the other at his waist, tugging him against her.

When his eyes dropped down to hers, he saw a fire matching the one he knew burned within him and any doubts he had of pushing her too far too fast melted away.

This wasn't the reserved woman who protected herself by separating herself from the world. This was the fierce woman he'd had the pleasure of dancing with at the masquerade ball.

He'd seen glimpses of her in the time he and Zanai had spent together. But tonight was the first time he'd seen her willingly come out to play without being coaxed.

"Darlin', we'd better make a move because whether we're here in the driveway or back in my cottage, I'm going to experience what it is to have my naked flesh covered with yours again."

She moaned, wrapping both arms around his neck and draping herself over him. "Trust me, Jayden. It can't be soon enough for me."

He nuzzled her neck, gently nibbling the exposed flesh there and smiling at the needy tremor that racked her body as he did so.

"I would love for it to be this very second," he said as he pressed her against his car, loving how her body molded to his. "I can only imagine how beautiful you'd look spread across the hood of this car. But since my mama is only a stone's throw away from us, that ain't happening tonight."

"You're such a tease for putting that image in my head and not following through."

"Dr. James, I do believe I've corrupted you."

"I'm pretty sure you have."

He bent down to kiss her again, needing to taste her sweetness one more time.

"Good to know, but since I'm not exactly prepared, we're still gonna have to take this show inside."

She pulled back from him and he could see eagerness that made his heart race like a shot of adrenaline.

"If you mean condoms, I have those."

He placed a sweet kiss on her lips, chuckling as he answered her. "Look at you being all prepared." She offered him a smile in return, soothing some of the burn he believed would eventually consume him if they didn't stop now.

"I'm very glad to know you're prepared for the fun we'll get into. However, I wasn't talking about condoms. I keep telling you, you're a queen. You're not someone to be used in a disposable way. Every time I'm buried inside you again, I plan to show you it means something to me. So, as much as my flesh is willing, I'm going to calm my ass down, drive you to my cottage and worship you the way you deserve."

He could see the disappointment sliding down her face like an ominous cloud. Part of him was delighted for it. No, he didn't want to see her needs and wants go unmet even for a brief moment. But, if she was this visibly disappointed and impatient, that meant she was just as into the idea of them re-creating the magic they experienced in New York.

"Don't worry, my queen. This is a good thing."

She shrugged, tilting her head as she looked up at him, trying to analyze his meaning.

"I don't see how getting me this aroused and then not doing anything about it is a good thing."

His hands tightened on the curve of her hips, and he released a desperate groan into the air. Hearing her speak of her arousal was just another thing to make him burn for her.

"I plan to do everything about it. Just not right this minute. Besides, you do realize that all the time we've spent yammering at my car, we could've been back to the cottage already playing at my new favorite activity."

She looked up, giving him a sultry smile that raised his ardor one more tick above scorching.

"Oh, yeah, and what exactly is your new favorite activity?"

"Pleasing you." The words slipped through his mouth without any hesitation, a fact that if he were honest, unnerved him a bit. This wasn't part of his usual MO. He was a "love 'em and leave 'em, content when he walked away" kind of guy. He kept things light. But as he stood there watching her, his body beside itself with need, even he couldn't delude himself long enough to ignore the fact that this was in no way keeping it light.

The worst part of it all was, there, somewhere deep inside of him, he was actually glad about that. And therein lay the problem. How deep had he fallen if he actually wanted to keep her near?

She pulled him to her, pressing soft lips against him, licking inside his mouth in a bold maneuver that made him fight to keep his control, and in that moment, he realized he didn't care how far he'd fallen. The only thing he cared about was keeping her with him for as long as he could.

Too lost in her touch to contemplate the future disaster he knew this could pose, he decided he wouldn't borrow tomorrow's trouble. Tonight, he'd allow himself to become intoxicated by the woman in his arms. A fact he was certain he would surely pay for later.

Twelve

They'd barely made it inside his cottage before they were tearing each other's clothes off. They took a brief reprieve to retrieve a condom from Zanai's bag, and as soon as the foil pack was in her grasp, they were plastered against each other again.

Too eager to be inside of her, he moved them toward the large sofa in the middle of his living room. They hastily discarded their last few articles of clothing. Jayden stopped for a moment. Standing behind her, he kissed the elegant curve at the base of her neck as his hands gripped her hips.

She was delicate, yet so strong. It hardly made sense to him that this woman had so much power over him. Whether she knew it or not, she was fast becoming an addiction for Jayden. He had his reservations, but the truth was, he was more and more willing to step off this emotional cliff she had him on if it meant bringing them both the pleasure they craved.

Refusing to let his thoughts temper the heat blazing between them, he encouraged her to climb onto the cushions until she was leaning forward with her front against its back.

"What is it with you and couches?"

He moaned softly, leaning down to nip at her earlobe with his teeth before whispering, "If you could see the view I have from back here, you'd get why there's no place I'd rather be than here with you spread across this very sturdy piece of furniture."

Before she could respond, he sheathed himself, plastering himself against her back before sliding his eager fingers over her hip, then between her folds. Her slick heat seared the pads of his fingers and he had to brace himself to keep from toppling onto her.

"Is all this for me?" He delighted in the shudder that passed through as he pressed two fingers inside her.

When she moaned as he slid his fingers in and out, he nearly came right there.

"No, it's for me. Now get on with it."

"So bossy."

"And you love it."

"Damn straight, I do."

He did as the lovely woman commanded, positioning himself at her entrance, slowly entering her from behind to give her body a chance to adjust to him.

When she dropped her head against the back of the couch, and pushed back against him, that was all the encouragement he needed.

With one knee bent on the sofa cushions and the other foot planted firmly on the ground, he gripped her shoulder with one hand and her hip with the other before he sank home.

That word wasn't just a euphemism either. Not the way her sex cradled him, gripping him so tightly, and certainly not the way she moaned with unadulterated want as he moved inside of her.

After a few slow strokes, he finally gave her what they both wanted, increasing his pace. She was close already. Her tight heat quivered around him, and he could tell she was trying her best to hold out, to deny the climax that was sneaking up on them both.

"Let go," he whispered as he covered her back with his chest. "Give in."

He dropped his hand from her hip, circling firm fingers around her clit until she cried out, falling headlong into her release.

Her body was tight and her jaw slack as she called out his name. She buried her face into the cushions, muffling the sounds as she continued to fall apart beneath his touch.

The sounds she was making poured gasoline on the inferno already threatening to consume them. There was no way he could resist taking his own pleasure soon.

He pulled her upright, planting a demanding kiss on her full lips before burying himself into her again.

He released her long enough to position her with her head on the armrest and her ass in the air, put on display just for him. The sight she made, like she was a gift waiting just for him, it tugged at every lecherous part of his personality, calling him to bury himself in her and finish this torture once and for all.

He positioned himself behind her, slamming into her, loving the loud litany of the word *yes* on repeat as his flesh slapped against hers, making the obscene sound of slick need their bodies created.

He could feel her spasming again, bearing down on his flesh in the most delicious way, triggering his peak. The electric shock waking up every nerve he possessed until his entire being felt alive. He rode that high until Zanai's demanding body clenched around him, and then he was lost.

Jayden's stride faltered as the tension of his climax built until it was a dramatic wave looming above him, its power both inviting and daunting. And at the very last possible moment when his mind shut down and his body took over, he surrendered himself to the inevitable force of his orgasm taking hold of him while the unrelenting pleasure her body offered consumed him.

He collapsed under its weight, falling against her back, circling his arms tightly around her chest as the waves of his climax pulsed through him.

When it was over, and he could finally find the clarity and the strength to swim back to cognizance, his muscles gave way. With exhaustion pulling him down against her back and into oblivion, he used the last bit of his strength to separate from her body, dispose of the condom and pull her on top of his chest. Circling his arms possessively around her, he swiped a lock of hair out of her face, cupping her chin as he stared into her satisfied gaze.

"We are definitely doing that again." His utterance garnered a sleepy smile from her just before she dropped her head to his chest and snuggled against him.

"We damn sure are."

"Details, please."

Zanai blinked, slightly dazed by the whirlwind that

was her best friend, Morgan. The last time she'd seen Morgan had been before she and Jayden had left for New York and before he'd brought her home to meet his family. That seemed so long ago.

The beautiful redhead appeared so abruptly, that Zanai had to look around the local coffee shop to see if any other guests were swept up in her friend's tailwinds.

"Spill what? The coffee I was just about to take a sip of?"

Morgan crossed her arms, her lips poking out without the slightest hint of amusement anywhere on her face.

"Zanai, I'm tired and irritable. While I was dealing with a busy store and annoying customers, you were off jet-setting with the very handsome Jayden Lattimore. I need details, and I need them now."

Zanai's laughter bubbled up, escaping her lips, and she was rewarded with a sharply raised brow from her best friend.

"I'd hardly call going to New York for the weekend 'jet-setting.'"

Morgan huffed, "Fine, does gallivanting work better for you?"

"You really are in a mood today. Everything okay?"

Morgan took a breath, some of her irritability bleeding out with the long sigh she expelled.

"I'll be fine. Like I said, the store was really busy this weekend and I'm just feeling a little tired. I won't dare complain, though. It's better to be run ragged with paying customers than to sit in an empty store."

Zanai saw a glimmer of her friend's usual upbeat personality shining through, helping her relax a bit.

"Enough about me, though. I don't have a lot of time

before I'll need to get back. I just wanted to catch up with you and see how your weekend went."

"It was fine."

That amusement that seemed nonexistent a few moments ago seemed to crack through Morgan's stiff countenance, resulting in a wicked grin on Morgan's face.

"Fine, my foot. What happened?"

Zanai sipped from her cup of coffee slowly just to get on Morgan's nerves. When she saw Morgan's brow knit, that was Zanai's cue that she'd taken things a bit too far.

"All right already. It was wonderful. We saw a play, had lunch in a really fancy restaurant and spent most of the night drinking champagne and getting naked in his hotel room."

Morgan's face lit up, her excitement over Zanai's account of her weekend activities chasing away the clouds of annoyance shadowing her bright eyes.

"Way to go, Jayden. I'm glad he's pulling out all the stops for you."

"All the stops? We spent a night in New York. I'd hardly call that anything spectacular."

Morgan didn't respond. Well, not verbally anyway. Her shaking head and tightly set mouth did all the talking for her.

"We both know Royal is a small town. If he were whisking any other resident away from here for overnight trips to New York, there's no way we wouldn't have heard about it by now. The only reason it isn't all over town already is that you're not a gossip and I would never betray your confidence like that."

A fact Zanai was most grateful for. The last thing she needed was this town, and by extension her father and his wife, finding out about her and Jayden. If things kept up the way they were, she knew it would eventually get back to Sanford. But for now, while it was still in its new and shiny stage, she wanted to savor this before the complication of her father became part of the equation.

"I think it's obvious Jayden really likes you."

Goodness, Zanai hoped so. The attention he paid her, the time they spent together, she'd been desperately afraid she was just seeing what she wanted to see. Although she knew it wouldn't be a lasting thing, to know that he genuinely wanted to be around her made her heart stumble in her chest.

"I like him too."

"And that scares you why?"

Zanai could feel the smile dripping from her face as Morgan spoke. When two people were as close as them, trying to hide anything was a fruitless exercise.

"Jayden is great and I enjoy his company immensely."

"But?"

"Eventually this will end and he'll find another woman to charm."

Her friend placed a comforting hand on top of hers, soothing the ache that Zanai wanted desperately to ignore.

"And you're okay with that?"

"I'll have to be. No sense in getting all worked up over something that isn't real. Instead, I'm just going to enjoy this wonderful man for as long as I can. I deserve that much."

For the first time in her life, Zanai actually believed those words. She deserved to be treated well. She knew it as intrinsically as she knew her own name.

"You deserve more than that."

Zanai nodded. "I know."

Morgan's face lit up with a soft smile that warmed

Zanai's entire being much more than the few sips of coffee she'd had.

"For the first time ever, I honestly believe you know that's true."

"Using the photograph you supplied, I was able to come up with a comparable likeness for the piece you commissioned."

Jayden smiled as he sat in a private room at the jeweler's. Mr. Danbury had offered to come out to the ranch to complete their business, but if his family saw the town jeweler on the premises, they'd jump to all sorts of conclusions he wasn't ready to acknowledge yet.

Mr. Danbury uncovered a velvet tray with a delicate platinum necklace with ruby and diamond teardrops. It was the perfect match to the earrings and bracelet Zanai had worn the night of the masquerade ball.

He couldn't say exactly why he'd felt the need to have this piece commissioned. They hadn't really been dating that long or seriously enough that expensive pieces of jewelry were warranted. But for some reason beyond even his own understanding, he wanted something of his close to her person. Something that would touch her, physically and emotionally, reminding her of how special he thought she was.

"Is it to your liking, Mr. Lattimore?"

Jayden blinked slightly, almost forgetting he wasn't alone in the dimly lit room.

"Mr. Danbury, it's perfect. Would you put it in a pretty box for me?"

"Most certainly, Mr. Lattimore."

Jayden paid for his purchase and waited patiently as Mr. Danbury placed the velvet jewelry box into a red gift box. When the gentleman placed it in Jayden's hand, he smiled as unexpected happiness began to bloom.

He didn't question it. He didn't even chastise himself for going too far too fast where Zanai was concerned. He just rode the high of good feelings rushing through his system as he left the shop, heading for his car parked a few doors down.

"Did you get anything pretty for my daughter while you were in with Danbury?"

Jayden's eyes focused on the tall man with brown skin dressed in a charcoal business suit and a black Stetson. He was leaning on Jayden's car, looking every bit the part of a Black J.R. Ewing with a deceptively sweet smile and easy manner.

"I'm sorry, Mr. James, I'm not sure I understand your meaning."

Sanford kept his pleasant smile pasted to his face as he stood to his full height, nearly reaching Jayden's eye level.

"The piece of jewelry you just bought from Danbury. I assume it's for my daughter Zanai, right?"

The hairs on the back of Jayden's neck stood up, prickling his neckline as he focused on Sanford's words.

"With all due respect, Mr. James, I'm not certain how what I do or don't buy and for whom I buy it is a matter that concerns you."

Jayden watched as the slick smile on Sanford's face began to slip as the man stepped closer to him.

"If it has to do with my daughter, it definitely concerns me. Especially since you've been occupying so much of her time and taking her to New York for special getaways."

Jayden's gaze narrowed as he glared at Sanford. "Are you having us followed?"

The older man scoffed, but didn't answer. Pushing Jayden further to the edge of his building anger.

Jayden didn't flinch, he held remarkably still as Sanford scanned him for a reaction. If he was waiting for Jayden to be ashamed, he'd wait for a mighty long time. Jayden had proudly enjoyed every moment he'd spent with Zanai, including those carefree times in New York.

"What do you want, Sanford?"

Jayden had had just about enough of whatever this nonsense was. He'd lost all his home training about two seconds ago. To make sure this stayed civil, he needed to end this sooner rather than later.

"I like a man that's direct. Your daddy taught you well, boy."

Sanford's cold laugh made the warm Texas air around him drop as if Jayden had walked into a meat locker.

"I want to know what your game is, young man. We both know my daughter isn't your type. She's awkward, and she's not cultured, and she wouldn't know how to land, let alone keep, a man like you if her life depended on it. So I have to wonder then why you'd waste time and money wooing her when she's so far out of her league. Are you planning to use her to get to me?"

At that, Jayden's neck snapped back as if Sanford had physically struck him. He may as well have considering how shocking the blow of his words was.

"What on earth could I possibly gain from using Zanai to get to you? I've barely said two words to you for the decade and a half you've been in this town. Why would you suddenly be the target of such a dubious plan?"

Sanford shoved his hands in his pockets, still keeping his gaze locked with Jayden's, not giving an inch in his accusatory stance.

"We both know I'm a hell of a lot richer than I was when I came to this town. Maybe you and that family of yours have decided there were too many of us skinfolks walking around in the same tax bracket. Perhaps the job fell to you to set a honeypot trap for my daughter to infiltrate me and my business. If that's the case, it won't work. I wouldn't let that mealymouthed, incompetent child of mine near any of my business matters. So your efforts are wasted."

Jayden held his jaw so tightly, grinding his teeth together so hard that it ached as if he'd been belted by something much harder than any man's right hook.

Jayden was the most easygoing of all his parents' children. But that also meant when he was pissed, he was much more likely to lose his temper and do something stupid like slapping the taste out of this man's mouth.

He could feel every muscle in his body tense and his hands ball tightly into fists at his side. He stepped closer to Sanford, watching the older man shiver just slightly as he did.

That's real good, Sanford. You do have self-preservation instincts after all.

"For the life of me I couldn't understand why such a beautiful, accomplished and compassionate woman couldn't seem to understand her own power. But two seconds of you in my face, and it's so clear. The problem isn't her. It's you."

Something dark flashed across Sanford's face. He looked like a cornered animal filled with a mixture of fear and anger. This was probably a good time for Jayden to walk away, but he couldn't. And there was only one reason that made him stand in this slimy excuse for a human being's presence any longer than it took to wipe crap off the bottom of his shoe.

Zanai.

"Whatever Zanai and I share is none of your business. She's a grown woman and is more than capable of making her own decisions."

Sanford swallowed and stepped back. The simple move gave Jayden sincere satisfaction. It was the moment a bully recognized he'd met his match.

"You don't want to make an enemy out of me, boy." The diminution didn't have the same bite as it had previously. Not with the almost imperceptible quiver in Sanford's voice.

"I think you'll find we're more evenly matched than you believed, Sanford. Take me on at your own risk."

When he couldn't scare Jayden, Sanford slipped his faux smile on his face again. "I'm trying to do you a favor, son. A man like you can't afford to get tied up with the wrong woman. You wouldn't want all that family prestige to go down the drain because my daughter can't hack it in your circles. She's—"

Jayden stepped close enough to Sanford that he could smell the scent of stale cigarettes on his breath.

"One more word, Sanford. That's what you've got. One more negative comment about Zanai and I'm going to lose the manners my mama taught me."

What little bit of self-preservation Sanford had must have kicked in, because he stepped back, making sure he was more than an arm's length away from Jayden.

Smart man.

"Who don't hear will feel, Jayden. Who don't hear will feel. Remember I tried to warn you."

Jayden stood stock-still for a few minutes after Sanford disappeared from his view. He needed that time to get his head together. He needed to talk to Zanai, tell her about what was going on. But before he could do that, he had to get his anger in check.

Sanford might be an asshole, but he was still her father, and if he didn't handle this well, it could become a wedge between them. They were finally getting closer, and the thought of losing Zanai over this made his anger bleed into fear. He couldn't lose her, not when he was so close to having everything he wanted.

Once he'd calmed down enough that his heartbeat wasn't thumping in his ears, he realized his phone was vibrating in his back pocket.

Without looking at the screen or putting on any of the usual charm he used when greeting folks, he answered the call with a short "yeah."

"Okay, who spit in your Cap'n Crunch today?"

The sound of Alexa's voice mentioning his favorite childhood cereal cracked through the residual anger lingering after Sanford's departure.

He huffed softly, trying to find his center again. "You know I don't play when it comes to the Cap'n."

"Trust me, we all know how ballistic you would go if one of us dared to eat your diabetes in a box."

He playfully grumbled. "I know you didn't call me to talk about my superior choices in breakfast cereals. What's up?"

"You sure you okay? You sounded a little off when you answered the phone."

He didn't want to rehash his conversation with Sanford. It would only serve to piss him off again.

"I'm fine. What do you need?"

Alexa's breathing became audible through the line.

"You need to get back to the ranch as soon as possible. Jonas Shaw called. He's coming over to update us on his investigation into Heath Thurston's claim."

A new irritation settled in his bones. But this went deeper than the blind rage he felt boiling up when Sanford was warning him off of Zanai. That made him angry. This, however, worried him.

Whatever Jonas Shaw had to say, it could very well mean the loss of part of his family's ranch. Jayden didn't want to entertain that idea. But like everything else concerning this entire convoluted issue, it didn't look as if life was going to give him much of a choice.

Thirteen

Jayden walked into the family room finding his three siblings, their parents and their neighbors, the Grandins, sitting with Jonas Shaw, the private investigator they'd hired to dig into this problem.

"All right, what did you find out?"

"Jayden, there's no need to be rude. Where are your manners?" His mother's voice held that sharp tone it had when she was chastising him as a kid.

"I'm sorry." He cleared his throat before taking the empty seat next to Alexa on one of the large sofas in the family room. "Hello, everybody." When everyone in the room acknowledged his greeting, he turned to the investigator. "Jonas. Do you have any news for us?"

Jonas gave him a reassuring smile, as if he understood Jayden's lapse in manners.

"Yes, Jayden. I do have news. But I'm not sure it will do anything but raise more questions."

His father sat stoic in his favorite armchair. The stern look reminding him of how serious he'd looked when all this nonsense with Thurston's claim had begun.

"I talked to the old surveyor," Jonas began, hedging his cadence as if to soften the blow of whatever he was about to tell them. "Henry Lawrence checked his paperwork and confirms there's no oil on the land." He picked up a folder and handed it to Jayden's father, Ben.

"This is a copy of Lawrence's records. It's all right there. There's nothing on either side of the land that would've warranted Victor Senior and Augustus turning over rights. The rights are useless."

"You said there's no oil on the land now. Was there ever any?" Jonathan asked.

Jayden could tell everyone else in the room was thinking along the same lines as Jonathan was.

"No," Jonas answered.

"I honestly can't make any sense of this," Jayden said.

Alexa nodded as she responded, "That's because it doesn't make any sense. If there's no oil, why would Augustus and Victor Senior sign over the rights?"

Jonas shrugged. "I'm afraid the only person who can give you any real answers is your grandfather, Augustus. If he can't tell you anything, then…"

"…then my grandfather, Victor Senior, took those secrets to the grave," Vic continued.

"Is everything okay?"

Zanai rushed across the threshold of Jayden's cottage as soon as he opened the door. He'd called her as usual just as she was leaving work. Expecting one of their playful chats, Jayden's stern voice filtered through her car's speakers instead, falling heavy against her chest as he asked her to come see him immediately.

"Jayden, is everything all right? Is anyone hurt?"

His penetrating gaze cut through her, pinning her to the spot in his foyer she was currently occupying as she waited for him to respond.

"No one's hurt." The belt of fear his voice had tightened around her heart loosened the slightest bit. But the stiff set of his jaw, the way his bright brown eyes had deepened into a muddy brown, still concerned her. This wasn't Jayden, at least not the Jayden she'd come to know and care for.

"It's been a rough day. Remember how I told you about Heath Thurston's oil claim against the adjoining land between us and the Grandins?"

She nodded. He'd given her a brief rundown of it when he'd invited her to the cookout. Although serious, it didn't seem to weigh on him as heavily as it did now.

"Has something changed?"

"Regrettably, no." His eyes softened a bit as he huffed, exasperation rolling off him in waves.

"My family's trying to sort out some issues with our land. We thought we'd have a lead today from our private investigator, but the so-called lead just brought more questions."

"I'm sorry, Jayden. This must be so frustrating to all of you."

She raised a gentle hand to his face, letting her thumb slide across the tight line of his stubble-covered jaw.

He covered her hand with his own, leaning into her touch as if it was a much-needed balm for all that was ailing him.

He took her hand in his and pressed a light kiss to her palm before leading her out of the foyer and bringing them to the large leather sofa in the center of the living room.

"Make no mistake," he continued, "this is a pain in the ass that could have some serious consequences if we can't get to the bottom of what's going on. As much as it concerns me, that's not why I asked you to come here."

Zanai tilted her head, letting her eyes slide up and down his form, then back again as she tried to decipher his meaning.

"Zanai, did you tell Sanford about us?"

Her eyelids seemed to be stuck on rapid blink mode as she tried to process his question.

"No. Why would I?"

Now it was her turn to be stiff as she braced for whatever Jayden would say next.

"To be clear, it wouldn't matter to me if you had. I'm not ashamed of anything we've done and you shouldn't be either. We're not a dirty little secret you need to keep."

She shook her head, pulling back, attempting to get a better understanding of whatever he was trying to tell her.

"Once you brought me to meet your family, I didn't think you were all that concerned about who knew about us. I've never felt like we were secret." She wrapped her fingers in his, needing the connection to help her feel anchored. Fear had robbed her of so much in her life, she didn't want Jayden to be one more thing it tarnished for her.

"Jayden, what's going on?"

"Sanford cornered me when I was in town today. He wanted me to know that he was aware we were seeing each other and he warned me to stay away from you."

Ice spread through her veins at the mention of her

father's name. No good had or would ever come from her father showing interest in anything in her life.

She fought the cold panic trying to take over. If she froze up, she'd never be able to think her way out of whatever Sanford was planning.

Think, Zanai. Think.

"How did he know? We've been around town having meals, but we haven't been overly affectionate in Royal. How could he possibly know?"

"He somehow knew we were in New York. I asked if he was following us. He wouldn't answer."

She fought to crush the full-body tremor threatening to rip through her being. Something dark and angry settled in his eyes and for the briefest moment, she couldn't tell if it was a residual effect from meeting with her father, or if that glare was directed at her.

"We both know that Sanford isn't the loving, protective type when it comes to me. So if you're angry enough that you're damn near grinding your teeth together, he had to have said or done something more than announce his knowledge of our relationship. What happened, Jayden?"

He moved closer. His body was still stiff with the barely concealed anger thrumming through it. But even though he was obviously out of sorts, his nearness calmed some of the anxiety her brain was having a hard time curbing.

"He told me to stay away from you. I would've understood it if he were just a father being protective of his daughter. But there was something sinister about it. He accused me of sleeping with you to somehow sabotage his business and get insider information. He didn't seem to care that I'm a rancher and the only businesses that concern me are those connected to land and livestock."

She dropped her head, shame pressing down on her back and shoulders so heavily, all she could do was slump down into the sofa cushions.

"I'm so sorry, Jayden. He was so out of line. He had no right to say something like that to you. I hope you know I don't believe you could ever be so callous. You would never do that to me."

He leaned over and kissed her gently, as if he understood if he offered her anything more, the dam would break.

"I know you trust me, Zanai. And I would never violate that trust by using you like that." He squeezed her hand to reassure her his words were true. "I'm not the least bit concerned about Sanford's baseless accusations."

He dropped his gaze before he spoke again. "Listen, Zanai," he started, then closed his eyes before continuing, as if whatever he had to say was so heavy, so difficult that he couldn't even look at her as the words dropped from his lips.

Worry crawled up her spine as she attempted to anticipate what he wanted to say.

"I know he's your father, but no one should have to put up with his crap."

The fear tightening around the bottom of her spine increased the pressure of its grip, numbing her from everything except the despair that was now spreading throughout the rest of her body.

He's leaving me.

The thought was so clear in her head, she worried she had spoken the words out loud. But since Jayden didn't react, she figured she'd kept them locked away.

Her chest hurt, like a vise was crushing her, preventing her from taking a breath. She'd known he'd eventually leave. She'd known from the very beginning she was a challenge for Jayden. That's the only reason a man like him, one who had money, good looks and could easily have any woman he wanted, would pay someone so disconnected from the elite world they lived in a second glance.

But although she'd told herself time and time again that he'd eventually get bored and move on, the thought of losing him, of not enjoying his lighthearted and playful ways, it shook her to the point that she gripped the cushions of the sofa to steady herself.

Her brain continued to spiral out of control as she tried to anticipate his eventual letdown and somehow that fear turned to anger, taking control of her before she could stop her mouth from opening.

"So you're ending this?"

As he turned his face toward hers, she closed her eyes, not wanting to see rejection there.

"All my life, I've dealt with Sanford hating me simply because I was too uncultured, too comfortable with 'slumming,' as he calls it. He's always hated me for my apparent affinity to what he sees as the ailments of poverty. I'm used to him rejecting me because I don't love the trappings of wealth the way he does. But I never thought you'd push me away for the same reason."

She felt him stiffen on the cushions next to her. Finally, she found the courage to open her eyes, determined not to let him see the hurt and disappointment cutting through her soul.

"What the hell did you just say to me?" Confused, she lifted a brow, sitting straighter on the sofa, trying to figure out where all this was leading. Rejection, she'd expected to see it. But there was bright rage that flamed so hot in the depths of his gaze, it shook her to her core.

"I'm done apologizing for not being the daughter he wants. I'm done with apologizing for not being born into wealth and for wanting to help people who are the most vulnerable among us because it somehow sullies rich people's need to enjoy everything their money can buy them. So if you're going to break up with me because I'll never fit into your world, just get it over with. I won't say I expected it, or even wanted it. But I for damn sure won't beg you to stay."

His jaw dropped as she glared at him. He seemed to be ready to say something, but he closed his mouth, taking a long, slow breath, as if he needed time to gather himself before responding to her.

"I was pissed because for the two minutes we spoke, he used one and a half to berate you. Standing there listening to the disrespectful filth he was spewing got under my skin."

The muscles in his face tightened until she could see his jaw flexing.

"But now I'm pissed for a whole different reason."

The fiery anger she was feeling gave way to icy fear. Had she misread things?

"Jayden—"

"Shut up." The words were quiet, yet so powerful she complied instantly. "Not another damn word until I'm finished."

Fire burned through him as he watched the vibrant, beautiful woman he'd come to care so much for accuse him of the vilest behavior.

"Zanai, how could you for even a moment think I shared any views Sanford could have about you? After all this time, how could you think I cared about something as trivial as you not being one of the spoiled brats born to the wealthy families of Royal?"

"Jayden, I didn't mean—"

"The hell you didn't." He barked those words at her. He wasn't prone to yelling, especially at women, his mother had raised him better than that. But the very idea that he could be so superficial and void of basic human decency pissed him the hell off.

"Zanai—" He stopped himself, whatever he was about to say leaving him as he met the confusion in her eyes. Her father had shaped her thoughts of rich people, had told her she didn't fit in and that something was wrong with her for wanting to be around people who didn't come from means. And now she was painting him with the same brush and he couldn't stand it.

"You know what? I'm going to show you better than I can tell you. Come with me." He grasped her hand, pulling her up from the sofa and leading her up the stairs to the standing mirror in his bedroom.

"What do you see?"

His voice was sharper than he intended. But he didn't apologize for it. He was too angry with Sanford for poisoning her mind against people like him, and he was angry with Zanai for buying into her father's bullshit.

It stopped tonight.

"Tell me what you see, Zanai."

"I see me."

He shook his head, folding his arms to keep his hands off her. As angry as he was right now, he couldn't trust himself not to try to shake some sense into her.

"No, you don't. You couldn't possibly see yourself, because if you did, you'd know there's nothing all the angels in heaven could tell me about you that would make me crave you any less. If you truly saw yourself as I see you, then you'd know the only thing Sanford made me believe today is that it would be thoroughly worth the risk of getting thrown in a holding cell at the sheriff's office just to have the satisfaction of popping that smug son of bitch in his mouth."

He unfolded his arms, stepping closer to her. Leaning down toward her ear as if he was whispering a precious secret to her.

"I'm so gone over you, Zanai, that I was ready to lay my hands on your father for disrespecting you in my presence. I'm so turned out that I had to war with myself about whether I would skip the emergency meeting my family had with the PI today or go to you and make sure you were safe and protected from Sanford's hate."

She visibly trembled, stoking his hunger for her, twisting it up with his anger to make it a dangerous mix of emotion and need that he was afraid he wouldn't be able to handle. But when he met her eyes through the mirror, and saw the same lust, the same need to consume and be consumed, he knew there wasn't a chance in hell of him walking away now.

"I fucking crave you, woman. Like air, like a vital nutrient my body needs to function. How dare you or anyone else try to diminish the dominion you wield so naturally over me? How dare you assume that my wealth and standing in this community is more important to me than you? I wouldn't care if you didn't fit into my world, which is the furthest thing from the truth, by the way. I'd turn my back on all of this bullshit in heartbeat just to be with you."

He let his thumb travel the supple line of her neck, loving the feeling of her racing pulse beneath her skin. He wrapped his opposite hand around her waist, pulling her against the hard wall of his body so she could feel him, feel what she did to him by simply being near him.

"I don't call you 'queen' because it's cute, Zanai." He unzipped the simple dress she wore and watched through the mirror as it slid off her body, exposing hard nipples through the lacy cups of her bra.

God, she was perfection. Standing there with her so close, he couldn't resist the need to slide his hand over her hip and finger the thin scrap of lace covering her mound. He fiddled with it until his fingers were beneath it, traveling down until they met the wet heat of her sex, drawing an audible moan from both of them when he slid so easily between her folds.

"I call you 'queen' because whether I'm in or out of your presence, the only thing I want to do is serve you, please you, protect you, worship you, sacrifice for you."

The circular rhythm of his fingers increased and her hips instinctively bucked, chasing the pleasure his touch gave her. "My devotion to you is proof that by divine right, you are majesty born. And if it's the last thing I do, I'm going to burn every negative lie Sanford James has ever made you believe about yourself and people like me until you understand that the only thing I could ever see you as is the powerful and compassionate woman that I can't get enough of."

She was riding his fingers now, her head fell back against his chest, her jaw hanging open as she moaned so beautifully for him. When she closed her eyes, he raised his free hand to her throat, applying slight pressure there as he spoke to her.

"Open your goddamn eyes. I want you to see what you do to me, what pleasing you does to me."

She obeyed and that fact made his dick so hard the jeans he was wearing were acting more like a tourniquet than clothing, cutting off much-needed blood flow. She was close, he could tell by the tremble of her thighs and the desperation in her wide eyes.

He moved his hand from her throat, filling it with one heavy breast, tweaking its nipple as she climbed higher, reaching for satisfaction.

"Do it," he whispered, his voice low and rough, scraping against his throat as the sound banged against the wall of his pharynx, through his mouth and finally floated on the air next to her ear. "Watch yourself come for me. See what I see every time you allow me to touch you like this. See how beautiful and powerful you are when you trust me enough to take care of you."

He scraped his teeth against the shell of her ear, tipping her over the edge. She screamed as she climaxed. The sound was animalistic, a roar that echoed across every wall and surface in his home, letting the world know she'd arrived, and was claiming everything, and everyone in her kingdom, because it was her right. And when she raised her arm, gripping her hand at the back of his neck, digging her nails into him, unafraid to mark him because he was hers to do with as she pleased, all he could think was *Thank you for finally realizing I'm yours.*

Fourteen

Jayden carried her to his bed, laying her down gently as if he was worried she would break.

That concern was understandable considering the way her body collapsed against his when she'd climaxed. She also understood that her track record of doubting him, and herself, probably made him uncertain of where her head was. She'd come to realize doubt was a joy killer. After standing in front of that mirror with him, so brazen and unencumbered with the weight of uncertainties, she decided she'd never miss another moment of happiness because she was too busy wallowing in the steady diet of doubt that Sanford had fed her for most of her life.

No more.

Whether Jayden stayed or not, watching herself come undone by his touch finally did make her see what Jayden had spent so much time trying to drill into her head. He wanted her. There wasn't any plan behind it, and he couldn't care less about what the rich and famous of Royal had to say about it. All he wanted…was her.

The confidence she'd displayed as she took everything she wanted from him broke the bonds of fear and doubt she'd struggled against for more years than she could count.

She was fearless as she stared at the wanton creature who had no hang-ups or misgivings about chasing the satisfaction she knew was within her grasp. It was hers to have, he was hers to have, and she would take as much pleasure and as much of him as she wanted.

Jayden quickly removed his clothing, positioning himself between her legs as he braced his weight on his arms.

"Every time I see you let your disbelief in me show, it's like a gut punch. I've done everything I can to show you what you mean to me, that I'm sincere. The fact that you still think I could be playing games with you, it's an insult, and quite frankly, it's really pissing me off. You're calling me a liar. I'm done allowing you to question my motives, my integrity. It's as simple as this—" his voice dropped down to its lower register, the deep baritone rumbling through her, breaking every chain of suspicion that lingered in the far reaches of her heart and mind "—I want you because you're everything, Zanai."

He spoke her name like a whispered prayer, reverent, sacred, necessary. It fueled her, emboldened her, making her reach for him, wrapping her arms around his broad chest and pulling him to her.

She draped her legs around him, using his surprise at her making such a bold move as an opportunity to roll them until she was straddling him.

She could understand the shock in his eyes. She'd held back for so long, only allowing glimpses of her true self to shine through for fear he'd reject her, or worse, criticize her and detail every way she didn't belong. But tonight, she could stop holding herself back.

The look of need burning in his eyes was the only permission she needed to do what she wanted. And right now, the only thing she wanted was to indulge in the delicacy that was Jayden Lattimore.

She started by capturing his mouth in hers. There was no hesitation, no preamble, only sheer lust. Her lips were insistent, demanding entry that he willingly gave her. His compliance was fuel to the blaze of need consuming her.

On a mission to satisfy the ache inside of her, she tore her mouth away from his, kissing down the sharp angle of his jaw, his neck and chest, licking and nipping his glorious, rich dark skin. She made her way down his torso, until she reached the coarse thatch of hair at his groin.

"Zanai, you don't—"

She didn't give him a chance to finish his sentence. She was determined to take what she wanted and the only thing she wanted was to consume the amazing man beneath her.

She eagerly continued, licking his length from root to tip, loving the full-body shudder, and the almost visceral "fuck" that escaped his lips. Satisfied he was just as into this as she was, she circled her tongue around the tip, gathering the pearl of his arousal, moaning her delight.

Too ravenous to linger, she wrapped her hand around the base of his cock, loving the feel of his girth in the palm of her hand as she slowly took him into her mouth, internally celebrating the long moan of satisfaction that escaped his lips.

Using her mouth and hand, she created an aching pattern of movement that had Jayden spreading his legs. At first, she thought it was just to give her more room to work, but soon, she realized it wasn't just for her comfort, but his need.

He planted one foot against the mattress, using it to gain purchase as his hips joined in the sensual rhythm she'd established.

She allowed him that boon, but refused to permit him to lead this dance. She wanted Jayden at her mercy the way she'd always been at his, and she refused to relinquish even the slightest bit of power now that she had him just where she wanted him.

She picked up the pace, one hand at the base of his cock, the other cradling his testicles with gentle pressure.

"Zanai." It was a warning mixed with a plea, and everything in her wanted to answer his need, to give them both what they so desperately desired.

She glanced up at him, taking in the beautiful image of the taut muscles of his body, of his face contorted by pleasure, realizing she'd never been so aroused or felt so powerful in her life. Without question, she knew this was where she belonged, with him, where every touch they shared was always welcomed and needed.

With one final twist of her hand she cupped her tongue against the underside of his cock. He laced strong fingers through her hair, as he thrust upward, calling out her name in sharp, broken syllables as he toppled over into bliss.

She swallowed his essence, licking him clean while humming softly against his flesh as his body relaxed beneath hers. She released him, kissing a path up his body, back to his mouth, loving how he pressed his lips against hers with such desperation, even after experiencing such a powerful release.

When they finally broke apart, there was something so intense swirling in the depths of his eyes, she nearly pulled away. He threaded his fingers into her hair, making sure she couldn't look away as he stared into her soul and said, "I love you."

She didn't have a chance to respond. He kissed her again, short-circuiting her brain, and eradicating any fears that tried to fill her skittish heart. And as he tucked her into his side, tightening his hold on her, she realized this was exactly where she needed to be. In his arms where nothing and no one in the outside world could touch her.

Daylight filtered through the curtains in his bedroom, dragging him from slumber. He stretched, smiling at the delightful ache of letting Zanai use his body in every way she wanted.

He was sure bruises and scratch marks would reveal themselves later, and he couldn't find a damn to give about it.

She'd taken everything she wanted. She didn't ask, she took, and it stoked his need so much, his dick was already rising with each sultry memory that danced across his closed lids.

He turned over, his hands instinctively reaching for warm flesh. When all he felt was cool bedding, he sat up searching the room for her.

The cottage was still, so much so, he instinctively knew he was alone. He quickly looked at the clock to see it was just past seven in the morning.

He ignored the disappointment growing in his chest, reaching for his phone and finding a folded piece of paper from Zanai waiting for him.

Two words were displayed on the flap: *Thank you*.

There was a finality to those words that hollowed him out like an empty piece of deadwood drying up in the Texas heat.

Brittle was the only word that even came close to what he was feeling. He couldn't breathe, he couldn't move, every thought of losing her beating against him like a merciless body shot, breaking something vital inside him.

He lay back down, looking at the irony of the situation. He'd wanted her to be confident, to recognize her worth. And now that she had, she'd found the strength to leave him and his heart behind.

He didn't even try to deny it. He was in love with her. He'd said as much last night. His heart belonged to her, and thinking she might not want it had him lying in bed, staring up at his ceiling, wondering how he was going to deal with all of this if her note was the Dear John letter his mind told him it was. Deciding it was better to know the truth than speculate, he opened the note and read.

Zanai opened the door to the house she lived in with her father and his wife, slowly cataloguing everything around her.

There were no pictures of her up on the walls, no moments from her childhood displayed with pride. It was as if she didn't truly exist in this place. The realization made her shiver. This wasn't her home. The people who lived here weren't her family.

She stepped farther into the house. Seeing the family

room and the kitchen were empty, she headed toward Sanford's office located in one of the more remote sections of the house. She knocked on the door, not waiting for an answer before she opened it and stepped across the threshold. She didn't care what he was doing on the other side of the door, Sanford was going to make time to hear what she had to say.

"Well, look what the cat dragged in. Since I didn't see your car last night, I assume you spent the night with that Lattimore boy, didn't you?"

She didn't dignify his question with a response. She was an adult and she'd finally realized she didn't need to share anything about her life she didn't choose to and it didn't matter that the person doing the asking was her father.

"You were out of line accusing Jayden of trying to use me to get to you."

Sanford glanced up at her, offering a nonchalant snort. "Did you actually come here to defend your little lover? I do assume that's why you've found the courage to barge into my office giving me *tone*."

The word *tone* was bathed in derision. Before Jayden, she would've cowered under that dirty look her father was currently throwing at her. But today, she was her own woman and she wasn't going to allow him to throw dirt on her or Jayden.

"Telling you that you were out of line with the disrespectful accusations you lobbed at Jayden and me is not giving you tone. It's telling you that you were wrong."

"I was wrong?" Both brows stretched toward his hairline as his question floated in the air. "I'll give that young man credit. He's actually got you believing you're more than the mealymouthed waste of time you've always been."

The words should've hurt a lot more than they did. But sadly, for him anyway, she wasn't the same little girl seeking her father's approval. As an adult, she now realized she'd never have it.

She huffed, mourning all the years she'd wasted because she hadn't yet come to that realization.

"Stay away from Jayden. My relationship with him is none of your concern."

"You walk into my house telling me what I will and won't do? Little girl, you forget yourself. You are nothing but what I allow you to be. And my benevolence is reaching its breaking point."

Rage, raw and blinding, colored her sight. This man, her own father, believed she was his to command.

"If you'd clear your head of all that boy's charm, you'd realize I'm actually trying to protect you. We both know you're not in that man's league. What other reason could he have to be with you other than to get to me?"

She dropped her gaze to the floor, not because she was afraid to look at Sanford, not even because she was hurt by his cruel words. Again, regret filled her as she thought about how much time she'd lost caring what this man thought of her.

"Would it kill you to support my decisions and show at least a small modicum of faith in me?"

"Would it kill you to give me a reason to?"

The nerve of this man was galling. Why she was surprised, she didn't know. Sanford had never shown her any kindnesses.

"Why do you hate me? What have I ever done to make you not love me?"

He casually laced his fingers together as if they were having a mundane chat that held no consequences.

"You're weak, Zanai. And I despise weakness. I've

tried my best to rid you of it and nothing has worked. I've given you everything, and all you've done is thrown it back in my face. You're too much like your mother, you still can't seem to find your backbone. And just like her, the world is going to chew you up and spit you out because you're so broken. Mark my words, it won't be long before you're taking the easy way out just like she did."

The mention of her mother in such a context made rage rush through her bloodstream.

"You drove my mother to killing herself and then profited off her death. Don't you ever speak of her like that again. You are a heartless creature that never deserved the beauty and grace she embodied. My only consolation is that life will deal with you much better than I can. When it does, you'd best believe I'm gonna pull up a chair, kick my heels up and chomp on popcorn as I watch everything you value burn to cinders."

It might've been a tad dramatic, but she'd meant every word of that tirade. She didn't know how or when, but he would get his comeuppance, the universe always balanced itself out. Knowing how her mother had suffered through their toxic relationship, there had to be a hell in which Sanford James was going to burn.

"Impressive." He nodded as he readjusted himself in his seat. "But I'm done. I demand better from you. On this I will not budge. You will end whatever this thing is you share with Lattimore and that's it. He's either trying to mess with my business, or worse, he and his kind are looking to make me look bad through you. Either way, I've worked too hard to let the Lattimores and their ilk take anything from me."

"He's a rancher for God's sake. What could he possibly want with your business?"

He shrugged. "Don't know. Don't care. But there's no way someone like him comes down off his perch to wallow in the gutter unless it will benefit him."

His self-centered paranoia made absolutely no sense. She realized trying to dig any deeper wouldn't yield any different results, so she tilted her head and asked, "Is that your final word?"

She widened her stance and braced herself as if she were expecting a blow. Sanford had never laid a hand on her throughout her life. That didn't mean that he hadn't left lasting marks on her soul.

"That is my final word."

"Well," she huffed, "that's too bad. Because there's no way in hell I'm letting the best thing that's ever happened to me go. Especially for some imagined threat your ego has cooked up. Contrary to what you believe, you are not a rival to the Lattimores. Not just in your net worth, but in your composition as a human being. You've got nothing on those folks. You've got nothing on me. And I refuse to listen to your garbage for one more minute."

A wry grin spread across his face until it morphed into the malicious laughter that was meant to do nothing but intimidate her.

"Zanai, I've used up as much grace as I care to on you. I'm done. This is my house; you are my daughter and you will obey me. Otherwise, you can leave my key on my desk and get the hell out."

She looked into his soulless eyes and realized he meant every word he'd spoken. The thought of homelessness should've frightened her, should've made her give in. She was employed, so of course she could carry the financial weight of being on her own. What should've been daunting was facing the world on her own terms. But as she saw the pleasure he took in bullying her, she realized there were worse fates than being kicked out of Sanford's house. The one in particular that came to mind was the threat of losing herself forever if she remained under his thumb.

She couldn't do it. She couldn't spend one more moment doubting herself and being tortured by the so-called family who was supposed to love her.

Without speaking another word, she removed the house keys from the metal ring securing them, and turned toward the door.

"Don't come back. Don't even think about taking anything in your room either. If it's in my house, it's mine. See what it is to truly fend for yourself."

Again, she didn't say a word, she simply opened the door and stepped through it and into her future. Now, all she had to do was convince Jayden to be part of that future and everything would be fine.

And as she stepped out of the house, smiling at the warm Texas sun sitting high in the sky, she realized that as much as it would hurt, as much as the thought of losing Jayden felt as if she would lose something precious to her physical being, she knew if it came to that, she would live. She was strong enough to face whatever came her way. And for the things she couldn't handle, she was fortunate enough to have access to the tools that would help her deal with them.

This was her path, and she would gladly walk it.

Fifteen

Jayden sat at his table holding the folded piece of paper between his fingers like it was a ticking bomb. Every time he opened it, rereading it over and over again to make sure he'd read it correctly, he felt like a timer was ticking away with each beat of his heart.

Dear Jayden,
Thank you for showing me who I am. Sorry to leave without saying goodbye, but there's something I have to do, something I've been putting off too long. It was the coward's way of running away like a thief in the night, but if I'd woken to see your powerful gaze, or your warm smile, there would be no way I could willingly separate myself from that even for a brief few moments.

He sat there, with the letter in one hand and his phone

in the other, looking back and forth between the two. He was stuck, he wanted to call and demand answers, but deep down he knew if he heard her voice, he'd be reduced to begging her to come back. And he couldn't do that.

He would not do that.

Sure, he wanted her. No, that wasn't right—he needed her. He needed her in his arms the way his brain needed oxygen and his lungs craved air. But if he asked her to return, he'd never know if it was because she wanted to be by his side, or if she was simply doing it because he wanted her to.

After everything, after every moment of pleasure they'd wrung from each other's bodies, after baring his soul to her in every way he knew how, she'd still left. The only recourse for him now was to respect her decision and let her be. Otherwise, he'd be no better than her father who'd tried to control her by withholding love and diminishing her fire, and manipulating her into believing she wasn't worthy of his love.

He would never do that to her. With that decision firmly made, the only thing his aching heart could do was continue to leak his love and joy until his insides were a bloody, inoperable mess.

He thought about how broken he was in this moment, and his face contorted into a derisive sneer. He'd told himself and Zanai this was just for fun. Developing feelings for her beyond the desire he instinctively experienced every time she was near was not in his plan. But somehow, he landed in this space where his entire world stopped spinning because she'd walked away.

In the distance, he heard a knock on his front door, but couldn't find the strength to get up and answer it. Whoever it was on the other side of it, he knew he didn't want to see them. He wasn't fit for company, especially not from one of his family members who would take one look at him and know something was wrong.

How could he explain that he, the master of relaxed and unbothered, was so tied up in knots over a woman that every breath felt like a laborious undertaking?

The knocking didn't cease, irritating his already foul mood. He pushed himself to his feet, taking hard steps toward the door, making the room around him vibrate from the force of his gait.

"Jonathan, if that's you, I'm taking the day off."

His brother didn't answer, so Jayden yanked the door open, nearly losing his balance when he saw who was on the other side.

"Jayden, are you okay?"

The sight of Zanai was water to a man wandering the desert aimlessly. He extended his hand, wanting to see if she was real or if this was a cruel mirage his battered heart had created, but stopped midway between them.

"What are you doing here?"

She braced against the question. Her knitted brows drew tightly together as she gazed at him.

"Didn't you get my note?"

"Oh." He spoke on a weak laugh that was filled with snark. "I got your note all right."

He stepped away from the door, leaving it open for her to walk in if she wanted. Even now, when he ached with this strange mix of anger and need, he couldn't find the strength to turn her away.

He flopped down on his couch, stretching out lengthwise so she'd have to sit on one of the armchairs. The scent of her was already far too enticing, having her near enough to touch was too much for him to handle.

"According to your note, you were leaving. What are you doing back here? I thought you were gone."

God, he could taste the acrid bitterness on his tongue with each word spoken. She'd changed him on a chemical level, and now his brain was stuck on stupid with disappointment and pain, leaving him unable to temper his speech and keep the emotion out of his words.

"To go take care of something," she responded, pulling his gaze toward hers. There was something about the way she said those words that gave him pause, like he was missing something important in the delivery of the message.

"But your note said you left."

"Temporarily, yes. I needed to see Sanford this morning and set some things straight before I could come back here. I was kind of hoping you'd still be asleep and I could slip right back into bed with you without you noticing. Except I didn't realize the slam lock was on and I didn't have a key to get back in, hence the loud knocking."

He sat up, locking gazes with her as he processed what she'd said. "You intended to come back?"

He could see the moment that something clicked in her head, as if she was finally understanding his words. She stood, taking slow steps to cross the small distance from her armchair, to the sofa he was sitting on.

When she reached him, she kneeled down between his legs, placing her hands on his thighs.

"You thought I wasn't coming back?" It was phrased as a question, but the stern glint in her eye made it a statement. She was declaring this, no doubt about it.

"Jayden, you've spent the majority of our relationship reassuring me. Let me return the favor. There is nothing and no one who will ever make me walk away from you. Not anymore."

He could feel the muscles in his jaw tightening. The mere thought of there being anyone who could separate them made his anger rise.

There wasn't anyone else. He knew that. The way her body craved his, the way she responded to his touch, there was no way she was involved with anyone else romantically. He'd stake his life on that.

But they both knew Zanai was skittish, always ready to turn and run from the things burning between them. Hell, she wasn't just ready to run, she'd actually done so. It was only through serendipity that he'd discovered the identity of his disappeared red queen.

"After last night, something changed for me, Jayden. It wasn't just about great sex. Something clicked into place the way it never has before."

She rubbed her hands up and down the ridges of his thighs. It was an absentminded gesture, but to him, the feel of her when she was so near stoked an almost Pavlovian response, him wanting to feel her bare flesh against him.

"I've spent so much time focusing on the problems of others as a means to avoid dealing with my own issues. As much as I love my job and the good it does, it's become a shield against the wounds I've spent a lifetime trying to cover up."

He opened his mouth to speak, but she held up a hand, silencing him.

"Please," she begged. "Let me get this out while I still can." He gave her a curt nod in response and she continued.

"The doubting you and myself to boot, it was all there because I feared turning into my mother. That fear was the reason Sanford has been able to make me forget who I could be."

She inched the fingers of one hand up until they were touching his, lacing them together in a beautiful latticework.

"From the moment I met you, you've poured your belief into me, and it's finally paid off because when you told me Sanford had cornered you, I was no longer afraid. Instead, I was mad. Mad enough, I needed to give him a piece of my mind. The only reason I was so angry was I knew Sanford was trying to take something away from me, something that was mine, something I deserved."

"Zanai," he huffed, his countenance wearing thinner every time her doubt in him surfaced. "I would never allow anyone to tell me who you are. Not after spending time with you, not after touching you. I knew everything I needed to know about you the moment we met. I wanted you, and if that were so, it was only because you were worthy of my desire."

A slow smile spread across her face, softening her features, making him want to pull her to him, and press his lips against hers.

"I know that now. I really know that. Because when I woke up this morning, I had to go see Sanford and let him know he couldn't turn you against me. That you'd never leave because of something he said. That I would never let you go at his command."

Those words unlocked the cage imprisoning his beating heart. The constriction of anger and fear fell away, leaving it room to pump as fast and strong as his love burned for her.

"I can't imagine he took that well." Jayden only knew Sanford by reputation and their brief exchange on the street. Neither scenario particularly warmed Jayden enough to the man to want to spend time getting to know what made him tick. But even still, the fact that Sanford was a bully, especially when it came to his own daughter, was unmistakable.

"He didn't. He huffed and puffed and when that didn't work, he threatened."

Jayden tensed, the idea of Sanford, or anyone else for that matter, bringing harm to her made every muscle he had stiffen in preparation for a fight.

But she raised a hand to his cheek, gently rubbing her thumb against the skin there, slowly stroking his anger away.

"He threatened me. But when he saw his threats fell on deaf ears, he stooped to the only tactic he had left in his arsenal. He threw me out."

Jayden closed his eyes and took a slow, deep breath, trying his best to keep his anger in check. Anger clouded his mind, and he desperately needed a clear head to listen to what Zanai had to tell him.

"Did you bring your belongings with you? If so, I've got plenty of storage space."

"That's sweet of you to offer." She leaned in giving him a brief kiss. It was so soft and fleeting he could hardly believe it happened, the resulting flame being the only proof of her touch. "But he wouldn't let me leave with anything."

"Your things, Zanai—"

"—are just things, Jayden." Her smile was so bright and charming, he couldn't see any pain or apprehension there. Whatever had transpired between Zanai and her father, it didn't seem to bring on the distress just the mere mention of his name created the night before.

"I've always known Sanford would get tired of me underfoot, sooner or later. Living rent free all this time has allowed me to put enough money away that I should be fine getting a place of my own. All of the really important things like my mother's jewelry and mementos, my identification, and my degrees and licensure, I moved into a safe-deposit box a long time ago. The only thing left in that house were clothes, and things that can be easily replaced. And since my bestie owns a clothing boutique, finding new clothes won't be a problem."

He went to speak, but she placed a delicate finger over his mouth, silencing him before the words could slip into the air.

"You don't have to worry about me, Jayden. That frail woman who was afraid to live her life outside of the confines of the prison Sanford locked her in, she's gone. I can do this."

There was determination in her eyes like he'd never seen before. A strength that always seemed to simmer just below the surface, but now, was on full display, intoxicating his senses.

"I've already contacted a Realtor. I'll start looking at some listings tomorrow. I just need a place to stay tonight. Would you be willing to let me crash on your couch?"

He quickly pulled her up from her kneeling position on the floor, settling her on his lap, then clasping his hand around the back of her neck, drawing her to him. Before she could say another word, his lips were against hers in a fierce kiss that sent him reeling.

This woman. This smart, sexy and infinitely capable woman had finally stepped into her own and he'd never found her sexier as a result.

"Cancel it."

She pulled back, her dark questioning gaze falling onto his face.

"Cancel what?"

"Your appointment with the Realtor. Stay here."

The "with me" part disintegrated on his tongue the moment he pulled her down for another kiss. She was free now. Finally free to fully step into her own, and he didn't want to miss one second of it.

"You mean, indefinitely?"

"I mean, as in move in with me."

"I couldn't impo—"

He kissed her again, stopping whatever nonsense she was about to speak into the air.

"I love you, Zanai. More than I thought I ever could. I want you with me all the time. If that's not what you want or if you don't feel the same way, I'll certainly understand. But I need you to know my intentions are to be with you and only you. Just give me the chance and I'll prove to you how much you mean to me."

She pulled his hand from her neck, burrowing her cheek into it as she moaned his name. And the sound of it, the way every syllable slipped from her full, soft lips had his cock aching to slide into her.

And he would.

He had all intentions of burying himself to the hilt inside the tightness of her warmth. But first things first, he needed to convince her this was where she belonged, by his side.

"You've already proven it to me, Jayden. Now it's time for me to prove myself to you."

She stared intently at him, as if to make sure she had all his attention. She needn't have worried about that. His attention was always on her.

"I love you, Jayden."

Those four words spoken so softly he could hardly believe they'd escaped her mouth, cracked his chest open leaving his heart vulnerable and exposed. Fear should be welling up inside him as a result. Instead, a calm assurance fell over him, letting him know everything would be all right.

"I want nothing more than to spend the rest of my life with you."

"That sounded vaguely like a proposal."

She giggled softly. "To shack up, not get married. At least not yet. Let's see how this living together thing works before we cross that particular bridge."

The languid sensation of happiness flowing through him curved his lips into a playful smile. "Then you'll give me pretty words and my ring."

"Then—" she paused, leaning down to kiss him, slipping her tongue into his willing mouth "—then, I will give you anything you want, for as long as you want it."

"Well, since you won't give me my ring right now, maybe you'll at least accept a small token from me. Sort of a pre-engagement gift, if there is such a thing."

He leaned over to open the coffee-table drawer, pulling out the red jewelry box.

He handed it to her, and her face lit up with anticipation. She carefully opened it and her eyes glazed over in awe of what she found inside.

"Jayden, when did you...? Why...?"

He took the opened box from her, removing the necklace from its cushioned bed, and carefully placed it around her neck as she held her hair up for him.

"After you fit in so well with my family at the cookout, I knew I wanted you near me as often as possible. And I wanted to be near you. So I gave the jeweler a picture of the earring you left behind and had him create a companion piece for your neck. I wanted it to be a necklace because I wanted to give you something that would remind you of me and how we met, and have it lay close to your heart."

Tears slid down her face as a wobbly smile curved her lips.

"This is stunning," she whispered. "I love it, and I love you."

His heart stuttered in his chest, stealing his breath and his ability to speak. This woman had changed him, made him reach for something other than "a good time." She'd burrowed underneath his skin and permanently nested her love inside of him, effectively taking control of his being.

That should've terrified him. It should've made him run for the proverbial hills. Instead, the only thing he wanted was to draw her closer and never let her go. His red queen had finally arrived to reign over his heart and he couldn't be happier.

"That, Dr. James—" he punctuated his words with soft kisses along the curve of her neck, drawing the pretty sounds he ached to hear from her "—is exactly what I wanted to hear."

* * * * *

COMING SOON!

We really hope you enjoyed reading this book. If you're looking for more romance, be sure to head to the shops when new books are available on

Thursday 10th November

To see which titles are coming soon, please visit

millsandboon.co.uk/nextmonth

MILLS & BOON

THE HEART OF ROMANCE

A ROMANCE FOR EVERY READER

MODERN

Prepare to be swept off your feet by sophisticated, sexy and seductive heroes, in some of the world's most glamourous and romantic locations, where power and passion collide.

HISTORICAL

Escape with historical heroes from time gone by. Whether your passion is for wicked Regency Rakes, muscled Vikings or rugged Highlanders, awaken the romance of the past.

MEDICAL

Set your pulse racing with dedicated, delectable doctors in the high-pressure world of medicine, where emotions run high and passion, comfort and love are the best medicine.

True Love

Celebrate true love with tender stories of heartfelt romance, from the rush of falling in love to the joy a new baby can bring, and a focus on the emotional heart of a relationship.

Desire

Indulge in secrets and scandal, intense drama and plenty of sizzling hot action with powerful and passionate heroes who have it all: wealth, status, good looks…everything but the right woman.

HEROES

Experience all the excitement of a gripping thriller, with an intense romance at its heart. Resourceful, true-to-life women and strong, fearless men face danger and desire - a killer combination!

To see which titles are coming soon, please visit

millsandboon.co.uk/nextmonth